The Wind Seller

Also by Rachael Preston

Tent of Blue

RACHAEL PRESTON

The Wind Seller

To Duncan,

with best wishes,

[signature]

Edited by Laurel Boone.
Cover image: Creatas.
Cover and interior design by Julie Scriver.
Printed in Canada.
10 9 8 7 6 5 4 3 2 1

Library and Archives Canada Cataloguing in Publication

Preston, Rachael, 1962-
The wind seller / Rachael Preston.

ISBN 0-86492-432-1

I. Title.

PS8581.R449W55 2006   C813'.6   C2005-906431-5

Goose Lane Editions acknowledges the financial support of the Canada Council
for the Arts, the Government of Canada through the Book Publishing Industry
Development Program (BPIDP), and the New Brunswick Department of
Wellness, Culture and Sport for its publishing activities.

Goose Lane Editions
469 King Street
Fredericton, New Brunswick
CANADA E3B 1E5
www.gooselane.com

For Ian

I

Thursday May 29, 1924. High tide, 2:30 a.m., 2:56 p.m.

Hetty awakens flushed and shaken, another man in her dreams, stroking, fondling, his breath slippery and warm against her neck. Her husband stirs and she tenses as his fingers trail a sleepy arc across her back, her hip, her thigh, before coming to settle behind the curve of her buttocks. She shifts away, then holds her breath before pushing it out, rhythmic and even. Patients wanting to avoid medicine or bed baths or even visitors would sometimes pretend to be asleep. Most breathed too slowly, a dead giveaway. Hetty presses her face into the pillow, hoping to reconnect with that other man. A vague shadowy figure, large callused hands, hair falling to his shoulders. No one she knows.

On occasion a dream insinuates itself more deeply. The man is real — one of the men from the mill rubbing himself up and down the length of her, Paul McFadden, the blacksmith, his thick, blackened hands gripped around her buttocks, the sinews in his neck glistening with sweat, inches from her face. Her sex is swollen, her quickened heartbeat alarmingly loud, her passion for her nocturnal partner disturbing, visceral. She wakes filled with dread. Guilt from adultery committed in sleep spills over into her waking life. But it is the dizzying strength of her lust for these men, known and unknown, the way such feelings, with their adolescent power, rock her to her core that unsettles her. Much more than the carnality.

The dreams take Hetty back to crushes on teachers — the librarian with the Cupid's bow lips, ripe for kissing. Tom, the delivery boy from the bakery. For Tom she began rising early to meet him at the back door, take the loaves warm from his hands. In braver moments, encouraged by a nod or a smile, she would brush the back of her hand against his long square-tipped fingers. She wanted to put them in her mouth. The desire to kiss the tips of his thick dark eyelashes burned deep in her belly. She counted out the money from the shortbread tin on the pantry shelf slowly, drawing out his time at her back door, drinking in the way his thin shirt pulled across his broad shoulders, the smooth planes of his chest. If she reached out and touched him she knew her fingers would meet a welcome resistance, because men's bodies — she could tell by the way their clothing both draped 'and clung as they moved — were harder than women's. When Tom left, Hetty stayed leaning against the door frame, eyes closed, tasting the scent of sweat and fresh bread he left behind, and imagined holding herself against him, imagined the feel of her hand, warm and secure in his larger one, imagined skip-stepping a little to keep up with him as they strode together along Hollis Street or around the flower beds and duck ponds of the Public Gardens.

Peter moves his hand to the dip of her waist. This is Hetty's cue, she could stretch awake, lean back into him, and the dream would loose its hold. Instead she remains still, feigning sleep until Peter rises to meet his day's work at the mill, unwilling to disturb the shadow of the stranger's imprint upon her body.

Laura is on her way out the front door but steps back inside as soon as she hears Hetty enter the kitchen.

"I thought you was having a bit of a lie-in this morning, Mrs. Douglas." Laura takes in laundry for several houses, and since Dr. Baker and his much younger wife moved back to the village last September she has been hired to clean their house once a week. But the greater portion of her workday is spent at the Douglas's, cooking, cleaning, washing and ironing. "So I cut you some fresh bread and left you a pot of tea warming."

"Thank you, Laura."

"If you'd like me to wait on while you have your breakfast, Mrs. Douglas, it isn't any trouble."

"That won't be necessary."

"But what about the dishes? If I —"

"Laura, I am perfectly capable —" Laura's face tightens. Hetty takes a long slow breath. "I'm sorry. I apologize. I'm a little tired this morning." She sits and pours herself a cup of tea, then pats the chair beside her.

"Come, sit with me." She doesn't particularly feel like talking. What with the dream and evading Peter's advances, she's a little off-kilter. But Laura clearly wants to natter, and while the woman can fill an entire morning with tales of the mischief her three boys get up to, as well as more solemn stories of her husband, a weir fisherman who keeps unsociable hours on account of the tides and for whom Laura holds grumbling affection, Hetty couldn't bear to lose Laura's confidence. Or her trust. Laura is fifteen years older and they have almost nothing in common, but she is still the nearest Hetty has to a friend in the village. Hetty pours Laura a cup of tea, then pushes her breakfast plate across the table. "Here, have a slice of this delicious bread I made in my sleep this morning."

She is rewarded with Laura's barking laugh plus the something else Hetty senses she's bursting with.

"You should take a walk down by the shore this morning, Mrs. Douglas."

"And why is that?" Hetty walks along the shore most days and figures everyone in the village already knows this.

"There's a schooner tied up at the wharf. Huge, it is. My Silas makes her a good hundred and sixty feet."

"And is that unusually long?"

"Not twenty years ago maybe. But this one is all smashed up and at first light she was sitting high on the tide." Laura pauses, reaching for another spoonful of marmalade.

"And that means?"

"She's nothing in 'er but ballast."

"Go on."

"So what's she doing here? Usually, schooners come in empty, they're picking up lumber or Murron's cabinets and Dominion chairs from Bass River, or sometimes fossil flour from them silica lakes. If she's just looking for somewhere to haul in for repairs there's dozens of ports between here and the mouth of the bay."

"Which is where you think she came from?"

"Where else? She's right built for the open seas. But she's from these parts original — full-bilged, you see." Laura demonstrates with her hands. "She'll ground out no problem," she adds, seeing Hetty's puzzled look. "Tide goes out she'll more or less settle on her keel."

Hetty still isn't sure but nods anyway; more sailing argot and she'll get a headache. "So you were down there yourself?"

"With half the village. And you know what? I figure she's hiding something."

"But you said she was empty."

Laura raises her generous eyebrows, slaps the kitchen table with her work-reddened hand. "Exactly."

Almost nine a.m. The tide will be out, having left behind a long wet rippled beach studded with shells and small rocks and seaweed. Hetty pulls on a jacket, it will be windy down by the shore, but when she opens the back door and breathes in the outside, the late May sun feels warm and welcoming on her face. She steps past the herbs in her kitchen garden and the violets that have sprouted in the cracks between the flagstones. She should spend more time out here: the mint is aggressive, the mother-of-thyme, a thatch of unruly hair smelling seductively of the sea, is already creeping through spaces between the chives and where last year's nasturtiums bloomed. Other spring scents follow in her wake: earthy, pungent, spicy, sweet. The kitchen garden, bordered by a field to the right, stretches easily a dozen yards to the stone wall that marks one end of the property and the dirt path that runs behind it. The path, part of an animal track as old as the land it inscribes, shambles its way to the woods, a dense and elongated thicket of trees that separates this end of the village from the water that was once its livelihood.

How to explain the draw of the Minas Basin and its tides? For Hetty there is something sublime about stepping across land that six hours hence will be submerged under forty feet of water, maybe fifty today with the spring tide. Watching its movement both soothes her spirit and feeds her restlessness. It has something to do with the way the water oscillates between one end of the Bay of Fundy and the other, as if a gigantic whale flipped its tail, as the Mi'kmaq legend goes, the outgoing tide never quite making it all the way out but forever being met by the waters rushing in, forcing the sea back through the funnel-shaped basin. And it has something to do with the cloudy red of the water, never clear because of the tide scrubbing against the red cliffs, wearing them down. Tinged with blood, Hetty thinks, the warning is in the colour. For the Minas Basin water is as dangerous as it is fascinating. Never the same twice, and, at this distance from the whirlpools and roaring seas at Cape Split, never what it seems. In places currents run so strong and deep they can wrench apart a fishing vessel. The tide moves swiftly, rising the height of a man in an hour, and fog glides down the basin in deadly silence, turning people out beachcombing or clam digging around. Drownings are common. But such danger Hetty can respect, removed as it is from the seedy and unpredictable violence of people.

At the end of her garden she hitches up her dress and steps lithely over the stone wall, no mean feat in a pair of Peter's mother's rubber boots, more than a size too big. Despite a pair of thick woolen socks, the boots slip on her heels with every step, reducing her walk to a kind of thud-scuff, thud-scuff. Wildlife flees long before her approach, though this morning a daring red-winged blackbird serenades her from a bower of chestnut blossoms. Insects, unperturbed by her noisy boots, whirr by her ears. Clover perfumes the salty air, spraying white and rosy swaths across the fields, and Hetty reaches out to stroke the heads of grasses grown past her knee. On this magnificent spring morning, she's overdressed. Perspiration is forming in the small of her back, the creases behind her knees. Her feet grow damp, begin sliding in their socks.

She glances around. No one for miles. She stops and pulls up her dress, unhooks her stockings one by one and rolls them down into her rubber boots. Her newly exposed skin tickles under the sun's warming rays, each cell limbering up, filling with fresh air and sunshine. A breeze runs up her legs, goose bumps in its wake, and catches the fabric of her dress, ruffling it against her skin in a tingling, teasing caress. The man in the dream, fingers strumming on her thigh, slipping between her legs. She glances around again, suddenly self-conscious, patting down her dress. What is wrong with her? Dreams are the province of sleep. So why is it that hers, unsettling enough in the confines of her marriage bed, now trail her during the day?

Walking faster, driving her heels into the path, she enters the woods. Eyes to the ground, mindful of the thickening new growth, tree roots and suckers lurking in the carpet of last winter's leaves, things that may trip her. A stray branch stabs at her face, startles her. A twig snaps. Behind? Off to the side? Is someone following her? Someone watching when she rolled down her stockings? She stops to listen, heartbeat blocking her ears. Probably a squirrel. And fancy being worried about who might see her bare legs. Still, she picks up her pace, grateful for the feel of the sun and the wind on her face when she emerges.

Something dark skulks in her peripheral vision, and Hetty turns to look down the bay. Masts rise above the grassy knolls. As she walks towards them, treading the path that winds along the shore, the masts lengthen until the forecastle and aft cabin and eventually the entire hull comes into view. Laura is right, the schooner is immense, bigger than Hetty ever imagined. High and dry on the mud flats, with every inch of the height and breadth of her hull exposed, she is quite literally out of her element.

When Hetty was a girl, schooners and their square-rigged forerunners moored cheek to cheek across the Halifax waterfront, as much a part of the scene as the Citadel and the town clock, their bows nodding with the swell, masts and rigging criss-crossing the sky from the north-end train station almost all the way out to Point Pleasant Park. Since she moved to the village Hetty has seen the odd ketch stranded, waiting patiently on the mud for the tide to buoy it up again. But never a vessel on this scale. There's something menacing in the way the schooner, painted black almost to her keel, consumes the wharf she is moored to, the way her bow angles above the horizon as if she's mounting the bank, threatening to climb ashore.

Drawing closer, Hetty makes out people on the tilted deck, leaning their bodies into the ship for balance, calling to each other; she catches only the cadence, their words hollowed out by the wind. The damage Laura spoke of appears confined to the bow. The jib sails hang shredded amongst twisted ropes and splintered wood, and the bowsprit is but a jagged stump. Perhaps the *Esmeralda* — Hetty catches the schooner's name as a gust billows the errant and tangled sails — has been in a collision.

As the path rounds the bow Hetty sees what was hidden from her view before, dozens of people milling about on the wharf. Normally she would avoid such a large congregation of Kenomee villagers, but today Hetty is as curious as her neighbours. And for once she isn't the focus of their gaze. Some nod at her approach, others step back to let her pass. As she wends her way through the crowd, she catches snippets of the men's conversations — "widow-maker's snapped right off," "squall in the bay," "if she didn't catch the flood." The carnival-like excitement in the air, the buzz of speculation, lifts her strange mood.

The halyards click and clang in the breeze, tapping a non-rhythm against the masts. A man labours high in the foremast rigging, apparently held aloft by his wits and the grace of God. Fear blooms in Hetty as she watches him swinging casually with the wind, a surge of fellow feeling she hasn't experienced in a long time. When with a stronger gust the sailor's hand slips from its hold Hetty gasps aloud, having in that instant envisioned him dropping, his head splitting open on the deck below. But his reflexes are greased, his loss of balance fleeting. Hetty's heartbeat has not quite returned to normal when she hears chuckling at her side and turns to see a spry white-haired fellow puffing on a pipe. Blue eyes sharp and pale as a winter sky. He winks at her. Does she know him? A sea of faces drifts by her every week at church, but the people are all spruced up in their Sunday best, smart hats and polished shoes, collars and ties. Identifying them the other six days has been a slow and at times embarrassing task. But then who's to say old blue-eyes even attends church?

"Don't you worry 'bout him up there," he says, taking his pipe from his mouth. "Tied up at a wharf, and not a drop of sea to toss him about."

Hetty glances back at the sailor, who now has one leg hooked around the mast. "But that was the wind."

"Days of the square-riggers, men were up and down rigging on the open sea and in all kinds of weather. None of this steam-hoisted sails business, it was all hands on deck."

"They didn't fall, ever?"

"Oh, they fell all right. You hit bad weather or an old sea out there, sometimes an entire watch would wash overboard. One minute there, the next gone without a trace." .

The wind cuts through her dress, chilling her bare legs, and Hetty pulls her jacket closed, rubs at her arms. People hurt themselves in so many ways: men fell down open pits, children speared themselves on treacherous railings, lurking nails. Mothers burned themselves on malicious stoves. How fragile the human body is, so easily bruised and broken; how vulnerable we all are. I used to be a nurse, she almost tells him, then wonders at her urge to share this confidence. Not that it's much of a confidence anymore. Almost everyone in the village seems to know who she is. Who she was. Or they think they do. Hetty isn't sure she knows herself anymore. The days since she strode with purpose through the north-end streets of Halifax, black bag in hand, knocking on her patients' doors, greeting their families, charting their progress, feel like another lifetime, something that happened on the other side of the world.

"See, I told you. Nothing to worry about." The old man nods towards the foremast and Hetty watches the sailor scurry down the ratlines, nimble as a rat himself. Her shoulders relax when his feet touch the deck. She would like to move away, take in the rest of the ship and finish her walk, but feels equally compelled to draw out the conversation. That the old man doesn't seem to know who she is, or isn't interested in bringing it up if he does, is enough of a novelty to stay her feet.

"I've never seen so many people on the wharf before."

Raising his nose to the air, blue-eyes sniffs. "Smell that? That's the scent of money."

Hetty follows suit, sniffing the air, and laughs as he chuckles at her clowning. Commerce. The men are down here looking for work, the women hoping to sell a few loaves of bread, a few preserves. The shopkeepers — there's Jed Harper climbing out of his truck — will be thinking along the lines of tobacco and rope, burn ointment and maybe even a new oil slicker or two.

They watch an exchange between one of the younger men on the wharf and a wiry man on the schooner. The village man leans over the edge and stares down at the ship's deck, which lies a good eight or nine feet below him. Then he steps backwards and disappears into the crowd.

"Surely he isn't going to — " Hetty never finishes her sentence, for suddenly the man is running full tilt towards the lip of the wharf. With more gusto than grace he leaps into the air, arms spread wide as if to catch the wind, knees angled to take the impact of his landing. Hetty cringes at the dull thud. A telltale second or so passes before the man pulls himself to standing.

"That must have hurt."

"That's Noble Matheson for you, always thinking he has to prove something." Blue-eyes pauses to relight his pipe. "It tells you they've trouble with their donkey engine, then. Matheson's no carpenter, that's for sure."

Now Hetty recognizes him too. Noble Matheson. Thin-faced and hawk-nosed, with a perpetual look of worry on his face. And perhaps most unfortunate, strawberry blond hair kinked in a full marcel wave — the kind of hair that looks better on a girl. He'd made a nuisance of himself when Peter briefly had the Model T last summer, forever wanting to tinker under the hood. It was as if he could smell engine trouble. The slightest hiccup — there had been many hiccups — and right about the time Peter started extolling the virtues, through gritted teeth, of horseshoes and hay, Matheson would suddenly appear from behind a bush or be conveniently strolling along the road. He would come over and stand behind Peter, peering over his shoulder and asking questions, giving unasked-for advice. Peter, accustomed to being the man in charge, the one with all the answers, grew so frustrated and fed up with being upstaged by the younger man — "being made to look a damned fool by some jack-of-all-trades in shabby shoes" — that he got rid of the car and bought another horse.

"And it's called a donkey engine because . . . ?"

"Does all the donkey work."

"Of course."

"Hoists the sails, runs the windlass, capstan, pumps, that sort of thing. It's down in the fo'c'sle." He waves his pipe at the bow.

"I see." Two nautical lessons in one day. This time next week she'll be able to sail the thing right out of the bay.

Matheson shakes hands with the wiry man, and a barrel-chested fellow with a beard and a hat strides across the deck to join them. The wiry man has a big red birthmark on his face. That or he's been in a fight. He calls down the companionway and the head of a fourth man appears from below.

"And the large fellow, that's got to be the captain." Though some pretend otherwise, everyone on the wharf is watching their man, and not simply because of his dramatic embarkation. It would seem that Matheson in his shabby shoes is the village's emissary, the first to break ranks and cross the us-and-them divide. If he can secure work, then so can others. The four men walk to the stern of the schooner. Hetty watches them disappear into the aft cabin.

"She looks as if she doesn't belong here."

"Who?"

"The ship." Hetty's face prickles. Didn't men always calls ships she?

"Well, she's not such a common sight anymore, I'll grant you that. But we used to build 'em that size here. Lay the keel and launch 'em right over there." He nods in the direction of Hetty's woodland path. He puffs on his pipe awhile then takes it out of his mouth. "Thought for a minute there you was talking about the girl."

"The girl?"

"The girl on the schooner."

"There's a girl on the schooner?"

"That's what I just said. Dressed up in men's gear too, like she's one of the crew. She's down aft, go see for yourself.

Hetty makes her way down the wharf towards the stern of the ship, where two crew members are furling a sail that has been laid out to dry. He must mean the one with the long tied-back hair. She isn't merely dressed like one of the crew, she's working alongside them: a girl on a ship, dressed as a man and working as a man too. Hetty is still gawping when the girl, as if sensing the attention, turns and grins. She can't be any more than nineteen or twenty years old.

"Hello there."

Hetty smiles back. She feels singled out and special. She too can blur the us-and-them divide. "I like your outfit, " she calls out. What she likes is the idea behind the outfit. Imagine the freedom to live in men's clothing, without the strictures of stockings and garters and girdles, without the exigencies and betrayals they cause. Imagine taking full strides, stepping out unencumbered by the proprieties that demand slips and high-heeled shoes.

"I like your footwear," the girl calls back, the trace of another country in her accent.

Hetty glances down at her rubber boots streaked with red mud. She points her toe like a fashion model. "They're all the rage," she shouts, then laughs, laughs until tears spring to her eyes, laughs so hard her belly aches. Where is this schoolgirl attack coming from? She can hear people tsk-tsking as they edge away, shaking their heads. Hetty sobers quickly, appalled at having drawn so much attention to herself. The girl's musical laughter carries through the air; Hetty can see her still standing at the ship's rail, one foot on the gunwale, hands on her boyish hips, head thrown back. But rather than be united with a stranger against them, Hetty has already stepped back into the crowd — excuse me, thank you, may I go past — intent on making her way back home.

II

The wiry man grasps Noble's hand in a show of strength, introduces himself as the first mate. His name is Spoon. Noble casts his eye down the row of tarnished teaspoons that serve as buttons on the man's jacket but is drawn back to his face. If he's going for nicknames, then why not Spot? The man's left cheek is an obscenity of dark crimson abscess, clusters of puss-filled boils bubbling at the surface. His pupils are pinpricks, and his pale grey eyes glitter. Has pain bled them of colour? It is difficult not to stare. When the captain strides over, Noble is grateful, now he has someplace else to look. The helmsman joins them, his name unpronounceable: Noble can call him Max. The captain points and Spoon heads for the aft cabin. The others follow but Noble hesitates, suspicious. What could be back there that requires his know-how? He scans the deck again. No cargo nets. No coal dust or wood splinters. And no fishy smell. There's something not quite right about the *Esmeralda*.

Below in the cargo hold, Noble's apprehension grows. He has never seen anything like it. At least not strapped to the keel block in a wooden sailing ship.

"It's an airplane engine." A water-cooled Liberty V12, the best contribution the Yanks made to the war effort. He wonders where in hell they got it but knows better than to ask. Likely war surplus, same as his truck.

Spoon fixes him with his bleached eyes. "I could've told you it was from an airplane, bright spark. Now can you fix it?"

"That depends on what's wrong with it." He can't move it, that's for sure. The thing must weigh close to half a ton. Which means working down here. He glances around. Ventilation is practically non-existent and the smell of gasoline is making his head thick. He worries there's a leak somewhere. Worries there's a bloody big gas tank sitting over their heads.

"May I?" He holds out his hand for Spoon's flashlight, shines it around the hold.

Spoon cracks his knuckles. "The engine's over 'ere, mate." Noble obliges, running the light along the length of the camshaft. Filthy. One of the pins holding the lifters is a bent nail, and the cooling pipe has a leak patched with a rag.

"I'm more used to cars, trucks, that sort of thing."

"I thought you said you knew engines. Now you're saying you can't fix it?" The air splits and fissures around Spoon. Could be he doesn't like confined spaces, or he's been sniffing the gasoline too long. Probably it's the carbuncle on his face, it's got to be throbbing something fierce.

"I didn't say I couldn't fix it." He'll learn. Fly by the seat of his pants. If these men are up to what he thinks they are, they have plenty of money to throw around. He looks to the captain and then Max.

"So you say she'll start no problem?"

The helmsman pushes his fingers through his hair. "She start. She run. But pushing down the throttle it is missing sometimes." Max mimes with his thick-fingered hands. "Duddle, duddle, phhs, duddle duddle phhs. And less power. When she is going faster, she is shaking."

"How fast you been pushing her?"

Max clears his throat, shuffles his feet on the dunnage. Spoon cracks his knuckles.

"Does it matter?" The cavernous space amplifies the Captain's baritone.

"It might." Noble bends to take a closer look and shift his face out of the crossfire. He smells mutiny. "You come through the channel on the flood?" Without raising his eyes to theirs he walks around to inspect the cylinders along the other side. "Tide turns on you it can put a hell of a strain on her, even a big engine like this." Four hundred and ten horses. That's some getaway power. He spots what looks like a silencer just before the screw. The gasoline in the air has been tossed about to hide another smell. Noble feels the thrill of danger tightening his skin.

"One of the cylinders has a broken lifter. See?" He turns and gestures, his finger on the culprit. They should see for themselves so they don't think he's some village con artist. Max takes a step forward and hesitates, trapped by the tension between the two other men. The captain's jaw is rigid. Why does Noble feel as if Spoon is in charge? He wipes his face on his sleeve. Spoon is using up all the oxygen, or his face is burning it off.

"Can you fix it?"

Noble turns to Spoon, fastens on the space above his right shoulder. "I'll need a little time."

"Take whatever time you need." The captain nods and turns to leave.

When Noble climbs the ladder to the wharf, the broken lifter tucked in his pocket, Spoon's parting words ringing in his ears — "Remember, village boy, I've got my eye on you" — Miss Murchie is standing there looking officious. For a brief moment Noble thinks she has come for him, to deliver in person the package he's been waiting for. He even checks to see if it's tucked under her arm. But Miss Murchie glances past him to the men on the deck of the schooner. In addition to being postmistress, Miss Murchie is also the customs officer for the village. As he walks away Noble hears her call out to see the ship's papers. Something else that probably isn't quite right about the *Esmeralda*.

Noble drives to the end of Shad Beach Road, then slows before edging his truck onto the tidal flats. Two hundred yards out into the basin stands Begging Dog Weir, a narrow, elongated V-shape of eight-foot-high birch stakes and woven brush whose uneven east and west wings together span more than two thousand feet. As the tide drops, the longer straighter east wing guides the fish towards the point of the V; the shorter and slightly curved west wing, the fishing wing, traps the fish once the water level has fallen enough to expose the tops of the stakes. The position of the weir has shifted slightly over the years to accommodate the basin's ever-changing tidal currents, but the track Noble follows, an ancient stream bed reinforced over the years with rocks and gravel, has not. A couple of feet on either side and man, horse and especially a truck would quickly become mired in the sticky red mud.

Noble pulls up near the edge of the shallow pool that the retreating tide leaves behind in the point of the trap. Bess is standing somewhere near the centre of the pool, seawater lapping over her fetlocks. She is dozing in the sun. Every minute or so the alignment of her rump shifts as she alternates her resting foot. Butler is a yard or two in front of Bess, bent to his task. Before getting out of his truck Noble changes into his rubber boots. He slams the door but Butler doesn't look up.

"Morning."

"Afternoon."

Noble rolls his eyes at the cloudless sky, then wades into the pool and grabs a dip net from the wagon hitched behind

Bess, which is already half-filled. At this time of year the catch is mainly cod, smelts and herring, though as the water warms gaspereau and mackerel migrate into the bay, followed by shad, sturgeon, bass flounder and then salmon. Butler's jacket and sweater are tied, arms together, around the horse's neck.

"They keeping you busy?"

"I haven't time to be pissing about, Matheson. If you're here to help then roll up your sleeves and get on with it." Noble kicks at the water and a couple of gulls at the pool's edge lift off, only to land again a couple of yards away, bend their beaks and resume pecking at the fish.

"Did you get a chance to check out the schooner?"

"What do you think?" Butler steps back, winds up and sends a startled skate, wings dark against the sun, hurtling over the top of the weir. Noble shades his eyes to witness the skate's trajectory over the wall of woven spruce and birch saplings. The skate, spinning like a wobbly tin lid through a forget-me-not blue sky, lands with a small splash, and Noble wonders if any of the skates and dogfish tossed from the weir as useless bycatch ever survive their ordeal. The gulls won't touch them. They probably suffocate long before high tide. He swishes his net through the water. Now he's worried about dogfish? — Lawson's influence. His brother has been on his mind a lot lately.

"Well, I did."

"Good for you."

Butler clicks his tongue and Bess pulls forward slowly, drawing the cart with her. Noble follows, tapping the seabed with his rubber-booted feet before transferring his body weight, feeling for flounder that may have burrowed themselves into the rich red mud. Up ahead, Butler executes the same strange dance. Bess takes it all in her watery stride. Bess was Butler's birthday gift from his father the year he turned ten. A playful two-year-old with a penchant for sugar cubes, Bess was bought to pull the cart to and from the weir twice a day. Not much of a gift then. Still, after sixteen years man and beast have mastered a working rhythm. Bess doesn't need tying to the weir while Butler fishes. Butler has so much faith in his animal he doesn't bother turning around to see if she's obeyed.

Bess stumbles and Noble runs a hand down her hind leg, watching her feet as they draw through the water. Could be she's tired, or at eighteen she's just plain getting too old for the job of hauling the catch every low tide, mid-May through October, not to mention the heavy winter work, hauling upwards of three thousand birch, maple and spruce saplings from the woods to rebuild the weir after the ice has ground out the previous year's poles.

"You should be thinking about retirement, there, old girl. Those feet of yours weren't made for toiling in salt water."

"She's plenty years left in her yet," Butler shouts at the weir.

"You should get yourself a truck. Join us in the twentieth century." Noble pats Bess's grey and white dappled rump. Her ears switch back and forth.

"And give myself another headache."

"What headache's that?"

"You're never done fixing that contraption of yours."

"It gets you around when you want."

Butler lobs a fair-sized cod at Noble, who ducks so that the fish sails over the cart and smacks Bess on the back of her ears. She never even flinches.

"That's animal cruelty. You don't deserve her anyway."

"We have an understanding, don't we, old girl?"

"Right."

"Listen, Matheson. When I get a truck it'll be shiny and brand new, not some jalopy tied together with baling wire."

Noble scoops up a cod with his net, dumps it in the cart. "Maybe I'll beat you to it. I got myself some repair work on board that schooner."

"You said you'd help out here. I need two pair of hands, especially these next few tides."

"I'll be here. It's just that this is real work for a change." The second the words leave his mouth he wishes he could call them back.

Butler straightens, a fish hooked through its gills dangling from each thumb — real weir fishermen don't use dip nets. "And this isn't work?" The fishes' mouths open and close in a mock jeer.

"I didn't say that." A toadfish breaks the surface, and Noble nudges it aside with the dip net, bends to chase the silver-blue back of an early shad. Or is the silver a trick of the bright spring sunshine?

"Funny, that's what came out your mouth. There's a village full of men'd be more than grateful to be lending a hand out here. Come to think of it, there's a village full of men better qualified to be fixing a damaged schooner than you. You don't know your awls from your planes."

"Aye, but I can rig a dodgy camshaft, strip a cylinder clean and put her back together without having anything left over."

"What're you saying?" Butler tosses the fish into the cart.

"I'm saying they've rigged up an auxiliary — a Liberty V12 with a silencer."

Butler's face splits in a grin. "Rum-runners."

"That's what I thought too. She's painted black, but it's all dull port side — little flecks of different coloured paint, you know, like she's been tied up alongside other boats out at sea. Thing is she's empty — a gaping great cargo hold with nothing in it but rock ballast."

"So what? They're probably between hauls."

"All the way up here? I doubt it."

"A rum-running expert now, are we? Go on then, what's your theory this time?"

"I figure they dumped the liquor on the way in."

"You been reading too many books, Matheson." Butler is bent over behind Bess, hands chasing another thrashing tail, but Noble can sense his friend's keen attention.

"No, think about it. It makes perfect sense. They drop it overboard on the way in and pick it up on the way back out."

"They dumped it in the water?"

"It's the perfect hiding place. And the cargo nets are gone. I make it sitting out there on the mud flats."

"It'd get dragged out with the tides."

"Not if it was weighted down."

"So it's anywhere from here to Cape Split."

"It's behind Moose Island."

"You got it all worked out, don't you?"

"They came in on the tide — no one would see them working a cargo boom at night, right? So think about it. In order to pick it up on the way out, they set anchor and wait for low tide. When the booze magically reappears, they hook it and haul it back in, sail out on the tide."

"And you think they'd do this behind Moose Island?"

"It's the perfect cover. Only the birds and a few rock crabs to see them."

"How bad's the schooner?"

"The bow's all banged up. Jibs are gone. Enough to slow them down, make navigation difficult. Someone had a good hand and eye bringing them in that sweetly in the dark."

"Full moon last night."

"True."

"How about the engine?"

"Broken lifter on one of the cylinders." Noble swishes his dip net through the murky water and scoops up the damn toadfish.

"You can fix this?"

"That depends on McFadden." He tips the wide-mouthed ugly brute back into the pool.

"McFadden?"

"I need a part cast."

"You asked him yet?"

"You have to pick your moment with McFadden. Liable

to get your head bitten off, you approach him at the wrong time."

"True. Get out, you vicious bastard." A thrashing in the water as Butler, two-handed, heaves a small dogfish into the air. He wipes his hands on his pants. "Wouldn't fancy being his kids."

"Or his wife."

"Wouldn't fancy being anyone's wife there, Noble."

Which is rich coming from a man whose own wife has to suffer his pathological skirt-chasing, much of which, conducted within eyesight and earshot, feels designed to drive her away. Noble watches the sand shark buckle and twist through the air. It's probably injured or they would have noticed it earlier.

"They eat them in England. You see that ever?"

"Wives?" Butler pushes back the brim of his salt-stained fedora and grins wickedly.

"Dogfish."

Butler pulls a face.

"God's honest. Some fish and chip shops. Battered and deep-fried."

"My friend, you can take home all the dogfish this weir can hold."

"No thanks." They hold dogfish in the same regard as carrion. Even one or two in the weir can make a mess of things, but they hunt in packs. In the Cheverie weir they caught over three hundred of them in one tide. This was a few years back. Smiler, Franklin Beattie's mare, walked herself home with what the men could salvage of the catch while Franklin and Bert Simpson stayed behind and tied all the dogfish they could get hold of to the weir before the tide chased them out. Noble can just imagine the look on his mother's face if he brought one home for supper, with its poisonous spines and its mouth filled with razor-sharp teeth.

"You should go see him soon as we're finished up here."

"Huh?"

"McFadden. Strike while the iron's hot, I say."

"That supposed to be funny?"

"Funny is my middle name, Matheson."

"Got any jokes I could use, then? Stories to soften a blacksmith's heart?" Something about Paul McFadden sets Noble's teeth on edge. There's altogether too much of him for a start, though Noble appreciates that size in McFadden's job is a definite advantage. But unlike Butler, who with his 6'4" frame can easily out-walk and outrun anyone in the village, the smith carries his size threateningly. At least around men. Rumour has it McFadden plucked out the hearts of Krauts on the battlefield with his bare hands, that he once dined on Kraut flesh. Noble thinks McFadden probably started the rumours himself; with his trade he would most likely have been on horse detail. Not that he wouldn't have seen any action that way. Lawson had always said that no matter what your duty, there was no way you could avoid hoisting a rifle to your shoulder and firing away at the enemy. His brother had fired his gun a lot. Still, there was a difference between shooting a man and killing him with your bare hands.

"He's not so bad."

"You've changed your tune. Anyway, you're a horse owner. I have a truck. To him I'm some evil portent of the future. He isn't the most enlightened man I've ever met."

"Enlightened? Portent? You swallow a dictionary or something, Matheson? Getting fancy ideas at Lillian MacAllister's Friday night lending library?"

Noble glances at his friend sharply.

"Remember, you want to tell a good story, you leave out the big words — they get in the way."

Noble bends to scoop a fish. Butler can't possibly have guessed anything, it's just his uncanny way of zeroing in on the truth. He seems to pick people's thoughts from the air, as if they were radio waves and he a giant antenna.

"What makes you think I'm interested in your kind of storytelling?"

"Women."

"Women?"

"They're all over me. I have to fight them off. Don't tell me you haven't noticed."

"Yeah. Five-year-olds."

"Accompanied by their lovely young mothers, older sisters and cousins, doting aunts and grandmothers. My stories charm women of all ages while the best you can do is lonely Lillian McAllister. You're jealous, Matheson."

"No, I —" He feels sorry for Eliza, though saying so will only get Butler's dander up. And maybe he is a little jealous. But not because of the women. It's the stories that spill effortlessly from his friend's lips, the way Butler blends fact and legend with his own peculiar twist, engaging his listeners' attention, whatever their age and station, and holding it.

"There's a girl on the schooner." Now why'd he go and say that? Butler will discover as much for himself soon enough. As will Eliza.

"Well, well. What kind of girl goes to sea with a ship filled with men, do you think?"

"I have no idea."

"Then use your imagination, bonehead."

He has. All he'd caught sight of was the length and sheen of her blue-black hair, her athletic carriage, unusual in a woman but far from mannish. He'd willed her to turn around but she was oblivious, talking and laughing with the Douglas woman. "She was wearing men's clothing."

"Men's clothing?" Butler wades towards the centre of the trap. "She pretty at all?"

"Couldn't say."

Butler weaves the end of a sapling that has worked itself loose back through the birch framework. The point of the weir's elongated V takes the force of the catch, and while its bottom is reinforced with rocks, the poles and brush frequently need mending. "Might be worth a gander."

"Well, I've already been down there once today. So you're on your own."

"Suits me fine. You'll cramp my style, anyway."

"You okay to split and salt this lot?" The tide is creeping back in and Bess's cart is full.

"I'm fine. The wife can help. You on your way to see Mc-Fadden?"

"Oh, so now you're taking an interest in my work?" Butler's no fool. Everyone has heard stories of the money to be made hooking up with the rum-runners. One of his cousins claims to be involved. He passed through early last winter, bragging and waving a clipful of cash around, trying to get a poker game going. He said it was dangerous work, but a deckhand could get something like sixty or seventy dollars a month, a mate closer to a hundred and fifty. Lunenburg and shipyards east and west of there were busy refitting schooners and building rum boats with engines and speeds the U.S. Coast Guard hadn't a hope in hell of keeping up with.

"I couldn't give a monkey's about your work, Matheson. Just wondering how long the rummies'll be around. See you tonight?"

"Eight-thirty okay?"

"Fine."

Noble walks back to the truck, sets the choke and pushes the starter. The engine turns over but doesn't catch. He tries again but the battery sounds run down. Butler, now sitting up on the edge of the cart and coaxing Bess to head for home, grins and doffs his hat.

"I rest my case, Matheson." Noble grabs the crank and gets out of the truck.

"Battery's low," he grumbles as Butler and Bess pull past him.

"Battery, choke, throttle, starter. It's always something, eh, girl?"

Noble pulls up twice on the crank, releases the choke and

she's fired. No kickback either. Where's Butler when you want him to be looking? Carefully Noble turns the truck around and heads back to the village. Halfway up Shad Beach Road he honks as he passes Butler and Bess, flashes the V for Victory sign. McFadden can wait. The mail should be in from Great Village by now. And Miss Murchie should be back behind her counter at the post office.

III

Hetty flexes her hands, imagines scaling the smooth sun-warmed wood of the ship's mast, the fibrous chafe of the ratlines against her legs, across the soft skin of her palms. How would it be to commune with the birds and clouds, wind at her back, sea spray in her hair? Imagine being able to journey beyond the horizon, to dodge icebergs and whales and round the infamous Cape Horn.

"You're very quiet."

"I'm not feeling so well."

"You look a little flushed. Perhaps you should have a lie-down after lunch."

"I don't want to lie down."

"Very well." Peter takes a slice of bread, spreading butter into every corner, spreading it so thinly Hetty doesn't know why he bothers.

"It's a lovely day. What are you thinking of doing this afternoon?"

Running away to sea.

"Laura and I plan to do some baking."

"Shall I look forward to a treat for dinner?"

Now she'll have to bake something. Though she can always

say she burned it and threw it away. Or gave it to Laura to take home. Baking. Needlepoint. Letter writing. Peter's ideas of how she should fill her days make her want to shock him: sit down at the dinner table stark naked, paint the outside of the house sunshine yellow or pink, take up mountaineering as a hobby, get her pilot's license and buzz the mill.

Upside down.

In February, not long after they'd returned from Halifax, he'd presented her with watercolour paints, paper, charcoal and sketchbooks. Still wrapped deep in her grief, Hetty had dismissed the gift as the gesture of a man cut adrift by the spectre of his wife's loss and trying to find a way back. In Halifax, the days had spun into one another, blurring at the edges, while Hetty had lain in her old childhood bed, afraid to open her mouth in case her mind slipped out as abruptly as her unborn child had slipped from her womb. And suddenly one day there was Peter, ready to take her back to the village. As the weeks passed she learned to move again, however woodenly, through the days, to eat without every mouthful tasting like straw.

But when March rolled around and Peter was still bringing his gifts to the breakfast table — "You might think about doing a little sketching or painting today, my dear. I set up a still life arrangement for you in the parlour" — she began to wonder if his behaviour had less to do with bandaging her feelings than with his notions of how women should behave, particularly women from upstanding Halifax families. Hetty had never picked up a paintbrush in her life, and charcoal was something to burn in a fire. Which, on Mothering Sunday, is precisely what she did: scooped up the unused sketching pad, the accusatory water-colour block, the tin of coloured squares, the box of charcoal sticks, and placed — not flung, she had no desire to appear hysterical — the whole lot on the fire that he had set in the grate that morning. She sat back down at the breakfast table, brought a piece of buttered toast to her mouth and stared hard at Peter's pale features, the bloodless line of his lips, silently daring him to retrieve his cargo of gifts from the flames. Peter finished his breakfast in silence.

But he was not to be deterred. The morning following his return from a business trip to Truro, a copy of Elizabeth Barrett Browning's poems was waiting for her between the teapot and the toast at breakfast. While the book remains in the dining room, placed with an artful casualness on the sideboard, Hetty, to her credit (and Peter's?), has read the volume several times through. Mrs. Browning was a champion of social causes, and Hetty has her favourites, among them "The Cry of the Children," which carries her back to Halifax's north end and its generation of the scarred and maimed. Even those children fortunate enough to escape the wrath of that December blast still bore the mark of their poverty in their stick-like arms and legs, their clay-coloured skin, their lustreless hair. Hetty turns these favourite pages carefully, wary of cracking the spine of the book or staining the pages with crumbs and butter spots and giving herself away to Peter, though why she expends her energy in such games is beyond her. As for *Sonnets from the Portuguese*, she reads wryly, if it is possible to read wryly, holding the book away from herself, one eyebrow cocked. How do I love thee, Peter? Not at all, I'm afraid. But then what did you expect from an arranged marriage?

"If you're not feeling yourself I could ask the doctor to call round."

"Doctor Baker's ministrations I can live without, thank you."

"If you're sure." He stirs the tea and pours them both a cup. "You could go to Halifax. Visit your family doctor if that will help you feel better."

"I'm not ill, Peter."

"But you said you felt tired. I think —"

"I know what I said." Why is she so tense? Because he surprised her by coming home to eat his midday meal with her?

Because he thinks he can cheer her up? Because he's inter-rupting her daydreams — the make-believe world she's been creating for herself since she first saw the girl on the schooner? Hetty pictures herself sweeping the dishes from the table to the floor.

"Don't you ever get fed up living in this village, Peter? Don't you ever wonder what's out there in the world? Don't you want to explore at all? Travel the ocean, see Europe?"

Napkin to his mouth. "I have seen it."

Four little words. How heavily they now lie over the dining table. On her skin. Who can compete with the war? Who can compete with an enemy that won't show itself? He will neither talk about it nor rail against it. Uniform under lock and key. Medals, likewise.

"I've seen some horrors too," she says, her voice small and sour. But she can't penetrate his mask. The war is Peter's to carry. As the miscarriage is hers.

Knife and fork together. Napkin on the plate. He gathers himself. "We could take a trip if you like. I usually take some vacation in July."

"Clara's wedding is in July." Why does he still speak to her as though they were virtual strangers?

"Yes, well, I can take the time before or after."

"It can hardly be before, now can it, seeing as I'm matron of honour. Weddings take an awful lot of planning and prepara-tion, you know." She stabs at the scrap of fish on her plate. How long had her mother planned her own and Peter's wedding? The length of time it takes to receive a telegram and compose a reply. Hetty pushes her plate to one side. How much planning and preparation had Vivian done? How much thought had she put into choosing the date? The venue? The groom.

"Of course. After Clara's wedding. We could hire a car and tour Cape Breton if you like."

"I've already seen Cape Breton."

"You have?"

"When I was a nurse." In her other life. When Kenomee Village was just the name of the place where her mother's cousin and his family lived. When Peter was — take your pick — a picture on the mantel, your second cousin, a good man, so handsome in his officer's uniform. Hetty had been qualified only a few months when she was chosen to work on one of two public health caravans that would tour the province carrying dentistry and surgery to outlying regions. Money left over from the Halifax Relief Fund, set up in the wake of the 1917 Explosion, paid for the project. The caravans had left Halifax in July of 1920. Often awake and on the road before dawn, Hetty and the others had spent six solid weeks on bumpy roads with torturous grades. Arriving tired and saddlesore in some remote hamlet, they set to work immediately, dispensing advice, giving public health talks and holding clinics. Hetty had helped examine the patients, many suffering from tuberculosis, and assisted in minor surgery such as removing tonsils and adenoids and extracting countless thousands of rotten teeth without anaesthetic from hundreds of mouths. She has been fastidious about her teeth ever since. The adventure had taken her to parts of the province never before travelled by motor vehicle. At Baddeck she had been invited to the home of Dr. and Mrs. Alexander Graham Bell and shown his great inventions.

"Anyway, you hate driving."

"I don't hate it."

"So why did you get rid of the car?"

"It wasn't practical."

"What's so practical about stabling a horse in two places and saddling it every time you want to go somewhere?"

"I prefer to ride."

"Then why even suggest driving around Cape Breton? The roads are terrible."

His chest and shoulders rise and fall in a deep sigh, but if Peter is irritated Hetty can read no signs of it on his face. He pushes his chair back and gets to his feet. "It's time I was going. I have a meeting."

The dining table stretches between them, an expanse of well-polished oak.

After he leaves Hetty makes her way to the kitchen. Suddenly, baking seems like a good idea.

IV

"This what you been waitin' for?" Miss Murchie produces a rectangular package from the small pile of mail sitting on a shabby sideboard against the wall and pushes both it and her receipt book towards Noble over the narrow makeshift counter — part of an old barn door planed smooth. The book's corners are curled and grubby. She points a wrinkled finger at the signatures column, a blank space next to her precise printing of his name. "Sign here."

Noble picks up the pencil leashed with a string anchored somewhere under Miss Murchie's side of the barn door.

"It's a book," she announces, in case he hadn't realized.

"I know it's a book, Miss Murchie." It's more than a book. Noble wants to grin but instead puckers his lips and fakes a frown. The box bears a printed label from the publishing house — The Author's Press — pasted in a skewed fashion, as if the sender were in a hurry, and two American stamps, one green, one orange, Auburn, N.Y. stamped in smudgy ink across Washington's faces. The package isn't sealed in any way. It is simply a box with a fitted lid and a cross of loosely tied string, both quite easy to remove and replace. Miss Murchie has perhaps already peeked inside. He narrows his eyes at her. And then what? The woman can broadcast news faster than a leaky shad boat takes on water. People will think he's getting ideas above himself. He tucks the box under his arm — his hands smell and there are probably still a few stubborn fish scales under his nails or clinging to the cuffs of his sweater — and bids Miss Murchie good day.

To appease McFadden's touchiness, Noble parks the truck around the corner, well out of the blacksmith's sight. Nearing the open doorway he hears first the soft nicker of a horse and then the low-pitched back-of-the-throat sounds of McFadden coaxing an animal. The blacksmith has an extraordinary touch when it comes to horses. Too many men throw their weight around with animals in their charge, thinking the only way to control a horse or ox or even a dog is to bully and punish. McFadden looks the horse in the eye, he clucks and coaxes, he strokes and pats. McFadden is gentle yet always in control. And while he is not simply a farrier but crafts tools, sharpens plow-shares, sets tires and welds axles, word of his way has spread to communities up and down the basin. If only the man could extend the same courtesies to people.

When he steps inside Noble can see that McFadden, busy tethering a roan mare to a ringbolt on the far wall of the smithy, has a small boy for company. Noble's heart snags, then settles in his throat. Though the boy, fawn-coloured knee socks pulled up straight, is staring into the flames of the forge, his back to Noble, he is instantly familiar. Jeremiah Baker Jr., Mary's boy. Noble glances around for the boy's mother but she is nowhere in sight. Jeremiah Baker Jr. is a brutal name to saddle a kid with. Besides, to Noble he doesn't look much like a Jeremiah. Walt maybe, or Joe. There's something disturbingly familiar about Mary's child. Noble can't help thinking he knows the boy from somewhere. He felt the same way at Harvest Festival last fall, not long after Mary and her doctor husband moved back to the village from Londonderry. Eliza, Butler's wife, had pointed the boy out, and Noble had spent the rest of the festival trying to shake off the uncomfortable sensation of déjà vu. Something of that same feeling is crawling around his belly now.

There's a satchel on the floor by the boy's feet; he must be on his way home from school. What do the kids there make of his drawn-out name? People never shorten Noble's name. Nobe. Who can blame them? Call me No, he'll sometimes tell strangers, but more often than not it's Matheson he goes by. "Which one?" he used to call out, swinging his arm about his brother's neck. "There's two of us." And he'd laugh, hiding the fact that his feelings were hurt. Lawson was always Lawson, or Paws to his friends, that is, to the entire village, a nickname bestowed on him because of the stray dogs he was forever befriending and taking home.

Noble stares at the satchel, almost afraid to look at the boy. The satchel is new and likely store bought. No hand-me-downs for Jeremiah Baker Jr. Probably purchased on a day trip into Truro or by mail order from Halifax. The stitching is still white and noticeable against the tan coloured leather, though Noble would bet the boy drags that new satchel through the grass and along the road at least part of the way to school, trying to get it dirty, worn in. There's a fine line between the shame of having something too new and having something too old that adults seem to forget when they become parents. Can't be much fun for a kid whose father's own childhood is buried way back in the last century.

"My name is Jem," the child announces self-importantly. Jem. Not bad. The kid has claimed an identity of sorts for himself. "What's your name?" Though the boy looks only about six years old there's an echo of authority in his voice, a trace of sharpness that suggests he is accustomed to adult deference.

"Mr. McFadden to you, son." The blacksmith doesn't look up from his work. Noble can't blame him; the master-addressing-servant tone is difficult enough to take at the best of times but just about intolerable coming from a child.

"And what's the horse's name?"

"Bracken." With a pair of long-handled tongs McFadden places a piece of bar-iron into the forge. He walks to Bracken's hindquarters and stands astride, facing away. Running a comforting hand down her leg he bends, grasps her fetlock, and swings her right foot towards him, cradling it between his powerful legs. All the while his trademark clucks and whistles issue from his throat. From a box at his feet he takes a tool and pulls the old shoe free. A pick to clean around the frog, pincers to remove the nails, then a rasp to quickly work off any rough edges. Next he takes a short knife and begins trimming the sole and hoof. Noble, who has seen such work performed countless times, is more interested in the child and can't get over the way Jem rocks back on his heels, hands pushed way down inside his pockets. Noble often stands just that way.

"Do the horses like it?" Jem's curiosity is getting the better of him, his voice is less shrill.

"Some do, some don't. They're like people, son." McFadden squints over towards the boy. He makes no sign of recognizing Noble, or even acknowledging his presence, though McFadden certainly knows he's there. The shop isn't that big. "Do you like having your toenails trimmed?"

Jem tips his head to the side and shrugs. One of Mary's gestures. "Not really." Me neither, thinks Noble. McFadden cleans and trims the other hind foot, then disappears behind the horse.

"Does it hurt the horse?"

Now McFadden is muttering into the mare's flank and Noble can't hear his response. Neither, probably, can Jem. If Jem had been raised doing any kind of farm work he'd know the answer was no. Fact is, he'd probably know a whole bunch of things, practical things, things you didn't learn being the son of a doctor and ordering servants around. Like how to help deliver a calf, and how to saddle a horse, how to whittle a piece of pine. Noble clears his throat, poised on the brink of shoring up the gaps in young Jem's education, when McFadden reappears, bearing a gift.

"Here, you take this," he says, handing Jem one of the worn horseshoes. "Nail it up over your door, it'll bring you luck."

Noble rams his hands in his pockets, finds the cracked lifter and flips it over and over with his fingers. He fixes on the back of Jem's head, the way his dark blond hair curls into the collar of his sweater. His mother used to leave Lawson's hair just so until he came home from school one day with a black eye.

Jem begins to shuffle restlessly from one foot to the other. "What's this for?" he calls out, walking towards the mandrel. Emboldened by the gift, Jem now wants to look with his hands, as Noble's mother would say. The cone of cast iron is almost as tall as the child. It's another perfect opportunity. Noble could easily step forward, introduce himself — *I'm an old friend of your mumma's* — explain how the mandrel is used to shape circular objects such as nose rings for oxen and cattle, hub bands for wagon wheels. *How do you know my mumma? Intimately. At least I used to.* Better to keep his mouth shut.

McFadden moves to the corner at the back of the forge without answering Jem's question and begins pumping the creaking bellows. The coals brighten, sparks launch themselves at the chimney, and the fire grows to a crackling, spitting roar. Unable to make himself heard anymore, Jem wanders towards the work bench along the right-side wall and, with his arm out straight from his shoulder, begins running his horseshoe across the surface.

McFadden lifts a piece of cherry red iron from the forge and lays it across the rounded corner of the anvil face. Keeping his hammer arm and movements perfectly vertical, he strikes the iron with precise blows. With his other hand he moves the tongs so that the piece is in constant motion. Sparks spray in all directions, but McFadden knows how far back to hold his head so that they fall uselessly to the floor or against his blackened leather apron. Noble, as drawn by the fireworks display as Jem, fails to notice that while the boy's eyes are trained on McFadden, his hand and, more dangerously, the horseshoe he's holding, still trail blindly about the workbench.

A hearth tool awaiting repair sets off the chain reaction. Hooked by the calks on the horseshoe, the broken-off handle becomes a hockey puck, shooting into the back corner of the workbench and toppling a hammer that rests against the wall. The hammer hits the bench and bounces, dislodging an over-sized horse rasp, which in turn topples the tall near-empty neatsfoot oil jar sitting on the end of the bench. The jar crashes to the flagstone floor with a dull explosion. Glass fragments shoot in all directions. Spooked, the mare rears, whinnying, the slipknot McFadden has used to tether her useless. She thrashes at the air. Cursing, McFadden leaps backwards, throwing tongs and the newly forged and still hot shoe behind him. Up and down the horse rears, snorting and tossing her head. Her pinched screams strike the floor and echo off the stone walls. Jem backs up, stumbling, and Noble reaches for the boy's shoulders, bends to scoop him into his arms and steps towards the safety of the doorway.

Just as the reverberations die and Noble's heartbeat slackens, a loud sharp crack rends the air: McFadden's fist connecting with Bracken's nose. The mare's head whips sideways, her eyes roll white, her feet dance and still. But for her breathing, hard and heavy, stomach expanding and contracting like a bellows, the shop is filled with a disquieting stillness. Jem trembles, strangled sobs caught in his throat. Noble's own throat grows so tight and painful it feels as if the smith just punched him. He pulls the boy closer. Who knew a child could feel so weightless and fragile? Over the top of Jem's head Noble catches a glimpse of McFadden, brooding and silent in the corner.

"Mumma!" Jem pushes back from Noble and scrambles out of his arms. When Noble turns around, there she is, gloved hands on her son's shoulders, pushing him outside. Mary. Noble stares but she won't meet his eyes. He hasn't been this close in years. She's filled out a little, sitting at the prosperous doctor's table, her arms are fleshier and her hips are less boyish. The doctor can afford to dress his wife in smart, fashionable clothes. She's wearing one of those hats that pull down too far and sometimes hide ladies' eyes. Though she's still a fine looking woman her mouth is pursed in annoyance, and Noble wonders how he'd ever been tempted by such pale, thin lips. There was a time when, standing this close, she could turn his spine to liquid.

"What happened here? What are you up to, Noble Matheson?" Her voice is sharper than he remembers.

"I was just . . ." Noble begins, but Mary isn't interested in explanations. Already her head is averted and she is pulling at Jem's arm. The boy's feet scrape along the floor; he's had a fright, yet he seems reluctant to leave this new world.

"My apologies to you, Mr. McFadden, I hope he didn't make too much of a nuisance of himself," she calls out without looking back. Obviously not that sorry. Or perhaps she's too shaken. They all are.

Noble watches mother and son retreating down Main Street. Though he can't hear the words of her scolding, fear has raised the pitch of her voice. They reach the hotel, then vanish around the corner.

"Cat got your tongue, Matheson?"

Noble starts, having momentarily forgotten where he is and his mission. There's a smirk on McFadden's face but his humiliation is visible too, like a faint bruising beneath his glittery eyes.

"Just looking out for the boy, that's all." The two men stand appraising each other. Noble feels strangely naked. He can't pretend he didn't see McFadden lose his cool.

"The apple never falls far from the tree." The blacksmith sneers and turns back to the roan mare, who has been standing quietly since the assault, an occasional shiver running over her quarters. He strokes her neck to reassure her and begins the clucking noise in the back of his throat that has made him famous. Noble has to fight the urge to sock the man hard and fast in the centre of his arrogant face. Or kick something over on his way out. He wants to stand in the entrance, blocking the light, and roll a cigarette, but he senses the tedium of this little drama. Adjusting his hat to a more rakish angle and scraping his heels noisily on McFadden's flag floor, Noble turns and strides back to his truck.

His muscles feel tight, his skin bound with irritation. Seeing Mary has unbalanced him. He used to think he was the one who owed her an explanation, an apology, not the other way around. But resolve fades with time. As do memories. When he heard she was back he barely gave her a second thought. She didn't matter any more. So why does he feel so wound up? He jumps in his truck and slams the door. The hell with McFadden. There's a blacksmith over in Five Islands who can probably help him out.

Noble swoops upon his mother standing at the kitchen sink and plants a loud kiss on her cheek.

"You had a good morning?" Sarah Matheson moves to the stove and lifts the lid from a pot, gives the contents a stir with an oversized wooden spoon. It is one of many objects plain and strange, practical and useless, that Noble's father whittled at during his sitting-on-the-porch days following his return from the Boer War. Noble was five years old when he first met his father. He did not remember that tall hollowed-out man from before, having been only three years old when his father left to fight. Lawson had been a baby.

"Good? Yes. It was good."

"What's wrong?" she says, bringing the spoon to her lips and tasting the soup.

"Nothing's wrong."

"Yes it is. I know you, Noble Matheson."

Does she? It's something every mother says, every mother believes. He pictures Mary's gloved hands pushing Jem from the blacksmith's shop. Sarah thought she knew Lawson too. But even Noble had trouble recognizing the man his brother became.

"Come on, spit it out." She turns from the stove, wiping her hands on her apron, and sees the parcel in his hand. It isn't that he was trying to hide it, but he would have preferred to slip it by her unnoticed.

"What's that?"

"Nothing."

She raises her eyebrows. "An awful lot of nothings for one morning. I hope you haven't been wasting good money on nonsense."

"It was free."

"First it was nothing and now it's free. Who sends free things in the post, I'd like to know?" She holds out her hand, and though he's inclined to refuse he knows there's little point keeping it from her now. He hands it over.

"It's a book."

"Another book? Lillian MacAllister has plenty books in that lending library of hers. What you need to be getting more books for?" She pulls the lid off. The sharp tang of fresh ink and unopened pages that escapes into the room is instantly swallowed up in the oily smells of fish soup.

"It's not that kind of book. It's not a story book."

Noble reads the title upside down: *The Elinor Glyn System of Writing* printed in gold ink, a swirl, some sort of glyph, then Book 1. Sarah lifts it out.

"There's more than one book here." She empties the box. Noble stoops to retrieve a letter that flutters to the floor. "Four books. You going to stand there and tell me these are free? No one sends four books for free. Not to anyone." Noble scans the opening of the letter.

> Dear Friend,
> Complying with your request, we are sending
> THE ELINOR GLYN SYSTEM OF WRITING.
> According to the agreement you signed, you
> are to remit a balance of $5 for the books within
> 30 days after they are received. This is payment in
> full for the complete System, including all the free
> services of our Advisory Bureau and Manuscript
> Sales Department, fully described in the enclosed
> booklet, The Three Magic Coupons.

Magic coupons. He wonders what Butler would make of magic coupons. Noble glances down the remainder of the page: $5 jumps out a few times, the word FREE, and another exhortation to remit payment at once. We promise to do everything we can to help you turn your ideas into cash. We will work with you shoulder to shoulder. Best wishes, Russell Dean Chapman (this signature in black pen), Librarian, THE AUTHORS' Press.

His mother is flipping through the books. Noble folds the letter and slips it in his pocket. While she might not be able to read, she has no problem with numbers. Or dollar signs.

"So are you going to tell me what this is all about?"

How can he? When he was a child, Noble's bookish ways exasperated his mother. "You'll ruin your eyes," she used to say. "Get your head out of that book and go and get some fresh air." She would even hide his books from him sometimes. They were always either schoolbooks or on special loan from his favourite teacher. "Why can't you be more like your brother?" she'd say, shaking her head while Noble searched in his bureau, under his bed, ran his hands behind the cushions on the couch and poked between the jars in the pantry. He still can't understand the umbrage she'd taken at his childhood reading; these days she enjoys nothing better of an evening than being read to.

"These some kind of learning books, then?" She begins fitting them back into the box, out of order. "That Lillian MacAllister been putting fancy ideas in your head?"

Foolish nonsense. He should know better. The puzzled incomprehension in his mother's eyes cuts him to the quick. She looks so small and lost Noble has half a mind to drive back to the post office right now. How many authors hail from illiterate homes? Sarah Matheson had to find someone in the village to read her sons' letters from overseas. But at the same time the trace of irritation in the line of his mother's mouth irks him, makes him want to prove something.

"I don't think I want to know," she says to fill up the awkward silence. "You should think about going to see Peter Douglas. Never mind Lillian MacAllister and her fancy ideas. She always did have notions too big for herself, that one. And he's a reasonable man, is Mr. Douglas."

"That doesn't mean he has any jobs going. There's been more layoffs this past month, from what I hear."

"You just need to talk to him nice and explain."

"What I need is for this village to move into the twentieth century. If more people had trucks and cars I could —"

"You could be waiting a long time, Noble Matheson."

"There's a fellow in Bass River needs me to look over his motor. And I got some work on the schooner that showed up."

"Peter Douglas could get you regular work. A steady wage."

"Mumma, I'm —" What? A grown man? Capable of looking after himself? Then why at twenty-six years of age is he still living with his mother? Because of Lawson? Who is looking after whom?

"Where you off to now?"

"Upstairs."

"Well, don't be long, your soup is almost ready."

Noble sits on the edge of his bed, his scalp tightening in the beginning of a headache. He brings the Elinor Glyn box to his nose and breathes in the aroma. Such an edifying smell, already he can feel his mind expanding. He pulls out the booklet, *The Three Magic Coupons*. Inside, a quotation from some foreigner. Noble has had enough of foreigners for any man's lifetime and quickly turns the page again. A photo of Elinor Glyn, her face turned down to the envelope in her hand and the letter she is pulling from it. A pretty face? He can't really say. She'd have to lift her head and face him so he could see her eyes. You can tell a lot looking at a woman's eyes, whether she was mean or petty or kind or if she wanted you. Though Noble has trouble reading Lillian's pale grey eyes. Her husband lies upstairs, his lungs so weakened from a gas attack at Ypres that he can barely speak and move. Waiting to die. It sickens Noble, but no matter how much he tries to push it away the thought comes back to him over and again: they are both waiting for him to die.

He stares at the booklet, decides Elinor Glyn could be handsome if her eyes were soft and kind and brown. Brown eyes are always kinder than blue and green eyes. And grey eyes? Otherwise she has a serious face, the kind of face that he supposes a writer should have. He practices a serious writer's face. It isn't so much different from his serious fisherman's face, or his mechanic's face, or even his millwright's face.

From downstairs comes the clatter of crockery and cutlery being taken from cupboard and drawer and placed on the table. He glances at the booklet again. Elinor Glyn says: *Many people think they can't write because they lack imagination or the ability to construct out-of-the-ordinary plots. Nothing could be further from the truth. The really successful authors — those who make fortunes with their pens — are those who write in a simple manner about plain, ordinary events of every-day life – things with which everyone is familiar. This is the real secret of success — a secret within the reach of all, for everyone is familiar with some kind of life.*

Some kind of life, yes, but some kind of village life? Surely people want to read about diamond-studded lives, glittering parties attended by the rich and famous. Or of events colossal and extraordinary, heroic adventures and wars that swallow countries whole and recast the shapes of others. Noble has lived in a city and reckons he knows a little of what educated and society people are interested in. And that doesn't include reading about unsophisticated country folk from a small Nova Scotia village, tales of chopping wood and fetching water, trapping rabbits and groundhogs, flinging skates and dogfish back into the water.

"Noble! It's on the table." He slips the booklet back inside the box.

But just imagine that a shipload of pirates turns up one morning at the wharf of said village, their schooner all battered and stinking of rum. Now that would be different. That might well be the kind of thrilling story city people would want to read.

V

Friday May 30. High tide, 3:17 a.m., 3:43 p.m.

Hetty rarely opens his closet. Laura does the washing and
ironing, Laura makes sure all Peter's shirts are returned to
hangers, his shoes, shined and treed, are lined up neatly in
pairs, the shoulders of his jackets sit straight, his pants hang
neatly pressed, creases sharp. She chooses a dark suit, a dusty
black, out of consideration for her hair and earthy skin tones.
Also black is dramatic, and the transformation, if there is going
to be one, demands some flair. She locks the bedroom door;
no one is due back for hours. Still, her skin thrills in anticipation and some fear. She slips off her dress and petticoat and
steps into the pants. They are of course much too large around
the waist, and when she lets go they puddle around her feet.
Stepping from them she unlocks the bedroom door and goes
in search of Laura's sewing basket, which she eventually finds
in the airing cupboard on the landing. Extracting half a dozen
long pins, Hetty returns to the bedroom and turns the latch
again. Four tucks, one on either side, front and back, and the
pants fit beautifully; at least they are no longer inclined to fall
off. Trailing six inches of hem she shuffles towards the long
mirror that hangs on the door of her wardrobe, an elegant

piece of oak furniture Peter had commissioned from a local craftsman once they arrived home after the wedding and he had taken stock of his new wife's expansive wardrobe. She slips on the jacket, fastens the buttons and appraises herself. She looks like a child, a boy dressed up in his father's clothes. How disappointing. She looks nothing like the girl from the stranded schooner.

A hammering starts up beneath her feet. Someone at her front door. Hetty clutches at the lapels of the jacket, knuckles white, heart whiter. Laura? Peter? Who else can it be? He knows what she's up to, standing in front of the wardrobe mirror dressed in his clothes. But how? And why would he beat on the front door like this? The hammering starts up again, louder still, the windows rattle in their frame. A neighbour perhaps, wanting to borrow something in a hurry. Hetty wills herself to move, fumbles with buttons, suspenders, pant legs, flings the lot on the bed and slips back into her dress. Bang, hammer, bang, the door jumps and thuds against the jamb, and Hetty, woman again, runs down the stairs, impatience gathering with every step. She has a mind to tear a strip off whoever is venting his spleen on her property. It's enough to summon her neighbours to their stoops, where they will stand, arms folded across ample chests.

Hetty yanks the door open, hand on her hip, words on her tongue, but is rendered wooden by the person standing in front of her. It's the girl from the ship. And standing behind her, hands thrust in his pockets, is Noble Matheson.

"Hetty Douglas?" Hetty can only nod. Noble Matheson's truck is sitting in the driveway, the engine running. Obviously he's given the girl her name and brought her here. Hetty can't bring herself to look at him.

"Noble here tells me you're a nurse."

"That's right. Well, I used to be." She's wearing a woman's blouse and what would appear to be a pair of riding breeches. Narrow-legged and tan-coloured, the pants hug the girl's hips, graze her calves. Hetty feels a shift in the air pressure, her world adjusting itself, preparing for change.

The girl reaches for her hand. Hetty flushes, surprised at the roughness of her skin, how wiry and strong her hands feel. Like a man's. The only girlish thing about her is the ring on her little finger — rubies in a heart-shaped setting.

"We need your help."

"My help?" Noble Matheson's presence is making Hetty uncomfortable. Village eyes and ears. She wants her hand back. God knows who else may be watching. She glances over the girl's shoulder and across the road, though the houses are too far away to detect twitching net curtains. Years of bucking propriety in Halifax have left her unprepared; it has taken this village less than twelve months to unhinge her insouciance.

"John James. He is very bad."

"I don't know any John James." Hetty pulls her hand free, fusses with the neckline of her dress.

"He's down in the crew's quarters. Please. Could you come with us now? Are you busy?"

"Well, no. But —"

"I told them you wouldn't mind being asked," Matheson says, steps from her stoop and makes his way back to his truck.

The nerve. Who is he to say what she would and wouldn't mind? The girl tries to take her hand again.

"What is your name?" Hetty stares into eyes the colour of honey, like a tiger's.

"Esmeralda."

"Like the schooner."

"My father's idea."

"Your father?"

"The captain." She tries out a smile, but her face is tight with worry. "Please?" Esmeralda tugs, pulling Hetty across her own threshold.

More intrigued than afraid, and strangely excited by the

rough feel of Esmeralda's hand gripping hers, the sharp point of the heart-shaped ring jabbing her, Hetty reaches for the handle and pulls the door closed. She lets herself be led to Matheson's truck, then almost changes her mind. Esmeralda gestures towards the passenger seat.

"I can sit on your knee or you can sit on mine." Muscles shift under the girl's skin, in her arms and neck. She is all planes, no soft curves.

Hetty looks away. "I'll sit on your lap."

The schooner is stranded on the mud flats, water lapping at her keel, the tide either on its way out or creeping back in — Hetty despairs of keeping track of the tide's daily hour-or-so change with the ease of the villagers, who count from the last new or full moon. Esmeralda climbs down the wharf ladder first, then extends her hand to Hetty, who struggles with her dress and worries about her shoes.

"It's easier to board on the tide."

"I would think it's easier to board in trousers," Hetty responds. She brushes her hands over her clothing, as much to rid herself of the disconcerting feel of Esmeralda during the ride to the wharf — thin, strong hand about her waist, muscles in her lean thighs adjusting beneath her — as to straighten and dust her dress.

"Possibly." Esmeralda seems even more distracted now they are aboard. Hetty, standing at a slant on the deck of the schooner she was spinning fantasies around only hours before, feels the same; Esmeralda's fretting is contagious, and Hetty is not without misgivings, is not naïve enough to believe her actions won't have consequences. Peter will want an explanation. His wife, hurried out in the middle of the afternoon by Noble Matheson and a beautiful young female sailor in men's clothing. Already she is editing the tale for his benefit.

Esmeralda vanishes down a set of dark narrow steps at the bow of the ship, and, her pulse racing, Hetty follows. At the foot of the steps she bumps up against one of the crew members and almost leaps backwards. The skinny man she saw that first day. Except that isn't a birthmark on his face. A carbuncle has spread its poison across the man's left cheek like a knuckled port wine stain, disfiguring him. Carbuncles, one of the doctors had said repeatedly during Hetty's years at the Nova Scotia Hospital Training School for Nurses, manifest themselves in the weakest part of the body but gather their corruption — here he rolled his Scottish r's with relish — from every organ, limb and digit.

"I'm sorry. You made me jump." The air is close down here, almost wet with moisture. He grins, but his eyes stay cold — like a dead fish, Hetty thinks, watching him disappear up the stairs. He isn't the patient she's come to see, but someone should lance and drain that thing on his face.

The dim light, the lack of air, the angle of the floor on which she is standing are all disorienting. Esmeralda has disappeared into the gloom. When Hetty reaches out to the side someone grabs her hand. Noble Matheson. Her first instinct is to pull away, but, her eyes still adjusting, she allows herself to be guided towards the bunk beds corralled on the side of the mess. Hetty smells the man she is here to tend before she can make out his form in the narrow berth. Breathing thickly through her mouth, she approaches the cot.

A young man. Someone standing in the shadows hands Esmeralda a kerosene lamp and Hetty takes in his sweat-drenched face, his pallor, his eyes, glassy with pain. John James is scarcely more than a boy.

"John James," she says gently. For some reason children always better handle their pain than they do their fear.

"J.J. This lady has come to make you better. She's a nurse."

"I'm not any —" Hetty begins but Esmeralda taps a warning on her arm. When Hetty turns around she all she can see is the lamp Esmeralda is holding. When she looks back at the comatose boy in the bunk, spots dance before her eyes.

"He has a bit of a fever. Not much, though, not enough to make him this ill. He is a strong man usually."

Man? Exactly how old is this man, Hetty wonders, with his plump lips, his skinny hairless chest and the faintest burr of a moustache on his upper lip? No more than sixteen, for sure. Esmeralda leans forward and, pulling the grubby sheet back from J.J.'s legs, reveals a wound in the flesh of the boy's inner thigh, just above his knee. The stench of rot is stomach-turning. Hetty feels her nurse's demeanour slip like a second skin over her face. Pustulence and the telltale blackened skin of necrosis. Part of this boy's leg is already dead. She squeezes his hand. J.J. doesn't stir; in fact he seems to have no sense of the people around him. How long has he been lying like this?

"How did this happen?"

A silence fractionally longer than it should be, and the back of Hetty's neck prickles. "This wound. What caused it?"

"He slipped on deck, the circumstances are a little confusing. Somehow he managed to impale himself on a grappling hook."

Somehow indeed. "The bone is shattered." Crepitus. She kneels on the floor of the cabin, not wanting to cause the boy more pain by disturbing the fractured bone. Her statement is met with silence.

"So there is nothing still in his leg?"

"Such as?" An edge has crept into Esmeralda's voice.

"Debris, a piece of metal. Even a shred of fabric, something from the pants he was wearing can bring on this kind of infection if it's left too long." Bullet. Only a bullet could have caused such destruction. She opens her mouth to say as much but it is as if Esmeralda has drained the air from the cabin and Hetty can no longer breathe.

"It was cleaned out," Esmeralda says eventually, and air flows back into the tiny cabin, Hetty's jaw unclenches.

"When was that? How long ago?" By whom? For she would like to wring his neck. It is just such meddling that has caused the infection. What had he used? A dirty penknife from his back pocket? Or had he taken the knife the cook just finished preparing dinner with?

"Yesterday."

"He's been sick this long? Why didn't you take him straight to the doctor?" She holds the back of her hand to his burning forehead. "J.J.," she says again softly to the boy, who might or might not be able to hear her. She takes his pulse as he mumbles in reply. Nonsense words. Delirium is a late symptom. His heart is racing. "He was fine until this morning." Now Hetty knows she is lying. This wound has been festering more than a few hours. "And then his leg swelled and . . . everything just happened so fast."

"He has gas gangrene." The cabin is deathly quiet. Gas gangrene. The soldier's nightmare. "See the bubbles of air under his skin, the bronze discolouration." She says it out loud, partly to reassure herself of her own diagnosis. Hetty hasn't had any real experience with gas gangrene, but she's heard tales. It is a front line disease mainly. Not that you couldn't develop it from an industrial wound, a cut from a ploughshare that turned because it wasn't treated quickly or aggressively enough. The wounds of boys she'd met in that last year of the war became infected because the mud they had crawled through had been farmed for generations, was contaminated with centuries of manure and now body bits — soldiers, horses, dogs. But they'd usually had the offending limb or limbs amputated in the Casualty Clearing Station in Europe long before they came under her care.

"I'll need some things," she says, her own pulse quickened with the act of taking charge. No time to waste. Blood poisoning is the next and, given the circumstances, fatal stage. The dead tissue needs debriding. A doctor's job usually, but she knows the procedure. "Iodine. Peroxide. Do you have any?" They should have something about for cleaning wounds, stuck out at sea for weeks on end. "Carbolic acid will do. Some clean rags. And a knife. It should be razor sharp."

Esmeralda turns and mutters instructions to the lamp bearer. The lamp is passed to Matheson and the first man scurries away.

Minutes pass and Hetty hears feet coming down the companionway. Now there's a press of people at her back, thickening the already stale air. Another lamp is lit, and a third. The lamps are held aloft. Other hands come and go, assembling the necessary items on an upturned crate by the side of the bunk. Esmeralda slips an apron over Hetty's head. Hetty mumbles a thank-you. She'd rather have gloves to protect her hands from J.J.'s wound, but she appreciates Esmeralda's concern for her dress.

Pouring peroxide on the rag, a much-laundered undershirt, Hetty wipes her hands: backs, palms, fingers, nails. Choosing the smaller of the two knives laid out for her — what looks like a paring knife — she sterilizes first the blade, then the handle, then braces her left hand on J.J.'s right knee for support, and approaches the wound. His skin is already cold. Hetty flinches, grits her teeth. Though J.J.'s unfocussed eyes roll in his head the fire is elsewhere in his body. Having long since lost all sensation in his lower leg, he does not stir at her touch.

Air thick with the high sweet scent of decay, hot and humid. Beneath Hetty's undergarments her skin is slick with sweat. More peroxide. She pours it undiluted over the wound, and begins scraping. Like a rotten pear the dead flesh yields to her knife and falls away; brown pus runs over her hands. Someone places a bowl on the bed beside her and she fills it. Knife, peroxide, another dripping rag. Quickly she is down to the bone, glistening white. It is always a shock, the healthy whiteness of bone. Peroxide again. She could run out before she finishes. Then what? But she doesn't have time to consider. Staring hard at the thin wavy red line on J.J.'s skin that marks the border of the gangrenous tissue, Hetty swears she can see the infection advancing before her eyes, creeping up his thigh, the surrounding flesh swollen hot and tight.

"Someone is going to have to go for the doctor." Why Esmeralda hadn't called for him in the first place is beyond her, given the severity of the boy's wound. "I can't treat him. It's too far gone." Esmeralda is biting her lips.

"There's nothing you can do?"

Hetty stares numbly at the red line on the boy's leg, feeling a part of herself retreat, wishing herself well away from here and the demands being made of her. She is a mill owner's wife now, her hands are soft and she wears pretty dresses and party shoes. She cannot summon what she needs here.

"Your village doctor, Dr. Baker, he's away delivering a baby out at a farm somewhere. It's too far away. His wife says she doesn't expect him back for hours yet."

Hetty wipes the sweat from her face with the back of her arm and bites herself, the edges of her teeth sinking into muscle, trying to stem her threatening tears. Why ever did she answer the damn door?

"Please say you can do something, that you can make him well again."

Make him well again. Who has put all this on her weakened shoulders? It isn't fair. Her back is so stiff and sore she thinks all she can manage is to lie down beside J.J. and weep until the pressure in her throat eases. Where is that feisty young girl who leapt at fate and threw herself into caring for the wounded the morning of the Explosion? Where the practical nurse in her sensible shoes, her black leather bag crammed with remedies and her head with no-nonsense advice? What have Peter Douglas and Kenomee village fashioned her into? Just who has she become? So many eyes on her, she can feel them on her skin, in her hair. Is she being selfish? She's only ever assisted once. She looks down at John James again. He is just a boy, with a mother somewhere, missing him.

"Do you have any laudanum?"

"Laudanum. We may have some." Esmeralda turns to one of her troops. "Laudanum. Go on. Go."

Hetty raises her hand from her lap and, well clear of the red line, draws a finger across J.J.'s leg.

"A tourniquet. Something strong, like a leather belt." A deep breath. "And I'm going to need a saw."

When Hetty emerges from the hold of the *Esmeralda*, she can tell by the angle of the sun and the length of the shadows on the shore that it is well past suppertime. Worried, Peter will have dispatched Laura and, depending on his degree of alarm, possibly others to go search. Her dress damp with sweat, Hetty shivers in the cool evening breeze. Her hands feel numb, her fingers gnarled and aching. She tries stretching them out but they curl back on themselves like autumn leaves. She stares at them: how had they ever held needle and thread?

Esmeralda follows her up on deck. "I'm so sorry about your beautiful dress. I should have realized that the apron wouldn't be enough."

"It's all right," Hetty says. The dress is ruined. Dark patches stain the skirt, and there is a small tear where the teeth of the saw had, in one jerk, caught the fabric and broken her own skin. It still stings, though the cut is whisper deep. Such a low pain threshold. She feels ashamed. How will J.J. feel when the laudanum and brandy wear off? She closes her eyes against a wave of nausea, feeling again the resistance of the boy's healthy skin before the sudden give, then the jarring pain in her own bones as she pushed and pulled the blade through his. And all through the brandy and the rag clamped in his teeth and the blood — so much blood! — the boy had moaned and hollered. Today she carved up a child. It isn't something she will ever forget.

"Here," Esmeralda says, pulling a hip flask from the waistband of her pants. She unscrews the lid and hands it to Hetty. "It will warm you up and calm your nerves."

Give her the courage to face Peter and those four walls that, only a few long hours ago, she had been roused to defend? Hetty takes the flask from Esmeralda's hand and tips it to her lips. Her eyes water but this is no backwater hooch, it slides silkily smooth down her throat, heat trailing in its wake. Hetty feels all her nerves snapping awake, her eyes growing wider, her skin tingling as blood rushes to the surface. She closes her eyes for a moment but J.J.'s face is waiting for her, head back, mouth straining at the gag.

"Take this to keep you warm." Esmeralda holds out a red and black patterned shawl with a long tasseled fringe. It looks like a relic from the stage. Hetty takes it and wraps it around herself.

"It's so soft," she says, fingering its velvety texture. Next to her skin the shawl seems transformed. "It's beautiful." She runs her fingers over the age-softened pile.

Esmeralda smiles shyly. "It was my mother's."

"But then I couldn't."

"Of course you can," Esmeralda says. "You're cold."

"No, really." Hetty begins removing the shawl but a sudden warm weight about her shoulders stops her. Noble Matheson's jacket. It smells faintly of tobacco and the damp.

"Thank you," Hetty says, as the warmth from the jacket relaxes her a little.

"You need it more than I do," Matheson says, voice flat. The two women share a wan smile.

Hetty has so many questions, but brandy can keep exhaustion at bay for only so long. She has a husband and a home to return to and she suddenly realizes she is lightheaded with hunger.

"I must be getting back."

Esmeralda takes her hand. "I can't thank you enough. You've saved J.J.'s life."

"He isn't saved yet." She'd been as scrupulously clean as possible but secondary infections are common.

Esmeralda presses her other hand on top of Hetty's. "He would have died today if you hadn't come. I won't forget this. None of us will." She pulls her hands away to produce a bundle of notes from the pocket of her pants. Hetty looks alarmed.

"Oh, please no. It isn't necessary." She shakes her hand in the air, shooing away Esmeralda's money.

"But my father insists. You have worked hard. We took you from your day. You deserve to be paid for all this. Besides, your dress is spoiled."

"Tell the captain I thank him for his offer, but I did what I could in the hopes of saving the boy's life."

"Which makes your services worthy of payment, surely?"

"Not at all. I wouldn't feel right accepting your money." Hetty rubs at her arms. She'll have to burn her dress.

"As you wish then." Esmeralda slips the notes back in her pocket and stares over Hetty's shoulder in the direction of the village.

Did Esmeralda sound curt just then or is it Hetty's over-wrought imagination? Maybe she offended the girl. Your money. Meaning dirty money. She stares at the deck and is now suddenly and horribly conscious of Noble Matheson in his worn-out shoes standing to one side in the shadows. Perhaps she should have taken the money and found some way of giving it to him. He could probably do with it. He's spent the day on board too, but Hetty hasn't noticed any payment changing hands.

"You will make sure the doctor takes a look at J.J.'s leg as soon as possible?"

"I'll take care of the doctor, don't worry. In fact it's probably best you both keep quiet about what happened here. It's the kind of day best forgotten, don't you think?"

Hetty musters the courage to look at Esmeralda. So it wasn't an accident after all, and she's probably right about the bullet too. What had young John James been doing to get himself shot? Matheson holds out his hand to help Hetty onto the wharf from the ladder. They glance away from each other. Keeping mum is hardly an issue for Hetty. She can't think of anyone she would want to tell. Peter has trouble with the idea of her cutting up beef shank for stew. There is no guessing how he will react to her newly acquired amputation skills.

"But the doctor should visit at least. He's going to need something for the pain. And anyway someone needs to check that I did everything properly."

"You did just fine."

Hetty and Noble begin making their way over to his truck.

"Remember!" They both turn to see Esmeralda raise her finger to her lips.

Noble opens the passenger door and Hetty sinks into the seat, even her bones ache from pent-up tension. She allows her lids to close while Matheson steps around to the driver's side.

"You did some work on the schooner?" Hetty says eventually. She could fall asleep sitting on a floating shoebox, but feels obliged to make small talk.

Matheson, hunched over the steering wheel, fingers tapping to some internal rhythm, clearly isn't driven by the same impulses. "Yeah, some."

"I saw you the other morning. Thursday." The *Esmeralda* showed up Thursday morning. Was it only Friday today? Matheson offers nothing more and Hetty gives up, relaxes back into her seat. He's probably sore about the money. They travel the rest of the distance to her house in silence.

The truck's headlights bounce about on the side of the barn as Noble and Hetty pull up the Douglas driveway. There's a light coming from under the stable door. Peter must be rubbing down Shadow or feeding her a bran mash. Such time and affection he showers on his horse. The thought swims up on her, unbidden: what an attentive, loving father he would have been. Hetty pushes at the door and scrambles out before Matheson can make a move to help her. She pauses to collect herself, removes his jacket and places it on the passenger seat. What to say in a situation such as this? Thank you? But is she thankful for today's experience? Matheson is staring at his hands, folded over the top of the steering wheel. He looks as uncomfortable as she feels. Hetty closes the truck door and enters her home.

VI

Noble watches until the Douglas woman lets herself in her front door. Lights go on. Electric lights no less. Nothing but the best for Pete Douglas and his fancy Halifax wife. His mail-order bride, according to the village grapevine. Though Noble would have thought a mail-order bride would be more desperate. There's another story there. He has to admit she surprised him today. Made of much stronger stuff than he'd given her credit for. To most people in the village Hetty Douglas had revealed herself for what she was at Christmas — a spoiled townie with no backbone. After the way Pete Douglas bundled her up in the postal wagon and told the driver to step on it, there were some who didn't even believe she was a nurse and thought that was the last they'd seen of her. Not that they'd seen much of her before, the way she kept to herself. And if he was pressed Noble would have to admit there had been a trace of something less than honourable in his bringing Esmeralda to Hetty Douglas's door. You found out the truth about people by putting them to the test. But if the village naysayers had seen her in action today, their doubts would be dispelled. She never even flinched. Just a matter-of-fact appraisal of the situation and she'd gotten straight down to business.

And what a messy business. At the sound of the saw rasping through the kid's thigh bone, the smell like scorched fingernails, Noble thought he might pass out himself. He's pretty sure he blanked out for a moment or two, eyes closed, swaying on his feet, though he couldn't have fallen over for all the men packed into that claustrophobic space. Christ it had been hot down there. He should have left once he finished his own job on the schooner, but then Esmeralda had approached, asking for his help. Her unlikely dress aside, Noble has never seen a woman like her. A raw energy charges her movements, the way her hips sway and her shirt slides over her breasts. She'd turned her gaze on him and pulled her hair back from her face, revealing the smooth line of her neck. Noble could no more have refused her than he could have spit in his mother's eye.

He backs down the Douglas driveway and heads into the village. He's tired and could do with a nap. It's been a long day, and he has to meet Butler down at the weir in a couple of hours. Wednesday's full moon means it'll be heaving with fish tonight.

Lillian.

Dammit. How could he have forgotten? Friday is her lending library night. He thumps the steering wheel. He could drive straight over there but his shirt is gamey, stiff with dried sweat. Home to wash up and change first.

Lillian opens the door and her pale, pretty face opens in a smile. The tightness in Noble unwinds in her presence. Tonight more than ever she is the salve to his abraded soul. He wants to take her in his arms and kiss her but has to content himself with an accidental brush against her fingers as she takes his hat and places it next to a lighter grey model already perched on the carved maple hat stand that graces her front entrance. While her back is turned he sniffs again at his hands, his sleeves, the front of his shirt. Despite a cat bath at the kitchen sink and a change of shirt, something of the afternoon still clings to him — the sweet smell of decay overlaid with a touch of ammonia.

Lillian's house soothes Noble too, despite the man upstairs. In contrast to his mother's almost Spartan decor — white-washed walls, plain and well-scrubbed wooden table and chairs — Lillian's house is all brocade and chintz and cushiony ornate rugs. Every sill and mantel, every occasional table is crowded with plants and porcelain figurines and framed family photographs, and in the warmer months a large cut glass vase crammed with flowers from her perennial garden graces the dining-room table. There are more pictures on the walls in Lillian's entrance hall than there are in Sarah Matheson's entire house. Dust traps, his mother would call all Lillian's ornaments. But to Noble they summon life. Sometimes, when no one is looking, he runs his fingers across the flocked wallpaper, strokes the tassels on the silk shades of the reading lamps set up in her library.

Lillian's library has outgrown her dining alcove, spread into the dining room itself and now commands nearly half the room. He follows her there. On six evenly spaced nine-foot-long shelves — shelves Noble cut, planed, stained, varnished, fitted and braced himself almost three years ago — Lillian keeps all her books and the books people have donated to her library over the years. Sitting in one corner on an overstuffed wingback chair, Stan Dean — the other hat on the stand — greets Noble with a distracted nod and returns to perusing the book propped opened in his hands. Agnes McVeigh turns from her spot before the bookshelves to acknowledge him, but the smile on her face appears rehearsed. Her expression pauses, as if she were mid-sentence and unsure whether to continue.

"Do you have a copy of *Treasure Island*?" Noble says loudly, nodding his greeting to Mrs. McVeigh and then edging towards the matching wing chair in the opposite corner.

Lillian follows and crouches by the lower shelf. "Did you finish *Adam Bede*?"

"Not yet." Noble's knees click as he crouches to join her. Lillian's eyebrows rise a fraction. Thick and dark and perfectly arched, they anchor her pale grey eyes in the paleness of her face. He can smell the cloves on her breath. "I found it a bit dreary." He isn't the only one having trouble with the book. His mother dozed off both evenings he tried reading it aloud to her. "But it's all about woodworking, Mumma," he'd crooned at her slackened features. "I wonder what Pete Douglas would say if he could see you now?" Sarah had snorted, twitched and resumed her gentle snoring.

"I can't seem to catch the rhythm of the way they speak." And so much of it is speech! A syntax and accent his tongue refused to bend around, a music his ears were deaf to. Boredom had set in while the story circled the room, refusing to settle. He couldn't understand Lillian's purpose in suggesting the book to him. Seeing her face fall, Noble blurts, "I much prefer Dickens."

"Of course you do," she says and places her hand on his. They are both taken by surprise at what she has done. Pulling her hand back immediately, Lillian stands and begins straightening the books on the shelves. Mrs. McVeigh clears her throat.

"I got the writing books."

Lillian's hands pause in their task. "You did?" A level of formality has entered her voice. "They arrived two days ago. There's four books altogether."

"Four." She turns and looks down at him for a moment. If he could just kiss her sadness away. "And how are they?"

"I haven't read much more than the introduction so far." He stands and thrusts his hands in his pockets.

"Oh."

"But I started writing already." In his head. That was a start, wasn't it? A small thump of shame at this white lie.

"You did?" Her eyes brighten and Noble has to stop himself from leaning over to kiss her nose. Her lips.

"I got this idea about the schooner that came in the other day." And how about the story he witnessed there today?

"Hence the interest in *Treasure Island*." Her eyes have drawn back to their pale depths again. Is she disappointed? She reaches to the bottom shelf and pulls the Robert Louis Stevenson volume free. Hands it to him. "I think you'll find the story more compelling than *Adam Bede*."

"Thank you. I'll bring the other back. Tonight if you like?" Agnes McVeigh edges closer and places a book between them.

"How is your husband keeping, my dear?" Her other hand clasps Lillian's arm, claiming kinship. Women's matters. Those who stood and waited. Mrs. McVeigh lost a son at Ypres.

"There isn't much change, I'm afraid, Mrs. McVeigh." Except in Lillian's demeanour. Noble can sense their meeting has drawn to a close.

"I'll take this book, then. Bring the other back some time later." Mrs. McVeigh turns to look at him. "Next Friday perhaps." Mrs. McVeigh's lips pull back in a smile. Her eyes are closed.

"I can write your name in the lending book for you." Lillian can't look at him either.

"Good. Well, I'll be moving along then." Stan Dean throws him a sympathetic glance.

"I'll see you to the door." Lillian steps away from Mrs. McVeigh. Stan turns a page.

Noble stands at the door, hating propriety and hating the sick man upstairs who holds both their lives in limbo. He hopes Agnes McVeigh falls and breaks her mouth walking home in the twilight.

"If I finish the first scene over the weekend, would you read it for me? I could bring it over on, say, Monday?" Lillian's eyes dart to the side. She nods quickly, begins closing the door.

Noble turns to walk away and then, remembering Lillian is a Sunday School teacher, changes his mind.

"Yes, Noble?" She tilts her head to one side. Her voice is barely above a whisper.

He buries his hands in his pockets. "I was wondering . . ."

"Yes?"

"Um, how old do you think the Baker boy is?"

"Doctor Baker's son?"

Noble swallows. "Yeah. I mean roughly."

"He's six."

"Six."

"Yes. He has his birthday in September. He's the oldest in his class."

"I see."

Lillian holds his gaze, but she has long since learned to keep her own features blank. He looks away, unable to tell what she's thinking, and his eyes brush down her dress. Tiny printed flowers. Not too modern, not too old-fashioned — a sensible dress. And then, taken aback by his own fickleness, by how his mind has made the leap, Noble finds himself wondering what Lillian would look like in a pair of closely tailored men's pants.

"Come on in, the water's lovely." At least Butler is in a good mood. And it isn't raining. "The evening is young, my friend."

Maybe too good a mood. As Noble wades into the tide pool Butler breaks into song. "A pretty girl is like a melody . . ."

"You've met Esmeralda, then?" Noble is surprised by the stab of jealousy that accompanies this observation.

"A girl in pants . . ." Between snatches of song Butler chuckles to himself, scooping fish and tossing them into Bess's cart. His full-throated tenor voice would be the envy of every church choir in the region — if any could persuade him to sing with them. Weir fishers don't keep regular hours, he tells them, but, while he might be able to reach the descant notes to "The Lord's My Shepherd," he would rather sing something bawdy and irreverent.

"So, been sniffing round the schooner playing Casanova, have you?"

"Left her arms not an hour since."

"Did you happen to mention to her that you're married?"

"What, and spoil my fun?"

"I spent the day with her, you know." They were linked by blood. Blood and high-seas drama.

Butler bursts out laughing. "You did? Good for you, Nobbie boy. Hey, she's a pearl, isn't she? Pretty damn gorgeous, eh?"

"I think she's very nice."

"Nice! I hope not. That girl has got to be the choicest piece of prime to sail into this lonely boy's life in a long while."

"Lonely? You?" Butler is married. He has children he can tuck in bed each night. Read stories to. How can he possibly be lonely?

"A girl dressed as a man too. That is some kind of tease. She's the captain's daughter, you know? And fiery. She's got spirit enough for a whole fleet of schooners. I can feel her legs wrapped around me already. Have her eating out of my hand — and lap — in no time."

"You're dreaming."

"And you're jealous, my friend. All those lovely curves, they're hiding an animal." He bares his teeth and growls. "She's a bit more exciting than your librarian, wouldn't you say?"

"I don't know what you're talking about."

"Oh yes you do. She's stringing you along there, Nobbie boy."

"Who is?"

"Don't be coy. Lonely Lil, who else?"

Noble sweeps the water with his dip net, careful not to aggravate his shoulder, which has been acting up.

"As long as her old man is still drawing breath with those messy lungs of his, you ain't gonna get any."

"Sometimes I think marriage has made you into one coarse bastard."

"Careful. Wouldn't want Eliza hearing you say things like that about her."

"I'm not saying anything bad about Eliza. I leave that to you."

Butler stops what he's doing a moment and leans over the side of the cart towards Noble. "I find it's always best you keep your nose out and your mouth shut concerning business you know nothing about."

"I could say the same to you."

"Different story, my friend. Entirely different story. When you've been conned into a shotgun wedding then you have room to talk."

Butler's admission taints the night air, thickening the rancour between the two men. They work in silence, Noble reliving the public moments of Butler's marriage in his head.

They empty Bess's cart into the first of two large crates on the back of Noble's truck. As Noble jumps from the tailgate, he sees the bottle. If Butler had been trying to hide what he was up to, he certainly isn't now, swinging the bottle to his lips and tipping back his head. Noble should have guessed. Since he arrived, his friend's mood, like the sands in the Bay of Fundy, has been shifting and changing shape.

"You're drunk."

"Drunk? Never. I'm merely merry."

Merry and angry and hostile and teasing and lascivious.

Butler slaps Noble across the shoulders and holds out the whiskey bottle. A peace offering. "For you, my friend, a swallow of Scotland's finest." In the moonlight Butler's eyes glitter with menace. Noble licks his lips, which have dried and cracked since this afternoon, and takes the square-shaped bottle from his friend. He recognizes the label. Bushmills.

"This is Irish whiskey."

"Irish. Scotch. It sure as hell beats Cyrus Warner's moonshine."

Corn liquor. Butler got his big mitts on a bottle once but Noble couldn't take the way it scorched his throat and the lining of his stomach. He wasn't much of a Scotch drinker to begin with — though Warner's hooch hardly qualified as such. He liked ale and not much else. Though he'd enjoyed champagne once. Lawson's doing. They'd shared a bottle during his brother's leave; it was shortly after Noble's release from hospital and just before the build-up to Vimy. Lawson told him how what was left of his company had stumbled into a shelled-out village and taken cover in one of the few remaining buildings with a roof. And a wine cellar. Empty but for a dozen bottles of champagne buried under a pile of wood. Five men grateful to be alive and one blissful giddy drunk. Laughter. Bubbles up their noses. The sweet smell of hay in the stable, a welcoming bed. Soft and dry.

Noble raises the Bushmills to his mouth and takes a swallow. His eyes water, but the kick behind his rib cage is welcome, as is the slow, delicious feeling that he's growing another layer of skin beneath his own. It's been a rough day. And it's been a long time. Because of Prohibition, any kind of legal alcohol has been near impossible to get hold of outside Halifax since the war, a fact that doesn't sit well with a few he can think of, and no doubt a lot more besides, no matter how it might have looked three and a half years ago to the vote-counters. He hadn't voted himself. Not many had if you looked at the numbers. Mainly the women and those with enough money to lay in a five-year supply before the law changed. Bankers. Lawyers. Doctors.

The two men pass the bottle back and forth between them and wade into the pool again. Butler clicks his tongue and Bess follows with the cart. Noble scoops an army of herring. They thrash and buckle in the net, silver skins shimmering with moonlight. He could fish all night.

"So where'd you get it from?"

"Where d'you think?"

"You just go down there and buy it? A bucket of fish for a case of whiskey?" How many more villagers had likely done the same?

"That's for me to know, Nobbie boy," he says. "But I tell you what. For all your hard work this evening, what d'you say?" Like a magician he produces another full bottle from thin air — it must have been stashed somewhere at the front of Bess's cart

The village's new currency, Noble thinks as he takes the bottle. He wonders briefly what the penalty is for being caught with contraband. Wonders how many more bottles Butler has managed to procure.

"Plenty more where that came from," Butler says, reading his mind. "Just take that home and you and lonely Lil have yourselves a real party." He grins. "I, on the other hand, have plans for the lovely Esmeralda."

"That so?"

"I've baited my hook. It's just a matter of time before it's set." Butler pulls out the half-empty Bushmills again and licks his lips. "I wonder if she's a nibbler or a swallower?"

VII

Saturday May 31. High tide, 4:03 a.m., 4:29 p.m.

Hetty struggles to push the stud through the back of Peter's shirt and collar. Her arms are beginning to ache and she's already snagged one nail. Peter keeps reaching behind with his hands to assist her. One more time and she swears she'll stab him with the damn thing.

"Tell Laura to loosen the buttonholes, then it won't be such a task next time."

"If you'll just wait while I fetch the sewing basket, I can loosen the buttonholes myself. It isn't more than a five minute job."

"Then let Laura do it."

"Laura has enough to do around here."

"You said it was a five minute job."

Hetty sighs loudly. Peter steps over to the mirror and finishes fastening his collar himself.

"I don't know why you agreed to go if it's so much trouble." Hetty bends to adjust the straps of her shoes, straighten her stockings at the ankles. "It would probably be more fun without you," she mutters at the floor.

"The invitation was addressed to us both."

"Then you could at least pretend to be excited. For my sake."

"Hetty, while you may find the notion of dining in a ship's galley romantic, I frankly find it abhorrent. And certainly not worth getting dressed up for."

"I'm sure we won't be eating in the galley." They couldn't. The smell alone down there would turn milk. The crew had been sleeping up on deck because of it. "And if you find the idea abhorrent, you should have said no."

"And you would willingly have stayed home, would you? Besides, the Bakers have been invited too, and I would rather not offend the doctor and his wife again."

His wife?

Hetty twists away to stare out the window before she says something she cannot take back. It's bad enough that Peter has been playing sycophant around the doctor ever since that misunderstanding at Christmas. Baker's misunderstanding. As if any amount of fawning could patch up that silly man's bruised pride. True, she hadn't wanted his country bumpkin hands all over her, not when she was coiled on the bathroom floor, impaled by cramps, blood draining away; not when the life she and Peter had created was gone, nothing but tarry clumps in the toilet. He'd leaned over to flush it and she'd leapt at his face, bloodied fingers curled like talons. Peter had hurried the doctor out of the house and, assuming that Hetty would fare better in more familiar surroundings, with her friends and family at hand, had then bribed the mail carrier to take them both to the Londonderry train station in his sleigh. From there Peter Douglas had carried his wife onto the train and held her, crooning and rocking her, all the way to Halifax. Hetty had unfolded herself against him, drawing comfort from the warmth of his body, the steady but quickened thump of his heartbeat in her ear, the feel of his lips in her sweat-dampened hair. Perhaps if Peter had stayed with her in Halifax, if he'd tried bridging the divide between her old life and her new, instead of leaving her adrift between the two, the wound festering between them might not exist. Who could say? What was patently clear on Hetty's return to the village, however, was Baker's coolness. The arrogance of the man. As if she had left to slight him, as if she blamed him for the miscarriage. That Peter seems to feel it is Baker, rather than his own wife, who needs accommodating chafes at Hetty.

"You're not in the least bit curious about the *Esmeralda?* The whole village is talking about her."

"What's so special about this ship, Hetty? It's just a schooner. Not so long ago the bay was filled with them. They were built right here in the village when I was a boy." You used to be young? Hetty mouths at the windowpane. "Some were much bigger too."

"How would you know that if you haven't even seen it?"

"What makes you think I haven't seen it?"

So he was curious.

"They built one over in Economy, the *Truro Queen*, must have been 1919. Eight or ten of us went from here in dories to see the launch." You had friends? Hetty thinks, but is no longer inclined to laugh. Were these people he'd known before the war? And where were they now? Married and moved to other towns and villages? To Halifax? Or had Peter's coldness simply turned them away? "And now everyone's behaving as if they'd never seen one before."

"As a businessman, surely you understand it's a matter of commerce?" Hetty watches his face in the mirror as one eyebrow arches almost imperceptibly. "How many men have you laid off from the mill since last fall?"

"Economics." He fusses with the knot of his tie. "There was nothing personal in my decision."

"I'm not suggesting there was." Hetty has to check the sarcasm in her voice. Even after all the money her father had poured into Peter's business to keep it afloat, the man was still making a hash of it. "But the winter has been hard on families.

And the *Esmeralda* and her crew have brought some excitement and gossip to the village." They've certainly brightened her days. "And some badly needed money. Think about it for a minute," she says, seeing by his expression that Peter considers this conversation over. "They've taken on three carpenters, plus a sail maker or whatever you call him, plus his assistant, to make repairs. They're buying from the weir families and clam diggers and staples and other goods from Harper's. Laura told me that Jed Harper drove his truck into Truro this morning to stock up because he's running low on all sorts of things. And some of the women have been down on the wharf selling their canned vegetables and preserves."

"Shouldn't they be saving them for their own families?"

Hetty shoots him a look of pure disgust. "That's the funny thing about children, it's never enough just to feed them. They grow, and they wear out their shoes." She stops, the muscles in her throat suddenly tight, her breathing shallow.

Peter's hands still. Hetty can almost see him turn from the mirror and step towards her, arms outstretched, the flat mask of his face falling away, and a part of her wills this to be so. The air divides, as if to guide him. But the moment passes, his soldier's mien overriding any emotion flaring in his chest. Peter pats down the front of his jacket, brushes the room's tension from his shoulders.

"One ship with a crew of what — eight or nine? — can hardly make that much difference."

"I think you're wrong. The arrival of the *Esmeralda* has been a blessing for this village."

"After this evening I would rather you had nothing more to do with the ship or its crew. You've done your part for the boy. It's the doctor's job now."

Hetty returns to staring out the window. The kitchen garden is a waste, mostly taken over with herbs Laura has either little inclination or little ability to use. Peter's mother probably planted them. She thinks about the kids of the families whose fathers Peter has laid off. She wants to help them where she can. Yesterday's adventure has reawakened the nursing side of her nature that has lain dormant these past twelve months. Though God forbid she turn into her mother, with her charity drives and bake sales. Something more direct. Maybe she should plant more vegetables. She could give them away to the needy. Though some people are too proud to accept charity. People like Eric Stevenson, with his gentle I-don't-wish-to-be-any-trouble manner. Though Eric had lost his home and all fourteen members of his extended family in the Explosion, he insisted on repaying through work every meal he ate and every blanket he slept under. "I'm not here for a free ride," he said over and again to Hetty, a raw recruit herself at that stage, taking from her the bloodied bandages and soiled bed sheets. He had even offered to restrain patients who needed operations for which there was no available anaesthetic. Staring at the tangle of weeds, Hetty understands that the only way Eric Stevenson probably knew of enduring his grief was to work through it. Or avoid it. She could start clearing the patch tomorrow. Or Monday. Peter has his own ideas of how post-church spring Sundays should be spent. Easy growers first—plants that more or less look after themselves: tomatoes, radishes, beans and cucumbers. Then, depending on how successful she is—listening to and observing the successes of others is different from gardening herself, which she's never actually tried—maybe a more ambitious fall crop of, say, Brussels sprouts and cabbage, or even cauliflower. Hetty startles when Peter, standing just behind her, places his hand on her elbow.

"I don't want a repeat of yesterday," he says softly.

Meaning what exactly? Hetty isn't sure, even with all the planning and foresight in the world that she could manage a repeat of yesterday. Or that she would want to.

By the time Noble Matheson pulled up at her house, darkness had fallen and the effects of Esmeralda's brandy were wearing off. Every muscle in Hetty's back and shoulders sang in pain. Laura had banked the fire with coal sometime earlier, and the warmth and quiet of the kitchen made her head feel heavy. But a fire meant there was hot water for a bath. Hetty retrieved her dinner, which, covered with another plate, had been left sitting in the oven, and stood picking at it, not trusting her ability to get up once she sat down. Muscle weary. But there was something else singing through her: the reward of a day's work, the feeling of being useful again. Today she had made a difference. She felt light-headed and giddy with that knowledge.

Peter didn't come in from the stable until Hetty had been soaking in the bath a good half hour. He knocked on the door and, when she called out in response, asked if she minded his disturbing her.

"Not at all." The door opened and closed again. Cool air swept into the steam-filled room.

"I trust your day was productive?" he said, and the soap slipped from her hands. She sat up in the water and went fishing for it, buying a minute to regain her composure. How much did he know? What shouldn't she reveal? Which, in Peter's eyes was likely to be the graver transgression, where she'd been or what she'd done?

Hetty did not trust herself to turn and look at him. "Productive?" She tested the steadiness of her voice. A white lie, or should she fabricate something entirely different? The problem was Noble Matheson. With her back and the nape of her neck exposed she felt vulnerable. "You could say that, I suppose. I was called on to help someone today. Someone who was sick."

"I thought attending the sick was a doctor's job."

"I am a nurse."

"You were a nurse, Hetty. Not any more. And anyway the sick in this village call on Doctor Baker."

"He was out delivering a baby."

"Well, what was so imperative that this patient — whoever it was — couldn't wait for Doctor Baker's return?"

"It was a fever. A bad fever."

"And at whose house was this fever? Hetty? Whose house did you go to? One of the workers from the mill? Hetty, who are you —"

"It was a boy from the schooner."

Hetty could almost feel the measured inhale and exhale of Peter's breathing across her back. "You were on the schooner? Alone?"

"Noble Matheson was there. And Esmeralda."

"Esmeralda?"

"The captain's daughter." And then, stupidly, "What's the problem, Peter? Don't you trust me?"

"That is hardly the point."

Like hell.

"What do you think people are going to say when they find out?"

"Why do you care so much what people think?"

"Why do you care so little?"

"He had a fever."

"So you put your health and reputation at stake for a fever?"

"He had an infection too."

"And that improves the situation?"

"I'm simply explaining."

"No, you are not, Hetty. Whatever you may think you are doing, you are not explaining anything." He sighed, and another draft chilled her back as he opened the door to leave. Then he changed his mind. "I'm not pleased with what happened today."

"Peter, you don't ever seem to be plea —"

"You are my wife and we have a position to maintain in this village. I am perfectly capable of supporting you in the manner to which you are accustomed. Perhaps Kenomee cannot offer a young lady the kinds of entertainment a city like Halifax can, but you want for nothing in this house. You certainly don't need to work."

Hetty didn't turn around, just held herself perfectly still, back rounded. Her face reflected in the water shimmered and shook with her breathing, jagged at the edges. "You think I did this for work? To earn a wage?"

"I can't see why else you would put yourself out in this way. And why you would willingly ruin your dress." The dress. Damn. She'd meant to get rid of it before stepping into the bath. She heard the garment drop to the floor.

"Then you understand me even less than I thought."

"Perhaps if you tried letting me I could do better." He paused as if weighing the wisdom of what he wanted to say. "When you've had some time to calm down," he began again, and instantly Hetty wanted to leap from the bath and pummel him in the face, "you could perhaps explain to me what you were planning on doing with my suit."

His suit? She could see Peter's suit lying askew on the bed where she'd tossed it when Esmeralda had knocked at the door. Laura's sewing kit on the floor beside the bed. It had completely slipped her mind. "I was just —" she began and turned around, but Peter was already gone.

"Hetty, promise me you won't go back."

Hetty crosses her fingers. "All right, I won't go back."

VIII

Noble takes one of the kitchen chairs up to his room and sits at his bureau, legs to one side. From the top drawer he pulls a book of lined writing paper purchased from Harper's a couple of weeks ago, in anticipation of the arrival of the Elinor Glyn books. Opening the dark grey marble-veined cover to the first blank page, he runs his thumb down the inside edge to flatten it. He unscrews the nib and bladder from the fountain pen his father used for keeping accounts back when the family owned the farm, dips the nib in a bottle of ink, squeezes the bladder and lets go. The pen sucks up the ink with a wet fart. He replaces the barrel, blots the excess off the nib and the indigo stains off his thumb and forefinger, and in bold careful script writes out his name in full on the inside of the cover — Noble James Albert Matheson. Across the top of the first page he writes, *Rum-runners of the Esmeralda*. Resting the pen in its stand, he sits back and picks up Book 1 of *The Elinor Glyn System of Writing*. In the introduction, Noble reads:

> *Helen clerks in a Department Store; her life is a*
> *dull, drear grind. In her little niche behind the notion*
> *counter, her girl's soul is slowly shrivelling. The drab,*

grey life, the monotony, the dull servitude from eight
to six is deadening every spark of hope within her.

His eyes scan down the page. The next paragraph begins with
George.

George is a bookkeeper. Every morning — rain
or shine, snow or blow — he must report at the
office, take instructions from someone else, do the
same thing hour after hour, day after day, year in
and year out —

George, old buddy, Noble thinks, that is a man's lot in life.

But he is not too tired to have dreams — no one is.

Which is what we're doing here, Elinor. Further on:

The girl who works can write.
The man who toils can write.
The businessman can write.

And so on. He begins flipping pages. The odd sentence jumps
out. *Don't get the mistaken idea that writers are super-beings,*
demi-gods, or rare geniuses . . . The average writer is no different
from you . . . Well, he'd hardly be sitting here with these books,
out his deposit and owing a further exorbitant five dollars if he
thought for a moment that being a demi-god was a necessary
part of his ambition.
      There are just as many stories of human interest right in
your own vicinity — stories for which some editor will pay good
money — as there are in Greenwich Village or the South Sea
Islands. Yes ma'am. He's lucky. Liquor and lawlessness are a few
hundred yards from his doorstep. If the scene in the hold the
other morning is anything to go by, Noble's life is practically

straight out of a swashbuckling high seas adventure novel: *Treasure Island II*. All the grizzled characters are on board the schooner, just waiting for him to transcribe their mannerisms and dress. He's going to need a full page just for the carbuncle on that Spoon fellow's face.

Thousands of people imagine they need a fine education to write. Nothing is farther from the truth. That's a relief. Grades one through ten in the village school, while better than many can claim, is probably not what Miss Glyn means by a fine education.

He skips the rest of the introduction, scans through the introductory chapter on the appeal and aims of the short story and starts on chapter two: "What Knowledge Must I Have To Succeed?" Noble is becoming impatient. He doesn't need to read about whether or not a college education is a prerequisite for a writer nor where to get ideas. Noble already knows what it is he wants to write about.

The *Esmeralda*, he thinks, taking up his pen again, came in on the tide Thursday morning, somewhere between one and five a.m. If Noble's hunch is correct the crew would have been able to unload her behind Moose Island before daybreak. But what were they doing all the way up here in the first place? So far from the open sea, and from the rum-runners' usual haunts? Why risk the treacherous currents and shoals in the Bay of Fundy? In order to pass through Cape Split they would have had to wait for the slack tide, which meant setting anchor anywhere from Spencer's Island to Port Greville. Unless by some fluke the winds and tides had synchronized perfectly with their passage. But then what? Minas Basin is a navigational dead end, their maps would have told them that much. Perhaps the Coast Guard had chased the *Esmeralda* up here? Or another rummy? Her damage suggests a collision. She could have been driven into a storm and then blown right to Cape Split. The Liberty wouldn't have been any use to them — the torque of a fast-revving engine in rough seas would have snapped the screw right off. Or worse, split the hull. And anyway its fuel was gravity fed. If the ship was being tossed about, the carburator would have kept cutting out. The donkey engine could have kept her on course. But what was her course? And was she here by accident or design? Noble sucks on the end of the pen. So many choices to make. So many factors to consider — including the possibility that the *Esmeralda* had come in empty. But that wouldn't make nearly as good a story.

He glances out the window to his right, sees the world fuzzily through the lace curtains his mother insists on putting up at every window, through the grime she can no longer reach and he can never find the time to clean off. Dark clouds have gathered on the horizon; they'll soon be in the thick of a squall. Which will make for a miserable night at the weir. To have the luxury of being able to turn Butler's work down: Sorry, I'm writing. Creating. Making decisions. I must finish this chapter. Figure out this character's motivations. Plot his next move.

Eyes back to the page. But how to get started? What should he put down first? Noble flips to near the end of the Elinor Glyn book, and in chapter nine spots this:

> *The young author may start to build his plot from any point he desires. There will be a certain situation, idea or intention in his mind that shines out with particular light.*

The arrival of the *Esmeralda* would make a fine opening: sails billowing in the breeze and craggy pirate types with eye patches and scars on their faces from various knife fights hanging from the rigging.

The *Esmeralda* — should he change the name? — ties up at the deserted wharf.

Deserted? Where did that come from? He decides to leave it for now. Deserted could be mysterious, perhaps even frightening. To a bunch of brigands? Was that likely? If they had something to hide, were escaping the law, then yes. So, do they stay on the ship or disembark? He places his pen back in its stand. Pirates don't disembark. They leap from the rigging and the gunwales, swords drawn. But who are these pirates, exactly? And where did they come from? Someplace exotic and foreign. Madagascar. Noble has no idea where Madagascar is but he likes the soft/hard combinations that roll off his tongue when he says the name. Madagascar.

His Madagascan hero is of course tall and muscular, with swarthy skin and long dark hair tied back with length of ribbon from his sweetheart. Noble picks up his pen again. No, better than the ribbon, a lock of her hair. Clever. He almost claps himself on the back.

H___ was born to be a seaman. Was actually born at sea. His mother was on a ship sailing to — He grew up on the coast of *Madagascar and had always loved the sea.* But that would make a man a sailor or a fisherman and not necessarily a pirate.

He was kidnapped by pirates while he was fishing/beach-combing/hawking trinkets/selling fish on the wharf. But if he's to be worth kidnapping then shouldn't he be rich?

He grew up in the capital of Madagascar — something else to look up *— the son of a wealthy merchant. But he always loved fishing/beachcoming/hawking trinkets —* This is getting him nowhere. Noble starts with a description instead.

H was a tall man with broad shoulders. He had a deep scar in the cleft of his chin left over from when a stray fishing hook nicked him when he was a boy. But the scar didn't make him less handsome. It acted like a warning, telling others that H wasn't a man who was afraid of getting in a fight and he wasn't afraid of getting hurt. The other warning was the long-barrelled pistol he always carried tucked in his belt. He stood at the bow of the ship with his feet planted apart and his arms folded across his chest and stared out to sea.

At what?

Another ship? A storm on the horizon? A marlin leaping through the air?

Maybe Noble should decide who the rest of the characters are before he starts making decisions about what they're doing and why. He decides to leave his hero for now and concentrate on the enemy. The British Navy? The Spanish Armada? The U.S. Coast Guard? Depends on where and when the action is set. Regardless, H needs an opponent. A stocky man, not as tall as H, and a little stooped. Hands like baseball mitts. A man not given to much in the way of words. He grunts and nods to his men more than he issues orders. But he's a watcher — eyes in his elbows — and takes things in that other people miss.

Noble pauses. Sounds a lot like McFadden. Same physique, minus the height; same caveman personality; same powers of deduction. He rubs his face with his hands, grabs the Elinor Glyn book.

Characters Must Be Interesting.

Well that rules McFadden out. Dull as cottage pie. He glances over what he's written so far. That scar from a stray fishing hook is definitely Lawson.

No one could accuse Lawson of not being interesting. "He's been here before," people used to say of him, and smile. And because Lawson was so much wiser than his years it was easy to believe. His air of sureness and charm was difficult to dislike. He was attentive and listened when people spoke to him. Really listened, with every ounce of his attention focused on the speaker. He could turn his hand to most things. To most animals. Even birds and insects. Noble had once seen Lawson coach a cardinal to take seed from his hand. Naturally he drew envy; there were some who described him as odd. Different. Though to Noble the difference came later. But no matter what, Lawson saw the goodness in people. Plucked it out, shone it up and handed it back to them. He'd find something good in the most ornery and sour-faced. It wasn't that he was oblivious to people's faults; it was more a conscious choice to ignore them in favour of a person's better qualities. You couldn't help but smile when he was around.

Lawson drew women too. Almost every girl in the village had had a crush on Lawson at one time or another. They would follow him home from school and dare each other to kiss him. They would knit him scarves and mittens and toques. Write him sentimental poems. Bake him cakes and decorate them with hearts. Even the older girls. Though he hates himself for it, Noble still wonders why God gave Lawson so much if he was only planning on taking it away so soon. He could have shared the looks out a little more fairly for a start. And it wasn't just the village girls whose heads Lawson turned. Town girls too.

Truro girls.

A picture forms in Noble's mind, a picture so clear he can almost step inside it. Sunshine. A breeze that whipped up the cinders of the sidewalk, making him squint. A Saturday in June, money from Lawson's first wages at the sawmill burning a hole in his pocket. He was allowed to spend it on himself, Sarah's rule, the same rule that had applied when Noble signed on at the mill eighteen months before. Lawson, in that golden-boy way of his, had decided to share his fortune with his brother. Briefly Noble had felt guilty for not having been as generous with his own first wages, then had climbed aboard the train for Truro with his brother, determined they would have a good time.

Noble saw the girls first, he was almost sure of it. Unless Lawson was faking. His brother had perfected a new walk. It was more of a swagger, Douglas Fairbanks-style, chest out, stomach in. He wore the all-American hero's open-mouthed smile, thinking that made him look more ravishing to the opposite sex. Noble had watched Lawson practising with his reflection when he thought no one was looking and realized then that young men were just as vain as women. Except a man could get farther in life without good looks. But with his face, Lawson was surely destined for greatness.

The girls, one brunette, the other with dark red hair, were giggling, arms linked, slim hands fluttering in front of their pretty faces. The brunette's features were more exaggerated than her friend's — big eyes, big mouth, lots of teeth. Noble was taken by the more refined looks of the shorter girl — how the sun picked out hints of burnished copper in her curling auburn locks, how she bobbed her head about like a filly. Girls didn't act that way in the village, not without getting laughed at or teased anyway. There was an aloofness about town girls in general, a sense of superiority in the way they held themselves that made a man think they were just that much more special. So that if you managed to court one, or even to get one to look your way, you felt proud of yourself.

Just as Noble was beginning to think they hadn't noticed him or his movie-star-handsome brother, the girls began crossing the road. They were walking more quickly and with purpose. Were they coming over? Speech rushed out a window in Noble's head. He wondered that the whole street couldn't hear the hammering in his temples. The brunette brushed her hair from her face before reaching into her shoulder purse. Lawson slowed his gait and turned towards the girls. Noble could picture the easy smile on his handsome face and felt his own smile slide away. Now the girls would have eyes for no one else.

And that's when he saw them: two white feathers, one each. The redhead must have had hers tucked up her sleeve the whole time, for it appeared suddenly in her hand as if from nowhere. The next few moments unfurled in slow motion. The girls' hands reaching towards the brothers. Their eyes meeting then flicking away. The crunching sounds made by their heels as they half skipped, half ran down the street.

Lawson plucked the feather from his shoulder and turned to face his brother. If the girls had slapped him he couldn't have looked more stunned. More lost.

"Just a couple of silly girls, Lawson." The day was ruined

though; Noble could already feel it, like a sack of wet sand about his neck. He swiped at the feather on his own lapel, ground it underfoot. "Don't worry," he said, "you're not even old enough to sign up." But his voice rang false in his ears, his mouth tasted of acid. The thing was, Lawson's height made him look older than his sixteen years. It was one of the reasons people rarely took them for brothers.

"I'm not a coward. " Lawson stepped back, his features twisted with an ugliness Noble never believed his brother could touch. "That's what this is supposed to mean, right?"

Why was he even asking? Noble squinted down the street in the direction the girls had run as if in half a mind to bring them back, demand an apology or at least an explanation. But his head was thrumming. Of course it had only ever been a matter of time before people started pointing their fingers at him. Pinning him with white feathers. He was old enough. His eighteenth birthday had come and gone two months ago. And though he'd watched his friend Butler and several others sign up and go off to war, Noble had felt no similar urge to rush headlong into that bloody adventure. But that didn't mean he was immune to the pressure mounting on all sides. Men, women, children. The old and the young. After all, it was 1916, and the casualty lists were growing. Disturbingly so. But something about the picture of his father whittling on the front verandah, his mind shattered, held Noble back. He wanted to grab Lawson by the shoulders and shake him. Yell, "So what?" Instead he thumped his brother playfully on the arm.

"What are you saying? You wanna sign up?"

Lawson whooped, his whole face lit up like it was Christmas and he'd just found the nickel in the plum pudding. "In a minute, my noble brother," he shouted, giving a mock salute. "This war's going to be over long before I'm old enough to serve."

"Then what are we waiting for?"

Noble's scalp is prickling, the tips of his nerves leaping, trapped by his skin. The sky rumbles outside. There's a knock at his door. He stands quickly, toppling his chair, which bangs against the footboard of his bed.

"You okay in there?"

"Fine, Mumma, I'm fine."

"You've been awful quiet these past days."

He opens his bedroom door to find her wearing a contrite smile. She holds out a book. "I thought you might like to read an old woman a few pages before your supper." *Great Expectations.* It's Noble's favourite book, one of the few he owns, and her way of making up to him.

"I would, except . . ." His reading out loud makes them both feel good. But Lawson's hand is on his shoulder, the stink of death on his damp breath. *When I close my eyes I can hear the horses screaming. And the dogs.* "I got a headache starting. I need to lie down." What he really needs is a hit of that whiskey Butler gave him last night. *Why d'you think that is?*

Chair rammed up under the door knob, Noble takes the bottle from his sock drawer. A sniff. A sip. The first swallow is like a punch in the nose. The next brands his throat. A delicious undertow of heat and Lawson retreats to the far end of the room. But he doesn't leave. Noble sits on the edge of his bed. Hold the whiskey in your mouth, run it over your teeth and gums. There, that's not so bad. He likes the way it dulls his senses, floats his life out in front of him so that he can see it in detail and with clarity but still far enough away that it isn't quite touching him. It's the bloody memorial celebration, of course, set for next weekend. No wonder his brother won't leave him alone. *You ever wanted kids, Noble? I did. A house full of them.*

And it hits him.

Jem. Lawson. Mary's boy reminds him of his brother.

He's dizzy, mind reeling as he adjusts, head and heart, to this new identity, to his new role: father. And as the enormity of this truth sinks in, Noble is forced to acknowledge that on some level at least, albeit buried fast and deep, he has known this since the moment he first clapped eyes on the boy at Thanksgiving. Jem is his. Strange how he can still feel the boy's legs around his waist, that small rib cage heaving with sobs, tears in his collar — how hot they were! He wipes his face with his hands, his skin clammy and cold, puckering with goose bumps. How had he not seen it before? Because Jem more resembles his dead uncle — the hair, the cast of his eyes, the one-sided dimple — than he does his father. And because Noble has been walking around for seven years with an image in his mind of the Lawson he last saw and remembered. A Lawson no one else in the village ever knew.

The apple never falls far from the tree. Jesus. If McFadden has made the leap then how many others have? His mother? What would Sarah Matheson do if she knew she might have a grandson? Might have. Even now Noble is terrified to claim the boy. But if Mary had upped and married the doctor because she was pregnant, then why hadn't she come to Halifax to tell him? She'd thought nothing of making the trip that January. She'd stayed a week. They'd holed up together in a cheap hotel and pretended they were on their honeymoon. Was it their age difference? Or had she misread his reluctance to come home as a rejection of her? He'd been honest with Mary. Truth be told he'd been honest in a way he hadn't been with anyone since. And far more honest than she'd ever been with him. Or about him. Hiding their relationship from everyone had been Mary's idea. Always Mary's idea. Noble had wanted to shout how he felt from the top of Economy Mountain.

So Mary had turned around and married a man nearly thirty years her senior. How desperate she must have been to give the child a father. Their child. His child. Jesus Christ. She could have written to him; he would have done the honourable thing. She knew that. And that's what hurts most of all. That he was good a roll, but — too young or too poor — not a man she would marry.

When he unscrews the cap on the whiskey bottle again his hand is unsteady. He fires an inch or so down his throat in one go. Coughs and splutters, eyes tearing.

"Nobbie? You all right in there?" Has she been outside his door all this time? Can't the woman give him a minute's peace? His mother wiggles the doorknob in vain. Noble wipes his eyes on his sleeve. The effect of so much Irish is instant. He can hear it in his thickened voice, feel it in his thickened tongue as he reassures his mother he isn't coming down with a cold.

Mary. Mary. Why so contrary? Why the hell did you come back here? He can see Jem as clearly as if he were standing in McFadden's doorway again. The way the boy kept stuffing his hands in his pockets, rocking back on his heels. Some things were just handed down in families, like flat feet and red hair. The muscles in the back of his neck feel tight; his shoulder is beginning to ache.

Noble had come sloping home just days before Christmas. He had to face his mother sometime. And now the war was over — though troops overseas wouldn't be back on Canadian soil until the following spring — there was no good reason to continuing hiding out in Halifax. He'd hitchhiked in from the Londonderry station. Had an Economy fellow take him right past his mother's house and drop him at Mary's. Mary. He'd been thinking about her all the way home. But Mary hadn't been thinking about Noble. Mary's mother told him her daughter had married the village doctor and they'd gone off to live in Londonderry. Then she closed the door in his face.

When? he wanted to ask. Did she get my letters? Or had they been opened and read by others? Some things we're better off not knowing. Noble had assumed she would wait for him. Why? Because she'd visited him in Halifax? Because he'd bought her a cheap brass ring and they'd passed themselves off as man and wife? Because she'd been moved to pity when he'd taken off his shirt?

Whiskey tastes better the more you get used to it. Chest and belly warm. A buzzing in his face. Noble thought Mary had understood when he explained how he couldn't go back to the village. Not yet anyway, not before he had something to show for himself, some nest egg saved up, though the truth was more complicated than that. But Mary had simply laughed and told him she'd be on the next train home if he didn't stop acting so serious. She was here to have fun. He wanted to give his shoulder time to heal so he wouldn't have to explain the injury. And then Vimy Ridge happened. A cause for celebration. Canadians had fought together and won together. The odds had seemed insurmountable, the losses negligible — to the pen-pushing, cannon-fodder-greedy high command at least. But for Sarah Matheson, holding the telegram informing her that her son was dead, a telegram she couldn't read though its black edges were story enough, the cost was too high. Lawson had died defending his country's honour. He was in some mass grave near Vimy Ridge. Big brothers were supposed to look out for their siblings. Noble put off going home a little longer.

When Noble knocked on Mary's mother's door that December in 1918, Jem was already born. He would have been nearly fifteen months old. Walking already. Uttering his first words. Mumma.

Dadda.

Except Dr. Stick-up-his-dried-ass Baker wasn't Jem's father. Noble puts his fingers to his temples. The pulse there must be visible from Mary's house.

Another sip. No burn this time, just a lick of golden glow.

He should pay Mary a visit. Tell her the ruse is up. She can't expect to live in this village and pass his son off as someone else's. And what kind of a childhood is Jem going to have with a man old enough to be his grandfather? The kid needs his real father. Fishing trips in the summer. Hunting in the winter.

Noble could teach him how to clean and load a rifle. How to aim. How to sit patiently and await your prey. He'd make a better man of the boy than a crusty doctor would.

Six years and not a word from her. Conniving little bitch. Never gave him the chance to do the right thing. But where is it written that he has to wait for her permission? One more splash. Liquid righteousness. Liquid anger. About time he had a few answers. From the pair of them. Mary and her old old man. What can she see in his buzzard's neck, his liver-spotted skin, shoulders rounded in the beginning of a dowager's hump? And how's his dick holding up these days? Or nights? Noble gets to his feet. Steady now. The bureau has moved. He grabs hold of the top drawer, hanging out like a dog's tongue, and finds his balance. Things are about to change.

Look out, hairy Mary. He stumbles to his closet and takes out a fresh shirt and collar. Might as well look decent for his new role. A tie too. Noble is amazed how clear his head his, how powerful and true his thoughts, how all he must do lies before him in startling clarity. Right is on his side. If Mary is going to start spewing lies there's no telling what he might do or say. He gives his only jacket a quick brush and decides at the last minute to change his pants. There's a stain on the knee of the pair he's wearing, and his mother will only ply him with questions if he stops to sponge them clean at the sink on his way out the door. He puts the whiskey bottle away, then takes it out again. Stuffs it in his jacket pocket — awkward on account of the bottle's being square. But it's a long walk. The Bakers live over the other side of Lower Kenomee.

Hat on, angle Madagascan. Noble smirks at the reflection staring back at him in the dresser mirror. He strokes his face. All he needs now is a scar. Or a carbuncle.

IX

The *Esmeralda* is sitting high on the tide, Esmeralda herself leaning against the gunwale at the ship's stern, looking for all the world like a romantic heroine who has struck a pose and is trying it out for effect. The wind fans her long tresses like marsh grass caught in a swift current. She is the colour of the sea too, wearing a dress of vivid greens she must have pulled from the same chest as her mother's shawl. Instantly Hetty feels guilty, she should have thought to return it. Esmeralda's wardrobe is probably quite spare and clearly from another epoch; at least her ankle-length dress, with its Empire waistline and paler-hued inner skirts, would not look out of place in an Edwardian drawing room. On a less confident woman it would look like a costume, but Esmeralda, who has left her post at the gunwale and now glides across the deck to greet them, is quite simply stunning. She must have been out walking in the fields earlier, for she has hooked a sprig of wild apple blossom in her hair.

Hetty introduces Peter from the wharf before ascending the ladder to the ship's deck.

"Your dress is beautiful," she says, once aboard; it's true, though when she draws closer it is apparent the garment has seen better days. Beneath the heady smell of lavender oil Hetty detects the faint odour of mildew. Still, it's easier to admire Esmeralda than pity her as she smiles at the compliment and touches her fingers to the flowers in her hair. In an instant she's gone, disappearing down the companionway into the ship's aft cabin. Too bad, Hetty thinks. She too would like to stand at the stern with the wind in her hair, staring out across the water, watching the storm clouds rolling in.

The accommodations in the main cabin of the schooner are far more luxurious than those in the forecastle. A table in the captain's dining room has been laid with a damask cloth of royal blue, crisp white napkins and ten full place settings of silver. Crystal goblets. Obviously the captain is expecting more guests than the Bakers and herself and Peter. Hetty glances at her husband but his mask is, as ever, set: the face of a gentleman determined to be surprised by nothing.

Esmeralda turns her honey-coloured eyes on Hetty and, as if the thought has just occurred to her, asks, "Would you like to see your patient?" She smiles winningly at Peter. "Your wife is quite the hero. You must be very proud of her."

Peter coughs behind his hand then clears his throat. "Indeed," he says.

"Perhaps we shouldn't disturb him." Hetty smiles to cover her panic. "He needs all the rest he can get, to build back his strength."

"But J.J. would like to thank you himself, seeing as he was in no condition to do so yesterday." Esmeralda takes Peter's arm.

How well did you know a person after a year? Peter isn't one to cause a public scene; Hetty has rarely heard him even raise his voice. But what he's about to learn might change all that. Mentally she kicks herself for not being more open about where she was yesterday. Who had she been trying to protect?

"Oh, I think he could probably manage a short visit, Hetty." In his wife's hesitation Peter has gathered his wits. "We won't stay long." He turns to Esmeralda. "If you think it wouldn't trouble the patient, I'd be very interested in witnessing the handiwork of a hero." He follows Esmeralda back up the companionway to the deck and across to the forecastle. Hetty trails behind, a sour feeling in her belly.

Esmeralda descends and waits for them at the foot of the forward cabin stairs. "It isn't just her courage that impressed us all, either. It was her handiwork, too. Such neat stitches."

"Stitches?" Peter, reaching up to assist his wife with the last two steps, squeezes Hetty's arm. Rather than meet his gaze, Hetty makes a show of resettling her dress.

Esmeralda manages to usher them through the galley and at the same time fill the air with a litany of praise for Hetty's bravery and professionalism without revealing any of the gritty details. Clever girl. When they reach the men's bunks, she lights a lamp. Hetty almost swoons as heat pours over her. The fetid odour of sickness still clings to the air, together with the eye-watering smell of decay. She licks at her dry lips, tasting last night's brandy. How was a person supposed to get well breathing such rancid air?

And then Esmeralda, leaning over J.J.'s bunk, steps out of the way. Hetty stares at the grey boy fading into the grey bed. John James Murray. His face drawn and aged, an old man's face on a young man's body. What is left of his body.

"You should say thank you to Mrs. Douglas, J.J.," Esmeralda commands. "She's the one who saved your life." Hetty feels heat in her cheeks, drops her eyes to J.J.'s leg, or rather his absence of leg, which is, she thinks, for Peter at least, the centrepiece of this tableau. The flap of skin she'd folded towards the front of his thigh and her tidy black stitches, like so many dead flies in a row. Too late and too slowly J.J. reaches for the sheet and pulls it to his waist. Esmeralda turns her attention back to Peter. "Your wife never flinched. Just rolled up her sleeves and got straight to work. She had the leg off in less than five minutes."

Five minutes. Was that all? The aching in Hetty's back and shoulders flares again. It had seemed to take so much longer.

Peter is ashen. Hetty glances at Esmeralda in dismay. In one glance — or was it his handshake? — she has taken stock of Peter and is deliberately trying to unbalance him.

J.J.'s voice is hoarse, probably from all the brandy and the screaming. Hetty, unable to make out what he's saying, steps past Esmeralda and closer to his bunk. She takes his hand between her own. "Shh, now. Save it for later. You need your strength." J.J.'s lips move and Hetty leans in to listen.

"My leg," he rasps. "What did you do with my leg?"

Gently Hetty lowers herself to perch on the edge of the bunk. My eye. What did you do with my eye? How many children had asked her the same question? "You had blood poisoning. If we hadn't amputated your leg you would have died." He's fifteen at the very most. How on earth had he ended up on this ship? Where was his family?

"Where is it? What did you do with it?" Hetty looks to Esmeralda. She has no idea. She remembers his screams as she tightened the tourniquet, the brief elastic pull of his skin, a rush of bright red blood, then the sudden release of the saw as it cut through the last of J.J.'s thigh. The way the leg fell to the bunk, heavier than expected, and her own momentary loss of balance. But hands took the leg away. Hetty tied off the big arteries and veins, pulled the skin together, closed up the stump. Gave no more thought to the leg.

Esmeralda shakes her head and it occurs to Hetty that it could have been tossed overboard or strapped to one of the brush weirs. Fish food. She turns back to John James. "The crew buried it. On the edge of the woods. It's safe there," she adds, not at all sure whether safety is his concern. But his face relaxes a little. "And before you know it you'll be up and around again." Hetty hates herself for uttering such platitudes, and John James looks away. There are huge purple circles under his eyes, which close now. Hetty stands and, leaving J.J. behind to bake and breathe in his own rankness, allows Esmeralda to shepherd them back towards the stairs.

The sky has darkened and fog has obscured the far shore, but when they enter the captain's dining room, the comforting aroma of food greets them. Covered chafing dishes sit on the sideboard. Candles flicker beneath, keeping their contents warm. Someone has set three candelabras at even intervals down the length of the table. Esmeralda gestures them to their seats.

"And Doctor Baker and his wife?" Peter has regained his composure. Hetty crosses her fingers for no more surprises. "They will be joining us, won't they?"

"The doctor sends his regrets," Esmeralda says, striking a match and lighting the candles. "He won't be able to make it this evening."

"Then the captain has others guests?" Peter is probably hoping they aren't some of his labourers from the mill.

"Oh, those are for the crew." The crew. Hetty is grateful she is already seated and for the softening glow of candlelight. "Mr. and Mrs. Peter Douglas will be the captain's sole guests this evening. Not to worry," Esmeralda says as she pulls up a chair. "It means there's more food for everyone."

"And it is much more cosy this way, don't you agree? Much more intimate." The captain. Hetty and Peter stand as a portly man enters from what must be his private cabin. His voice, rich and melodious, is characterized by the same blend of accents as Esmeralda's. He sweeps an elaborate three-cornered hat from his head and lifts a large thick hand to pat down a ruddy thatch of straw-like hair. If this is Esmeralda's father, his penchant for outmoded dress is where their similarities end. Hetty stares at the hat and the elaborate brocade that edges the captain's collar and cuffs, the shiny gold buttons down his jacket front.

"Captain Henry Woods." He holds out his hand, grips hers in both of his. "A pleasure, a pleasure. How do you do?"

The captain's smile, the way his eyes hold hers is so intense that Hetty is relieved when the rest of the crew files in and she can extricate her hand and rest her aching face. They all nod at Peter and shake his hand and do the same again for Hetty.

To their credit they are cleaner than the last time she saw them and have changed into freshly laundered clothes. In addition to setting the table, had laundry detail been part of Esmeralda's day?

Hetty sneaks a glance at her husband. Poor Peter. Even Esmeralda's charm and beauty — if possible more arresting by candlelight — are not enough to rub smooth the edges of this humiliation. No doubt he wishes that, like the doctor, he had said no. Obviously this is the sort of invitation gentlemen of substance refuse. But is Peter the sort of man to stand up and walk out now? She thinks not and can feel the dry heat he generates as he worries his hangnails.

A waiter, whom the captain introduces as Ambrose, appears at Hetty's elbow. Hetty recognizes him as one of the crew who had helped out yesterday, one of several sets of hands that had taken and delivered as she'd instructed. He has a clean butcher's apron tied high around his waist.

"And what is on the menu tonight, my good man?" the captain bellows. It is like being part of a costume drama. Hetty wishes she'd worn something more theatrical.

Ambrose beams and turns to take steaming soup bowls from a tray held by a short swarthy man with enormous bushy black eyebrows, presumably the cook. "To begin with, shark fin soup," he says, serving Hetty first and then Peter.

The captain bursts out laughing at their surprised faces. "A delicacy from the Orient."

Peter stares down into his soup, two small bits of shark fin floating on the surface. "We're not in the Orient." Now it is Hetty's turn to be embarrassed by his provinciality. "There are no sharks in the bay."

Having served the remainder of the table, Ambrose returns to the sideboard and the little man steps forward, nodding vigorously. "Yes. There is the small one," he says, putting down his tray and pulling his small pudgy hands maybe three feet apart.

"Dogfish," Peter says, raising an eyebrow and lowering his spoon. "The fishermen here throw them back."

"Well," the captain says, tucking his napkin into his collar, "and do any of these fishermen's families go hungry ever?"

Peter is saved having to answer by the reappearance of Ambrose at the captain's elbow with a bottle of champagne.

"Great courage calls for great celebration," the captain calls out, rubbing his ruddy-skinned hands together. "I propose a toast to the pluckiest nurse on the east coast."

"This isn't exactly the east coast," Hetty says quickly, sensing Peter's civic duty rising up and trying to avert it. But Peter isn't interested in geography.

The captain raises his glass. Ambrose pours and the rest of the crew follow and raise theirs. Hetty watches her husband and moves her hand towards her glass.

"This is a dry village."

"And this is a wet boat." The crew roars. Everyone takes a sip. Hetty rubs the stem of her glass with her fingers.

"It is the law."

"Then the law, Mr. Douglas, as a certain wise soul observed before me, is an ass. I cannot think of a better way to make an alcoholic of a man than to deny him access to alcohol."

"That doesn't make any sense."

"And neither do your laws. But some men will get rich from them because others will always seek what is difficult to find. There are ways, there are always ways, Mr. Douglas, to find what you want."

The ship bobs slightly, as if someone were pushing it to make it rock.

"The tide's on its way out," Hetty announces, for something to say, then takes a spoonful of soup. Surprisingly delicious. She ventures a smile at the captain. "I thought the food on ships was supposed to be atrocious. Your cook has outdone himself." Hetty nods at the cook, who, together with Ambrose, is now seated at the table and slurping quickly at his own creation. He scrunches his eyes up in a smile and carries on eating.

"But this is neither a merchant nor a naval vessel, my dear. On board the *Esmeralda*" — and here he turns to smile at his daughter — "we have a more egalitarian outlook. People will work so much harder for you if you treat them with decency and respect. Don't you find that so, Mr. Douglas?"

Peter pats his lips with his napkin. "Well, yes. To a point." For a moment, every soup spoon stops, suspended in mid-journey. Hetty lifts a small grey shark fin onto hers, then, sensing discord, lowers it into the broth again. "But they should not be allowed to forget who is in charge. That way leads to revolution. Mutiny."

"Mutiny." The captain nods and shakes his head a few times as if weighing the veracity of Peter's word.

Peter, having had time to absorb what the Captain has said, asks him, "If you are neither a military nor a merchant vessel, then what kind of vessel are you, might I ask? And if you've brought nothing to sell and don't plan on picking anything up, then what are you doing in these waters?"

"Ha, what indeed." Captain Woods pats his stomach and Hetty feels hers twist up inside her. J.J.'s leg wound is connected somehow, she's sure of it. "That's a fair question." The crewmen, rather than watching the captain to see what he says, have averted their eyes. Nervous, Hetty brings the glass of champagne to her lips. "The damage we sustained at sea —"

"Could be repaired anywhere," Peter cuts in.

"Oh," Hetty cries out in surprise as bubbles burst at her nose. Alarmed by her own response, she laughs aloud. Peter glares stonily at her, but then everyone is distracted as Ambrose gets to his feet and begins reaching across the table, clearing and stacking the soup dishes with a great clatter. Ambrose is an unlikely name for a rum-runner, Hetty thinks, having decided this is probably what the crew are, given the presence of the champagne and the tension Peter's question has generated.

The man with the carbuncle appears — he must have been on deck — and pulls the captain to one side in conversation. Hetty's eye is drawn to his jacket, fastened across the front with a row of tarnished silver teaspoons.

"Interesting buttons," she says.

"To remind me of what I didn't come from," he says, without so much as glancing her way. The other crew members chatter amongst themselves. Hetty blanches at his rudeness and then, preparing herself for the task of pulling Peter around, takes another gulp of her champagne.

"If you had any respect for me you would put that glass down and not touch another drop," he hisses between clenched teeth.

"If you're so bothered by what's going on, why don't you just get up and leave?" she hisses back.

"In case you hadn't noticed, I'm hemmed in on all sides by Captain Bluebeard and his merry men. They probably all have swords and daggers upon their persons."

"Redbeard." Hetty is finding it difficult not to burst into laughter.

"Excuse me?"

"The captain's beard is red."

Ambrose begins serving the main course: poached flounder with a cream sauce, potatoes, canned beans and an unrecognizable vegetable which the cook explains is early marsh greens, picked from just over here. He waves his arm behind him. While Peter's unanswered question still hovers above the table, the other diners, their appetites whetted by the soup, are hungry enough to postpone discussion and bend to the task of eating. With the exception of the odd mutter and mumble of praise for the cook and his delicious creations, the only sounds are of knife and fork against plate and the occasional chink of crystal. Somewhere between the clearing of the main course dishes and the delivery of dessert, a voice is heard.

"My name's Jem —" The rest of the speaker's words are

drowned in the wind. Several heads turn towards the portholes, for the voice has come from outside and somewhere nearby. Hetty turns and squints through one of the glassed apertures into the darkness but can at first make out nothing. Then she realizes she is staring at one of the wharf's support posts. So far down has the water dropped that the wharf itself is now several feet above their heads. The voice calls out again, the words completely muffled this time but not the laughter that follows. Some of the crew exchange looks and dart glances at Peter. The tension in the room rises again as people, unsure how to react, heads down, tuck into their sponge cake with preserves, purchased, no doubt like the beans, from one of the village wives who have been patrolling the wharf with their wares since the *Esmeralda* docked. The drunken reveller, for there is no doubt the owner of the voice is inebriated, shouts again, and Hetty nervously downs the remainder of her champagne. Instantly someone fills her glass again. Peter is coiled and ready to pounce. Hetty's head is swimming, waves of giggles rising inside her. She takes another swallow, and Peter grabs her wrist. He stands, pulling his wife to her feet.

"We thank you for your hospitality and lovely meal, but it's late and we really must be getting along." The absurd formality of his words and Esmeralda's wide-eyed expression are too much for Hetty. Buckled with laughter, she needs the assistance of more than one pair of hands to make her exit. The sight of the slippery wharf ladder, once they are standing up on deck, sets her off again. The very idea of making the climb in a dress and high-heeled shoes and with a head full of champagne is hilarious. But climb she must. With Peter behind her, one hand on her bottom to help her up onto each rung, Hetty gradually ascends to the wharf. Standing at the edge, she looks back down at Esmeralda on the ship's deck, waving and calling out goodbye.

"My hands are filthy," she cries out, laughing again. As she steps back to take Peter's arm, the corner of a rotten plank crumbles, and Hetty's ankle twists sharply. This time she cries out in pain. Peter helps her to her feet, and she can tell by his grip on her arm that he is angrier than she's ever seen him. He cuts off her apologies and won't hear any talk of the evening's events. Peter doesn't speak again until he has crossed his own threshold. His voice is low and barely controlled.

"You completely humiliated me back there."

Hetty steps into the house behind him, sobered by her silent and painful hobble home. "I think you managed that all by yourself."

Peter strides to his study and, without looking at his wife, opens the door and steps inside. "I will see you in the morning," he says, closing and locking it behind him.

X

It is not quite seven-thirty but it may as well be night, the day's blue skies obscured by bruised-looking thunderheads that have moved in from the water. Noble sniffs the air. A storm always carries with it a metallic taste that strangely sharpens all the smells of the village: the salt water, the split cod drying on racks, the sweet tang of marsh grass, animal dung, spring flowers.

Bloody truck on the fritz again, he sets off on foot, one in front of the other, weaving from shoulder to asphalt to shoulder to ditch. His coordination improves with distance, but his mood as he approaches the doctor's house, a rather grand L-shaped high-gabled farmhouse with a deep wraparound verandah, has degenerated. Vanished is the brave warrior of his bedroom, dashing, handsome and prepared for any battle. In his stead is poor old Noble Matheson, the guy who lost the girl to a more deserving opponent: wealthier, more established, someone with the means to provide a solid and respectable life. Better than a roll in the hay with good old Noble. Good young Noble. He disappears into the trees at the edge of the Baker's property, then raises the Bushmills to his lips, hoping to rediscover that earlier mettle. He stares at the side door and the warm orange glow from lights inside. Sneaking around.

Why can't he just walk up there and knock on the door? That's what comes of being a nobody, you have to sneak around, can't hold your head up properly, have to be careful, watch your Ps and Qs in public. Can't make too much of a fuss or someone might remind you what a failure you are, how you left your brother to fend for himself in all that godforsaken mud and shit and filth.

He's hot in his shirt and jacket, even though the evening is cooling. Sweat in his armpits, a sour smell. He can imagine Mary opening the door and recoiling. That is if Mary even opens her own door any more. Another nip. Just a small one this time. She sure as hell wasn't particular about opening anything back then. A forward little hussy when you got right down to it. Not that she necessarily had to get down to do it, either. Standing in a field, she'd pull her dress up and bend over, laughing at him, upside-down head between her legs. She'd laugh louder and higher as he fumbled with his belt buckle and suspenders, heart beating so fast in his mouth he thought he might choke on it. He'd place his hands on her hips, her skin always felt so smooth and cool, like rounded rocks when you picked them from the river, and guide himself into her, rocking her hips for balance in case his knees gave out. And when he knew she wouldn't protest any more, he'd pull out and turn her around, take her gently to the ground, all the while kissing her lips, her cheeks, her nose, her eyelids. And then he would make love to her.

The door opens and there's Mary, leaning over the rail of the fancy porch, peering into the twilight. He stumbles out of the bushes, her cries and whimpers still raising goosebumps down his back.

"Mary!"

She straightens up sharply. "Hello! Is someone out there?"

"Mary. Over here." He smiles and waves, but Mary's eyes haven't quite adjusted to the gloaming.

A pause. "Noble Matheson. Is that you?" Her voice has glass

in it, not what he was expecting. As he steps closer he can see no sign of friendliness on her face. "What in God's name are you doing here?" An angry crease appears down the middle of her brow. "And in that condition."

She's curdled in her middle years. That's what comes of living with that geriatric dog Baker.

"I was just thinking about old times." His lip has a mind of its own, curls in an ugly sneer. "Do you still like it from behind, Mary?" Then he laughs stupidly, giggles squeezing the muscles of his face together. It's outrageously funny, his being here before her after all these years, standing in her garden, asking her about how she likes the doctor to give it to her.

But Mary isn't laughing. She takes a step down from the porch. "You've been drinking, haven't you? You'd better not let the doctor catch you out here with alcohol on your breath. He'll have you in front of the magistrate before you know what's hit you. Now go on, clear off."

"I've come about Jem."

"If you're not off these premises in five seconds I'll start screaming."

Noble takes giant steps towards her and is surprised when she backs up the stairs. "Why didn't you tell me he was mine?" he growls, leaning into her face.

Mary turns so pale he thinks for a moment she might pass out. "I'm going to get my husband," she says. "Then you'll be sorry. You'll wish you'd never set foot on this property."

Hand on the banister. "He is mine, isn't he? I want an answer, Mary. I want you to look me in the face and tell me he isn't mine."

"He isn't yours."

"You're lying."

Hand behind her, reaching, she seeks the screen door handle. "I want you off this property now."

"Or else?" Noble is surprised by the vehemence in his voice.

"I'll bring the doctor out."

"I'm sure he'd be interested in learning the truth." It's as if the words are bypassing his brain.

"He already knows the truth. You can't frighten me."

"Then why aren't you running for him?"

"Jeremiah," she calls out, her foot holding the screen door. Noble leans against the post at the foot of the steps, pats his pocket with his hand. Time for a refresher? But then the door swings open and out steps the doctor. He's a thin marionette of a man with a long face and hooked nose. Staring down at Noble, he resembles a bad-tempered eagle.

"I don't know what your game is, young man, but you've no right to be on these premises and even less right to be upsetting my wife."

Noble looks him in the eye. "I've come about my son."

"Then you've come to the wrong house. No son of yours lives here."

"Oh no? How good's your math, doctor? Why don't you ask your precious wife whose bed she was keeping warm nine months before she gave birth? She wasn't even in the village. She was —"

Baker moves fast for an old man. He's down the steps, one strong hand under Noble's armpit, escorting him down the driveway. Noble has to concentrate on where he's putting his feet.

"Whatever you might believe about my son or my wife, Mr. Matheson, just remember they are mine, not yours."

"You can't own people, old man," Noble blurts as he's pushed into the road at the bottom of the Baker's driveway. "They're not things," he yells into the twilight at the doctor's retreating back. The verandah door slams and Noble is swallowed up in silence. He wonders what kind of a dressing-down Mary is getting from the old bird but then realizes he doesn't really care. Not about her at least. The boy is all he cares about now. Hugging the side of the road he unscrews the lid of the whiskey bottle. A faint headache nags in the back of his skull. Nothing a slug of Irish won't cure.

Noble stands in the shadows across the road from Lillian's house. There's a light on in the bedroom upstairs. Is she feeding him or washing him down, bathing his bedsores? Massaging his wasted muscles. Or maybe she's slipped out of that sensible dress of hers and is straddling him, riding him to Truro and back. Disgusted with himself, Noble makes for the wharf and tiptoes past the schooner. Lights are on inside, candles by the looks of the flickering shadows. He doesn't stop for a snoop even though no one appears to be up on deck.

"Thanks for the whiskey, fellas," he whispers. "Where you hiding the rest of it, eh?" Could be it's all gone now. Spirited away down the coast. Or back across the water again, maybe on its way to Rum Row and the Boston States.

He stands on a rock and stares out at the black expanse that is the mud flats, the shifting sea bed. He can picture the way Jem was standing just inside McFadden's door the other day. Marvellous, really. Those small hands and feet, that little mind already ticking over, making judgements and decisions and yet still so young and impressionable.

"My name's Jem. What's yours?" Noble calls out, holding the half-empty bottle aloft over the moonlit tidal flats. He laughs out loud. "My name's Jem." And in the midst of his laughter the tears return. Nothing maudlin this time. He's simply unbalanced by a surge of pride that sits fast in his throat like a hard smooth pebble. He mimics the lifting of that small chin. How sure the boy is of himself, how unafraid of the likes of McFadden. And why should he be afraid? He's been raised with more money and chances than Noble could ever give him. Not that Noble shouldn't be included in the boy's life. Hell, blood's thicker than a bank account. Isn't it? Noble stumbles over a tree root and, unwilling to let go of the whiskey bottle, lands face down in the dirt, mouth full of sand. He rolls over and sits up, rinses his gritty mouth with booze, spits it out between his legs in a graceful arc. He should go home, but not until he knows his mother is tucked up in bed. Would help if he knew the time. God knows what she'd say if she saw him like this. Not that he's so bad. He stands up. The ground dips and sways. Just having a minor problem with his feet. Be okay in a moment or so.

Laughter. Women's laughter. Such a magical sound. And coming from the *Esmeralda*. He squints in the direction of the schooner and can make out people on deck. If he takes it slowly perhaps he can get a little closer. There's Esmeralda in a dress, looking lovelier than a flower, softer than in her men's clothing. If Esmeralda can make time for Butler, who's married, surely she can for him too. He wants to step forward from the shadows, slip his arm about her waist. Certainly he feels courageous enough right now. But his mind is growing fuzzy, and the muscles in his face seem to belong to someone else.

People are getting off the ship. Now the tide is out, they have to climb the ladder that's attached to the side of the wharf. Voices call out goodnight. Pete Douglas and his wife. Hold onto your legs, fellas. Here comes the nurse with the bow saw. Her laughter sounds full and unrestrained. Maybe she's been into the sauce too. Now she's tripped and fallen. Instinctively, he takes a step forward. Still giggling, she must be okay. Her husband has picked her up, but now their voices cut the night air, sharp and angry. Marital disputes hold no interest for Noble. He slips further back into the bushes and sits on the damp ground just as the first spots of rain start to fall. It's the lovely Esmeralda he's here to see. And if he waits awhile he should sober up just enough to not make an absolute fool of himself.

XI

Sunday June 1. High tide, 4:47 a.m., 5:14 p.m.

"I'll go on to church alone. You should rest that ankle."

Hetty pulls herself up in bed. Scree shifts in a slow landslide behind her eyes. Even her teeth feel sore. Peter draws back the curtains and Hetty flinches as morning sunshine pours into the room.

"And you have a fine champagne hangover. I hate to say I told you so."

She covers her eyes with her arm. "No you don't."

"Excuse me?"

"You don't hate to say I told you so, Peter. You thrive on it."

"Perhaps if you get a little more sleep you might wake up in a better mood."

She could rouse herself for the occasion but really it's a relief not to have to go. Her ankle throbs like the devil, not that she feels much like sharing this information with her husband. And she suspects Peter's concern is less for her welfare than for the effect her boozy breath — her mouth feels and tastes like she's been eating raw onions — and her no doubt bloodshot eyes would have on the reverend and his congregation. And

Hetty's relationship with God has been in question for years. Ever since the Explosion. She can still feel the shape and fear of that morning, those small shocked bodies she'd tried to fold inside her own, rocking them. Can still smell the sharp iron tang of blood that gushed from between their fingers. Amy and Michael who, though blinded, somehow survived the assault of glass buried deep in their eyes. Lizzie, who did not. Lizzie, whose screams still tremor through her. What kind of God stood by and let such things happen? In Halifax it had been easier to hide her newfound atheism, there was always work as an excuse, or tiredness. Here in the village she's had to bite her tongue and simply go through the Sunday motions, though her heart is not in it. These days her marriage gives her six days a week to practice.

It seems to Hetty that she simply rolls over and Peter is back, telling her he is going out again and not to expect him for dinner, as he will be at the Bakers. He and Doctor Baker are having a meeting. Hetty pulls the sheet over her head. As long as it isn't about her.

"I've asked Laura to drop in on you later."

"I'll be fine, don't worry about me. Just go on and have a good time."

"It's hardly a good time we're after. We have serious matters to discuss."

The mutual grumblers society, tut-tutting over the presence of the *Esmeralda* and her rum-running crew. "Goodbye, Peter."

Hearing the front door close Hetty flings the bedcovers aside. She could spend the whole day in bed if she wanted. But what an utter waste of this unexpected freedom. She sits up. Too fast. Her head pounds in protest. First on the agenda, eat a little breakfast, drink plenty of tea. Then slip out before Laura shows up.

Hetty takes the short cut through the fields and the woods towards the wharf and the *Esmeralda*. She's told herself that she needs to check on J.J.'s progress and that the walk will do her good, clear her head. To that purpose the wind is having a spring-cleaning effect on her brain. But all she can think of is the camaraderie around the table last night, the laughter, the glow from the candles, the scents and textures of Ambrose's cooking, the giddy path of champagne in her blood. And even though the sun is shining, today feels flat, washed out, as if unable to summon yesterday's energy. The wind carries the sounds of hammering, carpenters at work. Clearly Sunday is not a day of rest for everyone. But who are these men, so long unemployed beyond a bit of fishing and a square of land to tend, to turn down a job even if it is on the Sabbath? These days everyone takes work where he can find it.

The wind on the bay whips her hair into her eyes, making them sting, and her tender ankle slows her progress. Unable to see where she places her feet, Hetty stumbles again. She is sitting in the grass rubbing her sore ankle when Esmeralda appears, back in men's clothing, coming towards her.

"I thought it was you I saw walking across the field."

"Limping, don't you mean? I was coming to check on J.J. And I wanted to thank you and your father for last night." She squints up at Esmeralda. "I had such a good time."

"Is your ankle okay?"

"It isn't even sprained, but it's a little sore from being jarred. I just need to sit here until the throbbing stops."

Esmeralda lies on her side in the grass next to Hetty, her head propped on her hand. Her pants and jacket accentuate the dip of her waist, the curve of her hips. "It's quite warm out of the wind." She smiles, pulling her lips together in a pout that Hetty witnessed her try on Peter last night.

"Is J.J. any better today?"

"He's no worse, except for the pain. Spoon went to your doctor this morning to ask for some morphine."

"So he went aboard?" Hetty wonders what Doctor Baker made of her handiwork. Esmeralda reads her mind.

"At the sight of your neat little stitches he raised one big bushy eyebrow and muttered, 'Not bad, considering.'" Esmeralda imitates the doctor's accent and mannerisms so well Hetty throws back her head and laughs.

"You don't like your doctor very much?"

"Not really. It started off as a misunderstanding that got completely out of hand. He misconstrued my actions, thought I was turning my nose up at his medical skills. We've locked horns ever since."

"Perhaps he feels threatened by you. A woman in his domain."

"I doubt it." She plucks grass and tosses it. Looks off across the bay. "A doctor jealous of a nurse? Besides, I don't practise anymore."

"Because you got married."

Hetty pauses before responding. "Actually, because they kicked me out."

"They?"

"The V.O.N. The Victorian Order of Nurses."

Now it's Esmeralda's turn to laugh. "A rebel. I knew it."

Hetty finds herself smiling at this new picture of herself. Rebel. At the sound of the word — the feel of it — something loosens and shifts under her skin. They'd branded her with ugly words at the time: depraved. Unnatural. Rebel fits better. "My mother was on the administration committee. It just about killed her when my name came up and they started baying for blood."

"And what did you do that was so terrible?"

To absolve herself through confession. Unburden herself to a stranger. How tempting. Would she be judged? Likely not. Esmeralda is a free spirit. But would her friend Clara understand such an impulse? Or would she feel betrayed? Lied to?

Esmeralda is thrilling and charming. But she's no priest; absolution is not hers to grant. Nor is forgiveness.

She shrugs. "Some minor scandal to do with a male patient."

Esmeralda wiggles her eyebrows and grins. "So . . . you became a nurse so you could run your hands over men's bodies."

Hetty blushes a deep red. "It wasn't like that."

Nurse. Nurse. Over here, nurse.

"No? And just as I was considering a career change too."

"I thought I could help them. Some of them were so damaged."

"Nurse. Nurse. Over here."

"Over here."

"No. Over here."

Hetty stood in the middle of the ward and shook her head, smiling. "Now which of you would be in the most need, do you think?"

"Me, nurse."

"Me."

"No, me."

"Over here."

Methodically she tended them all. Lovely lonely boys with broken bodies and ravaged faces. A wet cloth to a fevered forehead here, a shot of morphine there. She'd hold their hands — those who still had hands — squeeze their shoulders, rub their legs — those who still had legs. And she'd sit on the edge of their beds and whisper words of encouragement to the speechless, listen sympathetically to those whose consciousness the shells and the mud had split open and loosed a torrent of words and feelings. Flirt with them.

And then one night she let one of them touch her.

"So they kicked you out."

Hetty brushes grass from her skirt. "The profession is rather authoritarian when it comes to the morality of nurses. I mean, you need a certificate from a clergyman attesting to your character and church attendance before you can even be accepted into nursing school at Victoria General. And once you're accepted they move you into residence where they can keep an eye on you. There are rules about lateness and about making noise and laughing. Rules about wearing your uniform and keeping your room tidy. And rules about jewellery, and how you wear your hair, and who you can and can't fraternize with."

"Such as male patients."

"And doctors."

"Not that a few rules have ever stopped anyone."

"I suppose you're right."

"Of course I am. What are all the greatest love stories in the world about but men and women coming together despite the obstacles thrown in their way? Love conquers all. It's the most natural thing."

Could you talk to a lonely fellow?

Was that natural? It was no love story. It had just felt right at the time. Her gift. Her way of making their lives a little more bearable. But when, years later, Job Mitchell had gone running to the V.O.N., everything became twisted and sordid.

"People found ways around the rules."

"Except you got caught."

A sharp pain through her sternum almost takes her breath away, as though the stubby end of Job Mitchell's arm still pins her. "It was more that my past caught up with me."

"How dark and mysterious. Any regrets?"

"Of course. Nursing was my life."

"In spite of all those rules and regulations."

"But I loved the nursing. Helping people. Watching someone in my care pull back from the brink and grow stronger. Not that every patient is at death's door. But there's something powerful in being part of someone's healing. It's what drew me to the profession in the first place."

"So it wasn't all those men's bodies." Hetty plucks another handful of grass and throws it at Esmeralda.

"There was a war on and Halifax was filled with wounded soldiers. Suddenly nursing was something everyone wanted to do. Many of the men were horribly disfigured and broken, with minds that would never heal, injuries that had left them cripples. At first they repulsed me. Of course that all changed once I started nursing. You learn pretty quickly to accept what other people consider — what you yourself once considered — grotesque. In the beginning I felt pity, but not enough to move me to leave school and register for a three-year training program. And anyway, who knew how long the war would last? The Explosion changed everything." The warmth of the sun on her face soothes her aching head and she closes her eyes. "Suddenly the war was here and not just over there. This was my city, and people were hurt. They were dying. Dead. Some were burned beyond recognition." She turns to face Esmeralda and opens her eyes, sun-spots marring her vision. "These weren't soldiers who had been through the Casualty Clearing Station — who'd been bandaged and splinted and stitched together. This was the front lines. Worse. Two thousand people lost their lives, civilians, old people, men, women and children. The bodies were stacked six deep along roads where there used to be houses. I spoke to soldiers who'd been in the trenches, and they said it was like nothing they'd experienced overseas." She stares off across the water. "I expect that was because of the children. I don't think there's a sadder sight in this world than the body of a child." She stops to draw breath. "I'd been born and raised in Halifax, I'd always felt safe there. And suddenly it wasn't safe anymore. In an instant every life in the city changed."

"I'm sorry, I didn't know."

Why would she have heard of it? The world was turned upside down by war. And Esmeralda would have been, what?

Twelve years old at the time? Fourteen? And living who knows where.

"I was at school the morning it happened." Hetty sits up and hugs her knees. "The largest man-made explosion in the history of the world, right in the middle of Halifax harbour. Two ships collided near the shore. One was carrying ammunition. Massive amounts of ammunition. It seems hard to believe, but the explosion was so fierce it flattened the entire north end of the city, took out the docks and the railway station and every factory around them. One blinding flash and everything was gone. Peoples' houses vanished. Many of them were only wood so they just twisted into matchsticks and blew away. Or caught fire. What the Explosion didn't pulverize the fires took care of."

Hetty hadn't thought much at all when she first heard the Explosion. After all, men had been blasting out the land for the new railway for weeks. Certainly it was louder, a long low resounding boom, followed by a deep rumble from the belly of the earth, vibrations under her feet. And then the windows shattered, sprinkling deadly confetti over the staff and students of the Halifax Ladies' College, all gathered that morning, heads bent in prayer, in the gymnasium. The school shuddered and shook. An earthquake? A hurricane? Flakes of crystal hung suspended in the air. The symphony of shattering glass stretched so long — there could be no other sound so arresting, Hetty thought. And in the silence afterwards, the sudden and startling crash of pieces here and there, as if the music wasn't quite sure it was over.

And then pandemonium. Everyone rushing to the windows, winter morning air sharp in their faces. Glass crunching beneath their feet. Hands around the steel cages, built to keep the girls' tennis balls and basketballs from getting out, cages which today had kept them safe from flying debris. Over the harbour an immense filthy cloud snaked into the sky, expanding in billowy plumes, multiplying itself like a giant balloon filling up at the speed of thought.

As everyone watched, the cloud changed colour, shedding its darkness like a skin and appearing white, almost bright beneath, flashing with trapped lightning. And then someone began screaming in Hetty's ear. Clara. Her face covered in blood.

Esmeralda rolls onto her stomach, picks at a dandelion, petal by yellow petal. "All cities have their tragedies. I'm sorry I had not heard of yours."

"There's no need to apologize. You weren't here, how could you know?"

Esmeralda rests her head on her arms and Hetty leans back, stretches out her legs and closes her eyes. She tips her face to the sun and lets her mind empty until she is aware only of the smell of crushed grass beneath her and the sensation of it against her legs, the gentle heat of the sun and the breeze blowing in off the water. After a while she feels grass tickling her face and opens her eyes. Esmeralda grins.

"You okay?"

"I'm fine." Mouth in a tight smile. "It was a long time ago."

"I have a gift for you."

"Oh?"

Esmeralda pulls the heart-shaped ring from her finger, holds it out.

"What is this for? You don't have to give me a gift. It isn't necessary." Her mouth feels dry.

"It isn't necessary," Esmeralda mocks. "But I want to. Hetty the plucky nurse has earned a special place in our hearts, and I would like to give her something special in return." A wink? Or is she squinting at the sun? "I noticed you admiring it the other day. And besides, your pretty dress was spoiled, you deserve some sort of reward."

"It's very beautiful." And flawed. Now the ring is only inches from her face Hetty can see that the tiny ruby at the point of the heart is missing, and so is another of the smaller framing stones.

"I insist." Esmeralda presses the ring into Hetty's hand. Hetty turns it over between her fingers. The gold band is worn so thin it's almost translucent. Perhaps the rubies are really garnets. Maybe it isn't so valuable after all. She closes her hand around it.

"You shouldn't have, but thank you."

"It was my mother's," Esmeralda says, a wistful smile grazing her lips.

"Oh, then I couldn't," Hetty cries out, horrified. She tries to pass the ring back, but Esmeralda shakes her head.

"Once you've accepted a gift, it's yours. I want you to have it." She pushes Hetty's hand away. "My mother would approve, believe me. Think of it as a keepsake, something to remember me by."

As if she needs a ring to remember anything of this young woman, her ship, the events that have unfolded these past days. Burned in her memory forever.

"Try this one." Esmeralda points to the third finger of Hetty's right hand, grinning when the ring slides on easily. "Now we're engaged!"

Hetty, slightly hysterical, laughs along with Esmeralda. Why is her heart knocking so? Before their laughter quite dies away Esmeralda stretches and rises to her feet.

"What are your plans for the rest of the day?"

Hetty feels dizzy. "I hadn't thought any further than coming down to see you. And your father." Not strictly true. She'd been hoping for an invitation onto the schooner again. More than that, she'd daydreamed of sailing into Minas Basin, seeing the village retreat to a dot on the horizon as, sails unfurled and filled with wind, bowsprit steeved over the water and pointing the ship's way, the *Esmeralda* passed through the funnel of Cape Split into the colder Bay of Fundy waters and from there out onto the open sea.

"Why don't we go to your house?"

"My house?" What on earth could be exciting about going to my house, she almost says, then suddenly understands that, for a girl who probably calls a cabin you can't swing a cat around in home for most weeks of the year, going to visit someone's house must count as an adventure as big as Hetty's own sailing daydream.

"You said your husband is out for the day, and from his manner last night I'd say he doesn't exactly approve of me."

"He barely approves of me, and I'm married to him."

Esmeralda extends a hand to help Hetty to her feet. "Shall we go then?"

XII

"Spying on someone, were ya?"

Noble recognizes the singsong swagger of East London in the voice, its undertone of menace. He tries to sit up, but someone has fastened lead weights to his head, run glass through his eyes. Lips cracked, spittle dried at the corners of his mouth, tongue furred and foul tasting. Squinting against the painful sun — where is he and what the devil time is it? — he stares up at the skinny figure before him. Spoon. He kicks at Noble's feet.

"Time you were moving on, mate."

Noble holds up a hand, needing a minute. Though hard as hell the ground is still unsteady, and his stomach isn't happy with the sudden shift in his axis. What in God's name is he doing this far from his bed? It rained in the night, his clothes are damp. And he's as stiff and sore as a kicked dog. A thud by his side, a spray of sand. A water canteen. He takes it and empties the cool liquid down his throat. He licks his lips, then runs a hand through his hair. Pine needles and grit, bits of leaves.

"You're gonna be late for church, mate." Leaning his wiry body forward, Spoon scoops up the canteen from Noble's lap and walks away, whistling.

Noble turns his head and hurls up the contents of his stomach. He rolls onto his knees. On and on his stomach heaves. Cold sweat on his forehead and he's shivering, shuddering. Glances down the bay in the direction of Begging Dog weir. Tide'll be out soon. Butler will be all over him for not showing up last night. But he can't face work right now. Might as well be hung for a sheep.

Church bells begin pealing and Noble's guts lurch again. He can picture his mother's stiffened back, jaw tight as glass. Which is worse, being late or skipping the service altogether? The church door has a squeak that could set a schoolmarm's teeth on edge.

Had he walked down here last night? Staggered? He remembers lights in the cabin on the *Esmeralda*. What time would that have been? And the Douglases taking their leave of the luscious Esmeralda. Hetty Douglas was three sheets to the wind herself if all that giggling and tripping over her own feet was any indication. Sipping at the captain's private stash, which must be considerable. But how to explain his own presence at the wharf? What the devil had he been up to —

Mary.

And the doctor. Blundering about on their back lawn. Christ. What had possessed him to go over there last night? Booze, you stupid buggar. The better part of a bottle of Irish whiskey, the thought of which curdles his insides again.

Bad form, Noble old chap, shouting and carrying on like some spurned lover. It's coming back to him now, Mary's face, Baker's hand on his arm. He'd been making an utter fool of himself, no doubt, but what had he said? A cold dread sneaks up alongside his hangover. Something to do with Jem. His son. My son. There's an unreal quality to the words still, trapped in his head as they are.

"My son," he says aloud, then freezes, waiting for a voice of dissent in his ear, a hand on his shoulder. The damp air needles at his skin. "My son," he says again, thrilled by the bold new sound of the words. He prays that the boy was fast asleep the whole time. Prays the Bakers keep their mouths shut. Prays the village grapevine missed last night's events. Noble pulls himself to his feet and nods in the direction of the church steeple, apologizes to God for playing hooky this morning and stumbles into the village on wobbly legs.

Standing at the water basin in the kitchen, he washes his face and hands, the back of his neck. He'd like a bath but there's scarcely time enough to draw and heat the water, never mind have a soak and clean up the mess afterwards, before church spills out and his mother will be home, frowning at the waste. A Saturday night bath is fine if you plan on attending church the next morning. God, apparently, is the only event worth getting clean for.

Sleep presses at his temples, a band of pain across his forehead. Noble crawls upstairs; his bed beckons. He won't get in, just lie on top of the covers. A short nap is all he needs.

But the next thing he knows his mother is staring down at him, eyes doleful, lips narrow and straight, underlining the disappointment that is the rest of her face. Noble blinks and stares back but can think of nothing worth saying. His headache has settled behind his eyes like some cantankerous lodger and his lips feel as though the skin on them has grown together. He couldn't part them to whisper sorry if he tried.

"You should open the window," she says, turning away and going back downstairs. He listens awhile. No banging of cupboards or slamming of doors. Mother and son have both learned to tie down their feelings.

Noble climbs from his bed, straightens his clothes and walks quietly downstairs. Sarah is in the kitchen.

"Tea?"

He pulls out a kitchen chair, cringing as the legs grate across the floor. Tea he can stomach.

"Could you manage anything to eat?"

He shakes his head.

No lecture, no prophecies of doom. She doesn't even berate him for his crimes, the possibility and consequences of his being caught and fined, even jailed. Though someone would first have to find the bottle — where did he leave it, anyway? — and prove he was drinking from it. You couldn't be charged for having a hangover. Or could you?

His mother sits opposite him at the table, her hands around her own mug of tea, staring into its milky brownness. Noble watches how she still sits to one side, leaving room for Lawson. After his father died, Lawson, himself and their mother had all shifted sideways, filling up his empty space. It wasn't as if the man had expired suddenly, leaving them with a keen sense of loss; he had simply faded away. Noble doesn't have to wonder for long what is on his mother's mind.

"The memorial committee was all assembled there on the church steps after service this morning. They said they would wait on you."

Noble rubs a hand across his brow. "I completely forgot."

His mother picks up her tea mug, sets it down again. "Your brother's soul, God rest him, up there looking down on you, Noble Matheson. Makes a person wonder what he's thinking, you not there to do your duty."

Resentment rears in Noble, his fingers tighten around the mug in his hand. How can she always make him feel so guilty?

"I meant no disrespect to Lawson's memory, Mumma. You know that." It crosses his mind's eye sometimes: him grabbing her shoulders and shaking her, yelling, his mouth inches from her face, his spittle flying. *I miss him too. You don't have a monopoly on pain, Mother. I'm hurting too.* He takes a sip of scalding tea, hoping to burn the rage from his throat.

"Aye, but does the rest of the village know that, Noble? What about how it looks in their eyes? What you need to do is pull yourself together and get yourself over there." He rises from his chair. "Not now, not stinking the way you do."

He sits down again.

"There's water on for you to bath in. And you mind you scrub long and hard, Noble Matheson." Here her voice, so far under control, spills over. She stands and walks to the kitchen sink, rinses out her mug. "I don't want to know where you got it from, though I have a good idea. But just you make sure you scrub all traces of sin from your flesh."

The memorial committee meetings are held in the basement of the Methodist church, as if the Protestants have some kind of monopoly on lost and wounded menfolk. Or so Noble had once overheard Rose O'Flannagan complaining to Jed Harper down at the store. When Noble, his skin red and tingling, his hair still wet, makes his way down the stairs, however, he hears, not the voice of Reverend Walker, piping on about the memorial day preparations, but rather the censorious tones of the village doctor.

It's too late to turn and flee. An embarrassed silence greets him. Noble, rooted at the foot of the stairs by the scene before him, has to stifle the urge to laugh. It would appear that the regular tables and chairs have already been commandeered for next Saturday's ceremony, and so the committee is making do with the Sunday School furniture. The effect is of a group of large and sombre schoolchildren, bottoms hanging over the seats of their pint-sized wooden chairs, legs splayed beneath the kindergarten tables, dominated by the ornery Dr. Baker. Resplendent in his dark Sunday morning suit, hands linked behind his back and under his anachronistic coattails, Baker paces back and forth like a glowering raven.

Has he been regaling them with last night's sordid details? Why else would the man be here? And Pete Douglas, whom he now spots leaning against the far wall, arms folded across his chest. As a decorated officer and a four-year veteran of the war — few men could boast four years over there — Douglas is slated to give a speech Saturday. Though to Noble's knowledge he's never bothered showing up at any previous meetings. Noble hulloes the rest of the committee and does a quick head count. Bob Winters and Matthias Tweed, both carpenters, both of whom have been working on the *Esmeralda*, are missing. He wonders how many absentees there were from church, how many villagers have hangovers this morning. This afternoon, he corrects himself, remembering he's already slept away half the day. Is Baker avoiding his eye or is that just Noble's imagination? Exactly what had he been shouting last night?

"Glad you could make it, Noble." Marjorie McFadden, the blacksmith's mother. A large woman, almost as broad as her son, a woman who never seems to age or change in any way, a woman many villagers feel disinclined to cross. "We missed you in church this morning."

Noble bows his head in her direction. "Under the weather," he mutters. Absent-mindedly he rubs at his arm, feeling the press and outline of the doctor's bony fingers.

"But feeling better now, are we?" Her eyes are penetrating, like her son's.

"Much," he lies, with a weak smile. Oddly enough there's nothing at all funny about being interrogated by a big woman in a small chair. Noble steps towards the table, which barely clears his knees, pulls out his seat and sits down. He'd like to see Butler negotiate his long legs around this child-sized furniture with grace.

The doctor claps his hands impatiently. "I trust then, ladies and gentlemen, that I have painted an adequate picture of what may befall the village if the present circumstances are allowed to continue. Kenomee is a dry village, an edict voted for by the good people assembled here and other like-minded villagers. It is our duty to uphold the law." Nods and murmurs of assent around the room.

"I understand that as a coastal village we likewise have a

duty to assist mariners in distress. But I'm informed that damage to the aforementioned schooner has now been repaired. So the continued presence of the *Esmeralda* is, as I see it, a threat to the integrity of the Prohibition Bill as set out by our government." Noble stares at coloured pencil drawings of Joseph in his coat of many colours and pictures Lillian's soft pale hands pinning them on the wall, praising each child's effort, no matter how uninspired. He sniffs. The smell of Bushmills is seeping through his pores and into the humid atmosphere of the room. Rocks roll and slide inside his head as he concentrates on breathing through his nose. He hopes that now he's sitting no one will ask him a question.

"Then we all understand each other and agree that action must be taken?" More nods and murmurs. "I'd like a show of hands, please." Noble's eyes dart about. What is Baker planning? McFadden's mother and Jed Harper's spinster sister, Iris, raise their hands immediately, as does the minister and Marsh Bates, leader of the Truro Pipe Band, not that it's his village to be voting in. Noble would like a clearer picture of exactly what it is everyone's voting for. Marching down to the wharf and unmooring the *Esmeralda*? Armed insurrection? Asking means he'll have to breathe on someone and risk provoking the doctor's ire. One by one the other men raise their hands. Finally Noble raises his along with them. Who is he to stand against the majority? And considering the way he's feeling today, keeping alcohol out of the village is probably a fine idea. As long as it doesn't turn into a bloody witch-hunt, Baker, he thinks, lowering his arm now that the doctor is nodding his satisfaction.

Still, perhaps it won't come to that. The *Esmeralda*, bowsprit and rigging brand new and shining, as he's seen for himself, could be gone on today's tide. And maybe that is in part why it's easy for everyone to agree with the doctor this afternoon, the promise of Sunday dinner a few hours away, a seat on the verandah to watch the sun go down. They've already got what

131

they wanted from the schooner: money for loaves of home-baked bread and jars of preserves or a few days paid work or a bottle or two of booze to chase away low spirits.

Excusing himself to go look after his wife, whose nerves are a little frayed this morning — the doctor sweeps his hawk's eyes over Noble — Baker stands to leave. Reverend Walker stands too to shake his hand and thank him for coming and "for giving us all this little pep talk." Noble couldn't be more surprised when Pete Douglas takes his leave at the same time, the two men muttering together. The door has no sooner banged to behind them than everyone begins speaking at once.

"All the Swinton menfolk were missing from church this morning."

"The women too."

"Aye, but Allison and young Marie would've been too ashamed to show their faces alone. Too many questions."

"It was like party night in a brothel down at the wharf last night, so much noise. Surprised the whole village wasn't wakened by it."

"And what would you know of a party night at a brothel?"

"Nothing. I was just using it as an example, is all. I only know what I been told. A lot of carry-on like that in France."

"So you've been told."

"Aye."

Noble nods in the direction of the various comments, in half a mind to run after the doctor. And say what, though?

"Wasn't Pete Douglas down there? With his wife."

"My sister told me the whole shindig was some celebration in her honour."

"What honour? She hasn't got any, stuck-up young madam."

"She's not so bad. Has anyone given her a chance? Anyone here?"

Noble realizes he's spoken aloud. Faces round on him.

"Has she given us one?"

"Serves her right, putting on so many fancy airs."

"We were planning to go over the route of the procession and the music for the marching band." Reverend Walker, back from his goodbyes at the door, is once again seated and smiling, eyes closed and crinkled at the corners. Marjorie McFadden nods at the Sunday School chalkboard. Noble turns around and reads: ROUTE PROCESSION. MUSIC PIECES (MARCHING BAND). He pushes his hand through his hair. It's ground they've covered time and again. The band has been rehearsing for weeks, the route mapped out in every villager's mind. Baker's lecture is the real reason this meeting was convened.

"Is the rigging ready for the unveiling, Noble? The ropes and curtains?"

"All ready for set-up, Reverend." He can't meet the man's eyes. What a farce. The village has been prepared since well before Victoria Day, when the ceremony — the unveiling of the bronze statue of a soldier who stood to commemorate the village's dead, an uncommonly high number of bright young men — was to have taken place. But then Frederick Murray had succumbed to his war wounds. Adding the young man's name to the plaque became a point of honour for the villagers though they lacked the extra funds to stand behind their pride. Until Pete Douglas offered to pay for the recasting himself. When the new plaque failed to arrive in time it was decided by a majority to postpone the unveiling until the following week. Though not unanimously. Some held that the memorial celebration should proceed as originally planned on the day commemorating Queen Victoria. The first plaque could be temporarily mounted to the statue's granite plinth and the new plaque substituted when it arrived. The Murray family had bristled at the suggestion; friends and sympathizers had threatened to boycott the event.

"And you're confident the curtains will glide open without a hitch? We wouldn't want them to rip, or the entire installation to topple over onto someone, would we?" Noble forces a laugh, though the minister has used these lines several times now, and the rest of the group chuckles in response. It's as if the wretched schooner is in the room with them, seawater dripping from the rigging, and everyone is trying to ignore it.

"It is," Reverend Walker says, pushing back his chair a little and raising his chin, "important that the occasion befit the seriousness of the moment. This is the village's opportunity to formally honour its many dead." Here heads bow. "Far too many of our young men lost their lives fighting evil. We owe it to them to make next Saturday a serious and formal occasion."

Mary is sitting across the road on one of the village green benches when the memorial committee files out from the side door of the church. She has her back to the door, but it's obvious she's been waiting for the committee to finish up when she rises and begins walking towards them. And while she isn't looking at Noble, she is heading in his direction. He glances around for her husband, and just as he's about to dart sideways to avoid a collision her hand reaches out and takes his. Without breaking her stride she presses something into his fingers and is gone, greeting Iris Harper in a too-loud voice.

It's a note. Some sort of warning about last night no doubt. Stay away. Leave my son alone. But he's my son too, Mary. Blood thumps through Noble's ears. Feet moving in the direction of home, he waits until there's no one around.

I NeeD To TAlk To you. MEET ME DOWn aT tHe wooDs AS SOON AS yOu ReAd tHis. M.

So the doctor hasn't cured her rotten penmanship. He probably writes all her correspondence. Her shopping lists. She must be a source of embarrassment to him. Nice to get yourself a young wife who looks good on your arm and feels good in your bed, but you have to take the sand with the marsh greens.

If she just wants to tell him off about last night then he's disinclined to go; he even starts off back home. But on reflection Noble figures he probably owes her for last night. Staggering over there and chucking his drunken weight around, disturbing the peace, interrupting their sing-song or bible-reading or whatever it is they get up to evenings. More than likely she wants to talk about Jem. She's going to say leave the boy alone, stay out of his life.

But now that Noble has ventured down the Jem-is-my-son road, it's impossible to turn back. In his mind he has already begun shifting over and making room for this young soul, has already guided those young hands (clammy, for children's hands invariably are) in his own. He has shown him how to whittle an arrow and string a bow, how to climb an apple tree, how to select the best conkers, how to scoop a fish by its gills, how to saddle and bridle a horse. How to drive a car. He's walked with him through the streets of Kenomee, his hand on Jem's shoulder or tousling his hair, the boy looking up at him from time to time, face animated in a smile partway to a laugh, a non-stop barrage of question spilling from his mouth, feet skip-stepping to keep in time with his father's strides.

Noble pulls out his tobacco pouch and rolling papers and doubles back. He can always walk away if she gets hysterical.

From the stiff and self-conscious way she holds herself, walking towards him, Noble can tell that Mary feels as awkward and uncomfortable as he does. He grinds the butt of his cigarette under his heel and begins rolling another. Closer, he can make out the band of red that plays across her eyes like a mask

"You know," she begins, fussing with the collar on her dress. It cost a pretty penny, did that dress. As did her fancy shoes. Noble takes a bitter pleasure in the streaks of red clay across the toes. She must have stumbled making her way down here. "I could get the magistrate on you after that stunt you pulled last night." Briefly she looks him in eye. "And the doctor had a

135

mind to do exactly that. It took me half the night to talk him out of it."

Was he supposed to be grateful to her?

"The doctor doesn't like alcohol, and you fairly stank of it last night."

"This is why you dragged me out here? To tell me your husband doesn't like alcohol?"

"No." She looks away, and he can hear in her choked off voice, see in the wringing of her fingers — that's some fine jewellery she's got there — that she's trying to collect herself. "Jeremiah isn't yours. I don't know who put that idea in your head, but he's most definitely not yours."

"I can count, Mary."

"So can the doctor."

"Had us both at the same time, did you?" Noble is shocked at the sudden hatred he feels, expanding like heartburn. So she was being wooed by Baker before their Halifax tryst. While he was away getting shot at in the trenches — at least for all she knew he was getting shot at in the trenches — Mary was entertaining a man old enough to be her father. He has a fleeting urge to grab her fine dress by its oversized collar and rip it from her back. "You're a weak and stupid woman, Mary. Only I was too young and stupid myself to see it at the time."

"I've been a good mother to him."

"You've lied to him. You're still lying to him. You think that makes you a good mother?"

Her eyes glisten. She looks away in the direction of the woods. "He has a good home. He's happy. Why do you want to go stirring up a bunch of trouble?"

"I want to get to know him, do things with him." He does, but he hasn't thought this through. Sarah. What in God's name is she going to say? And the rest of the damn village.

"No. That's impossible."

"I could take him fishing, show him how to skin a rabbit."

"He's six years old. You want him slicing his fingers off?"

"We can go skating on Miller's pond in the winter."

"He goes there with his father."

"Hunting, then. All boys want to know how to hunt."

"A knife isn't dangerous enough? Now you want him carrying guns?"

"I'm his father, he should be with me." Noble's mouth is so dry and sour it feels as if he's taken a spoonful of baking soda.

"And what does the word father mean to you, Noble Matheson?" Hands on her hips. "Exactly what do you think it means? Because let me tell you this, it is much more than being the sower of the seed. Anyone can do that."

Sower of the seed. She was never this eloquent before. Obviously living with the doctor has rubbed off on her, or the man has spent hours correcting her speech and manners. Noble thinks he almost misses the cruder, brasher Mary. But there's another realization rattling around his head. She's almost as much admitted he is Jem's father. That his seed produced the child. Hasn't she?

"Nothing to say for yourself now, mister? I didn't think so."

She hasn't given him a chance. He's still collecting his thoughts.

"Well, mark my words. As long as I'm still in this village, Noble Matheson, he won't be with you. I'll make sure of that." And she's marching back towards the main road.

"You'll make sure how, Mary?" Fool. Bloody fool. Keep your mouth shut, can't you? But some part of him, unleashed in last night's whiskey-fuelled venture, has taken control of his mouth.

She stops, turns, and takes measured steps towards him. There's a trace of a smile about her lips. "Do you care about him?"

"Jem? Of course. He's my —"

"Then you'll think on what vicious gossip and rumours will do to him and you'll leave well enough alone."

Up close, her eyes sparking with passion, her features set with purpose, Noble is reminded of how attracted he once was. Without thinking he raises a hand to straighten the furrows on her forehead but she bats it away with her own gloved one. Finger pointed at him. "If you care you'll keep your distance. You know how cruel kids can be."

Not half as cruel as adults, Noble thinks, watching her walk away.

XIII

In through the back door, Esmeralda following on tiptoe, as if afraid of disturbing something fragile. Crossing Hetty's threshold she sheds wisdom and sophistication as she would a cloak. Now she's a child, exploring. Hetty stands aside and watches fascinated as this new Esmeralda pores through her house, touching things and lifting them up to look underneath, as if she half expects to find a story or explanation printed there, a price tag. But then Hetty would probably have acted similarly aboard the *Esmeralda* if her introduction to the schooner and its crew had been under more social circumstances. Esmeralda lurches. I'm still finding my land-legs," she says and giggles. Hetty, shackled by alarm, by how off-kilter Esmeralda seems — what if she breaks something? — feels suddenly years older.

Open doors may be welcoming, but there's none so intriguing as one that is closed. Now that she's finished inspecting the kitchen and front parlour, Esmeralda heads instinctively for Peter's study.

"Ah-ha. The lion's lair." She turns and grins wickedly as the door swings open with an obligingly theatrical creak. Though it's a room Hetty herself rarely steps foot in, she follows Esmeralda inside. How does Peter's world look through the sea-girl's eyes?

"My mother has a pair of these," Esmeralda says, moving towards the mantel. Her voice sounds soft and far away. She picks up the leather case and removes a pair of field glasses.

"Is she a bird watcher?" Hetty has no idea to whom the glasses once belonged — Peter's father or his mother — or whether they were employed for bird watching or for observing ships in the bay. The Douglases could have spied on their neighbours regularly for all she knows.

"She uses them to track the wind." Esmeralda seats herself in Peter's leather wing chair, the glasses at arm's length. She stares at them intently, as if this might somehow make her mother materialize in front of her.

"And why would she want to track the wind?"

"It's part of her job.

"Tracking the wind?"

"Actually, selling it. She's a wind seller. You know, a witch. She sells wind to sea captains — which is how she met my father, of course." Esmeralda raises one dark and handsome eyebrow. "Don't tell me you've never heard of wind sellers?"

"Well, of course I have. 'I'll give thee a wind,' the three witches in Macbeth."

"Right, wind sellers."

"But they're not exactly selling the wind. They're more controlling it. Using it for revenge."

"My mother is descended from a long line of Scottish witches who worked mostly for pleasure in an ancient art, calling up favourable winds for sailors' routes. Or unfavourable, as whimsy took them. They sold only enough to pay the bills. Which set them apart from other witches who would use their powers to accumulate great wealth. And that of course made them more feared — they couldn't be bought."

Hetty pauses and peers at her new friend. Where did she come from, this sailor-girl with her bookish vocabulary, her apparent education? "Esmeralda, they're just lines from a play."

"A figment of someone's imagination?"

"That's right."

"So sirens and harpies, sea monsters and sprites, they don't exist?"

"Of course not." Hetty searches Esmeralda's face, looking for signs of lunacy. Her patients sometimes babbled nonsense, those whose minds had been bent in sickness or accident. She conjures a mental picture of Esmeralda's flowing green dress, her father's elaborately dated jacket.

"Seamen have been buying magic hawsers from wind sellers for as long as anyone can remember. You think this is all just superstition?"

"We live in modern times. How many ships today rely solely on the wind?"

"A steam engine is more powerful than the wind?"

"That's hardly the point."

"What is the point then?"

Hetty pushes the ball of her thumb against the point of the heart-shaped ring. The empty claws leave matching deep red imprints. "You don't really expect anyone to believe in witches and wind sellers today, do you?"

"No." Esmeralda smiles, and the tension between them dissipates. "Of course I don't."

"So your mother isn't really a witch?"

"My mother is a school teacher on the Isle of Skye."

"And do you live with her when you're not sailing around the world?"

"My mother's temperament changes with the wind." Esmeralda winks. "Or perhaps it's the other way around. She isn't the easiest person to live with."

"Nor is mine," Hetty agrees, anxious to keep the conversation from straying back to the weird and the occult. "Mothers like to interfere, always thinking they know best. They'd arrange our lives for us indefinitely if we let them."

"Like your mother arranged your marriage."

Hetty's smile stretches taut across her face. "What makes you say that?"

"Why else would you marry Mr. Peter Douglas of Kenomee village? Anyone can see you're not in love with him."

Anyone? She reaches to take the field glasses from Esmeralda and put them back before they get broken. "You're imagining things."

"I don't think I am." Esmeralda's gaze is so level Hetty can feel fingers of red creeping about her neck and into her face. She fusses with the mantel's other ornaments, rearranging their order, checking for dust Laura might have missed.

"Since when has love been a prerequisite for marriage?"

"So I'm right?"

"You're direct, I'll say that much."

"Sorry. It must be the company I keep." Again the disarming smile. "It's a fascinating story, though."

"As is yours."

Esmeralda scribbles a headline in the air. "City girl thrown out of nursing, banished to a village miles from anywhere, married off to an older man."

Stated so baldly, how grim it sounds. "Peter is scarcely thirty-five."

"Which makes him at least ten years older than you." If only pinning an age on Esmeralda was so easy. One minute she's green, the next she has the wisdom of Adam. Or would that be Eve?

"Age isn't so important."

"Of course it isn't. So long as you're happy lying to yourself."

I wasn't the one just prattling on about witches and wind sellers, Hetty thinks. But whenever she suspects Esmeralda might be goading her, the girl turns on her smile. Her shadows vanish instantly.

"Your mother must have been pleased. Her little embarrassment safely out of the way of gossiping friends and acquaintances."

"I thought we were talking about your mother."

"Talking about yours is so much more interesting."

"I find that hard to believe." Hetty folds her arms and glances out the window.

"Why is that? I covet your life, you covet mine. Not that either of us would truly change places if the choice were presented to us. But it's fun to dream, isn't it?"

"It just feels as if you're making fun of me." Pulling at the loose threads. Unravelling the stitches.

"I'm not. I promise. It's just that, well, when you spend all your time with men, you forget that girls, women, speak differently. Behave differently. Walk in my shoes for a while. My wardrobe is from another era and I live on a wooden sailing ship with a bunch of misfits — all lovely people, in their own way, but, let's be honest, they'd be barred from polite company in most countries. Of course the rules and obligations of your life are fascinating to me." Esmeralda looks up at Hetty. "I find you fascinating. I can't help myself. Curious as a cat. It's just my nature. Do you forgive me?" Hetty doesn't think she's ever met a woman who can use her beauty to such advantage. Especially on another woman.

"Of course." This time when Esmeralda smiles Hetty has to look away. She pulls at the neck of her dress, feeling warm.

"So tell me" — mischief creeping back into her voice — "what's in it for Mr. Peter Douglas of Kenomee village?"

"Sorry?"

"It isn't as if he has a harelip or a hunchback, is it? Quite handsome really, if you're willing to overlook the cold fish qualities. And so many women are, aren't they?" Hetty can feel two bright discs of colour warming her cheeks and the disconcerting sense that Esmeralda has taken a walk through her head. "I mean, just look at this fine house and all your lovely clothes." She gestures at the room — female gestures with her manhands. "All the mothers of marriageable daughters for miles around must have had Peter in their sights."

"What are you suggesting?"

"What's the rest of the story?"

"I don't know what you mean." But she does. Not that it had bothered her so much in the beginning. Hetty wasn't the first bride to be offered up with a dowry; her marriage wasn't the first ceremony to be part of a financial arrangement. But at least she wasn't marrying a total stranger. Peter Douglas was Aunt Rachel's husband's sister's boy. A distant relative in, as it turned out, every sense of the word. They'd met at weddings and funerals over the years, he tall and gangly while she was barely in school. Peter had often been left in charge of the younger children at such events and had devised games and tasks to keep them busy. She remembered him as inventive and fun. Gradually his chest and arms had filled out, the planes of his face had shifted and thickened. Suddenly he was a man while she was still a child. He stood with the adults.

Once war broke out his likeness graced the mantel in a silver frame, the entire family inordinately proud of his uniform, his officer's stripes. So proud that when the V.O.N. committee began wagging their fingers in her mother's front parlour and Aunt Rachel suggested Peter Douglas as a husband, Hetty's mother leapt at the chance. The picture came down from the mantel. "Look how handsome he is in his officer's uniform." If Vivian had understood the irony in her approach she might have rethought her tactics.

But Hetty, as anxious as her mother to ease the situation, took the bait. Peter seemed the perfect road out of Halifax and the disgrace she'd suddenly found herself in. His mill was in a little financial trouble, nothing her father's bank couldn't see to, and so everyone would benefit. The wedding plans were drawn up and executed inside a month, their official line that Hetty had given up her job for marriage. She even began to believe it herself. And if Peter seemed a little stand-offish, she was willing to overlook this; after all the man had spent four years on the front lines, witness and perpetrator of all manner of horrors. Familiar with the vagaries and aberrations of shell shock, she knew she could warm him up.

And in those first weeks her enthusiasm, her willingness to please, to flirt, to pour her passion for nursing into her marriage, proved enough for the two of them. The coolness of her reception in the village didn't upset her. After all, it was simply proof she'd made the right choice. Wasn't it? Still smarting from her expulsion from nursing and preoccupied with how much her mother really knew, Hetty never thought to question how, in a world filled with girls and widows and not enough men to go round, handsome Peter Douglas had managed to make it into his thirties without finding a wife. She wound her days and nights around coaxing warmth and cajoling tenderness and never asked herself what was wrong with him. She simply skated on the surface of her marriage, growing fond of the awkward but gentle man, until the ice cracked in December and she found herself head first in icy waters. When she surfaced again, she and Peter were stranded on different floes, a lost baby between them.

"So what is Peter's deep dark secret?"

"I don't wish to talk about this any more."

"I'm sorry, I'm sorry. I'll change the subject, I promise." Esmeralda glances around the room as if looking for inspiration. Hetty holds her breath.

"I know. How about we try on all your clothes?"

"What a good idea." Hetty almost laughs aloud in relief. So eager is she to leave Peter's study she practically turns her ankle again lunging for the door.

"When would you wear something like this?" Esmeralda asks, holding up a cream and yellow dress with three-quarter-length sleeves. Against the olive tones of her skin, the colours seem discordant, the dress rendered drab and dated.

"Church, probably, or a luncheon."

"And this?" A navy blue and white sailor-style. Esmeralda wiggles her eyebrows and Hetty laughs at the absurd juxtaposition of her sailor outfit and the sailor-girl.

"Maybe you should try something on," she says. Clothes hang differently on a person. And darker, richer colours might be better, possibly more feminine styles; she's thinking of the dress Esmeralda had been wearing last night. Yet still, in skirts of chartreuse chiffon, scarf draped alluringly around her neck, Esmeralda looks strangely ordinary. Her beauty, like her wardrobe, seems to belong to another time and place. Esmeralda, running the fabric through her fingers and admiring herself in the mirror, doesn't appear to see what Hetty sees.

"Try this." Hetty hands her an evening dress. Perhaps Esmeralda's exotic beauty requires a touch of glamour. Esmeralda jiggles the dress on its hanger and giggles. Sequined and fringed in off-white, the not-quite-knee-length number swishes and shimmers. Daring, a little cheeky even. Most definitely a Halifax item. Or Montreal, New York, London, Paris. Hetty has had neither the occasion nor the inclination to wear it herself. Quickly Esmeralda sheds her male regalia and steps into the dress, but not before Hetty's sideways glance takes in the girl's lean legs, the way the muscles on her back ripple under her skin as she first bends and then reaches to hook up the side fastenings. Esmeralda spins, delighted, but to Hetty the result is the same: oddly disappointing. Current fashions sit ill on her new friend.

"It's great for doing the Charleston in," she offers. "The fringe swings back and forth in time to the music."

"The Charleston." Esmeralda begins moving her feet. Hetty pulls out a pair of shoes, and Esmeralda forces her feet into them. She minces over to where she's thrown her own clothes. "Now it's your turn."

Hetty shakes her head. "No. I don't think so." Esmeralda and Noble Matheson banging on the front door. Had they seen something? Could Esmeralda have possibly guessed what Hetty was up to that afternoon? Esmeralda pushes her shirt and pants into Hetty's hands. Though the twill of the pants is quite coarse, no doubt for practical reasons, the much-washed cotton of the shirt feels almost silky in its softness. The clothes smell like her, sweet and spicy.

"Go ahead, try them on."

"Oh, no. I couldn't." Hetty places the garments back on the bed.

"Please. Try them on for me. You'd look good with your short hair, more like a man."

Oh, who would know? It's only a bit of fun. Shy of changing in front of Esmeralda, Hetty turns away to slip on the pants and shirt and then faces the mirror. Is this the transformation she was looking for the other day? Esmeralda reaches over and ruffles her hair. Hetty regards the young man in the mirror. Esmeralda's clothes fall a little loosely on her. The two stand side by side. The gypsy and the lady. But Esmeralda is two or three inches taller than Hetty, so some of the effect is lost. Esmeralda looks about her, opens the door to Peter's wardrobe, and pulls out a wooden shoebox.

She places the box at Hetty's feet. Hetty steps onto it and grows from boy to man. "Now you may take my arm." Esmeralda holds out her arm for Hetty to link. The girl's skin feels so soft against her own the very idea of it makes Hetty uncomfortable. She stares at the couple in the mirror, the stiff young man with his face bleached of colour, a mild look of panic in his eyes; the long-haired beauty in a dress that is somehow all wrong for her. Hetty grows warm, can feel dampness in the hollow of her throat. Time stretches till she believes it might break, and then without warning, or maybe she's had all the warning in the world, Esmeralda turns towards her, cups her hands around Hetty's face and kisses her. Such a surprise, the softness of her girl's lips, the fullness of them, the curves of her face and the gentle down on her skin, so different from the resistance of a man's planes and angles, the pumice of bristles. Hetty feels Esmeralda's tongue dart across her lips and, when she parts them, the tease of tongue against her teeth, her gums, her own tongue.

Alarmed, Hetty draws back sharply. Esmeralda's mouth is drawn up in a sideways smile. A look of challenge? Conquest? Hetty steps from the box, turns her back, pulls Esmeralda's shirt over her head, undoes the waistband and buttons and shakes the pants from her legs as if they were crawling with ants. Everything is blurry. She yanks her own dress up over her shoulders and the sound of tearing fabric rips the air. She stares at the box on the floor, unable to risk a glace at Esmeralda. "Would you mind putting that back where you found it?"

"It was a bit of fun. Don't take it so seriously. It was a kiss. No harm done." Esmeralda reaches to take her hand but Hetty flinches and draws away. She stares at the window. No one can see in, she feels sure, and anyway the sun is beginning to set. Whatever is the time? Peter might be back any moment.

"You can have the dress."

"Do you mean it?"

"I have no use for it." She pushes past Esmeralda to her wardrobe, runs her hand across the myriad dresses and outfits her mother had, in a fit of relief or guilt, bought in Halifax and ordered from Montreal and New York last spring. She can afford to give up one or two. She selects a couple, places them on the bed, and when Esmeralda falls upon them exclaiming, pulls out a couple more. She won't miss them. "You don't even need to bother getting changed. Just leave in it. And here" — she selects another evening dress — "you can take this too. I don't need it." She begins folding Esmeralda's boy's clothes. "You should get going, it'll be dark soon."

"It's barely six o'clock."

"There's a fog on its way in. If you don't leave now you won't be able to see to cross through the fields and woods, not knowing your way."

"You could come with me. Hold my hand."

"Now I know you're making fun of me." Esmeralda opens her mouth to protest but Hetty holds up her hand. She's heard enough.

XIV

I remember him as if it were yesterday, as he
came plodding to the inn door, his sea-chest
following behind him in a hand-barrow; a tall,
strong, heavy, nut-brown man; his tarry pigtail
falling over the shoulders of his soiled blue coat;
his hands ragged and scarred, with black, broken
nails; and the sabre cut across one cheek, a dirty,
livid white. I remember him looking round the
cove and whistling to himself as he did so, and
then breaking out in that old sea-song that he
sang so often afterwards:

> *Fifteen men on the dead man's chest —*
> *Yo-ho-ho, and a bottle of rum!*

Noble's mother's lips twitch. "Go on," she says, looking up
from her mending. Perhaps it wasn't such a great idea reading
to her after all. Maybe he should have settled for the Dickens.
He stifles a yawn. Not quite the bottom of page one and the
man with the pigtail, not content to merely sing about rum, is
now calling for a glass of the stuff. Isn't *Treasure Island* supposed to be a children's book? Noble soldiers on, mouth so dry he
wonders if the Bushmills has seared his saliva glands closed.

He had taken me aside one day, and promised
me a silver fourpenny on the first of every month
if I would only keep my "weather-eye open for a
seafaring man with one leg," and let him know
the moment he appeared. . . .

How that personage haunted my dreams, I need
scarcely tell you. On stormy nights, when the wind
shook the four corners of the house, and the surf
roared along the cove and up the cliffs, I would
see him in a thousand forms, and with a thousand
diabolical expressions. Now the leg would be cut
off at the knee, now at the hip; now he was a mon-
strous kind of a creature who had never had but the
one leg, and that in the middle of his body. To see
him leap and run and pursue me over hedge and
ditch was the worst of nightmares. And altogether
I paid pretty dear for my monthly fourpenny piece,
in the shape of these abominable fancies.

Noble glances up at his mother. She's enjoying herself. The
story of course, but also, he suspects, the fact that reading
aloud is punishing him. Dinner felt good going down, but his
brain is back to aching, his bones to feeling tender. Maybe he
caught a chill sleeping rough last night. He drains his glass of
water and she takes mercy on him.

"I'll make us a cup of tea, shall I?" she says and disappears
to the kitchen.

Noble rests the book, spine up, in his lap and rubs a shaky
hand across his eyes, trying to push his hangover to the back
of his brain. A shot of that rum the captain is forever knocking
back would be more use than tea. A little hair of the dog.

"Hair of the dog," some sergeant had roared in his ear. He'd
been in a crowded lamplit pub. In the heavy gilt-edged mirror
above the bar he could see the low-slung pall of cigarette smoke
drifting above a tight scrum of heads. The hissing from the

gas lamps on the yellowed walls sounded like someone trying, through the dissonance of shell-shocked, battle-fatigued laughter, to get his attention. Noble didn't want to lose Lawson again but there was already something different about his brother. And not just in his face, which was leaner, with a line down either side of his mouth that cast his smile in parentheses. Quite uncharitably Noble thought how they made his brother more attractive, how now even more girls would throw themselves at him.

Noble hoped that Lawson had made it to the bar and was ordering them drinks. He was slowly elbowing his way between soft cap, hard cap, flat cap and bare head when suddenly a large red-faced sergeant blocked the way. The sergeant's eyes were focused somewhere on the space between Noble and the glass of whiskey in his hand, which found his mouth at regular intervals. With his right hand he clamped Noble's sleeve.

"Hair of the dog." The sergeant burped whiskey in Noble's face. "Hair of the dog," he roared again, in case his audience had missed it the first time. "Roman cure for dog bites . . . stuck hairs of the dog that bit you into your wound, they did." No one stared, despite his pitch and volume. Noble wanted to jerk his arm away and push on, but he couldn't, that damned English accent having reduced him to schoolroom obedience.

It was the sergeant who staggered off, Noble apparently not his ideal audience.

Past the curve in the bar, leaning against the back wall, Lawson was surrounded by a group of Lancashire Fusiliers. Like the sergeant he was drinking whiskey, a man's drink. But then at seventeen Lawson had already lived a life Noble could only imagine. He had killed men and watched his friends die. With his free hand he painted the air, his laughter and his flashing eyes punctuating his story. The centre of attention, as always. But something had changed. Noble could see it in the way Lawson held himself; something had reconfigured his stance, the set of his shoulders, the line of his jaw.

"If it isn't himself," Lawson shouted over people's heads, finally perhaps sensing the distant appraisal. "I got you a drink." Lawson nodded towards another short glass of honey-coloured liquid on the bar. After weeks of hospital food and tepid tea, Noble had been looking forward to the malty taste of ale, froth in his moustache, the weight of the wide-mouthed glass in his hand.

"You have it," he shouted back and called over to the barmaid for a pint. Lawson downed the extra drink in one backwards toss of his head. His new mates whooped and whistled, slapped him on the back.

The regulars began to thin out around ten o'clock. Noble felt gassy and bloated and more than a little light-headed. Lawson, who'd matched him pint for pint and knocked back half a dozen whiskies on top, looked cold sober. Stone cold. There was something unsettling about him. And as the others wandered away one by one and Noble found himself alone with his brother, it grew worse. The booze had loosened something in him. Whereas the other men seemed to forget, Lawson grew maudlin. He turned to Noble.

"When I close my eyes I can hear the horses screaming. And the dogs." He fixed Noble with blank eyes. "Why d'you think that is?"

Noble shook his head. His answer was likely to be wrong.

"Someone puts a bullet through their heads pretty quickly. No one can stand it. The noise. The whimpering. The screaming." He stared into the dregs of his ale. "Men ask you to do the same sometimes. But you don't. A man can only scream and cry for so long. Did you know that?"

Noble shook his head again. He wanted to shut his brother up, didn't want to hear what it was Lawson needed to say but was afraid to stop him.

"Soon enough it's all he can do to moan, mumble to his mama. Or his girl. Or God. Then nothing. But it doesn't mean he's dead."

"Time, gentlemen, please. Let's be having your glasses now."
The barmaid had disappeared, she was in the back maybe, the
landlord was left wiping down the bar. His skin was the colour
of cured plaster. It occurred to Noble that the man was probably dying. Heart failure.

"I was with a buddy out there when —" Lawson had his
elbows on the bar. He was in the landlord's way, a mess of
sticky beer rings corralled between his arms. "He had a wife
and kids. Two little blond-haired girls. Real cute they were.
Are. They still are. It's just him that . . ." He stared into the
bottom of his empty glass, as if he might find the rest of his
sentence there. "You ever wanted kids, Noble? I did," he said,
without waiting for his brother's response. "A house full of
them. Six, seven, eight. More. I always wanted a house filled
with kids' laughter and scraped knees and first steps and first
words, and bicycle rides and swimming, and me and the missus
watching them all walk down the road to school together. You
ever think about any of those things?"

"Not really, no. Can't say I have." It was a surprise to learn
that his brother had. Lawson was still a boy. Too young to have
kids himself, too young to be thinking about them.

"I got some champagne stashed for a little nightcap for us,
brother. Did I tell you about the night we spent in a champagne
cellar?"

It wasn't until Noble was undressing for bed later that night
that he realized Lawson had been talking about himself as if
he were already dead.

Christ.

"You look miles away."
He takes the mug of steaming tea from his mother's hands
and sips at it before setting it on the floor by his side. His mother settles herself back into her armchair. His bottle of Bushmills
must be somewhere in the bushes down by the wharf. If he

could just summon the energy to get up and walk down there. Whiskey would stop the trembling in his hands and ease the pressure in his head. His mother reaches for her mending and nods at him to continue. Noble picks up the book again.

His stories were what frightened people worst of all. Dreadful stories they were; about hanging, and walking the plank, and storms at sea, and the Dry Tortugas, and wild deeds and places on the Spanish Main. By his own account he must have lived his life among some of the wickedest men that God ever allowed upon the sea; and the language in which he told these stories shocked our plain country people as much as the crimes that he described. My father was always saying the inn would be ruined, for people would soon cease coming there to be tyrannized over and put down, and sent shivering to their beds; but I really believe his presence did us good. People were frightened at the time but on looking back they rather liked it; it was a fine excitement in a quiet country life; and there was even a party of the younger men who pretended to admire him, calling him a "true sea-dog", and a "real old salt", and suchlike names, and saying there was the sort of man that made England terrible at sea.

In one way, indeed, he bade fair to ruin us; for he kept on staying week after week, and at last month after month, so that all the money had been long exhausted, and still my father . . .

He jerks awake, his neck sore from having fallen asleep with his head slumped on his chest. He reaches for his tea, now lukewarm. His mother potters in the kitchen. The last of the sun's rays throw long shadows across the walls of the room, walls that feel uncomfortably close. The nausea has gone but his head still feels thick. He struggles to his feet, and his mother appears in the doorway, wiping her hands on her apron.

"Happen you should get yourself to bed early."

Happen he should. A glance at the clock. But not this early. He pads gingerly into the kitchen, grabs his coat from the peg by the back door and steps out into the windy evening.

Whitecaps have gathered in the bay. Waves slap against the sides of the *Esmeralda*, which in turn rubs and bangs against the wharf. Her jib stays, spanking new, tremble and twang in the stiff breeze. The jib boom lifts and drops, and the bow of the schooner shudders and creaks. Noble, intent on his whiskey hunt, ears filled with wind, does not at first hear the footsteps along the wharf. Then he stiffens. Could be one of the crew, or a villager on the prowl for another bottle. He hunkers down in the bushes, heels knocking against the bottle, which he grabs, holding his breath until the person comes into view. It's a woman, all dressed up in fancy evening attire and carrying some fancy wrap. Hetty Douglas? But then she pulls her hair from her neck and he can see it is Esmeralda.

Esmeralda in a sparkly dress and men's boots. A contrast that common sense tells him should look absurd but which instead is unsettlingly erotic. The dress, despite lines designed to hide her curves, slithers and shimmers as she moves. Swaying fringe at the hem grazes her thighs. There's nothing more seductive than a woman unaware she's being watched, Noble thinks. Was the dress for Butler's benefit? He hopes not, for Eliza's sake more than his own. But if Esmeralda has been with Butler, why is she walking back to the schooner alone?

He drops the whiskey bottle by his feet just as the wind dies. A clink of glass on stone, a small thud as the bottle comes to rest. Esmeralda's face tightens, and Noble, feeling both sheepish and underdressed, steps sideways from the shadows.

"Waiting for me, were you?"

"I'm sorry. I stumbled," he lies. "The wood is rotten in places." A half-truth. He worries the worn toe of his boot in the splinters on the wharf deck, embarrassed by his scrabbling in the bush like an animal. Esmeralda watches him, a smile gathering on her face. Noble cannot return her gaze.

"Why don't they replace it?"

"Too expensive." His eyes take in the length and breadth of the *Esmeralda*, which seems suddenly too big for her moorings. "There isn't the need so much anymore for a wharf like this. Yours is the biggest schooner to be tied up here in years."

"No big ships at all?"

"Some. But none as fine-looking a vessel as this. Mainly old ketches carrying salt, molasses, fabric, that sort of thing. One stops off here every few months or so."

"My father had her built to honour my mother."

"I thought she was named after you."

"She was named for my mother's famous green eyes. Even though my mother has never set foot on her deck."

"Not much of a sailor is she, your mother?"

"Once upon a time she was. Until my parents were ship-wrecked near the coast of Argentina. Now she lives alone in Mar de la Plata, has done ever since they found themselves beached there. She refused to leave even after my father had the *Esmeralda* built and christened for her. She claims she likes the heat. And the Spanish temperament. Some people say I look Spanish." A gust sweeps across the shoreline, ruffling the surface of the water, and Esmeralda reaches behind her neck to gather her hair, pull it from her face. The smooth olive-tinted line of her neck dries Noble's throat. "Perhaps that's why they live apart. "

It's an exotic story, like Esmeralda herself. According to the carpenters who worked on her prow, the *Esmeralda* was built on the Bay of Fundy. But he's standing so close, watching the words spill from those bruised-looking lips. Her malt-coloured eyes, the sweet spicy smell that exudes from her skin and hair — everything about this girl can set him off course.

"You've been shopping." From somewhere he draws the nerve to reach out and touch the dresses draped over her arm. Cool and expensive under his rough fingers.

"They were a gift. Like this one." The fringe dances as she holds the garments one by one against herself, strikes exaggerated poses, pirouettes. "Do you like?"

Noble nods dumbly. He likes a lot. She smiles the way no girl in the village ever learned to smile. He imagines burying his face in her neck, running his tongue between her breasts, his hands up and down her thighs. Feeling himself stiffen, he has to look away.

"Sit with me awhile?" She walks to the end of the wharf and perches on the edge, her long legs and mannish boots dangling over the water. Noble joins her, watching the fringe lift and dance with the wind.

"You didn't bring your whiskey?"

Heat rushes to his face and she starts to laugh. "Spoon mentioned he found you sleeping in the bushes this morning."

"Yes, well, I was three sheets last night."

"And feeling a little rough today?" Her mouth pulls up in a sly grin.

"I'm not a huge fan of whiskey."

"Me neither. Too medicinal-tasting. Give me champagne any day."

"My brother liked champagne. He shared a bottle with me once." Noble stares off beyond the stern of the *Esmeralda*.

"And did you enjoy it?"

Champagne didn't twist through your head the way whiskey did, warping your judgement and playing a maudlin game of roulette with your memories. Champagne, as he remembers, just made you silly, then left you with a headache.

"I enjoyed it well enough."

"Then champagne it must be." Esmeralda swings her feet back onto the dock. "Wait right here."

She moves with animal grace. Noble tracks every gesture, every nuance as she gathers her dresses and disappears aboard the schooner. Within minutes she reappears carrying glasses and a bottle of champagne, which she hands to Noble to open. Veuve Clicquot. "If you'd like to do the honours?"

The cork pops, and Noble's taste buds sharpen at the sight of the gas escaping over the lip of the bottle.

"To us." Esmeralda clinks glasses.

"To us."

"And to your brother."

"To my brother," he mumbles. Eyes closed, he tips back his head. Nectar sliding down his throat, bubbles dancing on his tongue. He can feel his head expanding, the tightness behind his eyes draining away. He fills their glasses again.

"You must be heading out soon?" He gestures to the prow of the schooner, the new bowsprit and rigging.

"Yes, it's just the sails left now. And they've been promised for tomorrow."

"The engine should hold — until you get to a bigger port, that is. I did the best I could but I wouldn't be putting it under any more strain than you have to. You might want to set anchor the other side of Cape Split, wait till the wind is right."

"I don't think that'll be necessary."

"Well, you managed just fine coming up here. That took some pretty skillful sailing, to get up the Bay of Fundy and through Cape Split with the kind of damage you had. I reckon some of your crew must be familiar with the area."

"Sometimes a whisper in the right ear can help." She leans towards him to demonstrate. "You know, a word with the powers that be, the sea gods, witches, whatever you want to call them." Noble can scarcely think straight for the heat of her breath on his neck.

"And then you'll be off on another adventure?"

She lifts a hand to stroke his face. "You would like to join us, maybe?"

He hears himself laugh as if from a distance. The champagne glass twirls between his fingers. "It must be a thrilling life. Not knowing where your next port is, calling the sea your home." How much more thrilling to be sequestered in close quarters with a woman such as Esmeralda. Unable to look at her for more than a few seconds, he glances down the length of the schooner's hull. One of the dories is missing. They must have taken it for fishing. "I don't know it's for me though. For a few days maybe, but weeks and months, it might get a little lonely or claustrophobic. I think I'd miss the feel of the ground under my feet."

"You'd miss your village."

He would miss Lillian. The thought is there without being summoned. And yet he's sitting next to Esmeralda. So close he can smell the evening on her skin. And his mind cannot move past her body. Though it's too windy, he wishes he could roll a cigarette, give his hands something to do. He pats his jacket pocket anyway, seeking his tobacco pouch. "No. Not the village, not really." A white lie. "But certainly the city life." An out-and-out lie. He's turning into Butler.

"You live in the city? I thought you lived here."

"I do. I was talking about Halifax. I lived there for a few years."

"Halifax. And have you ever been to a famous city like London or Paris?"

"London. In the war."

"You were in the war?" Her eyes round in sympathy.

"Yes. No. I was, um, we were stationed, well, training. Salisbury Plains. Horrible place. Nothing but rain and mud. You wouldn't believe how much mud . . ." His skin burns as shame floods through him. What about the mud at Ypres, at Flanders, at Vimy Ridge? He longs for the oblivion of another glass of champagne. Or a nip of whiskey.

159

"So you never were in London."

"London? Oh yeah. I was there. A bunch of us, on leave. And my brother."

"London is a grand city, beautiful too, when the weather is good. Did you see Buckingham Palace and the Tower of London?"

"We weren't exactly looking for history."

"No. I don't suppose you were." She leans into him, her breast pressing against his arm. Firm and full. Her dress inches up her thighs. Such long lean legs. He pictures his hand resting on her bare skin, can almost feel it travelling up and under her glittery dress. She smiles. "You were looking for girls."

He pauses. "Lawson was always looking for girls."

"Lawson?"

"Lawson was my brother."

"Who likes champagne."

"Who liked champagne."

She tips her head to one side so that her hair falls over her shoulder. Her eyes moisten and fill. "And —"

"He was killed at Vimy Ridge."

Closer.

"For your brother," she says. And now her lips are on his. So warm and full. He'd almost forgotten the softness of a woman's mouth. She tastes of salt and champagne. Her hands reach up and cradle his face. Surprising hands. Strong and rough-skinned. With her tongue she parts his lips and all the warmth and wetness of her mouth is open to him. Now his hand is in the luxurious thickness of her hair. He pushes into the kiss and she responds, kissing him harder, devouring him. His head is whirling, his penis so hard he fears his skin might burst. He has never wanted a woman as much as he wants Esmeralda. Has never wanted to take a woman as he wants to take this one, wants to pull her dress up over her thighs and push himself into her. He's losing his balance, the wharf is spinning, there's a roar inside his head, a fury peeling back his inhibitions. He takes his hand from the back of her head and slides it up the smooth soft skin of her leg. Esmeralda squeezes his hand and in one practised motion moves it away, pulls backs and gets to her feet.

She's leaving. He's hot and cold. Shaking. Suddenly fiercely jealous of the other men aboard the schooner, those who work side by side with her, those who spend every waking and sleeping moment close to her. He is angry with their lust, with the way they must press themselves against her cabin door at night, desire soaking their skin, listening for her night movements, picturing the rise and fall of her breasts in sleep, the curve of her thighs. How can he bring her back?

"I killed him." The words like stones in his mouth. "It's my fault he's dead." *You wanna sign up?* He can see his brother's mock salute, his face lit up as if he just found the nickel in the plum pudding. *This war's going to be over long before I'm old enough to serve.* Esmeralda turns. She's coming back, eyes holding his, the line of her sensuous mouth stricken ugly with pity. She stoops, brings his hands to her lips and kisses them; two long soft kisses. One for each hand. Her lips move to his ear.

"Your whiskey is in the bushes," she says, then straightens and walks away.

XV

Monday June 2. High tide, 5:32 a.m., 6.00 p.m.

Hetty wipes the heel of her hand across her lips, smearing her lipstick. The shade is too dark, the mirror in the station rest-room tells her, features pale and washed out from last night's restless sleep. Even pressing herself into Peter all night, trying to force him between herself and what happened yesterday after-noon, has not erased the imprint of the girl on Hetty's skin.

Or her mind.

She awoke this morning flushed and damp, another stranger in her dreams. Shadowy, wavering, a figure whose lines and contours she couldn't quite discern. Her fingertips tingled with caresses, her breasts, her thighs. Gradually the figure emerged from the shadows of sleep. No blacksmith from the village this time, no ropey muscled fisherman with darkened skin and sun-bleached eyes. But a tangle of long dark hair. Soft skin and curves, the heat and fullness of breasts under her hands.

Peter never mentioned her paleness over breakfast. But these days Peter seemed to notice little about her, and Hetty could tell once she had settled into the passenger seat of the doctor's black Ford, freshly washed and polished for the occasion, that her husband had things on his mind too. The details of his last minute business trip? Or did he need to concentrate on his driving? After all, he'd been entrusted with the doctor's car, and Peter is more comfortable with a horse and trap.

Wetting her handkerchief under the faucet, she rubs at her mouth, lips pursed in a ruddy bloom, but can still feel the gentle pressure of Esmeralda's kiss, the softness of her skin. Could the dream be a sign, as some people believe? Is Hetty, deep down, one of those women? How could she have been unaware until now? Or has she grown into this proclivity? Is it a reaction to Job Mitchell and Cabot Street, or a year of living with a man's desires? Was that how it happened? Or did those women simply always know?

Compact out, she tones down the clown-like redness around her mouth. Combs her hair, pulls her hat low on her forehead, pats at her dress, dusty from the drive. A voice over the loud-speaker announces something, she guesses the arrival of the mid-morning train from Halifax. Hetty pulls on her gloves and practises a smile in the mirror before stepping back into the bustle of the station.

Pale lemon cloche hat framing her heart-shaped face, Clara, looking like a warm summer's day, alights from one of the first-class passenger cars. The pleated skirt of her matching pale lemon dress swings expensively around her slim calves.

Today's fashions suit few women — straight lines and dropped waists sit ill on both the full-figured and the short and petite — but Clara's boyish figure is made for them. She appears flawless; looking at her, no one could possibly imagine the long filament of scar that traces her hairline. Clara's wound. A tidy white line hidden by fashion. Unlike the messy blue scars that mar the hands and faces of so many other Explosion victims.

Hetty rushes towards her childhood friend. Arms around Clara's back, she inhales the familiar scent of Worth perfume, anxious to replace the lavender and sea-salt smell of Esmeralda, which hangs in the air as if the girl had swept by just moments before.

"Is anything the matter, darling? You've got me worried, telephoning so early this morning."

"No, nothing like that. Peter didn't tell me until this morning that he was coming into Truro. And suddenly it seemed a perfect opportunity to get out of the village for the day."

Clara holds Hetty at arm's length. "Look at you. So bright-eyed and beautiful. And you've put some weight back on. Though I'd say you were in dire need of a haircut." Hetty reaches a gloved hand to the ends of her hair. Clara can see this through her hat?

"Are you going to keep me in suspense? Do I have to guess at your news?"

"There's nothing to guess at. Can't a girl simply invite her friend for a pleasant lunch?"

Clara threads Hetty's arm through hers. "Of course. Lead me to your best hotel. I'm in dire need of a cup of tea. And then you can fill me in on all your gossip."

"Whatever it is you're not telling me has put a lovely sparkle in your eye," Clara says once they are settled with menus at a well-lighted, draft-free table suitably distanced from the kitchen.

"It's country air," Hetty responds and smiles blithely at Clara's arch expression. "How are the wedding plans?"

Clara reaches into her purse and produces a square of fabric which she smoothes out on Hetty's placemat. Pink.

"It's shot silk." She wiggles her eyebrows, Charlie Chaplin-fashion. "Expensive."

Hetty fingers the fine fabric. It's like stroking water. "It would look nice in blue."

"Blue is a boy's colour. Besides, the napkins are pink, and the florist is going to make darling centrepieces with clusters of the tiniest pink roses. Even the place cards are pink." Clara pouts. "Don't you want to match my wedding?" Hetty imagines this is the way Clara negotiates with Jonathan. With all men.

164

Peter would laugh, not seduced in the least by such practiced charm.

When the waiter brings tea, Clara fusses with the ritual of stirring, straining and pouring, and Hetty chatters about the menu and the difference between Laura's plain cooking and the more elaborate meals that Frances, her mother's housekeeper, had accustomed her to. She's babbling but fears that without a constant stream of chatter, Esmeralda might slip into the silences.

"When are you coming to Halifax? Alice will have pieced together your frock by the end of this week. We should arrange for a fitting."

"Soon. I promise."

"Jonathan has made some investments in a new mining company, the Bayano River Syndicate, which is in South America. We're going to be fabulously rich."

Hetty glances over at the other tables. Flat-footed Jonathan stayed home and made pots of money during the war selling bolts of woollen serge to the army. Her resentment is irrational, but there it is, like a wall she can't scale or find a door through.

"Really, Peter should think about investing. I'll ask Jonathan to have a chat with him, shall I?"

"I'm not sure. Peter is rather cautious when it comes to that kind of thing."

"From what you've told me, darling, I'd say he's cautious about many things."

Hetty rearranges the cruet stand, spilling salt in the process. She scoops it into her hand, then brushes it onto the floor by her feet.

"But then he married you out of the blue, so there's an impulsive streak in him somewhere, right?"

"Clara, do you love Jonathan?"

"Don't be a silly goose. Why wouldn't I? Jonathan is handsome and rich and has all kinds of influential friends. We're going to honeymoon on the Riviera. Just imagine — hob-nobbing with royalty and movie stars! And he has the most exquisite house on Spring Garden Road, which I just can't wait to redecorate. Modernize. Honestly, you should see the décor now. So stuffy and Victorian."

"Yes, but do you love him?"

A tiny line of vexation marks the middle of Clara's creamy forehead. "Whatever is the matter with you today, Hetty? I thought we were going to have a nice girly chit-chat." Her eyes have darkened, and Hetty braces for tears.

"That's what we are having. Aren't we?"

"No. You're being beastly. At least Jonathan and I have known each other for more than five minutes. And Peter Douglas may well be some long-lost cousin of yours, but the first I heard of him was a week before your wedding."

"It was more than a week."

"And you sit there and lecture me about love."

"I'm not lecturing, Clara, I simply asked, that's all." She delivers this remark as a whispered hiss as she sees the waiter approaching with their lunches. Clara's salad and her cottage pie. He sets their meals in front of them and returns to the kitchen.

Clara picks up her cutlery. "Please don't let's fight, Hetty. I so hate it when you're angry with me."

"I'm not angry —" She waves away the rest of her sentence and cuts into her pie, despite the fact that any appetite she had has been replaced with irritation. Why can't Clara see what's in front of her nose? And has she always been so shallow? They are both a long way from those halcyon days at the Halifax Ladies College, where nothing mattered but high-sticking calls in hockey and passing Miss Ellis's Latin quizzes. After the Explosion, Hetty walked away from the college and never returned. Throughout her nursing days she put in an appearance at as many of Clara's parties and excursions as she could manage — or tolerate — but the truth is they've been living different lives for years. Perhaps her year away from the city has made all the difference in the world. That and the events of the past twelve months have pushed a wedge between them. Jonathan's money will eventually drive it home.

But for now they are still close enough to pretend their friendship is strong. Hetty watches Clara pick through her salad and wonders how long it will take her to arrive at the same conclusion, and wonders too how and why they've managed to cling so long to what is in essence a leftover from childhood, a friendship formed when their mothers, busy orchestrating Halifax social life, threw them together as little girls. If either had found a replacement friend they would have drifted apart years ago. Who will take Clara's place, Hetty wonders. Laura? And as if she's been waiting her turn all morning, Esmeralda is suddenly there. Centre stage. Her mouth. Those full lips. The colour of crushed grapes. *It was a bit of fun.* Then why is it so difficult to laugh? *No harm done.* Yet Hetty is here. Running away.

Finished eating, Clara pats her mouth with her napkin and moves her half-empty plate to one side.

"I'm sorry for being so sensitive, darling, that was unfair of me. I'm all jittery these days. Forgive me?" Clara's hand atop Hetty's. Cool, graceful fingers, neatly manicured, with polished nails. How different from Esmeralda's rough hands. "Am I forgiven?" Hetty draws her hand free, uneasy with the intimacy of the gesture.

Clara dawdles over the check and spends so long in the restroom reapplying her lipstick that by the time they reach the station, the train to Halifax is already pulling away. There isn't another scheduled for hours.

"Well!" She rolls her eyes. Hetty thinks she's been watching too many motion pictures. "I can't wait around here by myself, now can I?"

"I suppose not." Clara and the unwashed masses. Perched on the wooden benches in the waiting room twiddling her manicured thumbs. The lemon of her dress a sherbet oasis in a sea of dusty hats and drab overcoats. It's almost funny.

Peter is standing beside the large plate glass window of W.B. Murphy's Confectionary and Ice-cream Parlour on Prince Street. His shoulders straighten when he sees Hetty approaching with Clara in tow.

"Miss Turner." Peter lifts his hat.

"Mr. Douglas. How delightful to meet you again at last. I was beginning to think Hetty was deliberately keeping us apart. I'm so sorry we missed each other at Christmas." Peter's mouth constricts. Clara covers his hand with both of hers. When she releases him, Peter makes as if to reach for Hetty but at the last moment pulls back his cuff to check his wristwatch.

"Am I to take it, Miss Turner, that you've missed your train?"

"The next isn't until nine o'clock."

Hetty's cheeks are already aching with the strain of smiling. "Clara proposes we entertain her until then."

"Nine o'clock tonight?" Peter pauses. "I see. Well then, you must allow us to extend you a little Kenomee Village hospitality."

"But —"

"I'd be delighted."

"We can have dinner at home and then we'll drive you back in plenty of time to catch your train."

Clara in the village? Hetty opens her mouth to protest, but her friend has already excused herself to make a telephone call. To Peter she says, "It isn't your car to be promising rides in. What's your precious doctor going to say?"

"Dr. Baker and I have an understanding."

"Which means you'll be huddled in conspiracy with him for hours, I suppose?"

"Which will give you ample time to introduce Clara around the village."

"To whom?" *I'd like you to meet some friends of mine. They're rum-runners.* But isn't she done with Esmeralda and her games? And the schooner and her crew may already have left on this morning's tide. "I'm not exactly winning any popularity contests. Or hadn't you noticed?"

"We weave our own hair shirts, Hetty."

"I could say the same of you."

Peter flinches, and Hetty glances away. "By the way, you're dreaming if you think I'm coming back here again with you. I have better things to do." Clear the air with Esmeralda. Say goodbye. "You invited her to the house. It's your responsibility to bring her back."

"Sometimes I just don't understand you, Hetty. Clara is your best friend, I thought you'd relish the prospect of spending more time together."

"It isn't that. I just don't want her —"

"What?"

"Nothing."

"What else was I supposed to do, Hetty?"

"Offer to stay in town for the rest of the day. We could have gone for a walk. Or watched the tidal bore or something."

"I can't hang around here until nine o'clock tonight. I need to be back in the village. I have things to see to."

"Things that can't wait one more day?"

"That's right."

"Such as?"

"A meeting. You wouldn't understand."

"Try me."

"Let's just say I need to follow up on something."

"Mill business?"

"In a manner of speaking."

"More layoffs? You should try approaching my father again."

Peter glances down Prince Street and Hetty follows his gaze to see Clara waving from across the street. Peter waves back and points to the parked car. They begin walking towards it.

"We can talk about this later, Hetty. Right now you have a guest to entertain." Peter opens the rear passenger door for his wife.

"Entertain her yourself. You two have a lot in common." She yanks the door from his hand and slams it shut. "She's marrying for money too."

"Peter seemed rather anxious to get away. Do you think it's me? Am I too much for him, do you think?"

"Not at all. Though you're probably too much for most people around here."

"Laura seemed friendly enough."

"Laura isn't most people. And don't worry, Peter will be back as soon as he's sweet-talked the doctor into letting him keep his car a few more hours. Dr. Jeremiah Baker," she adds in response to Clara's blank look. "It's the doctor's car he's driving."

"I thought you had your own car."

"Not anymore. Peter would rather ride everywhere."

"Really? How Byronesque."

"Would you like some tea? I'll show you the stable later if you like."

"That sounds lovely, Het. But it was awfully stuffy in the car, and I feel headache coming on. Do you mind if I have a little lie-down?"

Hetty has to restrain herself from taking the stairs two at a time. Minutes after Clara is settled in the guest room with a glass of water and a blanket, the curtains drawn, she's by the back door in the kitchen shucking her shoes and stepping into Peter's dead mother's rubber boots.

"You're leaving me?"

"Clara!" Hetty almost leaps from her skin. "I was just going out for a walk."

"A walk in the country, now that should clear my head."

"It's muddy. And you haven't the proper shoes."

"I can wear those."

"Which?" Clara points at the pair of battered shoes Laura slips on to hang out the laundry when the ground is wet. Hetty fixes a smile on her face. It would be churlish to refuse her now. She'll keep her distance but take the path through the woods, just to check that the schooner is still tied up at the wharf.

As they near the wharf, Hetty's legs grow unsteady, her feet cold, as if she's stepped in water. A clutch of people are milling about on the wharf. Others are standing on the deck of the *Esmeralda*.

"What is it?"

"Something's wrong."

"Don't tell me you know these people." The captain, easily identified in silhouette by his paunch, is barking orders. Hetty picks up her pace and Clara falls quiet, perhaps sensing her distress. As they round the bow of the *Esmeralda*, another man appears from the fore companionway. Dr. Baker.

Hetty reaches the thick of the crowd just as the doctor climbs from the wharf ladder. He brushes his long hands across the front of his jacket and fixes Hetty with a baleful stare.

"In future you should leave off meddling in affairs beyond your ken."

Hetty clamps her hand over her heart to stop it leaping from her chest.

"Trained in field amputations, did you?"

A silence has fallen among those on deck looking up and those standing around her on the wharf.

"J.J.? John James. How is he?" At that moment Spoon steps backwards from the fore companionway. He's carrying one end of a stretcher. J.J.'s foot comes first, an incongruous sight, one where there should be a pair. He's covered in a blanket. Even his head. Oh dear God. Esmeralda appears from behind her father. Has she been on deck all along?

"See what your meddling has done?" The doctor's sanctimonious voice drills through her head. "Gone and caused that young man's demise."

"I only did what the moment called for." Her mouth filled with sawdust. "He would have died had I done nothing."

Doctor Baker gives her a withering look. "I'd tell you to stick to bedpans and dressings in future, but you're not even a nurse, are you?" He turns without waiting for a response, and the men around them part to let him through.

"I was a nurse for over five years, and a good one too," she calls at his retreating back.

"History, Mrs. Douglas. History," the doctor replies, his stride lengthening. "They threw you out on your ear."

"Het, they threw you out? You never told me!"

"Now is not the time, Clara." She can feel everyone's eyes on her, probing, trying to lift the surface of her skin. If they stare hard enough maybe her past will flash before them like a picture show. What kind of nurse, they want to know, what kind of woman gets thrown out of nursing?

"If you'd seen how fast the gangrene was spreading, you would have made the same decision."

This stops him. Half a dozen giant strides and he is standing so close she can count his nostril hairs.

"Young lady, it might behoove you to remember in future that nurses don't diagnose, and as a disgraced one you shouldn't even be nursing. Don't ever presume to know what I would or would not have done. I am a fully trained medical professional whereas you are merely a housewife. And from what I have gathered, not a very good one. If I ever hear of you interfering in a medical matter again I shall personally make sure you are brought before the local magistrate. Do I make myself clear, Mrs. Douglas?"

Hetty glares stonily at the back of Baker's head as he walks away from her a second time.

"Well, he got out of the wrong side of bed this morning. Het, are you all right?"

"I'm fine." But her hands are shaking. Pompous ass. She'd met more than a few of his kind during her training at Victoria General — men whose self-importance got in the way of their abilities and often obliterated any compassion they might have felt for the patients in their care. His wife is probably frigid, she thinks, clamping down on her lips to stop herself from shouting it out loud.

The stretcher bearing J.J.'s body is now being lifted by ropes from the schooner. It sways treacherously in the breeze, each clank of its metal poles against the wharf's pilings sending a shudder through the crowd. Hetty's skin grows cold. As she stares up Wharf Lane, watching the doctor disappear, a black Model T Ford turns down and begins making its way towards them.

"I say, isn't that Peter?"

So it is.

"You must tell him what that dreadful man said to you."

What possible business can Peter have at the wharf? A second car turns and inches up behind the doctor's Ford. Hetty takes in its high sides and length, the lack of windows in the back. The hearse. Peter steps out first. And though she knows he must see her standing with Clara, he neither acknowledges them nor glances their way. When the occupants of the second vehicle step out it is obvious why. Policemen.

"Could the captain of this vessel step ashore, please, and bring me the ship's registration papers and the crew's papers?"

Hetty watches as Esmeralda climbs the ladder to the wharf and strolls towards her. She can't begin to think what must be running through Clara's mind. Or how, under the circumstances, Esmeralda can find the composure to smile.

"You put a flea in that old doctor's ear."

"Yes, well, he said some unkind things."

"You can't feel bad about what happened. You didn't give J.J. the infection." She reaches out a hand and touches Hetty's arm.

Hetty can literally feel the wind as Clara's jaw drops. "Oh, would someone fill me in, please?"

Esmeralda acknowledges neither Clara's request nor her presence. "You made the right decision."

Clara could probably warm her hands from the heat rising to Hetty's face. "I hardly think —"

"Don't let the old windbag hurt you. What you did the other day took a lot of courage."

"I had a moral obligation."

Esmeralda shrugs and glances over her shoulder. "As it seems I now have a legal one. I had fun though. We should do it again sometime." A sideways tug of her lips and she's turned away, her steps neither hurried nor apologetic as she walks towards her father and a man who has just loudly introduced himself as the county liquor inspector.

XVI

The moon picks out the silver backs of the fish as they break the surface, twisting and writhing in the shallow tidepool. It isn't like Butler to be late. With the exception of his war years he has tended the family weir twice a day, May to October, for as long as Noble can remember. If he were gravely ill or passed out drunk, Eliza would be down here herself, or she would have sent word.

Noble slouches, wishing the truck's seats were more forgiving. Time stretches in a different dimension in the small hours of the night. Is Esmeralda lying awake in her Truro jail cell, chewing on her mind? Or worse? Why did it have to be Spoon who slipped free of the police this afternoon? It strikes him, not for the first time, that people don't usually get what they deserve. As for the *Esmeralda*, manned by the Coast Guard and a hired crew, she must be through the funnel that is Cape Split by now. On her way to where? What happened to rum-runners' ships? Were they sailed out into the ocean and scuttled? Stripped down and refitted for legitimate cargoes? Or simply sold to the highest bidder — more than likely another rum-runner who'd have it back out plying the same trade on the open seas as soon as the paint was dry on the new name?

And what of her cargo? He straightens in his seat, shakes the wool from his legs. Butler. He pushes the starter.

The Bentleys' homestead sits across from Five Islands. Noble crawls through the property, headlights off, and when the hump-shaped silhouette of Moose Island comes into view, he pulls up beside a thicket. He climbs from the truck and walks to the edge of the cliff. Below him the basalt rock face pushes out in a crumbling wedge that ends in two pinnacle shapes: Old Wife and Two Hour Rock, named for the duration of its visibility. From this vantage point, Moose Island, the largest and closest of the Five Islands — formed, according to Mi'kmaq legend, from clods of earth hurled at Beaver by Glooscap — stands like a protective elder sibling before the smaller Diamond, Long, Pinnacle and Egg.

Is Butler out there on the tidal flats, scooping up someone else's spoils? The tide is out, the crossing is clear. From where Noble is standing it would take less than thirty minutes to walk over to Moose. And another fifteen or so to walk around to the sheer cliffs that shape the seaward side of the island. But estimating the basin tides is a dangerous game, especially at night. The incoming tide is swift, knee-deep, and can carry off a child. By sunrise there'll be over forty feet of water out there. Butler's a fisherman; he knows these waters like his horse's behind, knows the full and new moons bring several days of higher high tides and lower ebbs. But tonight he's taking a chance. By tomorrow the tide won't be extreme enough and walking across will be impossible.

Noble combs the island, looking for lights. A childhood habit. Moose is supposedly haunted by the ghost of John Ruff. An alcoholic whose violence was legendary, Ruff was the first and only settler to have lived and died on Moose, though the lights people sometimes claim to see are more likely people digging for the pirates' treasure rumoured to be buried there. When he was twelve years old Noble walked across on a dare with Lawson and a couple of lads from the village. They were going to look for the treasure. Only the three younger kids had quickly decided digging was too much like hard work, it was far more thrilling to hide and spring themselves on Noble over and again, pretending to be John Ruff's ghost. The boys banged the shovel against a tree, mimicking the sound of an axe on wood. Ruff was felling a tree when one of his much-put-upon sons crept up behind him and slugged him across the back of the head with an axe. Or so the boy's youngest brother had told the police. But as no one had been able to prove that Ruff hadn't simply been killed when the tree in question toppled onto him, the accused son had walked free.

Trying to control three ten-year-olds had proved beyond Noble's abilities. He was unable to round them up in time to make it back to the mainland before the tide turned, and so they'd spent a miserable night huddled under an oak tree. His mother strapped him when they got back for being irrespon-sible and jeopardizing his brother's life. The whole thing had been Lawson's idea, but their mother would never have be-lieved him, so Noble had said nothing and taken the hiding.

The land slopes sharply towards the seabed as he walks northwards along the cliff edge, his gaze trained across the tidal flats. Despite the cool breeze off the bay his shirt beneath his jacket sticks to his skin, making him cold. There is no sign of activity. Nothing appears to be amiss. Still, unease settles like salt water in Noble's stomach. When the grassy bank is no more than four or five feet high, he jumps down onto the rocky beach and makes his way back in the opposite direction. The sticky mud sucks at his feet in places, threatening to take his shoes; this is a trip best taken in daylight.

He is less than half a dozen yards from Old Wife when he hears the rattle of harness and cartwheels. And then Butler appears from around Two Hour Rock, followed by Bess pulling a cart. Noble takes a deep breath before stepping into his friend's path.

Butler starts. "What the hell are you doing here?"

"I was going to ask you the same thing."

"I asked first."

"You weren't at the weir." Noble buries his hands in his pockets. "It's teeming with fish. What d'you expect me to do? Go back to bed?"

"Is that where you were Saturday night while I was out there hauling the catch by myself? How about Sunday lunch?"

Noble lifts a hand to stroke Bess's neck. "I wasn't feeling well."

"But well enough now to be out here telling me what to do?"

"You don't harvest it you'll lose it."

"That's my business."

Not entirely. It's most of Noble's livelihood too. But in light of his recent absenteeism, now isn't the time to point this out. He walks beside Bess.

"This is the cargo from the *Esmeralda*, isn't it?" Noble picks up one of the burlocks stacked two high on the flat cart Bess is hitched to. Wet and muddy, it smells of the sea. There must be at least fifty or sixty burlocks. More. At six bottles to a bag Butler's haul must be worth a small fortune. Jesus Christ. He savours the cool pulse of adrenaline through his veins. How is Butler planning to unload this much liquor? "Nifty package," he says. "Someone was thinking."

"Keep your voice down, would you?" Butler glances behind him.

"I told you it was out here."

"You guessed it might be out here. There's a difference."

"Which means what? Planning on keeping it all for yourself, were you?"

"You want a couple of bottles, Matheson? Is that what you're after? Fine. Take that package you have in your hands and clear off."

Which is what he should do. Does he really want to get involved in moving contraband? Dodging liquor police and courting jail time? But the scent of easy money is beguiling. By the time any of the *Esmeralda* crew get out of prison, whatever they had left sitting out on the mud flats would have been swept out to sea long ago. "Is there much more than this? What d'you reckon it's worth? Hundreds? Thousands?" He starts to laugh, giddy at the prospect of sudden wealth.

"For God's sake, Matheson, be quiet. If you know what's good for you, you'll go home."

"You threatening me?" Noble takes a step backwards. Butler's a big man.

"Warning you." Through gritted teeth.

"I thought we were friends." Butler clucks for Bess to move forward. "You need my help."

"Like hell I do. Out of my way."

"Next high tides you fish the weir, so as not to arouse suspicion. Use my truck. And I'll come out here with Bess and the cart. We split the work and split the money. Fifty-fifty."

"Come on, girl." Bess strains to get the cart moving again, its wheels sunk in the soft mud. All the muscles in her neck pull taut, her flanks darken with sweat.

"Sixty-forty then. You'd never have known it was there if I hadn't said anything."

Butler pulls on Bess's reins. "Go home, Matheson."

"You know that lunatic from the *Esmeralda*'s out here somewhere. Spoon. The one I told you about. The one with the messy face."

A split second pause. "I'm not worried."

"You should be. I'm telling you, I watched them all handcuffed and driven away this afternoon. All but him." Noble still can't figure out how he'd managed it. They'd both been in the cargo hold, running through checks on the engine. And then Esmeralda had popped her head down the hold and asked Spoon to help carry the kid's body off. But when the police arrived minutes later, Spoon had already vanished. No one had raised the alarm. It was as if they hadn't noticed. Or weren't counting. "He could be anywhere — hiding behind Old Wife, waiting to creep up on you. He's smarter than he looks. And he's dangerous."

"Never a truer word was spoken." Noble whips around. Spoon. "About yours truly." His mouth pulls back in a parody of a grin. "But a little correction, sunshine. I showed 'im where it was hidden, not you. Got that?"

"Got it," Noble hears himself say, mouth stuffed with cotton. He feels surprisingly calm. Possibly numb. It's as if his mind has wandered off without him and is hovering over the mud flats, looking on. Absurdly, Elinor Glyn pops into his head. She's standing to one side of their little assembly, hat low across her forehead, her striking face in shadow, nodding encouragement. *The wealth of your imagination will naturally grow from the extent of your experience of life . . .*

"I told you to stay on the island," Butler says to Spoon. "What if the lightkeeper sees you out here?" Noble stares at his friend. Whose side is he on?

"You should be more worried about yourself. You and your friend 'ere, and whatever you was planning behind my back."

Characters in stories undergo a very intensive and concentrated existence.

"I was getting rid of him. He's on his way home now, aren't you, Matheson?"

Noble nods, his tongue swelled fast behind his teeth . . . *characters must constantly be "in the frying pan."* He's still holding the burlock in his arms, the damp of which has seeped through his shirt and covered him with gooseflesh. Should he put it back on Bess's cart? Leave it on the ground? Or just walk away, nice and slow. He shuffles a step backwards.

"Not so fast, village boy."

Something cold and hard pushes against his cheek and

Elinor Glyn vanishes. Noble smells cordite. Recognizes the long narrow barrel of a Luger. Now he's scared. It's a German officer's gun. Lawson had one just like it. He bragged about all the treasures he and friends filched on trench raids.

"How do I know you two weren't plotting against me?"

A disparaging laugh from Butler. "Matheson's a coward. A mumma's boy. One whiff of danger and he's off. He even wounded himself so he didn't have to face the trenches." It's a Butler story, but still there's a sour burning in the back of Noble's throat. What's he up to? Appealing to Spoon's sense of God and Country? The man's a bandit.

"Then you won't mind if I blow his legs off and leave him here for fish food." Spoon cocks the pistol. The click echoes across the basin. A cold chill spreads across his crotch and Noble thinks he might have pissed his pants.

"He could be useful."

"Useful how? You just said yourself you don't trust him." Spoon walks around behind Noble, trailing the barrel of the gun under the brim of Noble's hat till he reaches the other side of his face. He probably tortured cats when he was a kid — if he ever was a kid.

"Well, for a start I need help getting these wheels unstuck. Bess can't do it by herself." Noble looks wild-eyed at Spoon, who nods at him to get behind the cart. But Noble's legs have turned to wet sand. It's a moment or two before he can move them. Once in position he rummages for flat rocks to jam in front of the wheels and then leans his weight into the back of the cart. Spoon joins him.

"How about we send him to Halifax instead of me?" Butler is saying. "He used to live there. He worked the docks, knows all the old sea dogs, don't you?" Noble can't find breath to reply.

The sand makes sucking noises before releasing its hold. Bess moves forward. Spoon straightens and begins waving his gun about.

"Halifax is your part of the bargain, mate. Your contacts you said." Noble glances over to the lighthouse and prays the keeper will spot them and raise the alarm.

"Still my contacts. But Matheson leaving the village would attract less attention. Only his mumma to miss him. I'm away from the weir too long, people will come looking for me. Look what happened tonight. And I still have to think up something to tell the old lady."

Noble could kiss his friend's feet. If he survives the night he'll give him the truck. He'll work the weir for the rest of his life.

"Matheson has a truck. No waiting around for trains. No one to see him leave. The quicker he gets to Halifax the quicker we get you a ship."

"There has to be a catch."

"No catch."

"Then I'll think about it."

Butler coaxes Bess up and over the rocky ridge from the beach to dry land. The load on her cart wobbles precariously. "You better get back," he says to Spoon, "or you'll be trapped here by the tide." Noble clambers up behind Bess.

"Where d'you think you're going, village boy?"

Noble looks to Butler, hoping for rescue. But Butler busies himself fussing with Bess's harness. "I'm gonna use your truck, Matheson, okay?"

"But you don't know how to drive."

"You'd rather see Bess try to pull this lot up the mountain?"

"How's she going to get home if you're in the truck?"

"She'll follow behind. She's a good girl is Bess."

"Let 'im use it, village boy. We'll call it your stake, shall we?"

"It'd be safer if I drove," Noble mumbles.

"Tut, tut. You didn't think I was going to let you go home, did you?" Noble can hear the smile in Spoon's voice, warm as a lick of brandy. But he isn't fooled. "Not a chance, fella. You're going to spend the night on the island where I can keep an eye on you."

Cold creeps through Noble's body. What is Spoon planning? Tomorrow, or possibly the next day, Noble's bloated, bullet-riddled corpse will be found drifting out towards New Brunswick and the Atlantic by some fisherman, holds filled, on his way home. Reluctant to discard any of his well-earned catch, the man will stick a grappling hook through the back of Noble's jacket, snag his skin, tear into his muscles, and drag him back to civilization that way. Or worse — after being smashed by the churning waters at Cape Split his body might be trapped by the Minas Channel tides, condemned to being pulled back and forth in that watery no man's land known to locals there as Cedar Swamp, nibbled on by fish until nothing remains. Who will mourn him? Lillian? His mother. His son? Jem doesn't even know Noble exists, and now he never will. Elinor, what say you now? Experience is all fine and good as long as you live to tell the tale.

As he turns and heads back out towards Moose Island, Spoon's gun aimed somewhere at his back, Noble waits for his life to flash before his eyes. But all that crowds his mind are the things he hasn't done, the declarations he hasn't made, the promises he failed to keep.

XVII

Tuesday June 3. High tide, 6:19 a.m., 6:49 p.m.

In the garden Hetty's soft hands soon blister. A sliver from the trowel handle works its way into the heel of her right hand, forcing her to dig with her left. Though the days have been warm this past week, and when the wind dies the sun has even felt hot, the ground still has the breath of winter in it. The damp cold seeps through her clothing and numbs her knees, spreading chilly fingers up her legs. She rolls her shoulders, the muscles in her back and arms deliciously tight and achy, and takes in her morning's work. A third of the vegetable patch is weeded and hoed, the earth surprisingly dark and loamy, and there's a fresh layer of green on the compost pile. The air smells peaty and fecund. Who would have guessed that gardening could be so therapeutic? Hetty almost smiles to herself, almost believes she has exorcised yesterday's events, along with her muffled rage, when she hears the thud of hooves along the dirt path. Her jaw clenches. Lunchtime already? She should have been paying attention to the sun, now almost directly overhead, but had assumed in light of yesterday's absence that Peter would be staying on at work. No, she'd been hoping he would stay on at work.

Shadow approaches at a loping canter, her dark head tossing, nostrils flared, her long mane catching the wind. Peter, sitting easily astride her, is a superb horseman. *How Byronesque.* An invisible touch to the rein and the mare collects herself and effortlessly clears the wall that divides the path from the field that adjoins the garden and makes up the bulk of the Douglases' four-acre property. On sleepless early mornings Hetty has stood at the paddock gate watching as time and again Shadow canters around the field and then, tail high, gallops towards the wall. Hetty believes that Shadow's horse brain has told her she can jump in the opposite direction, out of the field as well as into it. But at the last minute she always veers away. Why? Why does she never claim the freedom that could so easily be hers? Does she not strain against the needs that bind her to Peter — a warm stable, dry hay and a bran mash? Hands to break the ice on her water trough in winter? Or is there some less tangible reason, some visceral connection?

Criss-crossing the field, man and animal move as one fluid rippling muscle. Hetty, despite her rancour, is compelled to watch. Peter circles back to the stable and dismounts. He loosens the girth on the mare's saddle and removes it, unbridles her, rinses the bit, fills her water bucket, rubs her down briskly with a twist of hay, then strokes her muzzle and her long elegant face. Patting her rump he turns and advances on the wooden gate that separates garden from field.

Hetty stands, shaking pins and needles from her legs. They haven't spoken since dinner last night, a strained affair in which all conversation filtered through Clara. When Peter left to drive Clara back to Truro, Hetty moved her necessities into the guest bedroom and locked the door.

"She needed a run," he says when he's close enough to make himself heard without shouting. "She was wound up after spending most of yesterday cooped up in the stable." Shadow stomps her feet and tosses her head as if to underscore the fact.

"No one likes being cooped up, Peter."

"Clara caught her train all right last night. We were at the station in plenty of time."

"She telephoned this morning." Opening with a litany of questions about the scene down at the wharf yesterday. About Esmeralda and the dead boy. About Hetty's marriage. About the end of her nursing career. Awkward and largely unanswerable questions.

"We had time for an ice cream at Murphy's. You should have been with us."

"I had no appetite for sweets, Peter. Or anything else for that matter." Is he just going to pretend nothing happened? Expect her to join him in the conjugal bed tonight?

"Are those my pants you're wearing?"

Hetty glances down at her attire and then at her husband. "They were yours. But I suppose they're mine now. They wouldn't fit you anymore." She'd rummaged through his closet as soon as he left for work this morning. Taken them in on his mother's sewing machine. Increasing the seams, darts front and back through the waistband, a quick hem job, and she'd fashioned herself a practical gardening garment.

"I see."

"I've never seen you wear them."

"From a distance you look like a young man, with your short hair and everything."

Esmeralda. Hetty has to look away. She thought he was going to say, you looked like Esmeralda. And perhaps, more than any practical considerations, this is what Hetty's pants are really about, some act of defiance or solidarity. She's been trying hard all morning to fend off thoughts of Esmeralda locked up in prison — Esmeralda in her men's clothes, which Hetty fears won't protect her the way they would a man.

"There's nothing prepared. For lunch I mean. I wasn't planning on stopping for a break." Her stomach rumbles loudly, revealing her lie. She rubs the dirt from her gardening gloves; some has dried and cracks off and flies away as dust.

"Are those new?"

"I bought them in Harper's this morning."

"You were in Harper's?"

"Along with some seeds and a trowel. I charged them to your account."

"There are seeds in the basement, Hetty. Did you look there first? Mother saved seeds and propagated everything she could herself. There are a couple of trowels, and there should be at least one or two pairs of gardening gloves. Your hands would be about the same size."

Hetty shoves her hands, gloves and all, in the pockets of her trousers. "I'm already wearing her boots, isn't that enough? You'd begrudge me my own seeds, my own things?"

Peter fixes his gaze on the patch of garden Hetty has cleared and weeded. He seems on the verge of responding, but then his face shifts and Hetty senses another retreat.

"Mrs. McMannis and Mrs. Dunstable were in the store," she says. Staying her with disapproving glances, whispering loud enough to be heard from the far corner. "They were gossiping about the *Esmeralda*."

"Hetty" — Peter straightens his stance though he still can't meet her eyes — "I have no doubt the entire village is gossiping about the *Esmeralda*. Yesterday's events were rather dramatic."

"You enjoyed that, didn't you?"

"Of course not."

"Mrs. Dunstable said the police searched the schooner stem to stern but found no liquor other than the captain's private supply."

"Which proves nothing."

"Exactly."

Peter's face folds like a book snapped shut. "Hetty, please, my dear, you're being far too emotional about this. I can't discuss it with you, and the sooner the furor dies down the better." He walks away towards the house, turns and calls over his shoulder. "Are you coming in for lunch?"

The dining room faces north and is chilly. Hetty wishes a fire was lit or that Peter would stop his silly pretensions and eat in the kitchen as she does when alone. Still, he's not the kind of man who expects a woman to wait on him hand and foot. By the time she has changed out of her gardening attire and scrubbed her hands, Peter has set the table and arranged a lunch of bread and butter, pickles and cold sliced ham left over from last night's dinner.

"It's looking good out there," he says when the silence has grown oppressive. "I would say you've taken to gardening well."

"I simply put my back into weeding, that's all. Whether I can garden or not remains to be seen." She picks up her cutlery and flinches. Two of her blisters have burst and the heel of her right hand throbs, the spell elusive. She'll burn a needle with a match later this afternoon and dig it out, or, because she's not adept with her left hand, perhaps she'll ask Laura to do it when she returns later to prepare dinner.

"Lettuce and radish make good early crops. I would make sure to plant lettuce between the tomato plants. That way, when it gets hot and the tomatoes grow tall and bushy, they'll throw some shade to stop your lettuce from bolting and tasting bitter."

"Maybe you should be doing the gardening."

"Oh, you'll get the hang of it soon enough. Mother used to say that gardening is a patient art."

Hetty feels suddenly and intensely impatient. "Peter, right now I don't give a damn what your mother used to say about gardening." Alarmed to find her hands shaking, she sets her knife and fork down. "Perhaps I am being far too emotional for your liking, call me hysterical if you like, but I can't stop thinking about yesterday."

Methodically, Peter trims the fat off the slice of ham on his plate. "What's done is done. It's water under the bridge now. You just need to put the whole messy business from your mind."

"I'm having a difficult time with the fact that you lied to me about the purpose of your trip yesterday."

"That I lied to you?" He dissects the meat into bite-sized pieces. Irritation shuffles along Hetty's spine.

"We drive to Truro together, sit next to each other, pass the time of day, chat about nothing in particular, a bird here, a field there. Mill business, you said. And all the while you were planning on turning my friends over to the police."

"Those people are not your friends."

Hetty picks up her fork, stabs at the food set before her. "Peter Douglas, village hero and tattletale. I don't know how you live with yourself."

"I acted like any decent, honest and responsible citizen. They were in flagrant violation of the law. Law that I have a duty to uphold."

"Who do you think you are? Self-appointed guardian of the village's moral health?"

"They're criminals. Worse. They —"

"You can't control the whole village, you know. Remember what the captain said? If people want to drink they'll find a way."

"I'm not interested in controlling the village, Hetty, and I don't care what that sorry excuse for a captain has to say." Peter's face has turned the colour of the bread on his plate. "Those people were armed. The police confiscated several guns and long knives yesterday."

So she was right about J.J.'s wound.

"When I think of the danger you were in." He shakes his head, and Hetty feels a short-lived pang of guilt. "Did you give a thought for anyone else when you went aboard that day?

Amputating a criminal's leg, indeed. Which I don't need to remind you didn't save him anyway. Not that he's any great loss to society. They should all be hanged."

"I can't believe you'd even think such a thing. You shared a meal with them not three days ago."

"Against my will, as well you know. They're rum pirates, Hetty. Perhaps, to a lonely and grieving young woman, they might have seemed charming. But they are completely lawless. They could have put a gun to your head and pulled the trigger for making such a mess of things."

Lonely? Still grieving? Of all the patronizing . . . dizzy with anger, Hetty grabs at the seat of her chair for support. How dare he even think . . . what the hell would he know about loss? About grief?

"I don't understand why you got involved in the first place, why you willingly put yourself in so much danger. Is your life with me so dull and unappealing?"

An icy smile. "Your words, Peter, not mine."

He holds her gaze for the first time since they left Truro yesterday. "And what would your choice of words be?"

"Meaningless might just about cover it."

Peter wipes his mouth with his napkin and pushes his chair back. "I'm going to work now. Perhaps you should take a nap this afternoon. You'll feel much better once you've had time to calm down."

Standing in a rush of indignation, chair legs scraping, Hetty flees the dining room, heels resounding on the wooden floors. She stomps up the stairs, her anger cresting as the back door slams. In their bedroom she marches over to her dresser. Drawers open and close. Undergarments. A nightdress. A small overnight bag, something she can carry easily. She won't be gone long. Just long enough to ensure Esmeralda is being looked after properly. Long enough to teach Peter Douglas a lesson.

XVIII

Noble stumbles from the cliff edge and twitches awake, pulse jumping. He's cold and stiff from lying on the ground. And yet his legs ache as if he's been running for hours, men with weeping skin sores and wooden legs gaining on him. He shivers, clothing damp with dew and the residue of last night's fear, then struggles, shoulder cramping, to sit up.

The sun has broken over the horizon, threading the sky with mauves and pinks, but the woods that comprise most of Moose Island are still heavy with shadow. Who's out there? The ghost of John Ruff? Or that double-crossing snake, Long John Silver? Noble rubs at his eyes to clear his head, unsure whether he is still trapped in a dream or the pages of *Treasure Island*.

But the blanket-draped figure sitting across the scrubby clearing not ten feet away, back against a rock, head on his chest, is no figment of his imagination. Gingerly Noble straightens his sore legs. Spoon doesn't stir. Noble rolls his shoulder to loosen it, wiggles his toes. Could he creep away? Garner the strength to flee? How long would it take Spoon to gather himself and give chase? There's only so much land before Noble would have to deal with the sea, the currents and eddies that govern the basin. Not that he could manage the swim to the mainland, even in dead calm water. There is only one sure way of ridding himself of his captor, but Noble can conjure neither the mettle nor the physical strength. Even if he could, Spoon is the one with the gun. Which at a guess is tucked in the waistband at the back of his pants or hiding elsewhere under that blanket. If Noble rushed him now it's unlikely he would reach the weapon first.

Nature calls. As he shifts his weight to rise, Spoon grunts and wakes. He has the ashen thin-skinned countenance of a man who sleeps little; purple circles darken the sockets of his pale eyes, making him look ghoulish.

"I need to —" Noble nods towards the bush.

Spoon hawks up noisily and shoots a ball of phlegm in his direction. "You piss when I say you can piss."

He stands, the spoons on his jacket clinking against each other, and holds his gun aloft for dramatic appraisal. As if Noble was ever likely to forget he had one. Facing the water Spoon relieves himself, the sound of which increases the pressure of Noble's own bladder. To piss or to run? Noble stays put, the ineluctable truth of the matter simply that Spoon is far more Long John Silver than Noble could ever be young Jim Hawkins, fit, doubt-free and reckless, willing to challenge Silver's pirate authority by diving into the fray.

Spoon now seeks his morning repast. Drinks water from a canteen, reaches into the inside pocket of his jacket and pulls out a piece of ship's biscuit and a knife. Hardtack. The soldiers hated it. Lawson always gave his to the dogs. Noble concentrates on not pissing himself and wonders how badly he stinks from last night's accident. Spoon breaks off a piece of hard tack and pops it in his mouth. He grins, and Noble wonders that the man can manage even soft food, his mouth a ruin of gaps and greying, crooked teeth.

"Hungry?"

"No." Emptying his bladder is the more pressing issue, followed by thirst. He eyes Spoon's canteen. Spoon makes a performance out of twisting the lid back on and hiding the canister under his blanket. He pulls off his boots, toes curled up and heels ground down, and sits them together at his side, like shabby dogs at heel. Noble contemplates grabbing them and flinging them over the cliff edge, but there's no getting around the issue of the gun, or the sea itself. Spoon is sockless, his toes gnarled and his feet misshapen. He digs at his toenails with his knife. Noble's skin pulses in disgust.

His grooming finished, Spoon nods and waves his gun to indicate that it is now Noble's turn to relieve himself.

"That feel better, village boy?"

"Much."

"What do you say, then? What's the magic word?"

"Thank you."

"Nice to see your mother raised you proper. Be worried about you, will she?"

"I think so." Noble leans back against a tree stump. He longs to close his eyes against Spoon's taunting, against his hunger and his thirst, but his eyelids must have shrunk. It'll be noon before the tide is out again and they can walk back to the mainland. He watches clouds travel across the sky and conjures Lillian's pale face. He wishes he had kissed her so that he could remember the feel of her lips on his, wonders if her skin is as cool and creamy to touch as his imagination tells him it is. Would she know he's missing? Would she care? Probably not if she'd seen him Sunday evening drinking on the wharf, his hand up Esmeralda's skirt. A knife-edge of desire cuts through him as he recalls the feel of the pirate-girl's skin, soft but firm beneath his fingers. A tease. A woman like that would drive a man crazy with wanting her. And not for the first time since that night, guilt snarls at the base of his brain. Was it possible to be unfaithful to someone in your imagination? Was it possible to be unfaithful to someone who was married, someone you had only fantasized about? He pulls his hands through the dirt and grass beside him, trying to rid them of the memory of Esmeralda's thigh.

Gulls cry, surf breaks against the base of the island, the upper-most branches of the trees creak in the wind.

"Hungry now?"

"A bit." He straightens and stares in Spoon's direction, sun-spots dancing before his eyes. He prays Spoon doesn't offer him the hardtack.

"You could catch us something to eat."

"With what?"

"A spear. You're good at that, aren't you, all you colony types?"

"We cook anything over here the smoke will attract attention."

"And then what? You think anyone's going to bother coming out here to rescue you, village boy?"

"What about you? Aren't you worried about getting caught?"

"That's the beauty of the plan, see" — those ruined teeth again — "no one even knows I'm missing."

"You've got a plan, then?" Noble mumbles. But there's nothing wrong with Spoon's hearing. Before he can bring his knees to his chest in reflex Spoon has crossed the space between them. Noble catches a glimpse of the gun in Spoon's hand as it swings towards him. His head whips sideways in a flash of blood-red stars and searing pain.

When he comes to Noble's face feels drum-tight and hot, his head bruised on the inside, as if someone has been scraping out his thoughts with a Russell knife.

"Up you get, time to get going." Noble puts his hands to his head, convinced it must have grown to twice its normal size. So heavy, so unbalanced does it feel as he pulls himself to his feet that he worries it might roll off his shoulders. Spoon nudges him between the shoulder blades with his pistol, pushing him towards the water. This is it, Noble thinks. Spoon is going to walk him to the edge of the cliff and push him over. Or make him jump. With his giant head Noble will sink like a stone. But when Noble finds himself at the top of the steep and treacherous path he climbed in the small hours of the morning, he realizes Spoon has other ideas. There, hitched to a tree and riding the water, is the missing dory from the *Esmeralda*. It must have been sitting on the mud flats when he walked onto the island last night, perhaps tucked behind a rock; not that he'd been in a frame of mind to spot it anyway. Too busy minding his feet on the small rocks that slipped and gouged the surface of the path, unearthing other generations of stones; too busy looking for ghosts.

"Now you're going to row back across there, nice and calmly."

"Alone?"

"That's right, alone. You do as you're told. Now get in. There's a little surprise waiting for you on the other side. And remember, I have this." He strokes the barrel of the gun down Noble's throbbing cheek. A fresh burst of pain, a wave of nausea to buckle his knees. "I'll be watching you all the way across. So no funny business, no heroics, village boy, or I'll blow your arm off and enjoy watching you bleed to death. Got that?"

Noble scrambles down to the water's edge and clambers into the dory. Spoon unhitches the mooring sheet, tosses it into the boat, and Noble leans back into the oars. Despite his aggravated shoulder, his stiff muscles and throbbing face, and the pull of the retreating tide, he quickly puts several yards between himself and the muzzle of Spoon's gun. Water splashes over the gunwale as in his haste he steers the boat sideways to the waves. The sun makes a brief appearance, seeks out his swollen cheek and burns it as if through a magnifying glass. Noble rows and weeps, and Spoon and Moose Island gradually grow smaller. He eases up, his strength deserting him. Without sights, what are the chances Spoon could hit a distant target bobbing on the waves? But the man has the luck of the devil. Noble rallies himself, keeping half an eye on Spoon until he's no bigger than one of the tarnished teaspoons on his jacket.

Two Hour Rock breaks the surface as Noble passes. He sets his sights on Old Wife, then the mainland shore. Trembling with fatigue, he struggles to negotiate the quick-moving currents, which push and tug at the stern of the dory, spinning his weary bones first one way, then the other. And suddenly there is Butler dancing on the sand, the silhouette of his battered hat and long limbs a dead give-away. Noble pulls up his oars and drifts, staring at the shore and the figure Butler cuts as he spins his arm in a mock wind-up before releasing his invisible ball in a slow underarm pitch. Is he performing for the wind and trees, or does he secretly covet a career in baseball? And then the thwuck of stone hitting wood, delayed and amplified in the sudden stillness of a dip in the wind, clips Noble at the base of his worst fears. He strains to make out Butler's baseball partner against the backdrop of trees and red cliffs. Giddy, high-pitched laughter reaches him when the wind pauses again, and Noble's legs turn to waterlogged wood. How can you know someone your whole life and yet know nothing of the treachery of which he is capable?

"You bastard," he says, close to tears, sawing at the waves with his oars. "You piece of shit bastard." Noble is clenched in anger, the violence of which unbalances and shakes him, anger he can only swallow, worthless and bitter. He wants wings to cross the water and the body of a cougar to lunge at Butler's long conniving legs, teeth and claws to rip into his reckless selfish head.

It would be futile. For Jem, swinging his driftwood bat, feet dancing in excitement, is obviously enjoying himself. His laughter, his "come on, come on, throw it" now fills the shrinking distance between them. Under what lunatic pretenses has Butler managed to lure the boy out here?

When the dory scrapes the bottom Noble pulls his oars and sits, dizzy from exertion, postponing for a few precious moments the inevitable confrontation. Never has he had such a clear uninterrupted view of the boy. How beautiful he is, the shape and size of him. A fist of emotion pushes at his throat. The boy's skin glows. At least his mother doesn't keep him mollycoddled and tucked up inside. There's an athleticism to his build, lean and narrow, muscles that taper to tidy wrists and ankles. Jem steps forward into his batter's stance and then twists back to swing at the rounded pebble Butler has lobbed at him. He's the picture of Lawson. What love Sarah Matheson would shower on this child.

"What the hell do you think you're doing, Butler?" The question thumps about inside Noble's head but he hasn't the strength to utter the words. Any words. He stumbles from the dory, arms like dishrags, every bone in his body groaning. Butler meets him as if he hasn't a care in the world, as if nothing untoward has happened to shift the balance of power between them. Jem skips pebbles inexpertly across the water. Butler bends to take the bow of the dory, heave it up onto higher ground.

"Get the other end, will you?"

"What the hell are you trying to prove?" Noble manages to spit between clenched teeth. He sways and grabs at the vessel for support.

"We were having a game of baseball, weren't we, kids?"

Kids? A chorus of whoops and yells issues from the woods and suddenly the beach is filled with children. Three to be exact. Butler's three. They charge towards the water. Noble is still struggling to digest the idea that Butler knows about Jem; he's less than sure himself, so recently has he even allowed the boy to enter his thoughts.

"What happened to your face?" This from Simon, Butler's eldest son. The names of the other two escape him right now.

"I slipped getting into the dory."

"You're gonna have a black eye tomorrow."

Noble glares at his former friend. "What are you all doing

out here? Shouldn't they be in school?" Not that Butler, having spent little time there himself, is likely to care much about school.

"They don't go to school," says Simon, indicating his siblings. "They're still babies."

"Are not."

"Are too."

Butler ruffles his kids' hair and smiles, instantly smoothing the brewing spat. "We thought we'd all spend the day learning some more useful skills." One last heave and the dory is nestled against a low-spreading bush.

"Like baseball?"

"It isn't merely a game of baseball, my friend. We're demonstrating the value of pulling together as a team, in work as well as play." From beneath the bush Butler pulls out some old sacks and sawn-off branches and begins camouflaging the boat. Noble can barely keep the passage of events straight in his head but remembers the dory's been missing a few days now; how long has Butler been in cahoots with Spoon? "And soon we're off to the weir, right, kids?" They jump and circle their father, twirling around his legs and swinging from his arms, getting in the way. Are all children this energetic? The two younger ones are so alike they could be twins, though Noble suddenly remembers the middle child is a girl. Peggy. Peggy and Tom. "It's the perfect opportunity to show them how, when one person doesn't complete the task he's been given, the other members of the team suffer." Butler straightens and turns, raising one bushy eyebrow. "You get what I'm saying?"

"So why d'you have to come all the way out here?" Noble's eyes are watering.

"To tell us the story of the whale."

Jem. Noble turns to see cherub lips parted in a smile. Flecks of hazel dance in his green eyes. Noble's eyes. How could anyone looking at him not be struck by how alike they are? How must Baker feel every morning when he stares at his son across the breakfast table? How can this not sit between Baker and Mary, a reminder of Mary's past, her reputation?

"What whale?"

"A little local history. Another tale of teamwork. Do you know young Jem? Jeremiah Albert Baker Junior? The doctor's son?"

Teased by the recitation of his full and burdensome name, Jem kicks sand playfully in Butler's direction. Noble would settle for kicking his friend in the teeth.

"I can't say we've been properly introduced." Noble has never felt so naked, so exposed, and under such young eyes too.

"Jem, this is my very good friend, Noble Matheson."

A flash of recognition crosses his features and the boy flushes, stares at his feet squirming in the sand.

"We met the other day," Noble says, and the boy's face recedes further. Mentally Noble slaps himself for not grasping immediately that Jem would rather start afresh, would rather forget that afternoon in the blacksmith's shop and his girlish fear. Jem is leaning against Butler, the trust between them more than a few hours old. As the village storyteller, Butler is adored by all the kids, but is there something more between these two? Or is the connection simply because of the children? Noble doesn't have the emotional energy to puzzle it out. His mind skips to his thirst, the canteen that should be in his truck.

"You came from the island." Simon again, taking the driftwood bat from Jem and pointing in the direction of Moose.

"Our friend here was digging for pirates' treasure." Butler rolls his eyes theatrically and Jem and the other children laugh. "He was helping his friend Spoon."

"He's no friend of mine."

"Maybe you could all meet Spoon too. Would you like that?"

Noble's head swims. "Bad idea," he blurts out, halfway to collapsing. Has Butler taken complete leave of his senses? "Spoon hates kids."

"Where's your spade?"

"Huh?" Noble stares down into Jem's earnest young face. "Spade?"

"For digging up pirates' treasure."

"Oh, that." Noble stares back at Moose Island, rubs his arms. "I, um, left it over there."

"Why? Are you going back?"

He hopes to God not.

Butler steps in. "Not for a while. Mr. Matheson has a little business to attend to in Halifax first, don't you?"

"I don't think I have much choice."

"Uncle John, are you going to tell us the story of the whale? You promised."

Noble flinches, stung. *Uncle* John?

"Yeah, you promised, Daddy." Arms over her head, fingers stretching to be picked up. That's his little Peggy, dancing on her toes. Butler scoops her into his arms. "It was a long, long time ago, right?"

"That's right, princess." He blows a raspberry into her tummy and she squeals in delight. "It was a long, long time ago, long before you were born, when my friend Noble and I were just a little younger than Jem and a little older than Simon." That bloody storyteller's voice of his, it could charm the carbuncle from Spoon's face.

"Do you know the story of the whale?" Jem again.

Noble tries a smile in return and is alarmed to feel the muscles in his cheeks twitching. He glances away. "I might have heard something."

"Uncle John, we're ready for the story now. Would you like to hear it, too?" Jem asks Noble.

"I sure would." How polite he is. Noble has to resist the urge to reach out and touch the boy, convince himself he's real. He wonders if he has any right to feel as fiercely proud of Jem as he does.

Butler pulls at the knees of his baggy pants and sits cross-legged, holding his daughter. He pats the grass and the boys sit in a semicircle around him. Noble folds into the ground like discarded clothing, wondering if he'll ever get up again.

"There was a whale stranded on the beach at Five Islands the year I turned five," Butler begins, his voice strumming a silver rhythm. The rapt expression on Jem's face cuts through Noble like a betrayal. Butler would court this much trust in a child and then hurt him? It is almost too much to believe. But the cost of not believing? Noble doesn't even want to think about it.

The sun disappears behind clouds again and Noble shivers as the breeze cuts through his bones, knuckles at his throbbing face. Still, Butler's voice soothes, it's almost impossible not to listen to him.

"It was a mighty big whale, as big as a house." Butler stretches his long arms to either side of him, tickles Jem's ribs with one set of fingertips, his youngest boy's with the other. "And it lay stretched out on the beach as the tide went out, thrashing and blowing and heaving." He mimes the whale's last movements. Jem and the others copy him. "And all the people from the village came out from their homes and stood on the beach, watching and waiting for the beast to die. It took an hour or so before it was safe to get anywhere near it, because the whole time the whale was sending long wet quivers across its massive grey body." Butler steeples his hands together, points them in the air above his head and shakes and shivers. The children, shrieking with laughter, follow suit. "And the quivers that rippled across the whale's body reminded all the villagers of the motion of the sea. And some of them felt sad for the whale. He belonged to the sea, and now he was dying on their shore." Butler wipes an imaginary tear from his eye, then leans and wipes a tear from each of the children's. He licks his fingers and wiggles his eyebrows. Noble would like to leave Butler on the beach to thrash about, gasping for air.

"But then four men from the village decided they'd be clever and see if they couldn't work together as a team to turn a penny or two, and so when the high tide came back they hitched eight teams of horses and moved the whale up into the meadow. When they'd dragged it over the sands and over the rocks and over the grass, they fenced it in with great big bolts of canvas and huge long wooden stakes, so that the whale was in its own tent. And although this tent didn't have a roof, the men thought that the whale wouldn't mind if it rained because after all it had come from the sea. And anyway it was dead.

"Two of the men spread word up and down the coastline and in and out of all the villages in West Colchester and as far away as Moose River on the one side and Carrs Brook on the other. And when the people came they charged them each a quarter to see it. By Sunday they had a line-up halfway around the meadow and made over fifty dollars that one day alone.

"This was summer of course, and pretty soon after that the whale began to smell. Hour by hour the smell grew worse. Someone wrote about it in the newspaper and a constable arrived and told the men to move it. But the men knew they couldn't move it, it was too late, the whale had already started to rot. If anyone tried to move it, its skin would slide off and its body would fall apart into stinking slimy pieces."

Jem screws up his face.

"And its eyeballs would pop out."

Jem wraps his hands around his throat, rolls his eyes and puts out his tongue. Simon follows suit. His brother and sister, not to be outdone, add screams and groans to their clowning.

"And the eyeballs would roll onto the grass and down the meadow and back to the sea, looking for their mumma." Butler glances at Noble. "And their papa." Noble blanches. Jem mimes swimming, his forehead furrowed in mock distress. Noble wishes he could stay here forever, listening to the boy's voice and watching him paint the air with his emotions.

"And so the next day the constable came back, and he rounded up the four men and brought them all before the village magistrate. They were fined ten dollars each, but they didn't care, they were laughing under their hats, because their pockets were already weighed down with all the money they'd collected. And the fine made no difference to the whale. It continued to rot, and the smell got so bad folks living nearby had to move out. The cattle wouldn't go near it either. That year six acres of marsh hay went uncut."

"So how did it go away?" Jem asks. The other kids, beginning to annoy each other again, have obviously heard the story before.

"Well, what the birds and wild hogs didn't eat eventually rotted away till there were only the bones left."

"Where are the bones?"

"Well, some would have been eaten by animals, others could have been taken by folks around as keepsakes, so they would always remember the story of the whale that died on their beach. Some people may have decorated their gardens with them."

"That's silly."

"Maybe so. But some clever people would have taken them and made tools out of them. Whale bones are pretty big and strong."

"What kind of tools?"

"All kinds of tools."

Jem seems to contemplate this a while. The whale has whetted his appetite. "Can you tell us another story?"

"Yeah, another one," Butler's daughter echoes.

"Another one!"

Butler isn't the only one who can tell a story. Noble sits up and clears his throat. "Does anyone know the story of *Treasure Island*?"

Five pairs of eyes turn to face him. "Is that island where you came from?"

"He came from Moose."

"This is a much more famous island."

"What's it called?"

"*Treasure Island*, stupid, weren't you listening?"

"Don't call your brother stupid."

"It's a story about a boy called Jim Hawkins who finds a map to buried treasure." That damn tic in his cheek. Noble runs his tongue across his teeth, clears his throat again.

"And he finds the treasure?"

"Yes, but first of all he has to win a battle against some pirates who are also after the treasure." He glances at Butler.

"Who wins?"

"Well, Jim, naturally."

"Naturally." Butler's face is expressionless.

"Who are the pirates?" the smallest boy asks.

"Well, one of the pirates is called Long John Silver, and he walks on a wooden peg because he lost one of his legs, well, the bottom half of his leg." Noble mimes a chopping motion just below the knee.

"Like the boy on the ship, right?" Jem says.

The boy from the schooner. A pinching cold creeps through Noble's veins. "Who told you about that?

"My dad."

Of course. Who else? "Well, I guess like him. Except Long John Silver didn't die." Nor do men like Spoon. It's the young and weak who get in the way.

"The boy on the ship died." Simon.

"Who died?" Butler's little girl looks as if she's about to cry. Her tiny brow is crumpled and her eyes have filled. "Daddy, who died?"

"No one you have to worry about, precious," Butler says, getting to his feet and throwing her into the air until she giggles again. "Time to go fishing, what d'you think, kids? Tide's out."

"But what about the story?" Simon again.

"Another time. Now come on. On your feet. Let's go."

Noble thinks Jem would like to hear the story too. But Butler is already pulling the kids to their feet and he hasn't the strength to argue.

The two men cut back through the trees to where Butler has parked Noble's truck, the children chasing each other, weaving in and out of their path and the edges of the woods, playing a game Noble has forgotten the rules to. The children pile into the back of the truck and Noble climbs wearily into the driver's seat.

He drives slowly, trying not to jostle the children too much over the road's many potholes. He's quiet until they breech the crest of the mountain and begin the descent into Kenomee.

"Why are you caught up in all this?"

Butler shrugs. "A man has to make a living."

"Your family has the weir. Don't you make enough living from that?"

"Real living. Town living. You were over there. London, Paris. Even Halifax."

"But to get yourself involved with these people?"

"Don't be so preachy, Matheson. It doesn't suit you. Anyway, what do you mean by these people, there's only one of them. And I'm bigger than he is."

"A man with a gun. Who won't hesitate to use it."

"Problem with men like Spoon is they like the taste of their own poison too much."

"What about Jem?" Mouth dry, the taste of blood on his lips.

"What about him?"

"You'd better not harm a hair on his head."

"Wouldn't dream of it. He's a nice kid."

"And what about your accomplice? Think you can trust him, do you?"

"I can handle Spoon."

"You hope. You're not planning on taking his booze, are you? It belongs to someone, someone powerful, probably. You want them coming after your head?"

"It belongs to no one, that booze was stolen. They're rum pirates. You know, the girl was their best asset. She'd board the rum-runner first in those leg-hugging pants of hers and all the idiot crew would be winking and smacking their lips. Then she'd shake someone's hand and in the wink of an eye have his arm twisted behind his back in a hammerlock and bar, the tip of her knife blade pushing against his jugular."

Esmeralda and a knife. Noble tries to sweep the image from his mind.

"Who was it stolen from?"

"You worry too much, Matheson. The booze is a part load they got boarding another black off the coast of Boston. Stolen. Like I said. And it's been stolen again." He grins. "By yours truly."

As they enter the village, Noble is chewing the skin around his fingernails, a habit he thought he'd left behind in England.

"Well, well, well, if it isn't Lonely Lillian."

"Where?" Noble slams on the brakes then cringes at the thumps and shouts from the back of the truck. Her house is within sight but not Lillian. He hasn't seen her since the Friday night lending library. He hasn't written the scene he promised. And unable to think of a good enough excuse, he hasn't even called round to see her. Will she read his dalliance with Esmeralda on his skin? Does it matter anyway? There is no pledge between them. Only a war hero with ravaged lungs.

"There." Butler points. Lillian steps into road, waving her arms. Except it isn't Lillian. It's the nurse, Pete Douglas's wife. What the devil — ? The truck stalls and Noble takes his foot from the clutch, unlatches the window.

"I'm sorry. I didn't know you had passengers." She looks behind her, as if worried she might have been followed. "I need a favour from you."

"Mr. Matheson is on his way to Halifax. He doesn't have time for favours." Butler opens his door and climbs out. "Everyone okay back there?" He walks to the tailgate, begins helping them down. "We can walk from here."

Noble wants to call out to stop them but the Douglas woman is tugging on his arm. "If you're already driving to Halifax, well, I need to get to Truro. It's really important. I wondered if you could give me a ride. I'd pay you of course."

Butler sets Jem down, then opens the passenger door and sticks his head back inside the cab. "He'd love the company, wouldn't you, Matheson?"

Jem, running after the other kids, calls back over his shoulder, "Goodbye, Mr. Matheson."

Noble leans out of his window, looks Hetty Douglas straight in the eye. He blushes furiously and stammers an embarrassed apology. "Goodbye, Jem," he shouts at the boy's retreating back. "Hope to see you again soon."

"Well now, that's just going to entirely depend, isn't it?"

"You wouldn't dare." Noble has one eye on Hetty Douglas as she walks around the front of the truck to the passenger side.

"All you have to do is keep your end of the bargain."

"You don't have it in you."

"Don't push me, Matheson." Butler turns to speak to the Douglas woman. "One moment, ma'am, I just need to brief my friend here on a couple of errands he's running for me." He leans back inside the cab. "First thing you do when you get to Halifax is you look up a man by the name of Will Brooks. Just ask around down by the docks, real discreet, of course."

"And then what?" Noble has never felt so ancient, so helpless, so tired.

"And then tell him Esmeralda's bagged a Moose."

XIX

"What happened to your face?" Noble lifts a hand to his throbbing cheekbone. Sarah Matheson's eyes darken.

"It was an accident. Butler clipped me with the dip net." A frown pleats his mother's forehead. "I wasn't paying attention."

"Story of your life."

He starts up the stairs to his room, Sarah on his heels. "You seem to be making a habit of staying out all night."

"Eliza insisted. I went back with Butler to help him split and salt the catch, pack it in the puncheons, and she started making a bed up for me in the front room. Wouldn't hear of me going home." He could kick himself for including Butler's wife in his lies.

"So where've you been till now?"

"About."

"You expect me to believe Eliza Butler was up in the middle of the night, fussing around after you? And her with young ones to mind?"

A simpler lie would have sufficed. They'd be onto other topics by now.

"That bruise had better be faded by Saturday. I don't want you at that memorial service looking like you've been brawling.

Not when your poor brother's dead and without even a grave. The whole village is going to be there, honouring his memory, you know?"

And that of eighteen other poor souls, he'd like to add, but doesn't. He reaches for the holdall on top of his wardrobe and tosses it on the bed, trying to keep his gall in check. "It's okay Mumma, it doesn't hurt much." He opens drawers, pulls out a clean shirt and change of socks.

"What are you up to now?"

Underwear. He slams the drawer shut, picks up *Treasure Island*, then puts it down. What if he loses it? Or it gets damaged somehow? "I have an errand to run."

"An errand? What kind of errand is it you need to be packing a bag for?"

"I'll be gone overnight." He would slip the box of Elinor Glyn books into his bag, but his mother is breathing down his neck and he has neither the patience for a litany of tiresome questions nor the energy to invent responses. Not that he'll have time for leisurely reading. Or eating or sleeping for that matter. *Just ask around down by the docks, real discreet, of course.* What a gargantuan task Butler has set him. Impossible. Unfair. His temples pound. He should have grabbed Jem himself and driven off somewhere far away. But then what would the boy have thought of him? And there was Lillian to consider, and his mother. He rubs the whiskers on his chin. Halfway to a beard and furiously itchy. If he had the time he'd shave.

"What is that Douglas woman doing sitting in your truck?"

He whips around. His mother is at the window, the curtain pulled aside, peering down. Worried about the line of vision from the front windows, Noble had driven the truck as far up the driveway as possible. Too far. From this height and angle Hetty Douglas, sitting in the passenger seat, can be seen plain as day.

"It isn't what you're thinking. I'm giving her a ride into Truro, that's all. It's much more innocent than it looks."

"Innocent! There is nothing innocent about that woman, as sure as my name's Sarah Matheson." Her face has taken on that narrow, pinched look. "The biggest mistake Pete Douglas ever made was bringing the likes of her to this village. Who does she think she is, asking you to take her here, there and everywhere? Wants to go to Truro, does she? What does her husband have to say about that, I wonder?" She lets out a long, histrionic sigh. "When it comes to women, Noble Matheson, you haven't the sense you were born with. They'll be nothing but trouble come of you getting involved with the likes of her." Sarah raps on the window.

"Mumma. Don't."

"Don't what? Don't invite her in? I wouldn't waste my breath. Sitting out there like she's too good for us. Well, I don't want her round here with her city ways and her fancy clothes." She moves to his bedroom door but Noble blocks her way.

"I said don't."

Sarah's eyes slide from his. She juts out her chin and folds her arms. "What kind of errand takes you overnight?"

"I'm going to Halifax."

"Halifax?" Her face slackens.

"I'm coming back, Mumma. Don't worry." He reaches out to touch her, but she shrugs away, leaving her anxiety to drift between them. Muttering something about soup, she pushes past him to the stairs.

"Well, just you see you do," she says, halfway down.

Hetty, one eye on the Mathesons' front door, wills the truck quickly down the driveway. "I take it your mother doesn't approve of your travelling companion," she says, once they've turned onto the road, and are headed east.

"I'm sorry?"

"Your bedroom window was open. I could hear shouting."

Noble's headache is pulsing in time with his heartbeat. "What makes you think it was about you?" He grinds the gears. "She sometimes says things she doesn't mean."

"Don't we all?" Hetty mutters. Had she meant what she'd said to Peter? Meaningless. She'd heard Sarah Matheson's words plain as day. And maybe the woman is right. She glances down at herself, at her fancy clothes. She's turned into a clotheshorse, Peter Douglas's ornament. No wonder the women in the village have no respect for her.

"She's never gotten past losing my brother."

Hetty stares out at the passing view, the exposed red sands of Cobequid Bay. What meaning did her life here have?

"He was lost at Vimy." Noble repeats himself. Maybe she's hard of hearing. "That's why this weekend is so important to her," he says, a little louder. "The memorial celebration. His name is engraved on the plaque at the base of statue." The one your husband paid for, remember? "He doesn't have a gravesite." He's rambling. "They were all buried over there."

Hetty glances over at him. "It's heartbreaking to lose a child," she says. The air divides. "Children should bury their parents, not the other way around. J.J. has a mother somewhere whose heart must be broken."

"J.J.?"

"The boy on the schooner."

They lapse into silence. How heartbreaking is it to lose a child you've never had the chance to get to know, Noble wonders, a child you've only just discovered is yours. Hetty, picking at the sliver in her hand, is numbly aware that her due date has just passed. Thursday, May 29. The day before J.J.'s amputation. Another sudden dawning: their wedding anniversary. Peter hadn't mentioned that Friday had been their wedding anniversary. To commemorate it, Hetty had come home late, her clothes stained with blood. Happy anniversary, darling. She leans back in her seat and closes her eyes.

The truck's vibrations exacerbate the pain in Noble's cheek, which now radiates across his face, pulsing low across his brow and into his eyes. What if he can't find this damned Will Brooks? What then? How can Butler even think of leaving Jem at the mercy of an animal like Spoon? He has children of his own. Noble tries to sort his thoughts, but they keep straying away like driftwood on the tide.

Bass River. Portapique. For Hetty the motion of the vehicle and the silence is comfortingly stupefying. She gazes over the fissures and ruts in the road, clusters of dandelions along the shoulder, early lupines, the odd wind-twisted tree, her mind as empty as the rippled red sea bed. But as they reach a signpost for Great Village it occurs to her that Noble Matheson may neither share nor welcome her mood. After all, it wasn't his idea to have her along. She straightens in her seat and takes the measure of her travelling companion.

"How did you get that bruise? It looks sore."

He reaches a hand to his face. "I walked into a wall."

"That's what women used to tell me when their men had been beating them."

"No one beat me."

"You should get a cold compress on it. You need to take down the swelling."

"It's just fine. Thank you."

"I was only trying to help." She crosses her arms against the sudden chill in the cab. He's probably been fighting with that weir fisherman friend of his, the local pied piper. The tension between them had been palpable.

Clouds part and the afternoon sun, magnified through the window, heats Noble's head, thickening his blood, which he sees as a purple-orange bruise pumping sluggishly across the insides of his eyelids. His hands jerk on the steering wheel.

"Don't be falling asleep."

Her voice comes to him as if across the water. He blinks rapidly; the road rushes past.

"I thought you nodded off."

Christ, he's going to have to keep his wits about him. His face feels puffy, his skin tight. The swelling on his cheek has grown its own heartbeat. He rubs his eyes, flinching at the pain. "You might have to talk to me."

"I'm not very good at small talk," she says and wishes Clara were here. Clara, who, between Truro and Kenomee yesterday, had drawn more local lore out of Peter than Hetty had managed in a year.

Me neither, thinks Noble, but he's the one who's half-asleep. He should pull over and let the window down. Instead he asks, "What takes you to Truro?" The question feels inappropriate, and, his mother's dire predictions aside, he can't shake the feeling that driving Pete Douglas's wife about is courting trouble. If it wasn't for Butler he'd have said no. At least he thinks he would.

"Were you there yesterday? When they were all arrested?" Hetty is picking at her hand again. The skin around the sliver is becoming inflamed.

"I was down the hold. On the schooner." He senses her waiting for him to make a connection. He turns to look at her. "So you're going to see — ?"

"Esmeralda, yes."

And do what? he wants to ask but can't find his tongue. Esmeralda. Just the sound of her name is enough to set Noble's heart knocking. The backs of his hands tingle, his lips, as if the charge from her kisses still lingers there. Then he remembers Butler's piracy tale.

"Do you think it foolish of me?"

"Why should you care what I think?"

Why indeed?

Silence falls between them again. Noble considers other conversation openers, but the trouble with "How's your husband keeping?" is he doesn't really care. "What do you do with yourself all day?" sounds hostile. And "How do you find living in the village?" is a minefield he'd rather not chance crossing. In truth, a mental list of topics they have in common begins and ends with the *Esmeralda*.

"I heard what Baker said to you. Yesterday. When I was down the hold."

"Everyone on the wharf heard him, which no doubt means the entire village knows by now."

"I thought he was out of order. He'd no right to judge what you did or didn't do. He wasn't there."

Hetty's shoulders relax for the first time since she climbed inside the truck. Of course, a man like Baker would tread on all kinds of toes. A smile softens the corners of her mouth. "Ah, but doctors don't take kindly to nurses stepping in to do their work."

"I can't think of many who could have done what you did and not lose their nerve. You were a real professional."

"I lost my patient."

"I saw what you saw. The kid wouldn't have made it anyway. At least you tried."

"Thank you."

"And then you stood up to Baker."

"I wouldn't say I stood up to him, exactly."

"You answered him back. That's more than most around here can say."

"You don't like him either?"

"Can't stand the man."

They share a smile. "What takes you to Halifax?"

Noble's stares at the road ahead. It's an innocent enough question. But the answer?

"Just a bit of business," he says, voice gruffer than intended.

Hetty feels stung. They're all the same. Expect her to tell about herself, but won't return the same courtesy. She stares out the passenger-side window, watches a clutch of clamdiggers huddled out on the mud flats. Noble feels the connection slipping away.

"I used to live there," he offers.

"Me too," she says, face still turned to the window. Born, raised and banished from.

"It was a few years ago, though. I left about a year after the Explosion. They were just starting to rebuild." The Explosion. Hetty turns to stare at him. "The city must've changed a fair bit since. I might not recognize it."

"You were there when it happened?"

"Right in the middle of it." But not where he should have been. His mind shifts, stripping away the years. If it had been any regular kind of morning, Noble wouldn't be here telling the tale.

"You're lucky to be alive."

"Yes." He was lucky. He should have been down on Pier 8 readying the *Curaca* for a shipment of horses expected that morning. More animals bound for the European slaughterhouse. *When I close my eyes I can hear the horses screaming.*

"Steady." Her hand on the steering wheel. When did that happen?

"Sorry."

"You're tired."

"I'm tired. And . . ."

"It never leaves you, does it?"

His past lies in wait at the back of his mind, he sometimes thinks, unbalancing him as it surges forward unexpectedly — triggered by a familiar phrase, a movement, the turn of a head, a curl of hair on the nape of a young boy's neck.

"Did you talk about it? After it was over, I mean?"

"I tried to." How to explain the guilt that still binds him? Noble takes a slow deep breath. The look on his mother's face when he'd finally come home, two and a half years after he and Lawson had left to do their duty. He tried to tell her about that day, about the Explosion and its aftermath, about the cleanup.

And he'd tried to explain why he'd stayed away so long. In his mind the two events were connected, but not in his mother's. Sarah Matheson had turned and left the room.

"Me too." But by the time a degree of normalcy had been restored Hetty found no one was interested in talking about it anymore. Maybe it was exhaustion. Or pain. Some families had lost too much. She lifts a finger to her window, draws a circle. "It's odd how people act in a crisis. Everyone corrals together and gets the job done — and it's truly a miracle to be part of that — but then afterwards there's a kind of embarrassed silence about it all. As if for some reason we're ashamed to remember our naked selves. What shone truest in us."

Noble wonders what, if anything, has shone true about his behaviour since his return to the village. Six years he's spent dodging meaning and responsibility, and now he's paying the price.

"But I wanted to talk." Hetty's voice grows husky with emotion. "I wanted to tell anyone who'd listen how necessary and worthwhile it had made me feel. I remember explaining to my parents afterwards why I wanted to help people, why I had enrolled in nursing. They just sat there, they couldn't look at me, mother twisting her pearls, father rubbing his hands over and over, until I just wanted to scream at them both."

"My mother . . ." He trails off, his thoughts are perhaps unfair. "I used to think that some day I'd be able to write it all down, describe everything that happened that day. As a way of not forgetting."

"That's hardly likely, is it?"

"No." Noble pushes his fingers through his hair. The question was more whether you could bury it deep enough it didn't bother you any more.

"Do you still think you'll write it down some day?"

He shakes his head.

"Why not?"

Fingers stretched across the steering wheel. "How do you describe the end of the world?"

"Start with what you saw, I suppose."

But what he saw cuts too close to the bone. Bodies draped across telegraph wires. Hanging out of windows. How much easier to deal with cold statistics: when the *Mont Blanc* blew up at five minutes after nine on the morning of December 6, 1917, she was carrying twenty-three hundred tons of wet and dry picric acid, two hundred tons of TNT, ten tons of gun cotton, and thirty-five tons of extremely volatile high-octane benzol. And no one seemed to know about it. He'd memorized the numbers from the newspaper shortly afterwards but since then has never been able to find a way of bringing them into a conversation, let alone write about them.

Traffic has increased now that they are on the outskirts of Truro, and Noble turns his attention to the road, the pedestrians, the horse-drawn carts, the other motor vehicles, and even an ox pulling a hay-laden wagon.

"You'll be wanting the police station, then?"

"Would you like to come with me?"

Would he? For what? One last consoling hug. One brief kiss on the cheek — or the lips. Noble is having trouble shaking the image of Esmeralda holding a knife to someone's throat.

"No. You go." He'd rather remember Esmeralda as he last saw her, men's work boots on her feet, the fringe on her sparkly party dress swishing above her knees. Better to recall her taking his hands to her lips than to see her manacled and humiliated, desperately clutching prison bars.

"Will you be able to find a way home?"

"Yes. Don't worry about me." Noble isn't worried, but something tells him Pete Douglas should be.

XX

Hetty is pacing in front of the truck when Noble returns from the pharmacist, salve on his face and a small bottle of aspirin in his pocket.

"They've transferred them all to Halifax."

He opens the driver's door, but something in her voice prickles the back of his neck.

"It's worse than I thought. The charges have been upped to manslaughter and conspiracy to commit piracy. They're going to be tried in the Supreme Court of Nova Scotia."

Manslaughter. Noble tries to read Hetty's face. What of her role? Could she be held accountable too? Could he? "And I suppose you want me to take you to Halifax."

"Would you mind? I'd pay you extra of course."

"What about your husband?

"Mr. Douglas is my worry."

"I still think he'd want to know where you are."

"If you don't drive me I'll take the three-thirty train. How do you think Mr. Douglas is going to feel when he learns you abandoned me in Truro?"

Noble shrugs. "You'd better get in."

With Hetty quiet and brooding, Noble's mind strays to the difficulty and dangers of the task ahead of him, then, overwhelmed, draws back. He opens his mouth several times to reassure Hetty that Esmeralda will be fine. She's savvy and worldly wise. She's a cat with nine lives. But a person can hang for the crimes she's accused of, unless, cat-like, she can scale the walls of her prison. Or scratch and claw her way out. And of course there's the inherent danger of a conversation involving Esmeralda becoming a conversation about the village. About Spoon. About Jem. About Butler and his threat. The aspirin may be numbing the ache in Noble's face but the glut of unspoken words in the cab is driving a wedge of pain between his eyes.

An hour or so out of Truro they pass a sign for Stewiacke, a town, so he learned on that first train ride to Halifax, situated halfway between the equator and the North Pole. Noble has grown so accustomed to the hum of the wheels on the road, the vibrations of the truck's dash and gear shift that it takes him a moment to realize that Hetty has spoken.

"I'm sorry?"

"How close to the Explosion were you?"

"Little more than half a mile." He glances over at her. The Explosion has become the middle ground between them.

"What did you see?"

What indeed? He clears his throat against the telling. It's been a long time. "There was nothing to see or hear. Not at first anyway. Just a huge blinding flash of light." He pauses, remembering. "And then a massive windstorm. So much howling air rushing past your ears. And then everything you could think of — boats and people and the sides of buildings and trees — ripped from where they'd been and swept up the hill. The air turned black and oily, and rocks began falling from the sky — rocks that had been scooped up from the bed of the harbour. And burning bits of metal from the ship. And glass of course. There was glass everywhere."

Glass and eyes. Glass and skin. In the hours and days that followed the Explosion, Hetty had tended to dozens of burn victims, people with missing limbs, fingers or toes, with concussions and bruising. But it was the glass, wanton and treacherous, that inflicted the most widespread damage. It seemed every patient that came through Camp Hill Hospital had either a gash or a piece of glass buried somewhere in his or her flesh. And she saw a lot more besides who wouldn't hear of treatment. They were too busy helping others to stop; it was just a bit of glass, nothing to fuss about. When their cuts eventually healed they were left with hideous blue scars, the glass trapped inside. "Do you know, even after all these years slivers of glass still work their way out through people's skin?" She picks at the sliver in her hand. "Who needs to remember when your body does it for you?"

And what about the things that are trapped inside your head, Noble wants to ask, but doesn't.

"I still startle at the sound of breaking glass. It's almost a reflex. For weeks afterwards children would panic when the one o'clock cannon went off."

"For me it's horses." Noble and his brother have this in common, the screams of terrified horses. "I hear a horse in pain or panicking, it brings it all back. It's probably why I prefer automobiles."

He can feel her silent appraisal. "I was saved by a young man with a horse and dray," she says. "I've often wondered what happened to him."

"You were hurt?"

"No. Not that kind of saved. My friend was hurt, though. Which is why I was out on the streets in the first place. Taking her home. Our school was luckier than most. We were a long way from the Explosion, so there were only a few minor injuries when the windows shattered. But I can still remember how the air tasted that morning — of burning oil and soot — and how every house and every building we passed was missing its windows. And I remember how empty the streets were. That was the part that was so eerie and frightening. A city full of people. Where was everyone? I could hear people crying and calling out to each other, and now and again the sound of someone running. I'd never realized before what a lonely sound that is, someone running down an empty street."

Noble can hear the sound in his own head. Two girls. Running down the street. Can see the pair of white feathers they left behind.

"My friend lived up on Dresden Row. Her mother wanted me to come inside and wait with them, but I said I had to get home. And I had every intention of going home. I knew my parents would be worried about me. But I was at the top of Citadel Hill by that time, and there it was: all the horror of what had happened to the north end of the city laid out before me. All those flattened buildings. Everything black, except for the fire. So many fires, so many columns of smoke. And people moving about, slowly, dazed or hurt, still picking themselves up. But the city was on the verge of panic. I know I was. The screaming and crying was growing louder, the shouting, the howling. People were scrabbling through the heaps of ruins. I could feel a scream building in my own throat.

"And then the man with the horse and dray appeared, tearing down Bell Road. I stepped out of the way but he slowed down and called me over. He was frantic. I must have blanked out because it took me a while to realize he was yelling at me. And then I could hardly make out what he was saying. His skin was black and shiny and so I thought he must have come from Africville. But when I climbed on the back of his cart and I saw the woman laid out there, and her children, I understood it was oil and soot that had stained everyone's skin. The woman was bleeding to death, and her children were holding onto her. They were so small and frightened. Someone, perhaps the children, had placed rags about the woman's head, but they were soaked through already. She was in a bad way."

Noble's head has filled up with noise. What are the odds? She would have been a girl at the time, sixteen, maybe seventeen years old. A schoolgirl. He can still see the purple and white of her school uniform. Why would they recognize each other after all these years?

"The driver was trying to get to the Camp Hill Hospital. I couldn't understand how he'd missed it, but he was in such a dreadful panic. He started to weep. I directed him to turn around, we were only a couple of minutes away. The woman was so still and quiet. She was like a rag doll in his arms when he picked her up and carried her in. I thought she must have been his wife, but it turned out he didn't even know her name. When we got inside there were patients lying on mattresses and makeshift stretchers in the corridors. Bleeding and burned. Even the entranceway was filling up with victims. The stench of scorched flesh and rancid blood nearly took my breath away. And he laid her down where a doctor told him to, and then he said he had to leave. His work wasn't done. There were so many people out there who needed his help. And that's when I realized there were so many in the hospital who needed mine. So I stayed on and tended to the children. And then all the other children who came afterwards. Children with terrible wounds. They were all so good and brave. Even the scared ones were brave." She stares out the side window and dabs at her eyes.

"When the Americans came they turned my school into a hospital, but I stayed on, helping out at Camp Hill. I never went back. It sounds silly I suppose, but in a way it's as if the driver that morning called me to nursing. When I said he saved me that's what I meant. It scares me sometimes to think who I might have become if I'd just stood on the side of the road and screamed, if he hadn't reached out to me. Not someone I'm proud of, I'm sure." Someone like her mother, acting out of social obligation and the need to be seen doing good. She wipes her eyes again, brushes down her dress. "Anyway, I've always wanted to thank him. And to tell him that the mother survived."

There's an actual physical pain in Noble's throat, as if a hand has reached in and grabbed at his windpipe. He takes a long deep breath.

"Are you okay?"

"Fine. I'll be fine. You just gave me a bit of a shock, that's all." He rolls his shoulders and stretches his neck. His foot is numb on the gas pedal but his heart, heavy for years, feels lighter. Hetty Douglas has just given him a gift, and Noble feels he owes her the rest of his story in return.

"I was supposed to be helping load a shipment of horses onto the *Curaca*, down at Pier 8."

"The piers were all but destroyed."

He nods. "The *Curaca* was blown clear across the Narrows onto the Dartmouth shore. Over forty crew lost their lives. And all the horses." He touches a hand to his throbbing face. "The gaffer was cussing that morning because one of the trucks had broken down again. He asked me to hitch two old cobs to the dray and deliver some bales of cotton that were needed urgently up at the Dominion Textile Company."

"On Robie Street."

"You know the area?"

"Yes, of course. The Hydrostone District was my nursing beat. Patients used to tell me about all the factories in the area that had been destroyed. The friends they'd lost. But I interrupted you. You were talking about the horses."

"Ned and Princess. They were pretty old, a couple of characters, though. The gaffer had argued to keep them on after the owners had gone ahead and purchased trucks for deliveries. He was one of those men who didn't fully trust modern technology. The stables were there and the horses only required a bale or two of hay and water and a step out now and then. As

223

he was forever saying, what was that compared to not having any way to transport things every time those darn trucks broke down?

"Seth McCann looked after them normally. He was a retired longshoreman who wasn't past mucking out the stables and soaping up and polishing the tack once in a while. But Seth was off sick, and someone told the gaffer that I had a way with animals, that I was someone they'd come to rely on for loading shipments of horses. Of course they'd been cooped up for a couple of days by this point so they led me a bit of a dance while I got them harnessed up and ready. They were real eager for their heads once we got outside. Took all my concentration to rein them in.

"My guess is we were only about two blocks up from the waterfront when the *Imo* ploughed into the side of the *Mont Blanc*. Not that I saw it happen, with my back to the water. But by the time we were crossing Albert Street it was obvious something was up in the harbour. People were coming out from their businesses and houses and pointing towards the water, some were running to get a better view. A block or so further up a small crowd was gathering on Needham Hill. I took a quick look back and was shocked to see smoke, black billowing clouds of it, coming from one of the ships. So much smoke from such a small ship. That should have been everyone's first clue. I honestly never knew smoke could be so powerful, so furious. And then balls of blue and orange would shoot into the sky like fireworks. There's something about fire that makes it difficult to look away.

"I saw more people gathered on Campbell Road and some who had even stepped out onto the roof of the Acadia Sugar Refinery down at the waterfront. I doubt any of the poor buggers lived to tell the tale." He turns to glance at her. "I beg your pardon, I didn't mean to swear."

"Please. I've heard a lot worse."

"You know, when the Explosion happened all I could think

about was my brother." He'd cringed in the darkness behind the driver's seat, head to his knees as the air singed and hissed around him. Our Father who art in Heaven, he'd begun, teeth chattering, skin on fire. Our Father who art in Heaven, he'd mumbled, unable to reach the next line. "I figured this was probably how he died at Vimy, with all the smoke and mortar and all that gut-slitting shrapnel screaming around." What might Lawson's last thoughts have been? His last words? Noble couldn't begin to guess to whom they would have been addressed. "And then just as the smoke began to clear something big struck the dray and the horses bolted. It took me almost a block to bring them back under control."

If you could have called anything that was left a block anymore. Noble would have rubbed his eyes if his hands hadn't been so busy with the horses. All those buildings just gone. Or shifted, twisted into strange shapes. Trees robbed of their branches. Glass everywhere. And all the fires that started when people's stoves overturned and gas lines were ripped out. Some streets had completely disappeared under piles of rubble and debris. But for the hill and the harbour Noble would not have known which way he was facing. Nothing was where it should have been. The blast had even wrenched the clothes from people's backs.

"Princess was in a real state. Her coat was steaming and she was quivering and rolling her head. I jumped down from the cart and ran round to grab her, look her in the eye and try to calm her down. Both horses' flanks and legs were splattered with blood. I could see a shard of glass near the length of my arm had lodged itself in Princess's shoulder. It was in so deep it had cut an artery. Ned was bleeding where the shard had rubbed against him. He was badly scratched up, but she was bleeding rivers. I'll never forget the sweet coppery iron smell of it filling the air. Horses don't like the smell of blood, you know."

"No, I don't suppose they do."

"She was shuddering like she was taking a fit, and that spooked Ned. He started stamping his hoofs and rearing, rattling the harness and straining the running gear. He was going to break the shafts off the cart. I had to untie her. She'd bleed out before I could do anything, get any veterinary help. And there I was, concentrating on the horse, wondering what I was going to say to the gaffer, when people began wandering into the streets, stunned, most of them. They weren't saying anything. But then some started screaming that the Germans were coming. I could hear others crying and wailing. So many of them were bleeding. Ash was falling everywhere, making everything grey. And then there'd be someone wearing bright red — blood.

"I had to unfasten all the buckles and straps of Princess's harness and lead her away from the cart's shaft, even though my hands were numb and shaking. I slipped in her blood on the road, all thick and syrupy. And warm. Her eyes were still showing whites, but she was calmer, as if somehow she knew she was going to die. It tore me up to just leave her there by the side of the road, shivering and bleeding. But Ned was going wild, dancing sideways, dragging the dray and trailing Princess's harness over the ground. If I didn't do something he was going to catch his legs in the reins and break them. And then I'd lose two animals."

He pauses.

Eventually Hetty turns to look at him. "And then what happened?"

"I was trying to calm Ned down, leaning into his withers, reassuring him with my weight. I had one hand on his neck, stroking his face with the other, when I saw a woman coming towards me. She was being led by her children.

"I couldn't make out her face for all the blood streaming from a gash on her head. Her hair was matted with it, and she was crying that she couldn't see."

Hetty's face prickles, her eyes smart. Was it possible?

"At that moment Princess fell with a crash that shook the ground. I remember just standing there, staring at her blood streaming down the street, listening to her hooves scrape in the cinders as she thrashed. And then Ned screamed in a way I never knew horses could scream. It took all my strength to keep him from bolting again."

"Oh my God." She says it over and over again. "Oh my God." Noble forges on. Now that he's come this far, the rest of the story asserts itself, demanding to be told.

"I heard a man's voice. 'I got you. Steady there.' The dray rocked behind me. Someone was standing on the back of the cart, pushing off the cotton bales and helping the woman and her children up.

"I caught only a flash of arms, feet in workman's boots. 'I'll just see if there's someone else you can take,' the man hollered, and jumped down and ran back towards the ruins of what had once been Dominion Textile. The roof was entirely gone, and parts of the outside walls. The second floor had crashed through, probably because of the weight of the collapsed roof and the machines. And all those unlucky enough to be trapped below, no one could possibly have survived. But I couldn't just stand there doing nothing, so I threw the reins to the kids and told them I'd be back as soon as I could.

"The minute I stepped over the threshold I wanted to bolt. The place stank of oil and grease and dust and meat. Raw meat. That last smell made my legs rubbery. I couldn't understand. It didn't make any sense. The place had no roof and no walls to speak of, and yet there was this overpowering smell. And bodies everywhere, or rather bits of bodies, broken and smashed. I stood on someone's severed arm without realizing what it was, the hand at its end pulverized beyond recognition."

"And the woman and her children?" Hetty's voice is barely above a whisper.

"I honestly can't remember what happened next. Did I move forward into the building or back out? I don't know. I've no idea what happened to the man I'd followed. The next thing I remember I was standing at the back of the dray. The woman had stopped crying. She was just lying there. The little girl was cradling her head. There was a huge dark stain in her lap, like a blackened halo around her mother's head. There was a voice in my head yelling at me for not acting sooner, for letting the woman die, but maybe I was shouting out loud because the little girl spoke up then. 'She's still breathing,' she said. She sounded so much older than the little girl she was. She snapped me out of myself and I jumped back into the driver's seat and whipped Ned up as fast as he would go. All I could think of was getting to Camp Hill Hospital as soon as possible."

They still haunt him, the scores of dead and wounded he passed on that trip. A child pinned under rubble. A man trying to fit one of his legs where it should have been, blood trickling from his ears. People who followed him with their bleeding eyes. But Noble had kept on going, pushing Ned right on past them. It hasn't been easy to live with since, the thought of all those people he could have helped, people who might have lived if he'd had his wits about him.

"I thought I'd killed her, see, leaving her to bleed like that for so long."

"But you didn't. It turned out all right in the end."

"Because of you it did." She reaches out, squeezes his hand. "Your voice was so calm."

"It was?"

"You kept saying everything was going to be all right. But I didn't think it was."

Hetty dabs at her eyes again. "I feel overwhelmed, light-headed. Do you think anyone would believe us if we told them?"

"Probably not." He's having a hard time believing it himself. "They'd think it was too big a coincidence. It would make a poor story in that regard." No doubt Elinor Glyn has something to say on the matter.

"I think you're wrong. I think it's an amazing story. I think it's a miracle. Two miracles. And I think you should write it down some day. Even if it's just for yourself."

Noble stares hard through the windshield, fastening his attention on the approach to the city. "Do you think God saves people for a reason?"

"God?" Hetty tucks her handkerchief up her sleeve, smoothes her dress across her knees. "I sometimes wonder if He does anything at all."

XXI

The road approaching Halifax skirts Bedford Basin and then divides, each tributary branching into street after street filled with houses. Halifax is beautiful in spring. A different kind of beauty from the rugged red cliffs, the tides, the mud flats, the emerald green marshes of Minas Basin. Downtown is a red brick and sandstone kind of beauty, parks bedecked with flowerbeds and streets lined with spruced-up storefronts, freshly washed awnings and paintwork, goods beckoning behind sparkling glass. The sun glints off the water in the harbour, its reflection magnified by the buildings, the glass, the whitewash. The city pulses through her, thrilling her. How had she ever survived a year away? Christmas, that bloody, pain-distorted calamity doesn't count. Hetty had arrived in the dark, bundled in blankets and delirious from blood loss, and apart from the hospital and her parents' home had seen nothing of the city. The day Peter arrived to accompany her back on the train, a snowstorm had obscured the view from the window.

But this entrance marks a new adventure in her life. Lit up with anticipation, she turns to her travelling companion, then sobers at the lines of strain about his mouth. How anxious he looks. And tired. He takes Kempt Road. She regards him as they approach Young Street and then drive past the site of the razed Dominion Textile Company.

"They were still clearing this area when I left. I stayed over there." He nods towards the Exhibition Grounds.

"In the temporary housing?"

"Yup."

Of course, he would have lived in Richmond Heights, would have lost his rooms and possibly his friends, men he worked with.

"Do you mind?" he asks, already making the turn onto Robie Street. "I'd like to see it." The Hydrostone, he means, the ten-block area of houses too grandiose and fanciful according to some, *too posh for poor folk*, that had arisen from the ashes of the explosion. The same ten blocks Hetty had walked as a nurse.

"You're the driver," she says, lacing her hands across her lap. Her wedding ring turns loosely on her third finger, a poorer fit now than Esmeralda's flawed heart. She must have lost weight. She begins slipping it off — it'll be safer in her purse — but senses Noble watching from the corner of his eye. She slides the ring back into place.

"Look at them all." He whistles under his breath as the formidable rows of solid houses come into view. "You should have seen the places that were here before. No better than shacks, some of them."

What Hetty notices is how the yards' young trees have inched a little higher in her absence, how the shrubs have thickened. But the houses themselves still retain the stark grey quality of the concrete blocks, the Hydrostone, from which they are constructed and from which the development draws its name. Noble takes the truck slowly past the ends of each street: Hennessy, Kane, Stairs. Hetty finds herself wishing for a familiar face to appear, an old acquaintance to wave at her from a bedroom window or across a garden fence, but fears that in one short year she has become invisible. Richmond Heights has always been an area of transition. Families move in, break apart, scatter, come to rest somewhere else. Many rooms are filled with tenants and lodgers who follow jobs, moving on to other cities and provinces or south to the States. They pass Stanley, Columbus, then Merkel. Hand on his arm.

"Stop here, would you?" And he does, pulling over to the side of the road. Hetty stares down Cabot Street, down the crooked corridor of her past, though Job Mitchell would doubtless have moved on by now.

"Cabot Street. Isn't that the street the Prince of Wales visited?"

"I believe so."

"He came the summer after I left. They hadn't finished building all of this. He went inside one of the houses, inspected it from top to bottom. It was in the paper. I remember the name. Cabot Street."

So does Hetty. Number fourteen. But she's more interested in the house next to it, number twelve. She watches the door for a while, and then, just as she senses Noble forming another question, she turns and smiles, breaking the tension. "We can go now."

They ride through the city to Spring Garden Road in silence.

"Anywhere here will be fine. Thank you."

"Are you sure? There's no extra charge for door-to-door service."

She offers him a small wry smile. "Thank you, but I think my aunt will probably share your mother's feelings — about our travelling together, I mean. I'll walk from here." Noble draws the truck against the curb and slows to a stop. Hetty opens her purse, and taking out some bills, presses them into his hand. "Thank you again," she says, her hands still clasping his. "For everything."

"You don't have to pay me. I was coming here anyway."

"Please. We had an agreement."

"All the best with Esmeralda."

"Thank you. I'm sure everything will work out. I hope. My father has some pretty influential friends in this city. Shall I tell her you send your regards?"

He nods, waves and pulls away, and Hetty's courage withers. A room in a hotel might have been a better idea. Aunt Rachel had been touring in France over Christmas, so Hetty hasn't seen her since her wedding day, and while Aunt Rachel's correspondence has been regular, if thin on detail, Hetty has not once in the past year put pen to paper and written her back. Not even to answer her aunt's heartfelt condolence letter following the miscarriage. Now Hetty worries that she may not get such a warm reception as in the past. Aunt Rachel has always shored up her sister's maternal instincts. But it's possible her complicity in marrying Hetty off has compromised their relationship.

Aunt Rachel makes a valiant attempt to appear nonplussed by Hetty's unannounced appearance at her door but isn't as good an actress as they'd both like. "My favourite niece. How delightful to see you," she declares, pulling the door wide and opening her arms. Hetty smiles — it's an old joke, Aunt Rachel only has one niece — and bends to hug her diminutive aunt. Had she not been looking for it, Hetty might have missed Aunt Rachel's discreet glance over her niece's shoulder.

"Well, come in girl, don't just stand about in the doorway, you'll be giving all the neighborhood tongues something to wag about."

Hetty follows her aunt down the hallway. "So what brings you to the city? Is Peter not with you?" The second question follows the first so quickly that Hetty realizes her aunt isn't prepared for any proclamations she might be about to make.

"I came alone." Aunt Rachel leads Hetty to what she has always called her getting-things-organized room. "I'm here on some business."

"Business?" Eyebrow raised.

"Yes, you know, Clara's wedding." She isn't brave enough. Has no idea how her aunt will react to the truth. "I'm here for a dress fitting."

"Ah." Aunt Rachel's face relaxes and with it the knot in Hetty's stomach. "You should have called ahead of time, you silly girl. I could have had Beatrice make up a room for you. Now I feel completely unprepared."

"You're taking another trip." The ordered chaos in the room finally registers. Aunt Rachel's much labeled and battered trunk is standing open in the middle of the room. Designed like a miniature wardrobe, the trunk is shoulder height to Aunt Rachel. Jackets hang from the rod, shoulders squared like soldiers on parade; three pairs of sensible shoes sit in a row beneath. A folded pile of clothing waits on a nearby chair to be packed away in the trunk's drawers. A map is opened on the dining-room table, while a side table supports a small stack of books, France printed boldly on the deeper spines of the bottom two. Hetty cranes her neck to read the uppermost title. *THE SOMME VOLUME 1.* In smaller capitals across the top: *ILLUSTRATED MICHELIN GUIDES TO THE BATTLEFIELDS (1914-1918).* Someone has written a guidebook to the battlefields? Has illustrated it? She steps closer and picks it up. Guides. More than one, then.

"The Somme," Hetty exclaims aloud.

"Exciting, isn't it? I heard about the guides the first year they came out, in 1919, but I was too squeamish then. I suppose it was too soon afterwards. And now they've started rebuilding everywhere. It's all changing. So if I wish to see things at all, then now is the time to go."

"I thought you went there last year."

"Amiens. But it isn't quite the same thing. Look here," Aunt Rachel pulls a slimmer companion guide from a bookshelf and, standing at Hetty's side, thumbs through the opening pages. "'A Brief Description,' 'How the Germans Occupied Amiens in 1914,' 'How Amiens was Saved in 1918,' 'The Liberation of Amiens,'" she says, reading the subtitles and pointing to the photographs and maps. Then a page headed "Itinerary." "The Cathedral is prominent. It dominates the book. See? Description, facades, doorways, statues." A succession of photographs detailing the features of a building both vast and medieval in design and scope flit by. The flying buttresses bestow upon it a vague and forbidding majesty. Hetty finds herself wishing the building well.

"But see" — Aunt Rachel flips forward again; they are now more than halfway through the booklet — "It wasn't much damaged. Nine shells hit the cathedral in total but none caused any serious damage, and most of that had been repaired by the time I visited."

"So you didn't get to see anything." An edge of disdain has crept into her voice, surprising her.

"No, well, not as much as I would have liked." Aunt Rachel bends the booklet back at page thirty-six. "See, for instance, this picture of the Nouvelles Galeries showing how utterly destroyed all the stores were. Well, the rubble had been cleared away, but some of the ruined walls were still standing." Aunt Rachel's postcards were always cheery pictures of the French countryside and quaint inns, clearly the Before photographs. Hetty wonders whether the French sell After postcards too and is relieved her aunt chose the sentimental kind. What could you possibly write on the back of a picture such as this? *The view is marvelous, wish you were here.*

"Are many people doing this?" Stupid question. Why else would a company go to the trouble of publishing a guidebook?

"You know the Parisians came out by the thousands to visit

the Marne Valley battlefields less than a week after the battle itself. According to newspaper reports, there were still bodies of Frenchmen and Germans and English all piled up along the roadsides, many of them badly mutilated from the shells." Aunt Rachel sounds only mildly disbelieving.

"It's awfully stuffy in here, do you mind?" Hetty gestures towards the window, which looks onto Summer Street. She lifts the sash, gulps in the sea-city air. Hetty has seen Aunt Rachel's picture, the one with the bodies piled up at the side of the road. Except they weren't soldiers.

"I plan to go for longer this time, I think six weeks should do it. Time enough to get a proper feel for the place, don't you think?" Hetty turns back to the room, the Somme guide still in her hand.

"What is there to get a feel for, Aunt Rachel?" Hetty opens the guide and flips quickly past the advertisements for Michelin maps and the Michelin wheel. On page four she pauses a moment to take in a succession of pictures of the village of Ginchy, from village under bombardment to pockmarked countryside and white shadows where there were formerly buildings. *White shadows*? The gulf between the Amiens guide and the Somme is a wide and grey no man's land of bomb craters and makeshift graveyards.

"What are you going to see?" She shakes the book at her aunt, all but ripping the pages as she turns them. "Look at this. 'Albert Church in 1917.' 'Albert Church in 1919.' All that rubble." Over the page. "'La Boiselle. The sign is all that remains of the village.' Cemeteries. And what is that, a skull?" Aunt Rachel can hardly answer — her niece has the book in her hand. Hetty raises her other hand to the depression at the base of her throat, fingers on her rising hysteria. How can Aunt Rachel want to see this, to ogle these sites of wanton destruction? "A man in a motor car. Look, with his suitcases piled on the roof. Out for a Sunday drive. To see what? The ruins of Aveluy. But there's nothing there."

"Precisely, they're ruins."

"Oh, here's 'Panoramic view of the valley of the Ancre . . .' A panorama of what? Burned tree stumps. It looks like . . . like . . ." Her voice trails off. She can't quite meet Aunt Rachel's gaze. Hetty has never spoken so frankly, so emotionally to her aunt before.

"It looks like Halifax, you mean. After the Explosion."

"Why do you want to see these places? I don't understand. It's not as if you lost anyone over there. It's perverse."

"Are you saying I have no right to mourn?"

"What you're doing isn't mourning. It's gawking, it's making a mockery out of tragedy. Let's count the bomb craters. If we look hard enough we might find something of value. A gun, a belt buckle, part of a letter that never made it to a loved one. Souvenir hunting. It's carrion-eating. These things aren't public property to be picked over. Can't we just leave the dead in peace? And the effrontery of these Michelin people, making money out of tragedy. You're not going over there to mourn." Hot tears splash onto her cheeks. Aunt Rachel pulls Hetty's face to her shoulder.

"There, there," she says, stroking Hetty's hair and leading her to the loveseat by the window. "Everything's going to be all right. You'll see, my love." Hetty lays her head in her aunt's lap. She could wail like an infant.

"Can you forgive me?" Aunt Rachel asks after Hetty's sobbing subsides.

"Forgive you?"

Aunt Rachel strokes Hetty's hair, wipes at her tears with the cool back of her hand. "For not being here to help you at Christmas."

"It wasn't your fault."

"It wasn't anyone's fault, my love." The drawing room clock ticks loudly in the silence that follows. Hetty stares at the patterned carpet. A whisper. "Have you left him?"

"No." Where would she go? What would she do? Walk the

streets? Hearing all the doors slam in her face, she rubs her temples, the bridge of her nose, a headache beginning. "I don't know. I'm not really certain what I've done."

"Nothing that can't be undone, I'm sure."

"I don't know about that."

Aunt Rachel's voice drops a shade. "He's a good man though, isn't he? He is good to you, yes? I'd never forgive myself if he wasn't."

Hetty nods and shakes her head at the same time. "He is a good man," she manages, finally. "It's just that he can be so overbearing at times. And so cold. So unreachable. Is it always this hard?"

"Marriage? Yes, I think marriage is always hard."

"Even if you love each other?"

"Do you love him?"

"No."

"Do you think you ever could?"

"I don't know."

"It takes time, sweetheart. You'll settle into each other soon enough."

"But what if I don't want to? What then?"

"You'll have other babies, Hetty, and this phase will pass. And then all the things that upset you about Peter will seem insignificant and hardly worth the tears shed over them because you'll be so caught up in being a mother."

"Like my mother was, you mean?"

Aunt Hetty continues her rhythmic stroking. "She cares a great deal about you, you know."

"She cares a great deal that what I do and what I say doesn't reflect badly on her."

"She was heartbroken for you at Christmas."

"She has an odd way of showing it."

"Speaking of your mother, she doesn't know you're in town, does she?"

Hetty shakes her head.

"Have you eaten?"

"I'm not hungry."

"You have to eat, Hetty."

"I'm fine. We stopped for dinner in Fall River."

"We?" Aunt Rachel's hands stop their stroking.

Slowly Hetty pulls herself to sitting position and takes her aunt's hands in her lap. "It's a long story."

"They always are, my dear. They always are."

XXII

Once Hetty Douglas disappears down South Park Street and Noble is alone, the magnitude of his Halifax mission presses down on him. The chance of finding Will Brooks at work at this hour is slim. Not to mention that, after nearly eight hours of driving, Noble is stiff, sore and tired. The bowl of thick pea soup he ate an hour ago has curdled his insides and he's itching for a bath. But there's a picture etched in his mind of a carefree Jem swinging his makeshift baseball bat on the beach. *Do you know the story of the whale?* Noble understands his heart is no longer his alone; a large part of it is walking around with a tow-haired six-year-old boy. He heads down Spring Garden Road and turns right onto Barrington Street.

This southern end of Halifax has altered too. Streets that were once genteel are now shabby and run-down. More afflu-ent families have moved away since the building of the railway station and dockyards began, and now the whole neighbour-hood looks as if it could do with a scrub-down and a fresh coat of paint. Without the wartime bustle of military men and their sweethearts and families, the city feels oddly quiet to Noble as he steers towards Water Street. The roads are paved, which is new, but vanished is evidence of the war years' boom, the background din of sawing and carpentry, drilling and blast furnaces. It could simply be that he's arrived late in the day and that working men laid down their tools hours ago. But the emptiness feels more sinister than that.

The new deepwater terminals and docks being built in the harbour behind the South End train station — also still under construction — are quieter still. Noble parks before the foundation of what will be the new Canadian Pacific Hotel and steps from the truck. He stands and stares into the gloaming, one hand resting on the roof of the cab as if reluctant to let go, move forward into the unknown. It's a long stretch of water frontage from here to the Naval Shipyards at the foot of Richmond Heights, almost the width of the land the city encompasses. He has ludicrously little to go on. Who is this Will Brooks? Is he approachable or is he violent? What if he's part of a gang? If he hadn't been so stunned and sleep deprived, Noble would have asked Butler for more information, a description, a clue, anything to narrow the search. A wave of exhaustion almost fells him, courage draining through his feet. But he forces them to move, one in front of the other. The key to finding Will Brooks lies somewhere among these wharves and piers. He tries to rally his spirits, tells himself there's every chance of finding someone this evening who may know where Brooks is. He could be lucky: if Brooks has no family to go home to — though Noble has no reason to suppose he does or doesn't — he might even bump into the fellow.

But it is obvious within minutes that the place is deserted. By people. Rats rustle along the walls. A battle-scarred cat slinks inside a pile of broken pallets. He approaches the water, peers into the cavities of half-excavated docks and half-built graving yards. The wood no longer smells new, the scaffolding bleeds orange. His footsteps echo. The silhouetted armatures of unfinished sheds claw at the darkening sky like starved creatures. Glancing over his shoulder, he trips on a discarded bolt, and his imagination rears in panic. He begins to run, convinced someone is following him.

It will be completely dark in an hour or so. But Noble won't be able to sleep knowing he hasn't checked every wharf, ventured out on every pier, called down every alley. Returning to his truck he drives along Water Street a few blocks towards the city, parks and walks the waterfront. Drives, parks and walks again. North Atlantic Fisheries, Whitman and Mackenzie. Past Melville and Mitchell and Campbell Wharves and on through to City Wharf and Western Union. Circling back that way, he slowly he approaches the city centre. Now and then he calls out Brooks's name. Once, seeing a light, he jogs to the end of the pier. Another time he happens on a prostitute and her john, grinding against the wall. And on the same pier narrowly misses stepping on a pile of old sacks that turns out to be human. Sleeping, passed out or dead. Noble doesn't hang around to investigate. At the Dartmouth Ferry dock he spots a middle-aged man waiting on a bench, but the man's eyes widen in alarm at Noble's approach. He hurries away. Noble touches a hand to his bruised and unshaven face. What was he thinking? Night has fallen, and though reluctant to abandon his quest, he heads over to Barrington Street to find a room in one of the cheaper hotels.

In a steamy bath, Noble's muscles loosen, his mind flanking the edge of sleep. After towelling down, he pads back to his room, climbs into bed, cool sheets pulled into tight hospital corners, and then stares at the ceiling, his body thrumming like an electric machine. His eyelids burn. A streetlight pours through the thin hotel curtains. It reminds him of trying to sleep in England. He and Lawson had arrived in September. How late the sun went down. And how slowly. How long sleep had taken to come in the lingering daylight. How impossible he had found sleeping at all in that country after the accident. The thought of which prompts his shoulder to begin aching anew. He turns on his left side, skin pulsing with irritation, and rues leaving *Treasure Island* behind. He couldn't be more wide awake if it were morning. Fifteen frustrating minutes later, Noble slips from the bed, pulls on his clothes and leaves his room in search of a newspaper.

With its apron of light spilling warm and yellow into an otherwise dark section of Argyle Street, the bookstore looks inviting. Rows of handsome spines beckon, and Noble steps inside, breathing in the sharp scent of paper and ink and knowledge, the same smell he remembers from another lifetime when a quite different man sat on the edge of his bed and lifted the cover off a box from New York containing Elinor Glyn books. Glyn.

"Closing in five minutes," the clerk calls. Noble wanders past shelves and rows of books until he reaches G. He glances around. Two other customers are prowling the shelves. Both men. Women would do their shopping in daylight hours, resigned to spending the evening alone. Was it a stubbornness in men, perhaps, that they couldn't acknowledge their loneliness until the sun had gone down?

Finger across the spines. There it is. Elinor Glyn's infamous *Three Weeks*. Minus the dust jacket. He runs his eye down the white lettering on the spine. He's heard all about this novel, the sensation it caused when it was new, before the war. Shocking. A book that would never find itself in Lillian's Friday night lending library. A book he could never ask her about. Noble's ears are attuned to the shop assistant helping another customer with inquiries, yet still he imagines the man's eyes burning holes in his back. To glance behind him a second time might give the impression he's planning to steal it. Oh, what harm would looking do? He reaches up and pulls it free. Instantly the books on either side draw together in a puff of spore-filled air, as if they had had a hand themselves in pushing the book from their shelf. Out, vile volume. Noble pinches his nose to lessen his sneeze, which explodes instead from his ears and mouth. A fine spray of saliva now marks the red cloth binding.

"Two minutes to closing. If you wish to make a purchase, sir, you should make it now." Is he planning on buying it? This of all books? He needs to be in S for Stevenson, Robert Louis. Or D for Dickens. He could try putting Glyn's novel back, but he's being watched for sure, and the shelf looks stubbornly full. He glances inside the cover to where the clerk has scribbled in pencil the book's second-hand worth. Voices ring in his head. Lillian, Reverend Walker. His mother. He brushes at his neck, turns to make sure Sarah isn't standing peering over his shoulder.

Tipping his hat low across his brow, Noble approaches the cash register, absurdly grateful when the clerk slides the book inside a paper bag. He tucks the package inside his jacket and under his arm, where it feels hot against his skin.

Propped up in bed, Noble's thrill of anticipation is tinged with self-consciousness as he begins reading the tale of Paul Verdayne, a privileged young man who attends theatres and hunts. Paul commences a love affair with a parson's daughter, whose "hands were big and red." Ah, the lower middle classes frolic with the upper, a tale of debauchery. She was only the parson's daughter. After the ideals espoused in her *System of Writing*, Noble had expected more from Elinor Glyn.

He reads on. At his mother's behest Paul is sent on a tour of Europe. Isabelle, poor wretch, is now described as "quite six foot, and broad in proportion." Already Noble pities her. Paul tells Isabelle he loves her and a cuckoo calls from a nearby tree. Noble continues reading, titillation, or at least the rumour of it, drawing him on rather than any subtlety in Glyn's writing. And so to Switzerland; a bad-tempered Paul is ensconced in the dining room. But he is not too self-absorbed to take notice of the woman who comes to dine alone at the next table.

"She herself was all in black, and her hat — an expensive-looking hat — cast a shadow over her eyes." Was Glyn writing of herself? Noble recalls her picture in the front of *The Three Magic Coupons* booklet, the shadow cast by her hat. The mysterious woman's mouth is "red, red, red." Hardly subtle, but he supposes the mystery is not who the woman is so much as how the dalliance will begin. The narrator is trying to convince him of Paul's irritation with the woman, but Noble isn't fooled. Paul Verdayne is already under her spell. Poor Isabelle, how inconstant are this young fop's affections.

As the second chapter progresses Noble finds himself less critical. Paul, out on the lake for the day, glimpses the lady from the night before and tries and fails to pursue her. When Paul is unable to conjure a clear image of Isabelle's big red hands, Noble doesn't give her a second thought. On through one torturous evening when he dines too early to see her, and the following evening, when he dines too late. But later that night the mysterious lady invites Paul to her room. A sumptuous room, the lady's room, rich with brocades and flowers, a tiger skin flung across the sofa. The tease of conversation, unfettered flirtation. Noble devours it all. Eyes throbbing with fatigue, he reads on, his ears keen to every bed creak, every tap of rain against the window, every muffled shout and engine noise from the street below.

"Could a kiss wake a soul?" This from the lady's lips. "I think so," whispers young Paul, and Noble nods. For had Esmeralda's kiss not wakened his soul on the wharf the other night? A pang of longing cuts through him. Surely it is approaching midnight, but he must know where this kiss will lead.

The tiger skin in her room loomed large in Noble's mind, and so too, it would appear, in Paul's, for he purchases just such a skin at a nearby store and has it delivered. Noble dismisses his jab of envy that Paul has enough money to be buying a tiger skin. Noble once bought Mary a bauble when she'd visited him in Halifax and had been plagued with anxiety over both the money he'd spent and Mary's reaction. Quite physical as he recalls. What will Paul get for his tiger skin?

Answer: The lady, in a clinging outfit and stretched out on the bigger and better tiger skin in front of the fire, a red rose between her teeth. Footsteps at the far end of the corridor. Has he locked the door? He leaps from the bed to the door, against which he leans, left hand twisting at the already rigid key, right hand pushing at the fully-engaged bolt. He stays there, the thump of his heartbeat pushing through his temples and into the wood, waiting until the footsteps pass. Toes curled against the floor's unfamiliar grit, he tiptoes back to bed, lowering himself carefully so the springs don't give away his movements, and picks Elinor Glyn from his pillow. His breathing is absurdly loud and jagged. He focuses on the page but finds only more teasing. Paul must sit in a fancy chair she has procured that afternoon while the lady, now without her clinging dress, wriggles on the skin like a snake. Paul begins to beg the tiger lady to teach him the ways of love, yet still she wants to talk. How like a woman! And read poetry in Latin, though poor Paul has forgotten most of his, and then sing while quivers run up Paul's spine, and whisper in his ear until Paul — a man at last — finally cries out, seizes her in his arms and kisses her passionately. Noble is sweating.

XXIII

Wednesday June 5. Halifax.

Hetty has barely taken the first bite of her toast when the door opens and her mother glides in from the vestibule. Beatrice is out there? Or can Vivian walk through walls now? Perfume and chiffon trail in her wake as she crosses the room, leans to kiss the air beside her sister's cheek, and floats towards Hetty for the same. Vivian Landry Piers is a long lean woman whose crisp jawline and firm skin belie her age. Hetty pushes her breakfast away and sets her face before rising to greet her mother. They touch cheeks, an awkward, wooden gesture, then part and stand, beholding one another. Though Vivian's head is cocked at an engaging angle and her mouth turned up in a smile, her eyes waver between deprecation and terror. Hetty's own mask begins to crumble. She sits and pulls herself back to the table. How long has her mother been afraid of her?

"I have to find out from others that my own daughter is in town," Vivian says. Her voice sounds rehearsed, and an ancient heaviness settles on Hetty. Aunt Rachel makes tea excuses and disappears to the kitchen. Hetty wills her mother to sit down. Already her neck is beginning to ache with the strain of looking up.

"Your aunt tells me you're here on wedding business." Vivian smiles the smile that wins her seats on boards and committees throughout the city. Though too horsey-looking to be beautiful, Vivian was, according to Hetty's father, a fine catch. When the banns had first been read in church, he likes to tell people, one proprietary hand on his wife's arm, half the eligible young men in Halifax had gone into mourning.

Hetty mirrors Vivian's smile, feels her mother's veneer reshaping her own face. In order to deal with Vivian one must become Vivian.

"I took the liberty of calling Clara." Clever Vivian. Hetty dreads to imagine how Clara has translated the incident at the village wharf. "She asked me to remind you your dress fitting is scheduled for ten o'clock tomorrow morning."

Clever Clara.

"And I telephoned Peter to let him know you had arrived safely." Aunt Rachel bustles into the room with tea things on a tray, which gives Hetty somewhere to look other than at her mother.

"And how is he?"

"Very well. He hopes to be able to join us in time for dinner this evening."

"Perfect." A smile to match, vinegar in her mouth. A glimpsed weakness in her mother's fortifications is not sufficient basis for a coup.

"Six o'clock on the dot, then. I won't stop for tea, Rachel dear," she says, rising and pulling on her gloves. "I know you still have lots of preparations to make for your trip. I'll see you both this evening."

And she's gone. Hetty sits for a moment, dazed by what has just transpired, by the way she has allowed her mother in two short but devastating minutes to take control. No longer a child or in her mother's house, she pushes back her chair and rushes to the vestibule. Her mother is by the door. A pause to gather her wits and the necessary breath for protest. She raises a hand.

"I don't want —"

"Just the news that you'd arrived in town last night gave your father quite the fright, you know." Vivian's voice is low but penetrating, like the warning rumble of a large dog. The corners of her mouth turn up. "His heart isn't what it used to be." She grasps Hetty's arm. "We were so relieved to hear everything is fine between you and Peter."

Hetty stares at the door after her mother is gone. The woman campaigned for female suffrage, it's a wonder she isn't running the country. Hetty's hands feel cold. Her father's heart isn't what it used to be? Because of what she, Hetty, has done to her father's heart? Is that her mother's unspoken message?

Unable to face Aunt Rachel's pitying looks, her excuses for her younger sister's behaviour, Hetty sweeps through the apartment to the spare room where she spent the night in fitful sleep and sits on the edge of the narrow bed. She's past hunger, needs to be out walking somewhere, anywhere, to clear her head. Peter is coming to Halifax. Approximately eight hours from now he'll be here, facing her across the dinner table, wanting answers. Hetty can feel her resolve slipping away like water. How stupid to bolt like that without even leaving a note. He would have been worried sick. And now there is her father to fret over. Did she think she could run away and everyone would just let her go? That there would be no repercussions? Yesterday Hetty had felt so driven with purpose; the impulse to rescue Esmeralda had made so much more sense. But her old life isn't going to simply step aside so she can assume a new one. If assuming a new life is her intention. Beyond visiting the jailhouse, Hetty hasn't the faintest idea what she intends.

She stands and checks herself in the dressing-table mirror. The woman staring back appears so much calmer than Hetty feels. She combs her hair, and then, arranging her hat to cast a shadow over her face, she steps outside and makes her way towards Barrington Street.

The room is stark, the walls pale grey, the windows high and crossed with bars. The only furniture — a small table accompanied by two chairs — waits in the middle. Esmeralda is lounging against the back wall with a lemon-faced matron in sensible shoes, their heads bent together. But for the ring of keys dangling from a chain on the matron's belt, there is little to distinguish the difference in power between the two women. Everything about Esmeralda — her posture, the defiant casualness of her men's attire, the way her glossy hair, loosely tied at the nape of her neck, hangs over her shoulder — suggests that not an ounce of wretchedness has touched her: she might be leaning against the counter of an ice-cream parlour or the gunwale of her floating namesake, so composed, so unperturbed by her surroundings, by her probable fate, does she appear. In contrast, guilt marks Hetty's skin like a sunburn; it fashions every halting step she takes towards the girl. Just what had she been expecting? Some poor little match girl with stringy hair and smudges under her eyes? A bruise or two? As Hetty approaches her side of the table, a smile grazes Esmeralda's features.

"You came all this way just to see me?" she says, almost swaggering towards the centre of the room. "I'm flattered."

Hetty returns the smile but it feels crooked and insincere, as if it's sitting on the wrong face.

"When the police arrived at the wharf I . . . ."

Esmeralda's face hardens. "You felt responsible?"

They sit and Hetty fixes on Esmeralda's work-roughened hand, resting on the table between them. Dirt has collected in the crevices, under her short mannish nails, and Hetty wonders if it's been there all along, only she hasn't noticed it until now.

"I brought some things I thought you could use," she says. "They're in a parcel, which I suppose they have to inspect first. Soap, and a hairbrush. And a couple of dresses."

"How thoughtful. But I don't know that your fancy gowns will go down too well in this place, do you?"

"They're not mine. I bought them for you. They're quite practical." Plain, really. And a good deal less romantic than Esmeralda's male regalia. Why hadn't she purchased something bright and cheery? "I hope they fit."

"You should have saved yourself the trouble."

"How are you holding up?" Hetty asks, one eye on the matron, all folded arms and stern expression. "Are they treating you well?"

Again the inscrutable smile. "What do you think?"

The matron paces back and forth the length of the far wall. Hetty tries rubbing some warmth into her hands and wonders what she is doing here. Wonders why she has come all this way.

"I know it was your husband who turned us in." Stale prison air coats her skin, her tongue, her teeth. "That's why you're here, isn't it? You feel guilty. So you thought if you were kind to poor little Esmeralda, rotting away in the dungeon, you could make yourself feel better."

"No. Yes. A little. I thought you might need —"

"Your pity? No thanks."

"Some comfort. Some help perhaps."

"What kind of help would that be? You have any money?"

"Money?"

"Yes. Money. Cold hard cash. It's the only kind of help that carries weight in a place like this."

"I don't have money on me, I'm afraid. Well, a little, but it's in my purse, which I had to check at the visitors' entrance, along with your parcel. I could try and get you some. Though it might take me a day or two."

"I don't have a day or two."

Are you going somewhere? But her tongue hesitates over the words.

"What about the ring?"

"Sorry?"

"The one you're wearing. The one I gave you."

Hetty's face grows warm. "Oh. Yes, of course." She twists the ring from her finger and hands it to Esmeralda.

"The earrings too."

"My earrings?"

"No, the earrings on the woman standing behind you. Of course your earrings."

Hetty's cold hands fumble with the clasps. The matron shifts from her perch against the wall. "Everything all right over there?"

"Don't let her see what you're doing," Esmeralda hisses.

"We're fine, thank you," Hetty calls out, her voice tight and scared, not her own. She waits until the matron is looking elsewhere before handing over the earrings.

"I had no idea what Peter was planning. You have to believe me." She takes a breath. "In fact I've left him." She has? Her cheeks are burning.

"You won't be needing that then." Esmeralda taps her left hand. Her wedding ring. Hetty can taste this morning's toast and tea in the back of her throat. But if she wants to at least appear to stand by the declaration she has just made she can hardly argue to keep it. Esmeralda slips the jewellery inside her blouse. Will she not be searched? Hetty could have passed her a knife. How much experience did they have with female prisoners?

"You needn't have bothered, by the way."

"Needn't have bothered about what?"

"Leaving Peter. When Spoon gets ahold of him —"

"Spoon? I thought he was locked up with everyone else."

"Afraid not."

"Then where is he?" But Hetty has a sickening feeling she already knows the answer.

"Probably somewhere in or around your village."

"Where he might get caught?" Hetty's words sounds trapped

and tinny. "I don't understand. What does he have to gain in staying around?"

"Greed and vengeance. Qualities that make him a great asset to someone like my father, providing he's kept under control." Esmeralda's eyes never waver in their feline intensity. "Spoon would be a lot smarter if he didn't let his temper rule his actions." She lowers her voice, forcing Hetty to lean across the table towards her. "If he can find a way of getting to the liquor we dropped on our way in, he'll succeed no matter what."

"And Peter?"

"If Spoon's had time to cool down he may try and make it look like an accident. Otherwise . . ." She shrugs, blinks slowly.

Peter hunted down like prey. If Hetty could will her legs to cooperate she would leave. What if it is already too late to warn him? She makes to rise from her chair when Esmeralda grasps her arm.

"The charges are serious." And there she is at last, the frightened young girl behind the bravado, the poisoned words. Hetty brushes aside the picture of Spoon skulking around the village.

"I know," she says, and covers Esmeralda's hand with her own.

"As captain my father will hang for sure."

The collateral damage from Hetty's rash behaviour is colossal. Platitudes drift through her mind like dandelion seeds, but catching any of them for delivery seems pointlessly cruel.

"They could hang me too."

"It won't come to that."

"Yes it will. Don't think for a minute they're not going to enjoy making an example out of me. Helen says they're calling for the death penalty. They'd burn me at the stake."

"Helen?"

Esmeralda motions with her head to the back of the room. All her vivacity has fled.

"My father will help us," Hetty says. "He knows people."

"You're too kind, Hetty Douglas." Two fat tears slide down Esmeralda's face.

Hetty stares at her hand, covering Esmeralda's. How naked it looks without her wedding band. "Everything is going to be fine."

"You will be there tomorrow, won't you? At the bail hearing?"

"Of course I will."

"Promise?"

"I promise."

XXIV

A late supper, a strange bed, Elinor Glyn on a tiger skin. Or had he been rolling with Esmeralda? Noble opens his eyes, scratchy with lack of sleep, headache compressing his skull. His nerves jangle, his mind trying to catch up with the events of the past few days. A kaleidoscope of fractured sounds and broken images that flit by too rapidly for him to do more than watch: Spoon and the gun, Jem playing on the beach with Butler and his kids, Mary and her note, the doctor's hand on his arm, Esmeralda's kiss, last night's desolate walk along the dockyards, Elinor Glyn on a tiger skin. It's a wonder he slept at all.

Turning over, his glance falls on the book pulsing at the edge of his bedside table. He shoves it under his pillow, sits to extricate his feet from the tangled bed sheet, swings his legs over the side of the bed and pushes himself up. The room faces west; the wooden floor is cold. His legs shake as he stands and his shoulder throbs as if someone was swinging on his arm half the night. Stiff, he moves like an old man. *Characters in stories undergo a very intensive and concentrated existence.* Yeah, yeah, Elinor, that's for sure.

After using the toilet down the hall Noble pours frigid water from a crazed-glaze jug into a matching bowl on the washstand in his room, scrapes a square of hard soap over his skin and rubs himself down with the thin scratchy towel. He appraises himself in the dresser mirror, casting his eyes across his bare chest, the ravaged skin and muscle that is his left shoulder. It looks as if some wild animal has been chewing on him. Noble likes to think Esmeralda would have run her hands gently over the raw and angry-looking bumps and ridges, he affords her that much charity. Look at the company she keeps. Lillian would. Mary, once she'd overcome her initial distaste, had been fixated, had even seemed to enjoy the idea of his wound. In a braver moment Noble had started to tell her the story behind the injury but she'd stopped him before he could finish. She didn't want to hear it.

Washed, dressed, hair attended to with wet fingers, teeth the same. Noble glances round the room for anything he might be forgetting. What about me? the book screams from beneath the pillow. He has to admit he's disappointed. Not with the titillation, bravo Elinor on that score. But with the book's lack of subtlety. Where are all those high ideals espoused in *System of Writing*? About finding material in the most ordinary places. And choosing ideas because they mean a lot to the writer, they have significance that the writer wishes to impress upon the reader. Apparently she doesn't heed her own advice.

He should leave the book behind, hide it under the bed. He bends to look, grubby pockets of dust, a layer of grit. It would be a while before anyone found it there: weeks, months. They couldn't connect it to him. He straightens. Noble has made few purchases in his life. To leave the book behind without having finished reading it seems not only a thoughtless waste of money but wrong somehow. Perhaps he owes it to Paul and the mysterious lady to see their adventure through to the end. Of course it will end. Such affairs have no future, not even within the confines of a book.

When Noble steps outside, it is obvious he has slept in. He had wanted an early start, but the sun has already climbed a portion of the sky and Halifax is bustling. In the years he's been away from the city motor traffic has increased. And switched over to the right side. The street is filled with carts and trams and motorcars and delivery boys on bicycles, the sidewalks with pedestrians, shoppers, people all in a rush to go about their business. And beggars. Lots of beggars. Flotsam and jetsam from the war. Young men who don't look so young anymore. Those who made it back to their hometowns and villages are secreted away by their families. A spare room, the attic. Summers on the back porch. But for those still ambulatory, still capable of rage, their world is now the more anonymous streets of Halifax. They hold out their hands as people pass, impale them with their haunted stares. Those who have eyes, that is, for a goodly number of these men are blind. Others are amputees. Some are masked, or partially so, protecting the innocent once again. These men fought alongside his brother. They might even have known him. Noble considers stopping one or two and asking, but they smell of anger or despair or both; it rolls off their ragged clothes in toxic clouds, fouling the air. Their wounds make a mockery of his. It wasn't even a training wound. It was just a random accident.

He'd been walking down a country lane in the middle of the night. Noble and Lawson and some other men from their outfit. They'd been supping a few beers at the pub in the village. He heard the truck coming, but it was dark, and with the curfew and everything, its lights were off. He stepped out of the way. Or so he thought. The wing mirror was long and low. Pain arced through his shoulder and out through his mouth, blood in a spurt, the force cracking his shoulder blade, shredding muscles and tendons. His right arm danged uselessly, longer than his left. He'd spent six weeks in hospital, splinted and immobilized, and then he'd been discharged. The army had no use for a soldier who couldn't raise his firing arm above his shoulder.

Noble turns from the veterans, fingering the change in his

pockets, sorting it by size and shape, and makes his way towards the harbour.

Noble has to ask six or seven different people before he finds someone who may have heard of Will Brooks. Butler's information isn't as reliable as he thinks it is. Either that or Will Brooks is small potatoes in a city this size. The man points to an office atop a stone building. An office? Noble was expecting a shady doorway down an unpaved lane somewhere. The man up there may be able to help him. Noble opens the nondescript door and climbs a flight of stone stairs. In a room overlooking the water he finds a florid-faced, heavy-jowled man seated at a large oak desk. The man has a pencil behind his ear and a telephone receiver in his hand, either about to make a call or just finishing one. He replaces it in its cradle when he spots Noble.

"Can I help you, son?" Noble hasn't been called son since he can't remember when.

"Will Brooks?"

"Who's asking?" The man frowns, narrows his eyes, but not before Noble catches a flash of curiosity. A man with a prosperous girth, he shifts in his chair and leans back. Still, he looks ready to pounce.

"I've come from Kenomee village, up on the Minas Basin."

"And what might that be to me, son?" Noble had been hoping Will Brooks would be able to fill in the blanks himself.

"There was a schooner moored up there this past week." Brooks stares at Noble with the patronizing boredom of a teacher listening to his pupil's explanation. "The *Esmeralda*." Brooks straightens in his chair and leans forward, elbows on his desk.

"And this *Esmeralda* is where now?"

"Couldn't say. Somewhere between here and the Bay of Fundy, I shouldn't wonder."

"What's your name, son?"

"Noble. Noble Matheson." He wants to bite his tongue off. Why did he give the man his real name?

"And who sent you to see me, Noble Matheson?"

"The first mate. Fellow by the name of Spoon." Butler may know of Will Brooks, but there's no reason Will Brooks has to know of Butler.

Brooks steeples his hands in front of his face, sucks at his lips. "So you're here to tell me there's some cargo ready for pickup." He pauses a moment. "Some special cargo." It isn't a question, but Noble nods anyway. It's a relief he doesn't have to explain himself, but it makes him nervous to learn that other people know about the *Esmeralda* and the booze. He glances out of Brooks's window across at the docks. How many other people out there might be in on the game? And are any of them already on their way to Kenomee? What else do they know? A picture of Jem waving goodbye after jumping down from the back of his truck. Please to God no one else can connect the boy to him.

"Good enough then." Will Brooks reaches for the phone again. Noble is still standing by the man's desk. An awkward silence passes before he understands he's being dismissed. He came all the way from Kenomee for that? Couldn't someone have called Brooks on his telephone or sent the man a wire? In code? That would depend on who was on the warpath for all that liquor. He turns to leave. "Close that door behind you, would you, son?" Brooks calls out. "Oh, and by the way, I fired Will Brooks about ten days ago."

Noble, hand on the door, spins on his heel but receives such a cold blank stare that he thinks better of a retort and turns and picks his way back down the stairs.

Now what? He's not only no closer to finding Brooks but he's probably tipped someone else off. What an idiot he is. What made him assume the man was Brooks? He hadn't said so. Stupid, stupid. Why couldn't he have been more wary?

More suspicious? A great sleuth he'd make. Butler isn't going to be happy. Has Noble foolishly unleashed a course of events he'll live to regret? He steps back into the sunlight. He will recheck every loading bay and graving dock, ask everyone who crosses his path. He will find Will Brooks if it takes all day.

O'Malley's is in the building next door to the New Halifax Hotel. Noble glances up at the façade. He climbs the stairs to the second floor, knocks in the manner he's been told to and enters when the door is opened by a jumpy ferret of a man. Little attention has been given to decor. A naked bulb suspended on a cord from the ceiling casts harsh unequivocal light upon the room and its occupants. Grey complexions match the grey walls. A woman stands at a sink in the corner, her hands hovering over a jug. A makeshift bar of old bookcases separates her from the men.

Will Brooks, at least the man who fits the description Noble has been given, is drunk. He can scarcely keep himself balanced on the stool. Noble approaches the man but the woman steps into his path, her hand on the jug of rum. She pours him a glass and Noble forks over twenty-five cents, knowing that to refuse a drink will raise an alarm. For although the clientele are lounging half-drunk in and over the hodge-podge collection of stools and easy chairs, the proprietors are skittish and gruff with caution, poised at the first whiff of trouble to fling the illegal contents of their jug and glasses down the sink and bolt. Noble glances towards the tall window in the centre of the far wall. It opens onto a balcony, and he wonders if the drop is clear or whether he'd twist his ankle or, worse, break his legs if forced to flee. Conversely, if a liquor inspector were to suddenly appear in that window, having climbed up onto the balcony, could he make it back out the door in time? He cannot afford to add a conviction for consumption to his troubles. As it is he'll have to spend another three dollars on a hotel room, now that it's too late in the evening to start the long drive back to Kenomee. He regrets having handed over quite so much change to the men on the streets. He could sleep outside. But there are police patrolling the streets, this isn't the village, they have vagrancy laws in Halifax. He could try his luck with the veterans maybe, unbutton his shirt and show them his shoulder, claim a kind of kinship. But with the run of luck he's had so far, he'd likely end up in the city jail, closer to Esmeralda than he might wish to be.

Taking the small glass from the woman's chapped hands, he puts it to his lips, tastes the fiery molasses. His stomach heaves, not having forgiven him yet for the Bushmills assault. He saunters over to Will Brooks, sagged against the bar, feeling both the woman's and her partner's eyes trained on him the whole time. A new face. Not to be trusted.

"Will Brooks?" The man either doesn't hear him or pretends not to. "Your name is Will Brooks?" Head bobbing on his scrawny neck, the man turns slowly to stare at his interlocutor. Bleary eyes try to focus, lips part as if to speak, but no words come out. He belches a vile cocktail of stale alcohol and tooth decay. Will Brooks, whoever he is in the world of rum running, is rotting from the inside out. He places a shaky hand on Noble's arm, brushing the Elinor Glyn book in his unsteady trajectory. Noble flinches. "You are Will Brooks, right?"

"Who wants to know?" A voice behind him. The ferret man at his elbow. "He can't help you, whatever you might be looking for, mate. Comes in here for a quiet drink is all. Yous best be leaving him alone."

"I have a message for him."

Ferret man plucks the stub of a carpenter's pencil from behind his ear, offers it to Noble. "You got a message, you write him a note." Noble takes the pencil, wrinkling his nose as the man leans in closer. His clothes and skin reek, a more acrid and offensive smell than that of the begging servicemen. "Then you finish your drink and I'm gonna ask you to leave, fella. Nice and quiet."

Noble lifts his glass and empties a third of its contents into his mouth. His eyes water and his nose runs. "Good grog, this. Might be tempted to stay for a couple more."

"You finish that one, then you go."

The minute the man's back is turned, Noble is whispering Will Brooks's name again.

It's hopeless, Brooks is too far gone to comprehend language, and in the next instant, the danger he's in. The door bursts open and two men enter.

"Liquor inspector, no one move," the first one shouts as the woman dumps the contents of her jug. The policeman behind him bolts towards her. They struggle and the jug shatters on the floor at their feet. Ferret man, making for the window, briefly distracts the inspector, who, whether from excitement or stupidity, failed to lock the door behind him, and Noble seizes his chance. Grabbing Will Brooks by his jacket collar, he hoists him from the stool towards the door. Miraculously Brooks is able to put one foot in front of the other, at least he isn't tripping, and the two make their way quickly down the stairs and out into the street. Noble marches Brooks around the corner and into a nearby alley. But Brooks's cooperation, however involuntary, is short-lived. His feet stumble and his knees buckle until Noble is doing little more than dragging the man. They've covered only half a dozen yards or so before Noble has to lean him up against the wall so that he can rest his painful shoulder. Brooks slides to the ground and promptly passes out. Noble slaps him across the face a number of times, shakes him by his shoulders, but it's no use. Should he leave him and come back in the morning? But there's no knowing when Brooks will awaken or whether the police will find him in the meantime.

There's nothing for it but to get Brooks to his hotel room. Noble squats to shoulder the comatose man to standing position, and then the sound of hurried footsteps reaches his ears.

It won't be long before his pursuer discovers which alley he's dodged into.

Noble drops Will Brooks, cringing as the man's head bounces off the wall with a sickening thud. His first instinct is to run. But the picture of Jem playing with Butler on the beach is burned into his conscience. He places his fingers under Brooks' chin, searching for a pulse, and realizes he's still clutching ferret man's pencil. For the first precious seconds his mind is a complete blank. Then it comes to him: *Esmeralda's bagged a Moose.*

"Hey, you there. Halt. Stop what you're doing." Quickly he scribbles Butler's message on the paper bag from the bookstore and then, rum water fuelling his legs, takes off up the alleyway. Elinor Glyn would be perspiring under her hatband.

XXV

"Late or not, you could have at least finished dressing before you graced us with your presence." Vivian is upon Hetty before she's taken one step into the drawing room. One barefooted step. Feet burning, blisters wet with grief. The air fizzes and swirls around her mother's head.

She'd spent the afternoon walking the length and breadth of the city, anxious to shake the spectre of Spoon, free her skin of the prison stink.

"Dinner is almost ruined."

"You're looking well, my dear," her father booms from his perch before the fireplace. Vivian steps aside. "You have good colour in your cheeks." Hetty crosses the room to give him a hug and a kiss. "It must be all that fresh air and good country living."

"You should come and visit us then," Hetty says, noting how grey and drawn he looks. The dark circles that shadow his eyes.

"That would be nice. I'm busy with work at the moment, though your mother might be able to manage a trip out. You should have a word with her." Hetty smiles as if she considers her father's suggestion a good one. The sight of Vivian in gumboots squelching through sticky red mud might almost be worth the strain of her mother's undiluted company. But not quite. She leans towards him.

"I need to speak with you about something. Do you think after dinner we could — ?"

"Hello, Hetty." Peter. She sets her face and turns to greet him, place a kiss on his cheek, but with Esmeralda's grisly warning still ringing in her ears, she can't quite meet his eyes.

"How are you?"

"I'm well."

"I had no idea where you'd gone. I was frantic for a while."

Hetty can't imagine Peter frantic about anything. "I can take care of myself." *Can you?* Spoon's eyes, cold and glassy, bore through the back of her neck. Why can't she just open her mouth and warn him?

"Laura wanted you to know she's missing your morning chats."

"I only left yesterday, Peter."

He pulls at the cuffs of his shirt, inspects his fingernails. "She finished weeding your garden for you. We both did."

"I wanted —" *to weed it myself.* She hesitates to finish her sentence, knowing Peter will take it as proof she's planning on returning to the village with him. Why can't he ever leave her alone to do something for herself? Why does he feel the need to prescribe every moment of her day?

"Did you take the train?" Her face is beginning to ache. Is her father still standing behind her, listening? What about her mother and Aunt Rachel? She feels cornered by their sharp-eyed silence, her every move, every word monitored.

"Noble Matheson gave me a ride."

"I see. Your feet look sore."

"Feet and hands." She spreads them in front of her. "I'm a mess of blisters."

Peter takes her left hand. "Your wedding ring. Hetty, where's your wedding ring?" His voice, tight and, yes, fearful, echoes strangely inside her head. "Did you lose it?"

"No," she says quickly, pulling her hand back and checking her earlobes. Naked. "I didn't lose it."

"Then where is it?"

She massages the telltale finger, the groove the ring has left in her flesh. "I took it to the jeweller's. It doesn't fit anymore."

"We could get you another ring if you like." His eyes have a ragged, helpless cast.

"It isn't necessary, Peter."

"Time for dinner," Vivian trills, hand on her son-in-law's arm, leading him away. "Come, come, everyone."

Hetty slouches towards the dining room, dreading the small talk, the air already thick with her family's need for peace between herself and Peter. Her appetite sharpens as Frances lifts the lid from the soup tureen. When did she last eat a decent meal? But no sooner does she reach towards the basket of warm fragrant rolls than there's a knock at the door. Moments later Frances reappears.

"There's a constable at the door, sir." Peter cups her elbow, and Hetty is dimly aware of her father reaching towards the knot of his tie, Aunt Rachel leaning towards him, Vivian patting his arm. Their mouths move, but Hetty can hear nothing over the whoosh of blood in her ears.

"He says he's here to see Mrs. Douglas, sir."

They turn on her then, sisters with identical eyes — how has she never noticed before?

"I've shown him to the study, sir. Ma'am." She nods at Hetty, who is uncomfortable with Frances's newfound formality. They were practically playmates when Hetty was growing up.

Hetty stands. Peter follows. "Would you like me to come with you?"

"No — thank you," she adds at a sharp glance from Aunt Rachel. "I'll be fine."

"May I ask what this is about, constable?" Hetty's father says, holding open the door to his office. "Your timing leaves a lot to be desired. My family and I were in the middle of our evening meal." He steps behind his desk but remains standing.

"Our apologies, sir. The constabulary is conducting some enquiries into the death of a young boy aboard a pirate schooner that was laid up at Kenomee village this past week."

Richard Piers grips the back of his chair. "What kind of nonsense is this?"

"We have it on good authority, sir, that Mrs. Douglas was aboard the schooner in question."

Her father's eyes are turning rheumy. He must have aged a decade in the past year. Little wonder her mother resents her. "I sincerely hope you're going to tell me that the constable is mistaken."

"I'm afraid not." Wringing her hands. "They came to me for help."

"And you just consented to get yourself involved? Where the devil was Peter? What does he think he's — ?"

"It was nothing to do with Peter." Then. Now his neck is on the line. "It was my decision entirely. I thought they were harmless. Fishermen blown off course."

"If you'll allow me, ma'am," the policeman says. "I think there's some facts you mighten't be aware of. Sir." He nods at Hetty's father, clears his throat and pulls out a notebook for reference. "A ruthless lot of brigands they are, sir. The crew. They set upon the rum-runner *Alchemist*, stole her cargo, shot the bo'sun's feet off, and made the captain chuck him overboard." Hetty feels faint. What might Spoon do to Peter?

"The crew from the steamship were lucky the U.S. Coast Guard happened upon 'em so soon. They gave the schooner chase a good while, but then the weather came up in the Bay of Fundy and it got away from them.

"Rum-runners are a bad enough blight on our society, sir. But rum pirates are always armed and doubly dangerous. We wouldn't normally bother ourselves about it. You know, thieves stealing from thieves. But they murdered the bo'sun. And now with the boy's death and all, it's a Dominion matter now, sir."

"And how exactly is my daughter supposed to be involved?"

"According to our reports, sir, Mrs. Douglas amputated the boy's leg."

His heart. If it gives out now Hetty will never forgive herself. Her mother will hold her responsible.

"My daughter is a trained nurse. She obviously knew what she was doing."

"What she did isn't at issue, sir, it's what she saw aboard the schooner that's concerning the magistrate. Sir. Ma'am" — the constable turns to Hetty — "you will probably be called as a witness when the trial proper begins."

"Oh, now, I don't think there's any need for that, constable, do you?"

"Until such time I must advise you to stay away from visiting with any of the accused."

"As if the thought would even cross her mind."

The constable licks the end of his pencil. "And if Mrs. Douglas wouldn't mind answering a few questions?"

"I'll try my best."

"Just dates and times and anything that stands out in your mind. Any evidence of liquor onboard, that sort of thing."

"None."

"None?"

"Absolutely."

"And how can you be so sure, ma'am?"

Hetty's glance flits to the window, evening clouds pressing in from the ocean. "The woman who comes in to clean the house — she told me. Her husband's a fisherman. She said the schooner was sitting too high up in the water to be carrying anything but her ballast."

They watch his laboured note-taking, willing his pencil across the page. "The court requires that you inform them if and when you leave the city and return to your residence, ma'am. If you leave the province or the country without advising the authorities, you could be charged with contempt."

"Close the door, Hetty, please," her father says once they are alone. He sits and steeples his hands before his face. Her parents share the same gestures. Perhaps that comes from twenty-seven years of marriage. And what will she adopt from Peter? His bread-buttering habit? Or his throat-clearing? The way he worries his hangnails when lost in thought? Can Hetty envision twenty-seven years with Peter? She could be a widow before the weekend is out.

"Why did you lie to that policeman?"

"What makes you think I was lying?"

"You're my daughter. I know when you're lying. What I want to know is who you're protecting and whether you think any brigand ruffian is worth throwing your marriage away for."

"I'm not throwing my marriage away."

"Then what are you doing here, Hetty?"

"There was a young woman aboard the schooner. Her name is Esmeralda." Sensing a long explanation ahead of her, Hetty pulls a chair up to her father's desk. "I visited with her today. In jail."

"Go on." He has his bank manager's voice on.

"She's terrified. And the thing is, she shouldn't be there. She's too young to be in prison. Esmeralda is the kind of person who has never had any choice about what she wants to do in her life. Her father is the captain of a pirate ship, her mother is . . . her mother abandoned her when she was a baby. She's just an innocent victim in all this."

"This is what she's told you, is it? Prisons are filled with innocent people, Hetty. It's a wonder there's any room for the criminals."

"Esmeralda is a good person. I can feel it in my bones."

"She's a pirate. She's involved in violent crime."

"You don't trust my judgment?"

"Frankly? No. You're being dangerously naïve. This Esmeralda person is charged with a serious offense. She'll likely spend a very long time in prison, if she doesn't hang for her crimes. Rum pirates! Hetty, whatever possessed you? And what is she to you but a passing acquaintance? A flirtation with danger? The world doesn't need another of your damn crusades. God knows this family doesn't. If you weren't a married woman I would forbid you to have anything more to do her."

If I weren't a married woman, Hetty thinks, we wouldn't be having this conversation.

"I'll deal with your mother," he says as they leave his office. Hetty makes for the stairs.

Bathed and wrapped in a towel, she pads across the hallway from the bathroom and stops at the door to her old room. Hand on the doorknob, she starts to turn it, then changes her mind. Why pick at her scabs?

The guest bedroom has been dusted and aired, the covers on the bed turned down. Frances has even laid out Hetty's old brush and comb set on the vanity. On a hook on the back of the door hangs a navy silk peignoir and matching nightdress Hetty has never seen before. Something of her mother's? Or had Vivian, up to her old machinations, purchased these items today? Had Aunt Rachel?

She opens the drawers and then the closet, seeking something less alluring and romantic to put on. A surprise. Her nurse's uniform is hanging inside. She runs her fingers over the blue cape, its solid sensibleness. Her shoes, which would have saved her feet today, are lined up beneath. Why wouldn't her mother have tossed it out or given it to the rag and bone man? Had Frances burn it in the kitchen range? And who moved it from her old room? Had it been hanging here over Christmas?

Hetty slips on the uniform and beholds herself in the mirror. Nurse Piers. Older. She looks for signs that the past year's events have marked her in any way. A crease around her mouth perhaps? A line on her forehead. She steps closer and there it is, a hint of shadow in her eyes to mark the sadness and the changes. If she had known the far-reaching consequences of her behaviour back when she was at nursing school, would her life have veered down the same path? Or would she have acted differently and changed her destiny?

She removes her cape, touches her fingers to her reflection. All those poor boys with their broken bodies. If she closes her eyes she can remember the feel of their skin, the rough weave of the blankets that tucked them in. She had only ever wanted to make them feel better. Only ever wanted to help them forget. Brian had been the first. Brian Binns, a prairie boy from Brandon, Manitoba. While Brian had escaped outright disfigurement, his appearance was strangely unsettling: blue eyes in a gunpowder-reddened face, hair the colour of sun-bleached straw. He looked permanently startled.

But in the anonymity of darkness it was his large farmer's hands, his thick, ropy arms that unmoored her, cast her adrift in a sea of her own longing, her own undoing.

"Nurse?"

She moved over to his bed, stepping through the long rectangle of moonlight pouring through the window, then into shadow again.

"Yes?"

"Could you talk to a lonely fellow?" And he patted the bed. Hetty sat, first smoothing out the seat of her uniform, as her mother had trained her to as a child. Now it was a reflex.

"And what would you be wanting to talk about at this hour of the night?" she chided, a smile in her voice.

He set his hand in the crook of her waist, fingers hugging her hipbone. Heat rushed through her.

"Do you mind?"

Hetty closed her eyes a moment and brushed her fingers across her throat, grateful he couldn't see the flush of colour she could feel in her cheeks. "No," she said slowly. "No, I don't mind." His hand began kneading at her hip. She drew in a long and ragged breath and then Brian Binns moaned softly in the back of his throat. He took her left hand and placed it on his groin, his penis straining under the thin hospital blanket, the shiny over-washed sheet. Hetty had only ever imagined this moment. She grasped its hardness and began moving her hand back and forth. Brian Binns's hand slid down her leg and up under her nurse's uniform. Hetty shifted and his fingers slid inside her underwear and found her slippery wetness. They rocked together there a moment, a minute, a measure of time, and when Brian shuddered in release and his fingers stilled, Hetty was left trembling and unsated, her heartbeat clamouring in her throat, her body pulsing for something else, something more.

Corporal Brian Binns pulled her to him and kissed her hair, her lips, her cheeks. "You're a good girl," he whispered hoarsely. "A very good girl."

There had been so many lovely lonely boys after Brian Binns, and she'd made them whole again, if only briefly, seeking to make herself whole.

Not every young man was Brian Binns, though. Some were angry and hammered out their spleen on her body. Beneath her uniform she'd hidden her bruised chest and pinched thighs, the black marks on her buttocks. And once a ragged line of tiny blood blisters across her neck, which she'd explained away as too much starch in her collar. The soldier with the choking hands, Frank, a Cape Breton boy whose family had moved to Halifax in the mining slump and had all been killed in the Explosion, had taken out the remainder of his grief with a knife. He'd slit his wrists that night and been found the next morning by the duty nurse. The soldier in the bed next to his had complained all night of the smell of blood as Frank's veins had slowly emptied into his bed. Soldiers often complained they could smell gas and other impossible things, so no one had paid any attention until it was too late.

"You must miss it. Nursing."

Peter stands in the doorway where the light from the bed-side lamp doesn't quite reach. "You gave me a fright." Hand over her heart.

"I've never seen you in your uniform. You look very efficient and professional."

"I was," she says to her reflection. The comfort nursing had been but a stage. A short-lived temptation. A heart-thudding addiction.

"Your patients were lucky to have such a beautiful, con-scientious nurse."

"You came all this way to flatter me?" Hetty's words sound oddly familiar.

Peter steps into the room and stands behind her, a shadowy consort in the mirror.

"I was hoping to take you home."

Hetty would like to change out of her uniform, climb into bed and go to sleep. But something in Peter's voice gives her pause. He brushes a hand down the front of his suit, clears his throat again.

"I once sent a man under my command on a dangerous reconnaissance mission I knew he had no hope of surviving. I tried to pretend I had no choice, that he was the only man for the job, that the job was imperative. But the truth was I couldn't stand him." Hetty watches the shadows shift across her husband's face. "He was disruptive. I could always hear his voice above anyone else's. He never took an order without grumbling or backchat. He was happiest sowing doubt in the other men's minds, stirring discontent, inciting trouble. I'd had enough and saw a way of ending my discomfort."

"Did it work?"

"He never came back."

"And how did you feel?"

"I wasn't surprised. I knew it was an impossible mission. As did the rest of the outfit. They kept their distance afterwards. I never knew if I'd become someone they respected or someone they feared."

"Why are you telling me this now?"

"The army expects you to make decisions that aren't based on your emotions. They assume you don't have any."

Hetty holds Peter's gaze in the mirror. He moves closer.

"Sometimes people do the right things for the wrong reasons."

"Is this a confession, Peter? Are you saying you regret turning in my friends?"

"I regret what it's done to us."

"We were in trouble long before the *Esmeralda* and her crew showed up."

He reaches out and places his hand in the small of her back. The air contracts around them. "I wanted it too, you know."

"What did you want, Peter?"

"The baby."

"Why did you leave me here by myself?"

"I thought it was for the best, that it was what you wanted."

"Why didn't you ask me what I wanted?"

"I was scared. You were bleeding so heavily. I thought I was going to lose you too."

He looks so vulnerable in the soft yellow glow from the bedside lamp that Hetty turns from the mirror to perch on the end of the bed.

"May I?" She nods and he sits on the edge opposite, leaving an expanse of candlewick bedspread between them. "The house felt very empty last night."

"No emptier than it must have felt at Christmas."

"I wish I'd acted differently, Hetty. I should never have left you alone like that. If I had known it would mean losing my wife . . ."

"You surprise me, Peter. I wasn't aware you ever wanted a wife. Not nearly as much as you wanted a financial backer for your mill."

He glances down at his hands as if checking to see they're still the same length, that they haven't grown on him, or shrunk. "Your reasons for marrying me were no more noble than mine, but I don't keep flogging you with them."

She falters. It has never been clear how much he knows of her past, how much her parents or Aunt Rachel might have told him. God knows she could never bring herself to ask.

"No, you'd rather play the family martyr who married the fallen woman."

"Don't be ridiculous."

"Why did you marry me, Peter? What could a restrained man like you possibly see in someone like me?"

"This." He gestures towards her, hands open.

"What?"

"Your fire. Your passion. You live in the moment. Impulsively. Even recklessly at times. But I guess that's part of what attracts me so much."

"You have a strange way of showing it."

"Hetty, you frighten me to death half the time."

"I *frighten* you? Are you sure it isn't something else?"

"Quite sure."

"But I did things with other men, Peter."

"I don't want to talk about it. You must have had your reasons."

"What if it was more than that?"

"It was a different time, Hetty, a different world."

"Some need in me."

"I don't care." He reaches for her waist.

"I don't believe you."

"Believe me." His hand travels the bodice of her nurse's uniform, his fingers stroke the inside of her arm.

"Shameful things."

"It doesn't matter," he says, finding the nape of her neck, kissing her face.

"I touched them."

Hot breath on her neck, his voice gravelly in her ear. "Show me."

Heat twists through her. A damp pulse between her legs. She shifts into his arms, catching her breath as Peter's tongue grazes her skin. A soft moan escapes his lips, and as he buries one hand in the back of her hair, the other travels, rough and urgent, up her leg and under her nurse's uniform.

XXVI

Thursday June 5. High Tide, 8:04 a.m., 8:36 p.m.

Noble paces Grand Parade, from City Hall to St. Paul's Church and back, half a dozen times, mustering the courage to approach the police station. He needs to be sure Will Brooks is okay, that he received his message about the *Esmeralda*. Down the stairs, along Barrington and a quick left at Duke Street. The smell from a bakery follows him in through the police station door, nipping at his hangover. Will Brooks, it turns out, is in the prison infirmary. Noble's head feels cottony, his teeth sore. Visitors are not allowed.

"Friend of yours, is he? Relation?" The sergeant has the jowls of an ox and long baggy cheeks that hang down to meet them.

"Barely know the man." Noble begins backing up, but the stone door sill blocks his heels.

"Fighting with him last night, were you? Is that where you got that face from?" The sergeant stands and Noble turns, stumbles back into the bright morning light. Now he's responsible for a man's injuries. A suspected concussion. Doesn't mean he has one, does it? And how many are a few stitches? One or two? Three perhaps? Brooks hadn't hit his head so hard. Drunks could bounce down whole flights of stairs and wake up with nothing more than a thick head. Noble hadn't seen any blood. Not that he'd been able to see much of anything in that dark alleyway. Enough to scribble Butler's message on the paper bag from the bookstore, which he'd then shoved, book and all he later realized, into Brooks's jacket. When the police searched him, Brooks would have been guilty of nothing more than carrying a racy novel about his person. The message would mean nothing to them. Noble had made a worse gaffe yesterday at the shipyard office. There could be a rum-running gang on their way to Moose. Or worse, already in the village hunting for Spoon and the stolen booze.

The doors to Kenomee Village School open and children trickle out. They ran in his day, Noble thinks. Elbowing their way to the front, galloping across the playground and taking the wall (in his memory) like a herd of gazelle. He waits until every last student has left the building. No sign of Jem.

He hurries down the hallway. Through the spaces between the wavy lollipop trees and strips of blue sky Miss Bird has mounted on the door's glass panes, Noble stares into his old classroom. He knocks.

Miss Bird, hair feathered with grey, crow's feet about her eyes — isn't she Mrs. Someone-or-other now? — beckons at him to enter. "Noble Matheson. To what do I owe this pleasure?"

"Jem Baker. He's one of your students, yes?"

"He is."

"I need to see him."

"It may have escaped your notice, Mr. Matheson, but all the students have left for the day."

"He was here, then?"

"Never turned up for school this morning. Something he seems to be making a habit of."

"Is he ill?" He's too late. Noble feels himself growing cold. His hands are trembling.

"That would be a question for his father, don't you think?"

Miss Bird has no idea where the boy is either. He turns on his heel, is running back down the corridor.

"Are you a friend of the family?" she calls at his retreating back. "Could you ask one of them to come and speak with me?" he hears as he pushes open the front doors.

Are you a friend of the family? The words jostle inside his head as he pushes the accelerator to the floor. The truck rattles over the potholed road towards the weir. Noble's head bangs repeatedly on the roof. Some friend. Some family. Wheels inches from the lip of the tide pool, he yanks on the handbrake, wrenches open his door and charges into the water.

"You bastard," he hollers. Water churning, fish jumping. Gulls lift off in a screech, batting the air with their wings. Even Bess turns her sage head to watch him. "You piece-of-shit bastard." He's crying, snot and tears sliding down his face.

Butler straightens, dip net in one hand. "Matheson! You back already?"

The water drags at Noble's pant legs, pulling him down. Face in the pool, hands and knees in the mud. The long cool bodies of fish nudge against him. His hat floats towards the V of the weir. "You bastard," he pants. "I'm gonna kill you."

"Whoa there, Nobbie boy. Keep your shirt on."

Coughing and sputtering, salt water up his nose, Noble struggles to stand. "Don't mess with me, shithead. Just tell me where he is."

"No idea." Arms spread wide. "He's just vanished into thin air."

A guttural cry issues from Noble's soul as he lunges towards Butler, grabbing him at the hips and taking him down. He grapples for Butler's neck, squeezing hard, then, hand on his face pushes his head under the murky orange water. Butler is at first too surprised to resist. In seconds Noble has straddled his chest. The sinews and tendons in his neck shift beneath Noble's fingers as Butler struggles against his assailant. Noble strives to pin Butler's arms with his knees but he isn't fast enough, and his right shoulder lets him down. Butler is able to simultaneously wrench Noble's hands from his neck and curl himself to sitting position, roaring like a wounded bear. Noble, flung backwards, takes his second dunk into the water. A flounder trapped in the mud struggles with astonishing strength beneath him, its powerful rhythms thumping against his back. A toad-fish nuzzles his ear. Noble sits and spits up salt water, wipes it from his eyes. His cheek is throbbing like the devil again. And warm. He palpates the area gently. Is he bleeding?

"What the hell is the matter with you, Matheson?" Butler rolls onto his knees, trying to catch his breath. "Upset you couldn't find Brooks?"

"Oh, I found him all right." Noble spits again. "But not before I managed to tip off some big fat gangster about the whereabouts of the *Esmeralda* and her cargo."

"You did what?"

"A description would have helped. Skinny little fuck trying to drink himself to death. Don't talk to the fat fuck. He's not your man. Well, it's too late now. They're probably already prowling around the village, and Spoon's gotten hold of Jem and done God knows what with him, and it's all your fault, you stupid greedy bastard."

"Spoon hasn't got Jem."

"How the hell would you know who he's got? What he's done? You're down here with the fucking fish."

"I told you, he's vanished."

"Spoon? Spoon's gone?"

"Yup."

"Just tucked his Luger in the back of his lousy pants and hitched a ride to the train station? Where's he gone to?"

"Just gone. Don't worry. He won't be back."

"Like hell."

"I'd stake my life on it."

Noble scowls. "Your kids' lives?"

"Theirs too."

Noble stares over at Moose Island. He's spent two miserable nights on the place, more than most of the villagers around these parts can boast, more than enough for anyone's lifetime. Butler might be spinning one of his stories again, but Noble has no plans to row over there and check. Spoon could be anywhere. There was something of Long John Silver in the fellow. Like Silver he'd probably escaped into the wilds and would show up in some sun-soaked, palm-treed port on the other side of the globe. Or had Butler . . . Noble turns back to face his childhood friend but can read nothing in his weathered features, his loose-shouldered stance, the casual way he shakes the water from his hat and places it back on his head.

The instant Noble gets to his feet he wants to sit down again. The water is warmer than the air. "So then where the hell is Jem?"

"How'm I supposed to know? In school."

"His teacher hasn't seen him all day."

"Then go ask his mother. You're old friends, aren't you?"

"You shit. You were supposed to be looking out for him. You promised me."

"I was looking out for all of us. Jem is just fine."

"How can he be fine? You don't even know where he is."

"He's a kid. He'll show up eventually. He's probably bunking off with Simon and his buddies."

"He's six."

"He's a kid." Butler balances on one leg to pull off a rubber boot, tip out the water and push it back on. He repeats the procedure with his other foot, then starts dancing around the bed of the tide pool feeling with his feet.

"There's a big one in here somewhere." Noble gestures to where he was lying. "I felt it."

"I'm looking for the dip net you made me drop."

"Well, I've lost my shoes. Anyway, I thought you never used one."

Butler turns his back, moves down the pool. "So what did Brooks have to say for himself?"

"Nothing. The man was soused. Who is he, anyway?"

"He was in my unit. We demobbed together. Spent some days touring the blind pigs in Halifax. I'm surprised he isn't dead."

"He's pretty close." Suspected concussion. Four stitches tops.

"Can't believe he's still around, poor sod."

"I don't know if he got the message. About Esmeralda and the Moose. Can't say he'd be able to do much about it if he did." Noble flaps his arms to keep warm.

"Don't worry about it." Butler bends to retrieve the dip net.

"What are you gonna do now? What if these other people show up? What if Spoon comes back?"

Butler shrugs. "That's my problem. Like I said, don't worry. You won't see Spoon again." He pulls the net through the water, scoops a large cod.

"Don't worry! You threatened my kid to get me to go to Halifax and find this guy and pass on your dumb message, and now you tell me not to worry? What the hell?"

Butler dumps the fish in Bess's cart. "I was saving your life."

"Putting it in danger more like. Not to mention the kid."

"You honestly think I'd let any harm come to him?" Noble can feel the heat of Butler's glare. "Then you don't know me very well."

"So why even let a monster like Spoon know of his existence?"

"I didn't. But I was counting on you thinking I had. And you did. That's the beauty of being so predictable."

"What?" Noble's head is churning. "How the hell — ?"

"Close your mouth, Matheson. I did it to save your miserable hide. You wouldn't have left unless there was something at stake."

"So you used kid bait. My kid."

"You're not listening to me. He was never in danger. And anyway Spoon was on Moose and I had the boat."

"The tide goes out twice a day. He had a gun. He could walk —"

"You can't walk off Moose until the next high tides, you know that. Believe me, Jem was never in danger. And I had to get you out of the way."

"Why?"

"So's I could attend to a little business undisturbed."

"What business?"

Butler glances at the weir's brush wall and back at Noble. "Fish business."

"Fishy business, you mean. You were stealing the booze."

"Tying up some loose ends." A blank smile.

"So where is it now?"

"The booze? What you saw is, well, let's say it's been carefully distributed."

"And the rest?"

Butler gestures towards Five Islands. "It's still out there."

"The high tides'll get it. You should have anchored it to the back of Moose. There's a new moon coming up."

"What makes you think I didn't?"

Noble grins despite himself.

"Tell me, how d'you know about Jem?"

"Wake up, Matheson. The whole village knows about Jem. Like they all knew about you and Mary. Not that anyone has to do more than take a good look at the kid. He looks like you."

"He looks like Lawson."

"He's got your eyes."

They stand leaning against Bess's cart. Noble can feel his body temperature plummeting, his wet clothes like cement. He wants to be home tucked up in bed, but there's something he has to take care of first.

"You shouldn't be so hard on yourself, Matheson."

Noble shrugs. "You're right. I shouldn't."

"See you down here in the morning? Around five?" There's a wind fetching up, dark clouds rolling in.

"I reckon you owe me a new pair of shoes."

"Fair enough. Drop by the house later, I'll give you the money." Butler holds out his hand. "No hard feelings, then, Matheson?"

"No hard feelings." Noble smiles, grasps Butler's right hand with his, and delivers a solid left hook under his friend's cheekbone.

XXVII

"I just knew that colour would look fabulous against your skin."

Hetty turns in front of the long oval mirror, appraising herself. She has no objection to the style and cut of the dress, dropped waist with soft pleats and bell-shaped sleeves. Nor the fabric itself, with its shimmering watery richness. It's the unbroken yardage of pink she finds offensive. But Clara is completely carried away with her own cleverness.

"Alice has found the exact shade of dye for your shoes. Alice, do you have the cap handy so we can try that on too?" Who's we? Hetty thinks. Clara will be draped in much more forgiving white.

Poor harried Alice, on her hands and knees, pins in her mouth, nods and gets to her feet. "And bring my dress as well while you're at it," Clara adds in a mock stage whisper, hand shading her mouth. Hetty considers her pink reflection, her smiling face with its rosy glow — light bouncing off the dress, no doubt. Her cheeks are beginning to ache.

"I still can't believe you never called to tell me you were coming to town." Clara has left her chair and is standing behind Hetty.

"It was very last-minute."

Clara draws her friend's hair behind her ears, tickles her on the cheek. "Last minute is becoming your modus operandi, darling." They stare at their reflection.

Perhaps Clara has seen today's headlines: *Rum-Running Beauty Charged with Murder*. Hetty had only managed the first paragraph before her father whisked the paper from under her nose, claiming he needed it at the office. But she'd gazed long enough at the photograph to commit it to memory. A full-length shot of Esmeralda in her male attire, staring defiantly at the camera, hands on her hips, her wavy hair pulled to one side and spilling almost to her waist. The kind of photograph that sells a lot of papers.

"You remember the other day on the wharf?"

"It's hardly something I could forget in a hurry."

Hetty explains her reasons for following Esmeralda to Halifax, careful to avoid any details that involve Peter.

"You're going to court?"

"This afternoon."

"With Peter?"

"I didn't think he'd understand." What was it about mornings that recast the night before in such blinding, pitiless light? Hetty had woken weighted down with the warning that Spoon was on the prowl. But at the mention of Esmeralda's name she could see impatience knitting across Peter's face. So she'd slipped from the bed and left the house.

"Then I'm coming with you."

"There's no need, Clara. It's a bail hearing. It'll be over in minutes."

Alice returns with the pink beaded cap in one hand and Clara's dress on a hanger in the other. "A little shorter, don't you think?" Clara says, indicating the hemline on Hetty's dress.

"Shorter, yes, I think so." Anything to be rid of another inch of pink. She smiles warmly at Alice.

"I'm going with you," Clara mouths, then takes her dress

from Alice and disappears behind the change-room curtain. "No peeking," she sing-songs.

Hetty arranges her hair in the hope of disguising the cap. She tilts her head this way and that and worries Clara has pink stockings in mind. She's going to resemble a stick of rock candy.

"You look beautiful," she says when Clara steps from behind the curtain in flattering off-white silk. Alice has countered some of Clara's planes and angles with bias seams, soft folds and a layered handkerchief hemline. Seed pearls cluster in tiny rosebuds across the bodice, and the dress's delicate shoulder straps are edged in lace. Clara struts the length of the dress shop and back, twirling a matching cropped jacket with three-quarter sleeves.

"Isn't it just the cat's meow? And Alice the cleverest girl ever?" Hetty gushes over the gown and its tailoring, and when Alice shakes the veil from its box she coos a little more.

Parade over, a giddy Clara takes Hetty's hand and pulls her into the change room. She unfastens her dress and slips it from her shoulders. A shock of creamy skin, the line of vertebrae shifting beneath. Esmeralda, stepping into the party frock. *It was just a bit of fun.* Hetty spins away, but the change room is small and her burning face now grazes the curtain. Clara's cool hands tickle the nape of her neck.

"Like some help?" She begins unfastening the hooks and eyes in the back of Hetty's dress. Hetty's hands fly to her breasts as Clara's fingers travel down her spine. Her traitorous skin tingles with gooseflesh, her nipples contract and harden. *What on earth is going on?*

"You're awfully quiet." Hetty gasps as Clara clutches her shoulders and turns her around. "Hetty, whatever is the matter?" She pushes her hair behind her ear and steps from her dress. Her camisole is the sheerest silk. Hetty stares at the space above Clara's head.

"I'm doing it again, aren't I? Het, I'm so sorry. Rubbing all

287

this wedding business in your face." She passes the dress out to Alice and draws her friend into an embrace. "How unfeeling of me." Hetty's senses are so heightened that the air around her skin is surely now a part of her. Gaping open in the back, her bridesmaid's dress slips from her shoulders. And though her arms around Clara feel wooden and disconnected, Hetty is reluctant to let go. If she steps back the dress will puddle around her ankles. Then she and Clara will be standing inches from each other in their undergarments.

"Forgive me?" Clara squeezes tighter. Hetty feels lightheaded, a diabolical thrill at Clara's own nipples pushing through her silk camisole.

"Listen, never mind about all this wedding nonsense, most of it's Mummy's doing. And let me tell you, it was all I could do to fend her off this morning. She wanted to come with me to see how your dress fit. She's been a peach with all the planning and organization — the caterers, the linen, the band — but she can be so trying." Shaking her head in mock frustration, Clara zips herself back into her town dress. Hetty's throat unclenches, allowing her to breathe again.

The courtroom is crowded. Despite the high ceiling the room is warm and stuffy. Can these people all be here to see Esmeralda? Hetty has to shuffle over once again as yet more spectators squeeze onto the end of the bench. She scans the crowd, feeling proprietorial. Clara exchanges apologies with the couple to her right, then turns to her friend.

"Stop fidgeting, will you? People are staring." But Hetty cannot keep still. She crosses and recrosses her legs. Fusses with her bag, her hair, her hat, her dress, the fingers of her gloves. Worries she's seated too close to the proceedings, though it's too late to move now. A man behind them sighs impatiently and clears his throat. There are a lot of strained nerves in this courtroom, it seems, a glut of anxious people. Or perhaps it is Hetty's own anxiety that is spilling into the room, infecting others and skewing her perspective. For like the women who famously knitted while heads rolled from the guillotine, the spectators are here only out of voyeuristic craving. Besides herself, not one person cares a nickel about the fate of these prisoners.

A door in the wood panelling opens and guards appear from the bowels of the building, a clutch of men shuffling between them. The captain, in the lead, appears resplendent in his braided jacket, chin high, and yet his hair, unrestrained by any hat, stands out in bewilderment from his head. The rest of the crew follow in a ragtag huddle, unwashed and unshaven, a portrait of high-seas villainy. They seem a little off-kilter, still finding their land legs. Then Hetty hears the dismaying chink of leg irons. She prays Esmeralda has been spared this humiliation.

Ambrose, whom Hetty remembers as the waiter, glances around the courtroom as he enters. He catches her eye. Looks away quickly. The cook is wearing a scowl. Without Spoon and his outlandish jacket, his ravaged face, the others blur, indistinct from one another. People nudge each other and whisper, point at the prisoners. Who does the Pirate Beauty belong to? Which ship's mate is she, then? Men laugh self-consciously in lustful gravelly voices; one lewdly suggests she's with all of them. Hetty whips her head this way and that, searching out the heckler with her iciest glare.

Bringing up the rear is the matron assigned to look after Esmeralda. A collective intake of breath dislocates the air. Heads crane. It's the female pirate everyone has come to see. But the matron is alone. Where is Esmeralda? Whispers grow to a hushed roar. The crown counsel crosses the floor, his black gown billowing behind him. He and the matron exchange words, she shakes her head. And that's when Hetty sees the gold hoops in the matron's ears. She glances to the woman's hands, waving in the air, and spots the heart-shaped ring. And then her own wedding band.

You will be there tomorrow, won't you?

Hetty's world lists to one side.

The captain and his remaining crew file into the prisoners' dock.

The clerk's voice rings out above the throng. The crown returns to his table, beckoning the matron to follow. Silence descends as the judge enters and is seated. The crown counsel asks for permission to approach the bench, and the crowd smells blood. As he confers with the judge, rumours fly.

"She's sweet-talked the warden."

"Seduced him, more like."

"Slit the jailer's throat."

"Hid the key in her mouth."

"In her hair."

"Down her pants."

"She's long gone. Caught a ship to England."

The judge calls for order. The crown retires to his seat, black robes settling around him. The crowd simmers but won't be stilled. Esmeralda is too beautiful. They've all seen her in the paper, that magnificent hair, those figure-hugging trousers, that defiant stance. She's irresistible to men and women alike. Hetty understands that now, and the doubt that has rumbled through her mind like a distant train this past week fades to silence.

"Calling the matter of the King against Captain Henry Granville Woods, Esmeralda Catherine Joan Conseulo Marquez —"

"Well she can't be married to any of them," Clara whispers when the clerk has finished reading the names.

Marquez. And possibly she isn't related to any of them, either. Or to a wind seller. Maybe the hecklers are right. Hetty has no more idea of the sleeping arrangements aboard the *Esmeralda* than anyone else in this courtroom.

"My Lord, it's Robert Callahan on behalf of the crown. This

matter of a bail hearing is on your Lordship's list today. The charges are unlawful death in the course of an act of piracy."

"And are you and the counsel for the defense ready to proceed?"

Without Esmeralda? Is this hearing even legal? Hetty stands, and ignoring the tut-tutting and sighs of exasperation, makes her way to the end of the row, a surprised Clara in tow. In painful monotone the crown drones through the police report. His reductive descriptions of Esmeralda's machinations, of Spoon's depravity, scrape across Hetty's skin. Elbowing though the throng, she steels herself when she hears her name, and again on learning J.J.'s true age. Bail is refused, the prisoners dismissed. Hetty pushes out through the heavy wooden doors, and without waiting for Clara, picks her way down the courthouse steps and hurries towards her parents' house, hoping to find Peter.

Epilogue

Saturday June 7. High Tide, 9.53 a.m., 10:20 p.m.

Saturday morning dawns grey and cold. It has rained heavily in the night and the gunmetal cast of the sky means the clouds are not quite spent. But no amount of inclement weather can quell the anticipation amongst the crowd gathered along the parade route. Noble scans faces, on the lookout for Lillian. Having slept all through yesterday and the Friday night lending library, he's anxious to speak with her about the Elinor Glyn books. It was a nice idea, but he's sending them back. They mostly deal with photoplays, and after reading her fiction he knows she doesn't practice what she preaches. And anyway, he's already culled her best advice: "write in a simple manner about plain, ordinary events of every-day life."

He heads over to the food pavilion, thinking he might find Lillian there. Instead he spots Jem eyeing the cake table. A furtive glance around. No Mary. No Butler. He approaches the boy.

"Hey, Jem. Remember me?"

"Hello, Mr. Matheson."

"What adventures have you been up to lately?"

"Nothing much. Uncle John has a shiner just like yours."

"Does he now?"

"He promised me another story, you know. About pirates and buried treasure."

Noble shoves his hands in his pockets. "Speaking of pirates, you haven't seen any wandering around, have you?" He still expects to find Spoon lurking around the next corner. Butler insists that Spoon no longer poses a threat but he won't elaborate, and Noble can't find the words to form the next question.

"I don't know. What do pirates look like?"

"Well, this particular one wears a jacket with dirty old spoons for his buttons, and he has a big red mess of boils on his face."

Jem wrinkles his nose and shakes his head.

"Listen, Jem" — the sensation of the boy's name on his lips makes him light-headed — "here's fifty cents." Jem's eyes grow round as Noble hands him two quarters. "I want you to keep an eye out for this pirate I was just telling you about. And if you see him hanging around I want you to come and tell me, and I'll give you another fifty cents. Is that a deal?"

"It's a deal, Mr. Matheson."

"Shake on it." Jem holds out his hand. "And you're not to tell anyone about our deal. Are we agreed?"

"Yes, sir."

"Good man. Off you go then. And remember. Shh." He raises his finger to his lips and Jem follows suit, then disappears into the crowd.

"He's a lovely boy." Noble startles. Sarah's voice by his ear. "He reminds me a lot of Lawson at that age, don't you think?"

Noble looks at his mother to find her regarding him keenly. She holds his gaze, long and steady. Eventually he has to look away.

"You should lend him that *Treasure Island* book of yours. I make it'd be some kind of tale a boy his age would enjoy."

"He's a bit young yet for *Treasure Island*, Mumma." Can she hear his words above the clamouring of his heart? "And I'm not sure his mother could read it to him without butchering the story."

"What about his father, then? You think he could read it to the boy?"

Nobles shuffles his feet in the wet grass. "In a couple of years or so he'll be able to read it himself." And by then Noble may well have his own story for Jem. A story that will begin with the two white feathers.

Hetty Douglas yawns as she stands in the damp air surveying the back garden. Her neck aches and her eyes feel gritty. She has slept little these past two nights, twitching awake at every rogue sound in the night, worrying that Spoon might suddenly appear at the foot of their bed, brandishing a cutlass. She wants to ask Peter if they can get a dog, but he has assured her time and again that he's dealt with Spoon's type before, and anyway the man is more likely across the border already or halfway back to England than creeping around the village.

Her flowery dress touches the mud as she bends to peer more closely at the damp surface of the fresh earth. Peter, smart in his dress uniform, steps from the back door to stand beside her. Shadow raises her head and trots to the gate, where she nickers at her master.

"It'll be at least a week before any of those seeds are up," he says.

Hetty's shoulders tense. "But it's been warm these past few days."

"Not warm enough."

A sigh. "I was just looking, that's all."

"They'll be out when they're good and ready. And then you'll have to keep an eye out for weeds. You let them get too big, they'll choke your seedlings before they have a chance."

"My seedlings? From your mother's seeds? They wouldn't dare."

"Very funny. Are you ready to go?"

Straightening, she catches the tiniest hint of green. A curled green sprout — one of the peas — just breaking the surface. She smiles to herself.

"Then shall we?" Peter returns the smile and takes her hand. Hetty is at first too surprised to resist. But she stays her impulse to pull away and lets herself be led towards the village green, acutely conscious of her left hand clasped in her husband's right. If Peter has noticed that the wedding band pressing against his fingers is not the same ring he slid on Hetty's finger a year ago, he's keeping that knowledge to himself.

The sky is darkening, the weather will not hold. Whitecaps are breaking the surface of the Minas Basin waters, which have turned to pewter. The dogfish are happy and fed. And in the V of the weir, already half buried in the shifting sand, is a handful of silver teaspoons. The hallmarks on their necks are almost obscured by tarnish and grime. But there isn't a person who, having seen them before, would at once fail to recognize them.

ACKNOWLEDGEMENTS

I would like to thank my husband, Ian Warren, for his abiding interest in history and his love of collectibles. I had already drifted unawares past the dusty box of Elinor Glyn writing books in a Prince Edward Island antiques store, but Ian noticed them at once. When the sales clerk revealed the lid of the box in which the books were nestled, complete with mailing label — Noble Mattinson, Great Village, N.S., Canada — I sensed a story beginning.

Two events in Mr. Mattinson's early life intrigued me. His brother, Lawson, died at Vimy Ridge. And while Noble signed up during the Great War, for undisclosed medical reasons, he never served. The rest is fiction. The Noble and Lawson Matheson of *The Wind Seller* are products of my imagination.

For her assistance in answering endless questions on the geography and history of Economy, for arranging the fishing trip to James Webb's brush weir, and for risking being stranded by the tide walking with me over to Moose Island, I cannot thank Anita MacClellan of Economy, Nova Scotia, enough.

Thank you to the many other people who helped with my research, among them: Conrad Byers, Paul Hosek, Jeff and Meredith Layton, Katherine Lemmon, Mike Mines, Ted White, and the staff at Dalhousie University Archives and Special Collections, particularly Dianne Landry. I found the whale story in Will Byrd's *This is Nova Scotia*. For input on early drafts I am grateful to Judi McLeod, as well as Lynda Simmons and the other members of the Burlington Writers Group.

A profound debt of gratitude to my editor, Laurel Boone, whose ᶠt guidance has helped me make this a better book. And to my ᴴilary McMahon, for steering me clear of the shallows.

ᵗario Arts Council provided funding for this project, for ᵗeful.